T WO WHITE

QUEENS AND

THE ONE-EYED JACK

T0094668

TWO WHITE QUEENS AND

THE ONE-EYED JACK

20/200

20/100

20/70

20/40

20/20

HEIDI VON PALLESKE

DUNDURN
TORONTO

Publisher: Scott Fraser | Acquiring editor: Rachel Spence | Editor: Shannon Whibbs
Cover designer: Laura Boyle
Cover image: istockphoto.com/sbayram
Printer: Marquis Book Printing Inc.

Library and Archives Canada Cataloguing in Publication

Title: Two white queens and the one-eyed jack / Heidi von Palleske.
Names: Palleske, Heidi von, 1960- author.
Identifiers: Canadiana (print) 20200165518 | Canadiana (ebook) 20200165526 | ISBN
    9781459746787 (softcover) | ISBN 9781459746794 (PDF) | ISBN 9781459746800 (EPUB)
Classification: LCC PS8631.A444 T86 2020 | DDC C813/.6—dc23

We acknowledge the support of the Canada Council for the Arts and the Ontario Arts Council for our publishing program. We also acknowledge the financial support of the Government of Ontario, through the Ontario Book Publishing Tax Credit and Ontario Creates, and the Government of Canada.

Printed and bound in Canada.

VISIT US AT
 dundurn.com |  @dundurnpress | dundurnpress | dundurnpress

Dundurn Press
1382 Queen Street East
Toronto, Ontario, Canada
M4L 1C9

To the first twins in my life, mother Doreen and aunt Colleen, born of rape and full of rage and life; and to their mother, my grandmother, Vera, who was a warrior woman all the days of her life even though her youth was stolen at sixteen years old; and to my daughter, Cavanagh, who is brave enough to speak out and claim her voice. To all the daughters of rape. The cycle ends here.

The eye sees only what the mind is prepared to comprehend.

— Robertson Davies

ONE

HE WAS THERE WHEN JOHNNY fell from the tree. The crack of the branch, that double sound, a *cra-crack* warning before the final, disappointing snap. Then the slow-motion tumble through the air as the wood gave way. It was impossible to get to him. A slow-motion pantomime where the force of a turbo engine wouldn't be quick enough. He twisted and spiralled, taking leaves and twigs along with him. Those were the only sounds: the snaps, the cracks, and the rustles. Then, finally, the thud of his body touching down.

Hadn't they been warned about climbing? That smothering, mothering voice, "Well, don't come crying to me if you break your necks!" But that hadn't discouraged them. After Gareth emerged the climbing victor, up to the tippy-top and down again, it was Johnny's turn.

"Higher! Higher!" Gareth called out.

Johnny, being light and adept, was only too happy to comply. Until the top branches could not bear his weight. Surely it was not high enough to break his neck. It was only a few feet over their heads. An oversized bush, really. A hawthorn, Gareth thought, but perhaps that's just because of the word *thorn* following "haw, haw, haw." But no one was laughing. No one ever laughed. And no one ever mentioned how Gareth had called Johnny a "scaredy-cat" that hot afternoon.

The scream sent Gareth running. After an initial pause of frozen realization, his legs moved on their own until he was nothing but pounding heart and pounding feet, faster and faster across the field, over the fence, past the barn to the driveway and up the newly painted steps.

"Gareth, I told you! I just painted those!" Johnny's mother, Hilda, shrieked, but one look at Gareth's face and she began running in the direction from which he had just come. Finally, Gareth just stood there, catching his breath, squeezing his eyes, willing it all to go away.

He didn't go back to the tree that day. Didn't want to see the blood or his screaming friend clutching his eye. He turned his face toward home. To the understanding embrace of his mother.

"Good thing it was his bad eye," his older brother, Tristan, declared when Gareth delivered the awful news.

"What do you mean, Trist?" their mother asked.

Tristan regarded his mother with the weak disdain that only first-borns possess. He tossed back his mass of blond curls and planted his feet squarely, hands on his hips. His knowing look to his younger brother, then his inhalation followed by a slow exhaled sigh, all pointed to the fact that he had been alive an entire year and a half longer than Gareth. He knew things. He knew all sorts of things.

"Well, if he can still see then he only hurt the lazy eye. It's not the eye that does all the work." Then Tristan took his hand and covered one eye and then the other to make his point. "You know. Try it! See ... can't see ... see ... can't see."

And so on one hot day at the start of June, Gareth's best friend lost his eye to a thorn bush and it was discovered that Gareth's older brother was blind in one of his.

It was far easier dealing with his brother's blind eye than his friend's. Nothing had really changed for Gareth's brother, after all. Tristan didn't think twice about it. He was used to being monocular, having had single-eye vision since birth. Sure, their parents fretted over it, but deep down Gareth knew that nothing had changed for Tristan that day. He was blind in his left eye when he woke up and still blind in his left eye when he went to bed. Besides, the dud eye functioned as though it were a seeing eye. It moved as the good eye moved, following the stronger twin. Never letting on that it was in any way less.

But Johnny was another story. His new eye was, for the most part, unmoving. It was freaky how it sometimes stayed, staring blindly ahead, while the other did as it pleased with no regard for the replacement eye. Gareth assumed that his friend's old eye hated the new one. It must have missed its matching eye and begrudged the new eye's placement in his friend's head.

Johnny underwent surgeries and procedures throughout that entire summer. An enucleation to remove the eye happened just days after the accident, and Johnny was required to wear a patch to cover where the eye had been. Gareth didn't understand why the eye had to come out, why they didn't just let it get better. His eye always got better when he accidentally poked it! Sure, this was worse, but why not give it a chance?

"Well, Gareth, his eye had too much damage. They had to take the eye out because if they didn't then he could go blind in the other eye," Johnny's mom explained to him carefully with her deep, strange voice.

"Why? He didn't hurt the other eye."

"It's a strange thing that happens. When one eye goes blind, sometimes the brain gets all mixed up and then the other eye goes blind, too. Especially with kids," Hilda explained, although she, too, didn't quite believe it. She had wanted to wait and see. Perhaps his eye would be fine. But the surgeon had been insistent. So she sat outside the surgery door. She waited. Even when her husband suggested they go have a coffee, that they should take a break, Hilda stayed behind, feeling those first pains of separation. How could she leave her son to those consoling strangers with their sharp scalpels?

"But my brother is blind in one eye and the other one didn't go blind."

"That is because he didn't suffer a trauma. It's different." She wanted to let it drop, not wanting Gareth to feel responsible for the accident. Not wanting to remember.

Eventually, the patch came off and Johnny was allowed out to play. He had a pair of glasses on, for protection. Gareth stared at his friend in shock. It wasn't the strangeness of sudden glasses that bothered him; it was that the bad eye had been replaced with something that seemed to have a drawing of an eye on it. Unmoving. Hard. And just a little bit creepy.

"Not catch, Gareth. What if that baseball hits Johnny in the eye? But you can look at comic books together. I got the new Spider-Man one for the both of you."

Gareth didn't know if Johnny's mom was more worried about the fake eye or the seeing eye. If the ball hit the seeing eye, and Johnny got a shiner, then he wouldn't be able to see at all, not till the swelling went down. But what if it hit the fake eye? Gareth imagined shards shooting out of his friend's eye socket. Like the crystal vase that had slid from his hands when he was helping with the washing-up. Hundreds of sharp little splinters that cut into his hurrying fingers as he tried to pick it all up before anyone noticed.

"We want his eye to get better, don't we Gareth?" Johnny's mother asked, her *w*'s sounding more like *v*'s than the way other mothers said words starting with the letter *w*.

Gareth nodded. Of course, he wanted the eye to get better, but he knew deep in his belly that the eye wouldn't get better. It would never see again. Gareth wondered why Johnny's mother didn't know that, as well.

* * *

Gareth's feet didn't quite touch the ground. They dangled somewhere between the seat and the floor. He swung them back and forth, counting how many times each foot passed the other. Why did he have to go to the eye doctor with his brother again? Boring, boring, boring.

"You could colour. There are colouring books and crayons over there," his father, Mark, suggested, hoping Gareth would settle down.

Gareth scowled, his full bottom lip in a petulant pout. How many times did he have to explain to his dad that he only colours the things that he draws himself? Whoever drew those many pictures in the fat paper book should colour his own stuff!

"I'm not colouring someone else's stupid pictures!" Gareth's young sense of justice was slighted at the suggestion he should do someone else's work.

"Higher, higher!" He suddenly remembered his words and his stomach clenched, reliving his friend's fall from the tree. He knew it was all his fault, and yet he still resented all the attention Johnny was getting. At least his brother's eye problems weren't his fault. "Go on, you're almost there, don't be a scaredy-cat!"

Gareth put his hands over his ears but it didn't quiet the voice in his head. And so his leg-swinging took on more vigour until every exchange was punctuated by the *whish, whish, whish* sound of corduroy ribs rubbing violently against each other.

It was only when the two matching girls walked in that Gareth stopped counting the swings of his legs. His hands dropped from his ears and he could not help but ask out loud, "What are they?" His father swatted him on the thigh to make him hush.

"Tristan?" The woman in the white pants, the white coat, and the white shoes spoke his brother's name, as she opened the door separating those waiting from whatever strange happenings might be occurring inside, beyond the barrier. On each previous appointment Gareth was invited in to join them but he always shook his head *no*. He had glimpsed the large machines and could only imagine the torture his brother had to face. It was bad enough that he would have to see his brother's dilated pupils.

Tristan and their father went through the magical doors, leaving Gareth in the presence of the two white girls. He waved awkwardly at them. His hand doing that childlike side-to-side gesture that is always accompanied by a courageous, unnatural smile. A smile of hope. A smile that says, *I made the first move, do not humiliate me by not mimicking it back*. But the girls took no notice of him; they just talked to each other in whispers. He couldn't quite make out the words, but what snippets he did hear were gibberish to him. A foreign language from some faraway place.

"Den snippet up zen blondish boy?"

"Yes, him den snippet gooden still."

They seemed the colour of snow, with straight hair that blended in with their skin so that you couldn't tell where their foreheads ended and the soft, downy strands of their hair began. And downy they were, with hair more like goslings' feathers than actual hair, pulling off their faces and into tight, long, white braids, each secured with a blue bauble-band popping out violently from a sea of white. Behind their thick glasses, Gareth could just catch a glimpse of pink eyes, circled by thick, snowy lashes. The pink ovals darted side to side quickly. He looked from one twin to the other and, yes, both girls had pink eyes, with dark reddish-black pupils, moving back and forth, back and forth, rapidly, in small, slightly jittery movements. *Bunny eyes*, he thought. Scared bunnies. Like the ones Johnny's mother had in hutches. Pets until they vanished, only to show up skinned and headless in the freezer.

Gareth glanced at the colouring books. They were so close to the pale creatures. If he could only pretend to want one, he could creep closer, get a better look. Figure out who and what they really were.

"Don't stare!" an old man bellowed in his direction. "Not po-lite to stare!"

The old man turned his attention to the girls. Swatted them both on their backs and ordered that they sit up straight. The girls improved their posture, straightened their backs, and tried to focus their vibrating pink eyes in front of themselves.

"I … I … just wanted a colouring book," Gareth stammered.

"Oh, for Chrissakes, they don't bite. Get off your heinie and get one, then! Clara, hand this idiot a colouring book."

One of the matching creatures reached over and picked up a book. She brought it close to her face, to her vibrating pink eyes, and examined it. Then she discarded it. She picked up another and repeated the process. Each time she seemed to smile a bit more, enjoying the power she was building as she reached, lifted, examined, and discarded. Finally, she settled on the fourth book and, smiling broadly, held it to her chest as she crossed the waiting-room floor before offering it to Gareth.

It was only when he looked at the book with its missing cover that he understood her hidden message. There, flying amongst the flowers, was a pair of winged fairies. Outlines, no more, with uncoloured insides as white as the girls looking over at him.

Changelings. Switched at birth and expelled from the fairy world. Forced to live with the evil, fat, old ogre. Gareth quickly glanced at the old man sitting there. White ribbed socks, patent leather shoes in black and white, Bermuda shorts, and a stained, improperly buttoned polyester shirt.

"Ya need some crayons with that, don'cha?"

Gareth shook his head. The uncoloured fairies were perfect just the way they were.

* * *

The albino twins were ready and waiting. Their hair was combed and braided perfectly. Their clothes, matching, were their best dresses. They had put on fresh white knee socks. Even their shoes, Mary Janes, were polished and shiny! After all, their mother was coming home for a visit, so everything had to be perfect. They saw her only intermittently, weekends mostly, when she was well enough to see them. On those days they would ride in their uncle's second-hand station wagon with its fake wood sides and backward-facing seats. They always took those seats, looking at what had already been, what they were leaving behind. They would hold hands as they watched the scenery fall away from them, as they sped toward the little yellow cottages on the shores of Lake Ontario, past Lynde Creek where the swans and geese nested, beyond the Girl Guide camp where city Guides and Brownies could experience the joys of nature away from their concrete lives, and then along a gravel road that wound past a small hospital and weaved, benignly, to the little yellow cottages. They thought it unfair that their mom got to stay there on her own, staring out at the water, while they were shuttled between disgruntled relatives. And worse, they had to go to school to learn things, like how to lie low, how to seem invisible, and how to be deaf to the jokes made about them.

What did she do there all day, their mother? Probably not much since she said and did so little at home. Just stared ahead, counting the minutes. The only difference was that when she was home the girls had to "put a special effort" into behaving. No fights, no bickering, and not too much noise. Then, only then, at the end of the day, she would come and kiss their foreheads. Tuck them into bed. Snug as a bug in a rug.

Clara and Blanca thought of what it would be like if their mother never came home again. If she just decided to stay, forever, in her yellow cottage. Then they could be adopted by someone else, escape their reality and move far away from their grandfather with his ashtray of smokes, his greasy fry-ups, and his stinking farts. They could find new parents. A mother and a father who would be there every night when they got home from school, ready to help them with their studies while they sipped hot cocoa or tea. Maybe they could even be home-schooled, away from bullying nicknames, in the safe embrace of these new parents. The father would smoke a pipe and puff, puff, puff while he threw out words of wisdom or turned on his hi-fi to play something from his collection of records. And there would be a mother who baked cakes and pies. A mother who could sing like the dark-eyed woman who lived in the main floor apartment, two floors below them. Yes, they would be the perfect parents, the couple downstairs. Esther and David with their music and art! Imagine being tucked away in that mysterious lower apartment that smelled of wood polish, baking, and lavender.

The twins did not have to say this to each other as they zoomed along. They knew what the other thought and, when one didn't, they had a secret language. A language that kept them safe.

Blanca rubbed her foot along the colours. They were so intense that even she could differentiate between the reds and purples and golds. It was a woven garden, with vines reaching past the flowers to the edges of the carpet, and all the way around there were fringes, tied rope or wool, or whatever it was, stretching out along the shine of the polished hardwood floors. She took off her sandals. Pressed her bare foot into the plush of the rug, felt the soft wool pile embrace her tiny foot.

The two girls had been invited for tea in the downstairs apartment the day before, when they came home, again, with downcast stares and pouting mouths, because their mother hadn't come back with them. They hadn't even seen her. She'd had one of her episodes again and was in the big building being watched after a treatment. To the twins, it was just another disappointment they could lock away in their treasury of childhood memories. And so, when Esther saw them, she gave them each a piece of poppy-seed cake and told them to come by the next day for high tea. "After church," she had said. And told them not to change out of their Sunday clothes. That's how the girls knew how special high tea had to be!

Clara sat waiting, her tiny body trembling with anticipation. She had never had high tea and didn't know quite what to expect. She only knew that manners were in tall order. It all sounded so special. As special as the pictures on the walls. They had to be special because there were huge gold frames around them. Clara got up from her chair and approached one of the paintings. As she got closer she saw that it wasn't flat like the pictures they had in school and at the library. It had texture that seemed to swirl toward her. She wanted to get closer, to run her hand over the paint, feel the three dimensions. But then, when she got close, she realized that the woman in the painting was completely naked. *Why*, she wondered, *didn't she put on her underwears before she was painted?*

They had never been all the way inside the lower apartment before, only glimpsed what they could whenever the door opened, always too quickly for the girls' curiosity. Still, they had seen things. Knew that the first-floor apartment was a world apart from the attic one their grandfather had. How could two apartments in the same big old house be so different? Smell so different? But mostly sound so different? Clara looked over at the piano. It practically looked like another table, but higher up. She had never seen a piano so large and wide. She wanted to go to it, touch the keys with her sticky little fingers, just to hear what sound it would make. She imagined stretching her small hands as wide as possible so she could play a chord. She wanted multiple notes, all at once, and for them to sound pleasant, resonant, and accomplished.

"We can play the piano after tea," Esther Perlman announced. Clara knew she was found out. Caught staring, with a covetous eye, at the instrument. Hopefully, Mrs. Perlman wouldn't prefer her sister now like everyone else did.

"Clara wants to play the piano, but I want to sing!" Blanca announced.

"Well, we can do both," Mrs. Perlman said, smiling.

Gosh, she was wonderful, even if she had a funny way of pronouncing words.

"You know," she said, moving closer to the girls, confiding, "I used to practise both before I had to leave Hungary."

"I'm hungry!" Clara blurted out, misunderstanding.

Esther took the cue and poured out the steaming tea from a gold-trimmed, fine white teapot and offered the girls each a plateful of cake.

"Eat as much as you like, but let's make sure we leave one piece for David when he gets home."

"Is David your husband?" Clara asked.

Esther nodded.

"Why don't you have any children?" Blanca inquired.

"We were not blessed with children," Esther stated flatly so that the girls would not know how that great regret lived within her every day of her life.

"I wish we could come here whenever we're sad," Clara blurted out, spitting crumbs across the table.

"Are you sad often?" asked Esther.

"Well, we're sad we have to go back to school soon. Everybody makes fun of us."

"Well, have some more cake and let's not think of that for now. Come as often as you like during the summer and on weekends when you go back to school," Esther soothed and secretly thought, *What strange little creatures they are!*

When summer ended Johnny worried about going back to school. There would be real classes now, a full day from nine till three thirty with a lunch break and two recesses. There were so many new responsibilities that came with being six. Lunch buckets with Thermoses. Different subjects. And paperwork to bring home almost every day. But Johnny didn't worry about any of those new responsibilities. He only worried that someone might make fun of his fake eye.

It was not to be his final eye. Johnny's eye was a temporary conformer, placed over the orb, to fill in the roundness of the eye that had undergone enucleation. It was small, half an almond shell, placed behind the eyelids to maintain an eye-like shape after the surgery. A match, as close as possible, hazel with a grey outline, was found in a drawer. And while the socket was healing, the fake stand-in seemed to ooze and crust over like a captive reindeer's weepy eyes. Of course, the infection came from somewhere deep within the cavern of the socket, far away from anything his classmates could ever see or imagine, but it seeped forth through every unfit space like spoiling leftovers in a Tupperware container with an ill-fitting lid. And so he began to cover it with his hand, hoping no one would notice it.

"Does it hurt, Johnny?" She was a new teacher, fresh from college. She wore bright colours and lipstick on her ever-smiling mouth. Her voice was high and airy, like a cartoon. Not a squeaky cartoon, but a princess in a cartoon. One of those drawings with the long spiralling curls and pointy boobs. Miss Argyle had both. The hair, an ash-blond colour, fell down to where the points began and all of it was accentuated by the bright salmon- or seafoam-coloured cashmere twin sets she wore, a single strand of imitation pearls floating between the neck and inevitable swell. Both Johnny and Gareth loved her right away and laughed when one or the other accidentally called her Mom.

"Does it hurt?" Miss Argyle asked again, as she reached out to touch his hand softly as she moved it away from his unseeing eye.

"No, ma'am."

"Don't be ashamed of it. You had quite the ordeal! You know something? I think you are the bravest boy I've ever met. Your new eye is a badge of honour. You should never feel like you have to cover it."

At that moment Gareth disliked his friend's new eye almost as much as he believed Johnny's good eye did.

Hilda tossed in her bed. Her prince lay in the next room, asleep, his seeing eye as blind to the world now as his other eye. She knew it would be a restless night. Knew that the only cure would be to pick herself up, move away from her husband, and creep into her boy's room. How much more sturdy her girls were, playing double dutch and clapping hands! What was that rhyme they sang, over and over again? "Miss Mary Mack, Mack, Mack, all dressed in black, black, black, with silver buttons, buttons, buttons ..." How much easier it was for this generation. Protected by games and optimism. Protected by a look to the future. Her girls faced life head-on, both eyes open. But not her son. Not him. Even when he had two eyes, he was always just a bit more hesitant.

She opened his door, the knob whining under her grasp. She went in to have a look. Peaceful and still. With eyes entirely closed, he looked normal to her, handsome. An angel, perfect, unmarred, and content. Did he dream with the perspective he once had, with two seeing eyes instead of just one?

Hilda couldn't remember the last time she dreamed or the last time she slept through the night. She had been avoiding sleep as much as she had once embraced it as a child. When she was young no one ever had to suggest that it was bedtime to her. She would finish her evening meal and then take herself to bed, eager to experience the world of her imagination. She believed that her imaginary dream world was every bit as real as, and a lot more inviting than, her waking world. She had been bullied when she was young. Teased to try harder, go further.

She had grown up in a small town just an hour drive outside of Hamburg. Bad Oldesloe. "Bad," not meaning naughty but meaning "bath." And there were baths, old Roman baths, in the village, with steam rising from the concrete, and the faint smell of sulfur. The baths were a greenish colour, but healing. When she was a young girl she went there with her mother and watched as her mother walked the perimeter of them, putting her hand on rocks or trees, as if invoking something. Something so old and foreign to the new regime that had taken over. Something beyond threats and politics and horrors. When her mother completed her ritual, Hilda felt safe and secure. Protected. As though a circle had been drawn around her, so strong and so invisible that nothing could ever penetrate it.

Why hadn't she done the same for her own son? Why hadn't she drawn the protective circle for him so that the old gods could watch over him? Gods who could have caught him when the branch broke, to ease his fall. She secretly knew what had stopped her from practising the old ways. Optimism. Yes, that was the obstacle! She had been seduced by hope, believing she was in a new world, with a new chance and a new beginning. Surely, the protection of old spirits had no place in Canada.

Hilda stared at her one-eyed son in his Spider-Man pyjamas, sprawled crossways along the twin bed. It was only recently that he took to sleeping on his own, and that was certainly not her choice or his.

"It's time," her husband had announced to their son, wanting his wife to share their bed with only him again. "You are a big boy now. You're going to be going to school full-time soon. You don't need your mama to protect you from the dark!"

The very next day, Johnny tumbled from the tree. No, it wasn't the dark that was the problem, but rather the false security of daylight.

Hilda preferred the night hours, anything from twilight on. In darkness and in sleep there were no rules, no orders. Daylight meant obeying. It meant schedules and rations. Hilda remembered the years of bringing sandwiches stuffed with potatoes to school because meat was needed for the brave soldiers, and so her mother, wanting to give her more than dry bread, added potatoes, leftovers from the main meal from the day before. Large houses were divided and roomers were allotted. Hilda could not think of a time when there weren't old men and lonely women on the third floor or in the attic. There had been a woman who helped with peeling the potatoes who always wore an apron, even to bed. She had her long grey hair in double braids that wound in coils around her head and, when she smiled, a glint of tooth-metal could be seen. She used to reach out to tickle Hilda and, terrified, Hilda would run as fast as she could, around the corner, sliding on the hardwood floors and up to the wide, winding staircase, first grabbing the newel post with her left hand to whirl that last turn before racing up two at a time. But never did she fall or tumble or hurt herself. Yes, girls were the far more resilient sex.

There had been another man there. Much younger than the others, almost a boy. A boy-man who could stand on his hands and even walk on them. He used to perform this for young Hilda, lifting one hand then the other to amuse her. Hilda would then try to do headstands and handstands in her room, using the wall for support. As she flipped upside down there would be a *thump-thump* as each heel hit the plaster. Her skirts would descend over her upturned head, and there she would, again, feel safe in a skirt tent, happy in her topsy-turvy world.

But there was something else about the acrobatic young man. He had a special purpose. And as Hilda Wagner looked down at the discarded prosthetic eye on her son's night table it all came back to her. The young man who did handstands had been an ocularist for the German army.

TWO

BY THE LATE NINETEENTH CENTURY, the only country that made glass eyes was Germany. Italy had turned its gaze from the eye to the vase, France had its perfume bottles. Only Germany had the wherewithal to dominate the entire world in the artistry and manufacturing of the glass artificial eye. Precision and perfection were the hallmarks of the German ocularist. Each pupil, each vein, each nuance of colour, was a different shard of carefully blown glass. It demanded patience. It demanded precision. It demanded the obsession to create perfection for something that would always benefit the onlooker more than the host.

Siegfried had learned from his father, who had learned from his father. Siegfried could trace oculary back five generations. He had always been surrounded by eyes. Even as a toddler, they blindly watched him. His father's creations were so plentiful in their house that it seemed odd to Siegfried, when they went visiting friends, to sit in a place without eyes staring at him. From shelves and work tables, from counters and opened drawers, there they were, protecting him. Watching over him. They must have been. That is why he lived when the others didn't.

When the fire from the sky ripped through the clouds to strike the heart of their house, Siegfried was alone in a room full of eyes. He stood on one side, in the oculary, while his family were already sitting at the table for their four o'clock *Kaffee und Kuchen*. Siegfried could smell the *Apfelkuchen*, hear the chatter and his name being called, until there was a deafening ripping sound and then only silence. There, and then gone, and all around him smoke and debris. And discarded, misplaced eyes.

There was no point in finding him a home or putting him into an orphanage. He was fifteen, almost old enough to join the army and fight, and so off he went to the front lines with his pockets full of glass eyes. When a mine exploded and an older boy lost an eye, it was Siegfried who knew how to do the enucleation. It was Siegfried who fashioned an eye from his pocket, matching as close as he could, promising that when the war was over he would make a perfect match to the one that was left. When the eyes were used up Siegfried was sent back to Germany, put into a house safely away from the cities, and outfitted with the means and tools to make eyes for the many soldiers who would need them. Germany may have been losing ground on the battlefield, but they would win in the field of ocular replacement. While Siegfried made more and more eyes for the boys in Hitler's army, the Allies were denied the German glass eyes. Gunshots and mine wounds were sewn closed by the Allies, while carefully blown glass eyes were outfitted for the Germans.

There would be no more killing for young Siegfried. His world was nothing now but the shaping of hot, treacly molten glass into concave segments. He never brought the eyes into the new house, though, he kept them in drawers in an outdoor shed. They wouldn't be able to protect his new family any better than they had his old one. But when the war ended, he took his favourite eye and had it fashioned into a necklace that he gave to Hilda's mother. She wore it around her neck till the day she died.

Hilda, what had happened to her? That reckless girl of the house who was always running up stairs and sliding down banisters? That skinny girl who hid behind doors or furniture and listened to the adults talk? Oh yes, she ran away to North America. That barbaric place where they make eyes from acrylic in readied moulds. Now, where is the artistry in that?

The ocularist knew he was one of the last of his kind. He stood in front of the mirror, an overhead light bearing down on him. Even now he could see how the light illuminated the thinning strands of hair escaping the top of his head. He really should just shave it all. Make it a choice of baldness, instead of a slow, sad farewell strand by strand. But it seemed so unfair to the strands loyal enough to stay. The ones that survived when the others fell away. Those strands that hung in there and didn't betray him.

Would more hair make him more attractive? Lessen the height of his forehead? Take away from the new fleshiness his jowls had taken on? Make his nose seem smaller, his skin less reddened, his eyes more alert? His eyes. There seemed to be a change creeping into them. He had to go up a few points in his prescriptive reading glasses, from a plus-one to a one-point-five. His eye doctor had even suggested he may need bifocals at some point in the future. Bifocals, imagine that! How ugly that would be. How old and ugly!

Siegfried had secretly been making his own replacement eyes, just in case. Every year he created two new ones, a left and a right eye, to match any changes the passage of time may have brought on. And if he never needed them, *Gott* willing, what would he do with the drawers of eyes that lay in the dark, waiting just in case? *Actors*, he thought. *That is what they are, just understudy actors, waiting to go on in a pinch, to take over from the real stars. Always hoping that no one notices the replacement.*

Who will take his place, though? Who will replace him? Who will learn from him? In his forties and no wife, no girlfriend, no prospects. His art could not die with him. But without love, there is no immortality.

Siegfried opened the third drawer from the top. He reached in and, eyes closed, he pulled out a smooth oval object and turned it over and over in his palm like a worry stone.

Johnny looked out the tiny window. Below him were clouds, big and fluffy and porous. Above him there was sunshine. And nowhere in sight was there earth, solid, safe, and predictable. He'd had to go pee for almost an hour, but what if he stood up and his shift of weight unbalanced the plane? What if, suddenly, the plane dipped to one side because he upset the balance? Johnny wished that his friend Gareth was with him. He'd know what to do. He always did. Like the time the teeter-totter wasn't even. Gareth scooted from his seat and moved a bit, just a tad, toward the centre until the two sides were level and unmoving. He understood perfect balance. When he walked over the diving board in swimming class, when he rode his bike with no hands, and when he climbed a tree, Gareth was always perfectly balanced. That's why he didn't fall that day, why he still had two eyes.

"You should shut your eyes. Try to sleep," his mother, Hilda, said, putting a protective arm around him.

They were lucky; not a full plane. And when the stewardess saw the woman with the tired-looking one-eyed boy, she brought them to where there were three empty seats.

"More room to stretch out," she had said. "It's so tiring travelling with young ones."

Hilda looked at her boy. His eye must have been irritating him. He was rubbing the replacement. His lids were red, a bit swollen and, behind the irritation, an unmoving, fake-looking eye. It seemed that Johnny was allergic to the eye and his entire system had been spending the past three years rejecting it. It may be a replacement, but, to his body, the eye was an invasive species, wreaking havoc with his physical ecosystem.

Hilda knew that the three seats weren't really for them. What seemed a generous offer was actually to make sure that the other paying travellers felt comfortable. She graciously took the three seats, not really wanting the extra space. She didn't mind being squashed by a stranger on one side, her son on the other side, by the window. She had behaved as though she was thankful for the extra space even though it meant that she'd have to take a seat farther back. Back, farther away from first class. Back, where it takes longer to get your dinner. Back, where it is only a few rows till you are in the smoking section. Already she could smell that familiar sulfur smell of a struck match. The rising smell of smoke, the tobacco, and the pungent air. It wasn't like there was an invisible wall between her row and the smokers! It would all find its way to her. Envelop her, cling to her hair, her blouse, her nostrils. How she would rather be cramped with a complaining child and a disapproving stranger than have to smell that familiar scent when she was already so anxious about flying!

God, she wanted a cigarette. But she had given up the habit on her wedding day. It was a deal they'd struck. She would give up smoking and he would be neat and tidy. More organized.

"Just going to stretch my legs a bit, sweetie. You okay?"

Johnny nodded as he watched his mother rise from her seat and walk toward the bathrooms at the back of the plane. It didn't tip! Didn't dip at all! And Johnny knew that his mother would never truly understand him because she was as balanced as his friend, Gareth.

Johnny sat very still in his seat. He didn't risk looking back at her as she walked away. Didn't see her bum a smoke from a man with the piercing blue eyes and an accent as strange, as thick, and as wonderfully foreign as his mother's.

*   *   *

Johnny had never been in a taxi cab before. No reason for it; if he couldn't get somewhere by foot or by bicycle, then there was always his dad's truck with its long Naugahyde bench seat and three faulty seat belts that they only pretended to buckle if a police cruiser cruised by. When his sisters were in the truck, as well, Johnny would duck down, head near their laps, so he wouldn't be seen. And then there were the rides in the school bus. Again, bench seats and no seat belts. He and Gareth would rush for the back seat to catch the bumps as the bus zoomed along the gravel streets. Of course, the bumps were never big enough for them so they would bounce up and down, exaggerating the anticipated fun. Or, perhaps, encouraging it.

This was so different. The seats had the same smell as his yearly new Buster Brown shoes. Tan-coloured. And they felt warm in the sunlight. Soft to the touch. The outside of the taxi cab was sleek, and shiny black, with four separate doors and a deep trunk where his mother let the man with the blue eyes put her suitcase before he slammed it shut. Before he suggested Johnny ride up front with the driver, to get a better view.

And that was the last thing Johnny understood. From then on, it was a series of sounds that seemed so strange to him that he had to look back to make sure that it was indeed his mother responding and not some other woman who had sneaked into the car in her place. When the laughter started and he heard a back-of-the-throat *ch-ch-ch* sound, he looked back and saw the man squeeze his mother's knee. His mother put a reassuring hand on Johnny's shoulder and Johnny turned from her, focusing only on what was in front of him.

A box. He had never seen anything like it. A metal handle, almost like a flag, emerged from it and on it were the letters *FREI*.

Johnny had no idea what *FREI* meant, only that when it was flipped up by the driver the box came to life and every few seconds the number on it increased just a little.

An important event in the history of the taxi was the invention of the taximeter by Friedrich Wilhelm Gustav Bruhn, a German engineer, born in 1891 in Lübeck. Johnny knew nothing about the invention but he did know all about Lübeck and had secretly hoped, from the time it was announced that he would be going to Germany, that Lübeck would be their final destination. Lübeck was the place where they made marzipan. Sometimes his mother would tell him how the entire town was built on marzipan. Johnny imagined hills of the almond paste and rivers of rich, dark chocolate. He thought that buildings would be sweet morsels, but safer than the house that had tempted Hansel and Gretel. There would be no witches in Lübeck. Just German grandmothers. *Omas* with aprons and white hair and smiles that never left their mouths. That is how he imagined his own *oma*, a woman who used to send packages at Christmastime, filled with gingerbread, marzipan, and a new Steiff Bear every year. That was the Germany of his mind. A *Chitty-Chitty-Bang-Bang* Germany, but without the evil baron and baroness. But this? This wasn't the Germany he held in his mind's eye. This was cold and concrete and busy with zooming cars, darting randomly in and out of the lanes. He suddenly longed for his orchard and the lake. He longed for his best friend. But mostly, he longed for his mother because, deep down, he knew that from the minute the plane had landed, his mother had changed. She was the woman of her youth, more carefree and more animated. Johnny understood that he had not existed in her youth and so he had no place with her in this strange land. He felt as separate and as dragged-along as her worn suitcase.

Johnny counted between the number changes on the strange box. One, two, three, *click*. One, two, three, four, *click*. How high would the numbers go? Was there a limit or could the numbers go all the way up to infinity? Like the number pi.

He hated Germany. He hated the blue-eyed man. He hated all of it. He didn't want a glass eye! He just wanted his mother back.

Hilda climbed the stairs to the top. Already she was giving herself over to the twisting staircase, the polished dark wood banister, the thick but worn runner leading the way up, up, up to the little room they would share. Of course, there wouldn't be a private bathroom, but a shared one at the end of the hall. Johnny would have to carry his own toothbrush there and back, walk the hall alone, and be responsible for his soap and washcloths. Good. He had been mollycoddled by her for far too long. He was ten now; he needed to start to learn some responsibility. She wouldn't be there forever to take care of him.

She knew his childishness was her fault. She held to him too tightly, fearing the day he'd grow and leave her. Her girls were already gone, at least emotionally. They were more interested in boys and parties than doing anything with her. They had their own secrets. How they hushed when she walked into their room to leave them their folded laundry. Only as she retreated down the hallway could she hear them laughing again.

Had she ever been that way with her own mother? Of course, she had more chores to do than her girls ever had. All those boarders meant extra meals, more dirty dishes, and a weekly polishing of the wood and antiques, rubbing linseed oil into the huge, round table, bringing it to a high polish with her elbow grease. How she had dreamed of the day when she'd have daughters of her own who would polish for her. But they never did. She didn't even have a grand, round table in Canada. Just a long, knotty pine slab on four legs. Four chairs around three of the sides and a long pine bench across the back. Of course, the meals were rushed. Of course, there was no discourse for hours on end. The table was too casual. Too taken for granted. Too convenient.

Already she could feel the past entering her being. How freeing it felt to know that breakfast would be served at a specific time. That the eggs would be in an egg-warmer, each one in its own quilted compartment, in the centre of the table. There would be no coffee from a convenient machine. No, it was all about process and time. Water at just the right temperature, carefully poured over freshly ground beans and strained through a white porcelain filter holder, releasing the bitter aroma into the air. How excited she was to share these rituals with Johnny. Her girls were already lost from her world, in the modern world of transistor radios, miniskirts, and junk food. But maybe, just maybe, this trip would reclaim one of her children. Maybe not all was lost for Johnny. Maybe he would be the one to truly know and understand her.

"Do you like the room?" she asked Johnny as she swung open the door.

He shrugged. "It's okay."

"What's not to like? Look at that big fluffy eiderdown. You know when I was a little younger than you I had one like that and I would fling it on the floor and then jump from the bed into the feathers. It drove my *mutti* crazy!"

Johnny just shrugged again. He couldn't care less about the big fluffy comforter (not a comforter, an *eiderdown*) or the stairs or the wood.

Hilda placed her raincoat on a chair, kicked off her shoes, and threw herself into the thick swell of the eiderdown.

"It's heaven, Johnny, come try!"

He wanted to punish her for ignoring him earlier. But the bed did look cozy and comfy, and he would feel so much better snuggling into her.

"Mom?" he said, burrowing his head into the crook of her arm.

"Mmm?"

"What if the glass eye isn't any better? Then we came all this way for nothing."

"It'll be better, I promise."

"But what if it isn't? I'm scared."

Hilda rubbed her hand through his soft dark hair. How like hers. Dark, slight wave, widow's peak. The girls were strawberry blond like their father, with that easily freckled skin and green eyes. But Johnny was like her. Dark hair, skin that could tan, and astonishing pale hazel-grey eyes, in contrast with the hair, the dark lashes, the olive skin tone. That acrylic eye didn't do him justice. It didn't have the luminosity their eyes held. That glow. That liquid look that said, "Look at me, my eyes float on water." For almost four years now, Johnny has had one liquid eye, full of life and movement and one dull, opaque eye, lifeless and flat. It was replaced every other year, but the fit was never quite right and his eye was forever irritated. He had infection after infection, and a constant buildup of mucus, which Hilda patiently cleaned nightly. For all the trouble and fuss, she had hoped that the eye would have been worth it. But no, it was an affront, a mockery of his soul.

"Don't be scared. Soon you will meet the only man who can help you. He is an artist beyond compare. If he can't help you, no one can."

"That's why I'm scared, Mom."

If Siegfried had enemies, they were John and Charles Erickson. Viking blood. They probably couldn't help but pillage and destroy wherever they went, wanting to possess kingdoms. In the late 1940s those Viking descendants, those brothers, those mere dispensing opticians from Tacoma, Washington, saw a market and they systematically went from optician to optician, in every surrounding state, flung open their drawers, threw down their money, and then scooped up all the glass eyes. What joy they must have had, those pillagers, as they broke and crushed each pupil, each innocent orb.

Even now when he thinks of the travesties committed all those years ago, Siegfried cannot help but shudder in horror. At least fifty thousand glass eyes, smashed and destroyed, by those avaricious brothers. Those money-grubbing artisans. Yes, artisans. Wannabe ocularists! But not the real thing. They were not artists who learned from their fathers and grandfathers. They were businessmen, *betrüger*! They didn't know what it meant to blow the glass, lay in the individual colours. What did they know of reflection, depth, and the liquid quality shared by both the human eye and glass? After all, glass was a liquid! But how would those Vikings know that?

The eye is the only organ that can possess and also behold beauty. There is nothing that compares to the eye. *It is*, Siegfried thinks, *indeed the mirror of the soul. And is not a mirror made of glass and not cheap plastic, for crying out loud!*

> Glass eyes are no good in a cold climate. A man in midwest America could leave his house on a cold winter's day and that glass eye could crack in his head. In fact, I have heard of such a story. Not so with acrylic. Nope, glass eyes have no place in America. We custom-make each to fit the individual. Form it — no, mould it, actually — for a better, more comfortable fit. Germany is behind the curve. The future is in plastics.

Those were the words repeated at the ocularist convention by the American ocular representative. *Gott*, he hated the New World. A world of hula hoops. A world of bubble gum. A world of plastic. *Gott*, how he hated plastic. Cheap, cheap, cheap, and disposable! Of course, Siegfried hadn't gone to the convention to actually learn anything. He hadn't gone to — what was it they called it? — schmooze. No, he went to find someone who loved his art to the level he did. He went in search of an apprentice. Someone he could teach. Instead, he saw the way things were going. He saw the moulds, the dull plastic materials, the opaque replacements with their threaded veins. Oh, the best of them could match colour very well. They could add the veins as threads in the whites, subtly, and use what seemed like children's pencil crayons to colour and shade, but the eyes didn't breathe, they didn't shine. They did not reflect the soul. All Siegfried could do was to despair that he was becoming the last of a dying breed in a world that was destined to accept so much less than it deserved.

"Mirror, mirror on the wall," he said, doing his morning tradition of shaving, and caring for those last strands on his head. "Who's the fairest of them all?"

There is a boy coming. He is the fairest. And you will know him by his mother, for he has her eye colour.

Siegfried smoothed his hair, splashed cold water on his freshly shaved face, then, for the first time in ages, he opened his medicine cabinet and took out his aftershave. A twist, a sniff, and he thought better of it. Old Spice was for sailors. Not ocularists.

Hilda stared at her reflection in the mirror. Her lips were still full, her skin still soft, her teeth still straight and white. But there, at the sides of her eyes, she could see those crinkles creeping in. Laugh lines, they called them. But hers were not just from laughing. How many tears had she cried, alone, when the house was asleep? Tears for her son. Tears for her marriage, tears for the life she left behind, and tears of boredom. Indeed, her nightly habit of leaving her husband's bed so that she could cry had become the most seductive aspect of her life. Nobody noticed her sadness. They didn't notice her at all. Her cloak of invisibility was already woven and ready for her.

Invisibility has a way of waiting and then slipping stealthily into a life. It begins when the meal is taken for granted. When the kids' needs come first. When a husband is too tired to fuck you, and then too distracted with worries to fuck you, and then just too distant to fuck you. You become a stranger in his bed, seen only as a mother, a wife, and a financial partner. Anything but a woman. *Why?* Hilda wonders. *Why is it the sacrifice that every woman must make for her children? A sacrifice that will only be repeated again by her daughters and then by theirs, throughout the generations?*

Hilda put some kohl pencil around her eyes, darkened her already-dark lashes, smeared a warm red across her lips. She knew that Johnny had seen the stranger's hand on her knee when they were in the cab. Why did she allow that? Why didn't she slap the hand, or at least remove it? It would lead nowhere. It was just a flirtation in the back of a shared cab. But still … still. It was like an ignition button being pressed. Not a fire, but the first spark of pos-sibility. It was the first time in years that anyone saw her beyond her function and related to her as a woman. As a human.

Of course, she didn't make this trip back to Germany for that. It wasn't to trace her youth and reclaim her identity. No. It wasn't to hear a language that still existed deep, deep in her soul, but was forgotten a little bit each day. No. And it wasn't to wear nice clothes — city clothes — and to touch the sweeter parts of her youth. No. It was to help her son. To get him an eye that would stop the bullying and the pain. To give him a new start.

But still …

Still, she couldn't help but wonder if Siegfried would remem-ber her. If he would be happy to see her.

The boy looked ten or eleven at most. His hair flopped over his high forehead. Siegfried noted the long limbs, the awkward body language, the shy and cautious smile when spoken to. How like his mother he was! Siegfried remembered Hilda, spying on him from behind the door, thinking she couldn't be seen that first day when he had arrived at their house, a thankful soldier away from action. How old was he then? Perhaps five or six years older than the boy before him.

"Come over here, young man. Do you speak German?"

Johnny shook his head *no*.

"Then I have a good chance to practise my English, but you must promise not to laugh at me if I get some words wrong."

Johnny lifted his downturned gaze and smiled openly at the older gentleman. It was only then that Siegfried could look into the boy's eyes. See his perfect hazel-grey orb reflecting the light and shining with his emotional responses while the dull acrylic replacement sat lifeless in the other socket. How uncomfortable it looked! How foreign! What a mockery it made of the boy's emotions and thoughts. A well-crafted, perfectly painted mockery. And all because of those American Vikings from Washington! What blasphemy! What hackery! How dare they, those pillaging bastards!

"Now, I have a very important question to ask you."

Johnny was ready for this. The endless questions. What happened that day? Did they remove the eye right away? Was there ever an infection? Do you clean the eye regularly? Properly? Do you feel pressure at the back of the eye? Any pain? Discomfort, irritation, dryness? Johnny knew all the questions and had practised the answers over and over again.

"Do you eat marzipan? Because I have some."

Johnny smiled and nodded. The ocularist reached over to Johnny's ear and seemed to pull a red, tinfoil-wrapped chocolate out of nowhere.

"I will tell you a secret now, Johnny. I once tried to be a chocolatier instead of an ocularist, but it didn't turn out so well."

"Why not?" asked Johnny.

"Because all my bonbons looked like eyeballs! You see, we all have a destiny and you can deny it all you like and, when you do, life gives you a push. You fail or fall. Funny how in English those words are so alike! You are lucky, you got your push very early in life."

"I don't feel very lucky."

"Well, I didn't feel very lucky when my marzipan chocolates all looked like eyeballs! But there you go! So what, you fell from a tree. So what, you have only one eye. It brought you to me, didn't it? And I just pulled a marzipan from your ear!"

Johnny looked at the ocularist for what seemed a very long time. He didn't want to admit that he didn't quite grasp the concept of destiny. Unless destiny was part of the long list of things you could no longer do after you fell from a tree.

"I think that I would love to eat marzipan eyeballs."

"Come, let me show you something."

As Siegfried passed his almost closed door, toward his storage drawers, he caught in his periphery the only too familiar shape of Hilda, spying from behind the door. He passed by without a word. That would be another secret kept to himself. He put a finger to his lips as he opened a steel drawer, the metal screeching against metal. He motioned for Johnny to come closer, for him to peer inside.

A hundred eyes stared up at Johnny. Each with a light of its own. They glowed, they reflected, they seemed to move when Johnny moved. How was that possible?

"You have lost your external sight in one eye and, for that, you may mourn. But there are two types of seeing, my young friend. There is the outward-looking and the inward-looking. Now you must do both. You will appear to the world to be not quite as special as you are because no one else will know that you can see in two directions while most of us can see in only one. Now we both have work to do. I will make you the best eye possible, and you will have to start doing the seeing. Inward-seeing. And that, my new friend, is called insight."

Johnny wasn't sure what it all meant but he felt a rush through his body. A tingle that started somewhere in his gut and spread, in circles, outward.

"*Bewahre doch vor Jammerwoch!*
Die Zähne knirschen, Krallen kratzen!
Bewahr' vor Jubjub-Vogel, vor
Frumiösen Banderschntzchen!
Eins, Zwei! Eins, Zwei! Und durch und durch
Sein vorpals Schwert zerschnifer-schnück,
Da blieb es todt! Er, Kopf in Hand,
Geläumfig zog zurück.
Es brillig war. Die schlichte Toven
Wirrten und wimmelten in Waben;
Und aller-mümsige Burggoven
Die mohmen Räth' ausgraben," Siegfried recited, his voice low and full of dramatic intonation. Johnny stared at him, eyes wide, rapt. He had never heard anything so strange.

"Do you know this poem? I am sure I have mixed it up a bit."

Johnny shook his head *no*.

"It is very famous. The 'Jabberwocky.' Some people call it a nonsense poem, but I think it makes a lot of sense. It is about fear and finding courage. It is about defeating the monsters that stop you from being all you can be."

Johnny wiped his crusted eye. Whenever he was uncomfortable he touched his unseeing eye. All this talk of monsters made his eye itch.

"One day, one day, my boy, you will find your courage again. You are destined to defeat the Jabberwock himself!"

Hilda listened while Siegfried addressed her son. She had agreed to wait outside while Siegfried did his initial consultation with Johnny. That was after they had that awkward first meeting where they each regarded the other middle-aged version of the young people they once were.

"What happened to your wonderful hair?" she had blurted out when she first saw him.

"You have gained so much weight! You were such a skinny girl!" he had responded.

Hilda had thought to herself, *No wonder I went to North America. German men are so blunt. No tact.*

Siegfried had thought to himself, *No wonder I never married. German women are so blunt, so tactless.*

But now, as she listened by the door, she experienced something else. Something so rich in familiarity that she felt herself being drawn into every word he spoke. His kindness was weaving a web around her and she felt panicked. She was claustrophobic and filled with regret.

What had happened to her marriage? It all began so well. There was a time when they couldn't keep their hands off each other. In the beginning, the differences between them only ignited the sexual match. She was on an adventure, away from her homeland, away from her mother's watchful eye and, with John Sr., she could finally be herself in all her unbridled passion. He could just walk into a room and she would feel a dampness, an urgency, rushing through her body. It would take her over, as if their love was another vibration altogether, freeing their true selves. The rest of the world didn't exist in those moments. Not bills or responsibilities. Not past sorrows or heavy secrets. It was only then, during their lovemaking, that she was capable of being in the moment, mindful of the now. It was only then that she felt safe, desired, and loved.

It was easy to think that the change started when Johnny had fallen from the tree because the grief was just too much for both of them. John could not bear to look at his son's wound. He never cleaned the eye or dealt with Johnny's endless infections. He never consoled him when he came home, embarrassed that he looked different from the other kids, sad that he was no longer good at sports, teased and destroyed. Oh, what brutes children were!

Hilda knew that her husband still loved their son, but she also knew that the grief was too much for him. He spent more time talking to his daughters, where he could navigate safely, and Hilda became the only support for the boy. As the couple's bond became more about grief than passion, John had to find flickers of joy elsewhere. Well, why not? Hilda had become as heavy as a German dumpling! Not physically, of course. Oh yes, her hips had become fuller with each child. And yes, she wasn't as thin as she once was. But she was strong. Fit. What they would call a handsome woman. Handsome, strong, striking even. But not soft and pretty. And because John could not bring comfort to his son, he looked for distractions in women who needed him. Women who could make him feel strong. Women who were less than his wife. His distractions were all softer, weaker, easier. Distractions that could alleviate his guilt for being a father whose usefulness was ebbing each and every day. Distractions that could see him for the man he was and not the sadness he was destined to carry.

Hilda knew this. She was bonded to her husband although she knew that somewhere along the way he had stopped seeing her, even before the accident. It started drop by drop, event by event. A child born and suddenly her breasts were vessels for feeding a baby and not something her husband enjoyed fondling anymore. Then another child and the endless work, the bills, the tiredness. It was with the second that sleep became more inviting than sex. By the time Johnny was born, their roles were well-defined for a functioning home. She was a mom. A homemaker, a maid, a caregiver, a cook. She served a purpose and, in doing so, had ceased to be a woman.

Unlike Miss Argyle. Pretty Miss Argyle, who had a smile uncontaminated by the worries of motherhood. Miss Argyle, who could be breezy and optimistic even as the house of cards was scattering all around them. Young and fresh Miss Argyle, who hadn't lived through a war, hadn't had to deal with rations, or boarders in her home. Miss Argyle, who never had to see her father executed for war crimes. How delightful to be so very free. How delightful to be the foam on the top of a cappuccino!

"Do you like marzipan?" she heard Siegfried ask young Johnny. She knew that Siegfried would pull a sweetie out of her son's ear and that he, in turn, would be enchanted by the magic, just as she had been when she was his age and Siegfried was a young man, a teenager, really, but in those days, a boy was a man by the time he was sixteen.

Hilda felt the tight grip of regret squeeze at her heart. She waited for that tight fist to loosen, but it wouldn't. It just kept squeezing. What had she sacrificed, and for what? Oh, how she would like to believe in magic again. She would like to have the faith of childhood restored to her somehow. She would like to find that protective circle of her girlhood. *Gott*, how she wanted to believe that there really was magic and not just sleight of hand.

But if her ocularist friend from her past could give her son an eye, he would also give him confidence. And for that, she would trade everything. For that, she would make herself believe in magic again.

There are no ready shapes, no moulds. No set standards. Each eye is a work of art. A one-of-a-kind blown-glass piece, with a delicate touch of coloured glass placed exactly at the right moment. A glass eye is alchemy and art. It requires patience, precision, and a finicky attention to detail.

For Siegfried, it was more than that. He had his tools of the trade, the many cylindrical tubes of cryolite glass, the colouring glass, the Bunsen burners, the shaping tools, the pliers. He had scars on his fingers from burning them as he turned the glass, rolling it at an even pace to shape the small masterpiece. Yes, a masterpiece! Every glass eye had to be a masterpiece of his making. How many times had he blown air to shape the orb? How many times had he spun the hot glass into the required shape? How many times had he purified with fire, mated colour to colour with touch, and then detailed it all with precision?

Cryolite is the only glass material used for the prosthetic glass eye. The milky-white glass becomes translucent at high temperatures, becoming malleable and easy to manipulate. The moment the white cryolite changes to clear, a perfect sphere must be blown. It stretches slightly into a delicate bubble and then it is cut away from the tube. Next, coloured glass is put onto the whitening sphere with an array of colouring rods, by touching and inlaying coloured glass into the hot cryolite. Eyes are not merely blue or brown or green; eyes are a kaleidoscope of little shapes and colours, as layered and as dense as an Impressionist painting. From a distance, an eye may appear one colour or another, but the art is to see that each iris is a tapestry of hues and rings and specks. Every shade, every fleck, is another bit of glass, carefully chosen, heated, and placed. Layer by layer by layer by layer. After the iris, it is time for the pupil to be added. The ocularist uses a shiny black glass, and this is perhaps the trickiest moment. Get the pupil wrong and an eye will look crossed, wonky, off-kilter. Its placement must be exact to the seeing eye, not a fraction off. Finally, the anterior chamber of the eye, the cornea, must be reproduced. Through this, the design of the iris gets its own spatial depth which should complement the sitter's seeing eye, giving the person, repossessed of an eye, balance, confidence, and beauty.

For Siegfried, the process was never the alchemy. The alchemy was in the unknown. Something he could never explain to the makers of acrylic prosthesis. The eye had to be a reflection. Something from the sitter's soul had to be present in each and every eye he made. A glass eye didn't just match the other eye, it had to do much more, and, although the glass eye could not see, it also could not lie. The eye might be said to be the mirror to the soul, but a seeing eye could also evade, look away, and deny. Siegfried's creations would never do that. Because he always captured a little of the wearer's soul, trapped it in the darkness of the pupil, his glass eyes reflected an inner truth.

What had Siegfried seen in Johnny's soul? At first, he seemed just a shy and unassuming boy. Hesitant and polite with just enough curiosity to see him through the adventures of life. But after two or three visits he began to see something else. The boy who climbed too high then fell to the earth was another Icarus. He was insecure and unassuming because his eye, his current acrylic eye, did not reflect his soul at all and so his true nature was half hidden. His soul was deep-thinking and poetic, but it also had a desire to reach higher heights, to reach toward the heavens even if it meant the failure of a fall. What did the boy need most? Courage. And the only way to force courage was to display an honest truth at all times. To strip away all artifice, and to lay bare every vulnerability.

And so he began. The flame was a blue hot torch. It engulfed the glass, encircled it like hellfire. But Siegfried had never feared hellfire. He used it. He harnessed the flame, used it for his own purpose. The flame that destroys is the flame that creates and the glass that melts is the glass that forms. The layers of colours are the many layers of one's understanding, and the black of the pupil is the depth of a soul.

Siegfried worked through the night, both eyes straining for exact precision. That is the irony of it. A man with one eye could never be an ocularist, because spatial awareness, balance, and the ability to see well enough to work in infinitesimal detail were required.

How many more masterpieces would he be able to make before he grew too old, too shaky, too tired or until his eyesight lessened? He had time yet. Maybe twenty years or more. But who would learn from him? Who would make this boy's replacement eye when he became a middle-aged man and Siegfried was no more?

He could cry from loneliness. Cry that when his parents died they left him to carry the torch, but he had somehow let them down. Generations of ocularists, and it all stopped here with him, in his work studio. Alone.

He put down his torch, waited for the boy's eye to become cool to the touch and then held it in his hand. Yes, it seemed fine indeed. He could almost see the entire boy in the eye he held. Tomorrow he would know for sure. Tomorrow would be the test. He would know if he succeeded when Johnny opened his newly placed eye, looked into a hand mirror to see, from the other eye, his new glass eye reflected back at him. Equal. And balanced.

What had she run away from? Shame? In the innocence of her youth, she believed that shame would not cross the ocean. It would not find her in a new world. There, she could re-create herself, be whomever she wished to be and have a new lease on life. Yet here she was, back in the home of her youth, and the pull, the yank on her heart, was strong.

She was back in the land she swore she would never see again. Not back for herself, but for the good of her son. That was the desire, the impetus of her trip. And yet, it seemed to be affecting her on a cellular level. She knew that every memory was being reopened because of Siegfried. Here was a man who knew the sins of her father and yet, even with that shame, he still treated her with kindness, still seemed to listen to her, to drink in her words. Here was a man who seemed present.

She could come back every other year for a new eye as long as the boy was growing. She would have a reason and, with that, the thought of a two- or three-week escape every other year, she could endure the rest. The indifference. The invisibility. Her husband's wandering eye.

Bowling! That's what it came down to. She could see no point in it. A big, hard ball, hurled down a laneway in order to knock things down. Pins. That is what they were called. Pins. But why knock them down only to have them set back up again? What was the point? And the noise in those places as the balls rolled along. And people yelling out, "STRRRRRIKE!" It wasn't as if it were a real sport where one gets fit! Just a stupid pastime where people could eat too many french fries and drink sweet, fizzy pop. And laugh too hard at bad jokes.

And flirt.

Yes, Miss Argyle was part of his bowling team. Every week her husband went, straight after dinner, to help out the team. What about helping around the house? Dishes washed after dinner or the table cleared?

"You could come if you wanted to," he once said to her. But when she got her coat, pretending that she might join him, he suddenly changed his tune. Said that there were no more spots on the team.

"I could record the scores," she'd replied.

"Naw, that's Jean's job."

"Jean?"

She didn't really have to ask because she knew that Jean was Miss Argyle.

So what was it about Siegfried? Why did he seem so different from her husband? And wasn't changing men like swapping deck chairs on the *Titanic*?

For one thing, Siegfried didn't assume. He asked questions. He listened. Like the time he had taken the two of them to the Heidelberg Castle to see the ruins. A little outing, he had called it. A bit of sightseeing, a bit of fun, before getting to work on the eye. And so he drove them all the way to Heidelberg to see the castle. Gosh, how he marched about with such confidence, as though the castle had once belonged to him.

"We can take the boat down the Rhine, too!" he had enthused to Johnny. "But be very careful because we will go past the rock where the Lorelei wait and their singing could drive you mad."

"Who are the Lorelei?" Johnny had asked.

"Ah, the Lorelei! Some people think there are three maidens who brush their long golden hair and some think it is only one."

"What do you think?"

"I think that they are beautiful sisters who have all had their hearts broken by men who were not worthy of them. And so they sing a haunting song of their sorrow and then, only then, do they remember that they have power."

"Magical powers?"

"Oh, yes. You see they have beautiful pale hair and they brush it. It is long and it falls down to their waists in waves like the waves of that river over there. And when men hear their song and see their beauty they are enchanted and they lose their souls to them. But I think that any man who loses his soul to a beautiful woman actually wants to be caught by her!"

"The Lorelei wouldn't catch me! I don't care about music. A song would never catch me. Just some sad girls singing. It's silly!" Johnny had been adamant.

"I wouldn't be so sure, young man. A beautiful woman can catch you with many things, including a song."

And it was at that moment that he had glanced at Hilda for perhaps a few seconds too long before looking away, awkwardly.

"See here?" He then pointed at a small statue of a dwarf. "This is the famous Perkeo. He may have been a very small man — a dwarf — but he drank between five and eight gallons of wine every day. Every day! He died one day when someone offered him a glass of water. Anyhow, he was a great court jester and had been loved by all. Even though he drank so much of the castle's wine!"

"What is it with us Germans? There is always a dwarf in our folklore and literature." Hilda had laughed and when Siegfried laughed with her, she couldn't help but notice how straight and white his teeth were.

"It is a throwback to the myths and stories of the Black Forest. To the days of trolls and fairies and witches."

There had been a spell woven around Hilda that day. The Rhine, the castle, the perfect weather. So far away from worries and so close to hope. And every time Siegfried had mentioned myth or legend, magic or love, she could feel herself yielding to an otherness that the day in and day out of domestic responsibility had eroded away. But hadn't that magical thinking been the very thing that had made her flee Germany in the first place? Wasn't that magical thinking the cause of the war?

"Come on, we will go and eat something. Maybe some knackwurst and mustard. Have some fun because tomorrow we make the long drive back and then I will have to work, work, work all day long."

"Doing what?' Johnny had asked.

"Making the very best eye I have ever made for the most important person you could ever imagine."

"Who are you making an eye for tomorrow?"

"For you, of course! Now, want to see if I can still walk on my hands?"

And then Siegfried had winked at Hilda before turning upside down with all the grace and sprightliness of a much younger man. Hilda knew that he was showing off for her, but she had gone along with it, hugging Johnny as he clapped with joy.

That had been only a few days ago, but now it felt like a lifetime had passed. She knew the magical time was ending. She would be going to him this last time, with Johnny, to see the finished eye, to place the eye in Johnny's vacant socket, and to take the eye away to Canada. Hilda knew, in her heart, that every time she looked at her son, she would see the eye Siegfried had made and she would think of him.

*   *   *

Hilda didn't open the envelope for at least a week after she returned. She put it aside, out of sight. She would be attentive, a good wife, and she would push all thoughts of romance out of her mind. They were just old friends. That was all. They shared a past. A past she had chosen to run from. But Siegfried hadn't run, as she had, abandoning her mother in her darkest hour. No, Siegfried had stayed, remaining as a renter, being a comfort to her mother through the shame and loneliness. Not even as her mother suffered heart failure did Hilda return home. She couldn't. She knew that the shadows would swallow her up.

It was a secret that Hilda had pushed as deep down inside her as she could so that it was in such a faraway dark place of her soul that she could deny it, pretending it had never been there. She had created a world away from it. She had hidden it so well that even she could not remember where she put the memory and, in doing so, she knew that she would somehow protect her children from that dark seed and keep them away from the Black Forest of the soul.

But Siegfried knew. He knew only too well and he shone a light upon it and somehow, in his presence, it didn't have quite as much power over her.

"I can only imagine the sorrow you must have felt. The shame. You ran from all you knew and loved and you chose oblivion over comfort," he had said to her, finally, on her last day in Hamburg.

She remembered how he had used the word *love* that day. Love, without expectation or apology. It was a sweet way of using the word, seeming more like a fact than a seduction.

"You do not understand," she'd responded. "You see, I did not know my father, it was always just me and my mother. I never missed him. I never thought of him. Only in his dying was I forced to consider him. And I hated him. I hated him so much that I had to run. Not from the shame but from my hate. It frightened me ... how much I could hate."

Siegfried took her face in his hands and nodded.

"I know," he had said to her. "He was a monster. And he betrayed you."

Hilda could smell that familiar combination of chocolate and aftershave that German men exuded. Canadians were campfires and beer. Italians were garlic and red wine. But a German man, yes, he was aftershave and chocolate.

"It wasn't the fifteen American prisoners he killed for no good reason. It's what he did in Poland. Unspeakable. They hanged him for the wrong reason."

"You must know that the sins of the father do not become the sins of the children," he had consoled.

"No, that is not true. You throw a rock into a pond and the ripples travel. My children must not carry that shame and that is why I have a life in Canada. Why I will never live in Germany again. It is as much for them as it is for me."

"And how will your children ever know you?"

"It is better that they are safe in their oblivion."

And there it was. Secrets shared. Hilda opening up, after her years of silence, to someone who knew her as the child she had once been. A child free from worries, unaware of the war all around her. A child who spent hours practising headstands in her room, protected from the horrors she would learn later.

How did the locked gates of secrets suddenly open? A touch of his hand was all that was needed. That was the key that opened the past and now there it was, present, and the only place where she could feel safe from her past was in the touch of his hand.

Hilda couldn't open the envelope because she feared that the secrets of her past might somehow tumble out and follow her to the New World. And yet she yearned for that connection to her youth.

The first night that her husband, John, invited young Johnny to bowling, leaving Hilda home on her own, she sat for what seemed an eternity, holding the envelope in her hands. How bold and broad the letters were, fountain pen, navy-blue ink against the stark white envelope. The funny way of writing the letter *H* that only Germans do, with the loops on the sides instead of the clean lines of North Americans. She stared at the letters he had written with his square hands. Those hands that had touched her forehead. Those fingers that had lifted the tears from her cheeks when she cried and those fingers that brought her tears to his lips, where he could taste her pain, her grief, her confusion. She held the envelope, heart pounding. Then, as she glanced at the door, she slid her silver letter opener along the seam of the envelope and slowly pulled out the paper inside.

> Hilda, do not forget to clean the eye regularly. I would say that a rinse in salt water will suffice. The glass does not hold germs like the acrylic eye did, and it does breathe and so there will be no buildup like his old eye. You should not get any crusting. If he complains at all then he is growing and you must return right away, and I will create a slightly different fit for his comfort. He will need it changed every year to two years for optimal comfort. It is enough that you pay for the trip here. I will cover the cost of the eyes.
>
> Yours, Siegfried.

And there it was. No more than a note on how to care for her son's eye. No mention of how nice it was to see her again, to reconnect. No talk of how he felt when she was leaving. It was just a practical note. Necessary. What a foolish woman she had been! How foolish to desire that someone might still desire her! How foolish to hope for a bit of attention at her age! But a small compliment, perhaps … anything at all, to acknowledge that she existed. That her breath, her life, her being might have some worth on this earth.

Was there something between the words perhaps? A hope that she return every year or two? The kindness of not charging for the glass eyes. Any romance in that? No, it was just kindness, nothing more. How she had misread it all. How it had been no more than the kindness of an old friend. Kindness born of shared experiences. Of past.

Hilda folded the note carefully and opened the envelope to return it to its resting place. It was only then that she noticed something small at the bottom of the envelope. She reached in delicately, with two fingers. Slowly, slowly she took out the small token. A pressed blue cornflower. A flower he must have picked the day they were at the castle. A flower he had said was worthy of the Lorelei to wear in their hair.

THREE

A YOUNG MARRIED COUPLE, Katherine and Mark, travel by small airplane and are forced to land in a small, out-of-the-way town. The people there behave strangely, and Katherine and Mark want to leave but they can't. They are trapped by a force field that prevents them from leaving. They are held prisoner by a large bubble …

Gareth reached over and grabbed a fistful of popcorn from his older brother's bag. It was always the same, him opting for the candy then craving the salty. Tristan knew the routine only too well and so he always ordered a size up. He always placed the bag near his brother so that he didn't have to ask for it. He could just take it as he liked. He had never seen him take the popcorn, though. Both his brother and the popcorn have always been on the unseeing side. Not something he ever consciously chose to do, but something that was so much a force of habit that he didn't even know that he was doing it. His compensation was natural, unlearned, easy. By putting the popcorn on the unseeing side, it left the good eye, the eye with the periphery, on the public side. He knew if someone came and wanted to be seated, or if someone was struggling with their own popcorn and drinks, he would see them and could easily accommodate them. These instinctual reactions stopped him from blindly bumping into others, from knocking into what he didn't see, and from jumping, startled, from an unforeseen surprise. It was all second nature. No big deal. No one ever realized that he was even blind in one eye.

The hand stealing his popcorn did not bother Tristan. But Gareth was irritating him more than he could possibly imagine. Every time his brother jumped or yelled out "Too cool!" Tristan bristled. He had no idea what his younger brother was on about. It seemed to Tristan that they were not even watching the same film. He took off his 3D glasses, wiped them on his trousers to clean them, replaced them, but still nothing. No magic.

He looked at the glasses, one red lens and one blue. The red lens covered his blind eye and the blue his seeing eye. Perhaps if he switched them? He turned the glasses upside down so that the blind eye had the blue lens. Still nothing. Nothing at all.

Tristan had never considered his blindness in one eye. He hated all the talk of operations and procedures to recover his sight. Finally, it had been agreed that they would try the patch procedure. It was explained that Tristan had something called refractive amblyopia, a decreased vision in one eye due to abnormal development of vision in his infancy, possibly a condition caused by his premature birth. His vision loss occurred because his nerve pathways between the brain and the eye weren't properly stimulated. As a result, his brain favoured his good eye and his brain reacted only to the visual stimuli from that one, ignoring what was blurry and weaker, until it learned to not accept any information from the less-seeing eye. In time the brain accepted it as blind, but, with effort, Tristan could force the brain to accept the weaker eye, he could force his brain to accept that it could see, though in a blurry fashion, if, and only if, the good eye was limited. By using drops to blur his vision in his strong eye or by patching it in order to blind the good eye, the brain would be forced to acknowledge the weaker eye until the pathways were stimulated once again. Eventually, he would get to the point where he could wear glasses, one lens quite clear and unnecessary and the other very strong and thick. Then he could have two working eyes. Two seeing but unequal eyes. But why? Why all the pain and fuss? And why hamper the strong eye? Why make it feel like less just so that the weaker could have a chance, and feel better about its inadequacies? Why handicap the better of the two? To Tristan, it seemed like a punishment of the good eye. It was like the time when he won a first-place ribbon for being the fastest in his class, but then all the other kids got ribbons, too, just for participating, and suddenly his red ribbon, the ribbon he had won fair and square for being better than the rest, didn't seem quite as valuable. He had one brilliant eye. Why not just let it be brilliant in its own right? And so he argued with his parents. He stomped his feet. He started to become rude and petulant to the doctors. He didn't want any more drops and prodding. He didn't want any more lights shone into his eyes. He didn't want more of his afternoons used up. He was fine just the way he was! He didn't need to change.

Tristan didn't understand why there was all the big fuss over Gareth's friend, Johnny. Johnny lost one eye and that made him just like him. But from that day on, Johnny did everything with fear that he might lose the other eye. Always took precautions, like wearing glasses when he could see perfectly well. Why? Tristan imagined his heart. Only one of those! But he didn't approach the world with trepidation because there's only one heart, not two. It never occurred to Tristan to be fearful in case he were to lose the other eye. When he played outside with his friends or when he did sports, he always took off the protective glasses the ophthalmologist insisted his parents make him wear for the safety of the good eye. For him, it was, and would always be, a monocular world. The eye patching of his good eye to train his blind eye, the blurring drops, the discomfort, the embarrassment, he was done with it all! Oh, how the kids teased him at school when he arrived with that patch. "Pirate, pirate!" They all laughed. And even when he threw the patch away the nickname stuck. He hated it. And he saw the world better using only the more gifted eye, anyhow. Why go through all the procedures for something he had never missed?

Until now.

He felt excluded in the cinema, a place he had always loved, with its smell of popcorn and the sticky floor beneath the seats. He loved the beam of light that carried the magic to the screen and the way the dust and smoke in the air could be seen dancing within that beam. The cartoons, the trailers, the short film, and then the feature — it was all magic! At the movies, he could travel to other worlds, be anything the characters were, live other stories, and imagine a life of adventure. He had wanted so badly to experience 3D for the first time. He was the one who chose the film, convinced their parents they should go. He imagined he'd be in the film, a part of it, with the action all around him. But try as he might, he saw the picture the same with or without glasses. A fuzzy blur where a sharpness should be. And everything about it seemed just silly. Things falling for no reason. Things pointing toward the camera for no reason. And without the effect of 3D, the story was just silly and pointless.

The world had always been accommodating for him. He had never felt disabled. He rode his bike fast, sometimes over ramps, he played sports, ran hard, swam far, even learned to shoot a rifle, for which he never had to close an eye, but there, in the darkened cinema, a world he loved to share with his younger brother, there he was discriminated against. There the magic of 3D was withheld from him.

Gareth jumped again and laughed. On the screen, a huge rock was tumbling toward the lens.

"It's great, isn't it?"

The giant bubble closes down on Katherine and Mark and the edges of the bubble reach off the screen and into the audience. Gareth shrieked, thinking he would be caught in the bubble, too! He grabbed his brother's hand. He had no clue that he was experiencing something his older brother would never know.

Tristan couldn't see the posters he had collected and taped to his wall. But he knew where each one hung. He knew exactly how each looked. He turned his blind eye to each in its turn, mustering up the image in his mind, willing his dead eye to see what was there on the wall. The first poster, a goldish brown with a robot woman down the centre. Very art nouveau. Very imposing. And the words *EIN FILM VON FRITZ LANG*.

Tristan ran through all the things he had learned about Fritz Lang. He was born in Vienna, in 1890. He trained as a painter. He was the master of dark and shadowy heart-pounding psychological thrillers. He was known as the father of expressionist cinema …

Tristan then whispered out loud, "And he was blind in one eye."

Tristan turned his head a bit, centred his dead eye on the next poster. Willed it to show him a fuzzy outline of a feisty redhead with the top buttons of her shirt undone as she pulls away from the strong and silent man who towers above her. John Wayne, Maureen O'Hara, and the word TECHNICOLOR, much larger than the director's name, which is written simply and unpretentiously at the bottom: John Ford.

Tristan again ran through his knowledge of the director, itemizing to himself the facts.

John Ford went to Hollywood because his brother was an actor there. Became known for making westerns. He won six Oscars …

"And he was blind in one eye."

The third poster has mountains and a sepia-toned black-and-white picture of Humphrey Bogart and Ida Lupino. Bogart is all dangerous as he looks into the lens and Lupino stands all sexy-like behind him, the way any moll would. At least that is what Tristan always imagined, though he wasn't really sure what a moll was. Just a beautiful woman who stands mysteriously behind a man, but probably way more dangerous than the man is. And at the bottom, again, is the director's name. Raoul Walsh.

Raoul Walsh. Directed films for fifty-two years. He was known for crime movies. *High Sierra* was the first film that cast Bogart as a leading man. Yup, he could sure see talent ...

"And he was blind in one eye."

Tristan knew there were only two more posters to go. Then he could take the patch off his eye. He tried to focus on the next, a huge poster of Bugs Bunny, that giant, saucy rabbit, chewing on the end of a carrot. Tristan could almost hear him say, "Eh, what's up, Doc?" And who created him? Director Tex Avery. Yup, he directed all the great animated characters, including Porky Pig and Daffy Duck ...

"And he was blind in one eye."

Tristan saved the best for last. He rolled over on his bed, focused, and strained his sight for all he was worth on his last and favourite poster. But nothing. There was no fuzzy outline. No sense that somewhere there was the smallest amount of vision at all. His brain just wasn't buying it. Just wouldn't be tricked into believing his good eye was doing anything more than resting. And he was tired from it all. Tired of training his brain and focusing an eye that wouldn't cooperate, all while his other eye was wanting to burst free from behind the patch, to take over the task. It was almost screaming out to him, "I can do it! Let me do it for you! Why get an amateur to do a pro's job?"

Tristan peeled off the patch, carefully put it, secretly, into the drawer beside his bed, and let his good eye adjust to the light. It took no time at all to recover, to jump into the game and take over, doing what the other could not.

YOU HAVE NEVER BEEN SCARED TILL YOU'VE BEEN SCARED IN 3D.

The words are written so that they got smaller as they recede into the distance, giving a 3D effect on a two-dimensional poster. A girl in a 1950s swimsuit runs out toward him. Vincent Price stares malevolently down at him.

"Hello," Tristan said. "Lookin' good, Vince!"

When Tristan had first heard that *House of Wax* was the most successful 3D film of all time, he wanted to know everything about it. He went through comic books and he sent away for items from the back of magazines. He went to the library. He spent all his time trying to find out whatever he could. He even went to the local theatre and asked to speak to the manager, who brought him into his trust, showing him his own collection of movie memorabilia in the projector room. And it was there that he first heard the name of the man who made 3D happen in a full-length feature film: André De Toth.

André De Toth decided to become an actor after he'd already studied and graduated with a law degree. Then, after putting in his time emoting on the Hungarian stage, he turned his eye toward the film industry, first in Hungary, then in Hollywood. He worked as an actor, editor, and writer before even attempting to direct. His films were edgy for the time. Violence was realistic, not glamorized, and not subdued. Brave and in-your-face. But above everything else, he was best known for his film *House of Wax*. The first successful and critically acclaimed 3D film ever made.

"Directed by a man who was blind in one eye!" Tristan said aloud, no longer whispering.

What a victory! What a feat! What an inspiration!

All around Tristan were his heroes. Men who, like God himself, could create worlds from nothing. From light and imagination. Here were his gods. And one day, one day, he would walk amongst them. A Cyclops god in a world in need of his vision.

* * *

Grandfather was ranting on about the evils of the world. Nothing was safe. The police department was corrupt. The store down the street always ripped him off. The liquor bottles seemed smaller. His favourite shows were cancelled. And those city people who bought the house were putting up his rent! Why was the world conspiring against him?

"On yer knees, girls. Time fer some God intervention!"

Clara and Blanca stopped rolling the ciggies. It was Blanca's turn to use the contraption and Clara's turn to measure out the tobacco from their grandfather's pouch. A half a fistful, a squeeze to remove the excess, and that would be good for three. Three at a time, rolled and twisted off, until there were ninety-one in total. Thirteen for each day of the week.

The first one of the day would be smoked before breakfast, with a cup of warmed-up Sanka. Only once the last drop of coffee was downed and the last puff exhaled would their grandfather consider getting breakfast for them. On weekends it was a fry-up of bacon with canned beans on the side. But on the days of the ranting and raging, the coffee would stale in the cup, the cigarette would burn away in an ashtray, and breakfast wouldn't happen at all. On those days, all the girls could think about was the tea they were always served in the downstairs apartment. The little sandwiches, the petits fours cakes, and the etiquette lessons that accompanied the delectables.

"Prayers, girls. Prayers! The world is going to hell in a hand-basket and yer mother isn't gettin' any better. But yer safe with me, I'll take care of you. Who else would want ya?" He laughed. "Now get yer little white asses off them chairs, we gots some askin' to do!"

The list was long. The people who needed guidance to see things the way he did. The obstacles that needed removing. A new adult-sized tricycle to replace the one that was stolen.

"'Cause I need it for business. No wheels means there's no supply for the demand."

The twins slipped off their chairs and put their bare knees to the floor.

"A little help with the racing bets would also be nice," he added as he sat on the edge of the twin-sized bed that doubled as a sofa when the girls weren't sleeping on it.

Clara reached for a nearby foam pillow to place under her bruising knees and their grandfather saw her. Slapping the back of her head, he yelled out, "What in the devil do you think yer doing?"

"Just trying to be a bit more comfortable!" Clara answered him.

"Prayers are not about being comfortable. Prayers are to bring comfort. It is not about comfort for yer body, but comfort for yer soul!"

Clara had not been aware until then that her soul was in discomfort but, from that time on, she knew that fate had nothing to do with the white, white skin she wore, or her pink, anxious eyes, or even the bone-bleach natural colour of her hair. Her discomfort was deep in her soul and the only reason she looked the way she did was that her outward being was a reflection of what was wanting within. Clearly, obviously, her twin suffered the same deep soul melancholia. But how to expunge something she could not put a finger on? How to right the sin that was percolating through her DNA?

Music.

Clara understood that her ear for music had to be a gift from the angry god her grandfather wanted so badly to appease. The only way to soothe him, to remove the mark she and her twin bore, was to create a sound so original, so formidable, that they would blossom in colour and purity. Blush would slowly come to their cheeks, their pale eyes would stop reflecting the pink of the blood vessels hidden behind their pale orbs, and their hair might even change from snow white to a pale yellow blond. Even their lashes would darken and their brows would fill in with a light ash colour.

And then maybe, just maybe, they might experience lying out in the sun, warming their skin to a tan shade while boys walked by and noticed them in their bikinis. Maybe one day they might be like other normal girls. Maybe one day the stares would stop, the whispers would cease, and they could blend, unnoticed.

Clara and Blanca had been going downstairs to Esther's apartment, listening to music, training their voices, and sharing meals with the Perlmans, for almost five years. While other twelve-year-olds were holding transistor radios to their ears, tuning in AM pop music, they listened to opera and folk songs. They had become lessoned in classical music, everything from Rachmaninov to Mahler. They had practised their vocal exercises at home, challenging their vocal range and experimenting with sound and tone. Yet still, they looked as though they had just emerged from a tub of bleach.

"Why did you ever think that singing and playing the piano would make us look like everyone else?" Blanca finally asked her sister.

"I don't know. I just did."

"Maybe we can sing the way we do because we don't look like everyone else."

"But why do we have to pray so hard, then?"

"Because our grandfather is a mean and crazy old man."

He wasn't always mean; the girls had seen moments of kindness and gentleness. Beautiful party dresses bought for them on their birthdays. Chips at the chip truck when they wanted. And almost weekly they took stale bread to feed to the ducks and geese at the lake. That was him at his best. But then, some memory would return. Someone would diddle him for a few dollars, a cigarette wouldn't be rolled quite right, and this other man would emerge. The girls learned that it was best to walk away. To slip out of sight because the mere look of them would only escalate the self-pitying rage. Their grandfather could spiral into Hell before their eyes and the only thing a spiralling man wants, they learned, is to take any innocent bystanders down with him.

"Oh, I guess you are going down to that Jew-woman downstairs again. To have yer heads filled with her highfalutin lah-de-dah. Remember where youse come from! Yer not bloody royalty! Miss Lady Janes, the both of youse!"

But that was just the point. Esther told them not to slurp, just in case one day they were to be invited to Buckingham Palace.

"Oh, we'll never be invited there!" they had responded to Esther. "Not in a million years."

"You never know, dear girls. Art can open many doors that would not open to you otherwise."

"But we aren't artists. I can't even draw very good."

"It is 'very well,' Blanca. Not 'very good.' And there are many kinds of art. Music is art."

"Music is art?" Clara had been stunned by that revelation.

"Yes, you can create a feeling, and even an entire image or story, with sound just as you can with paint. Art is about creating another world. Another reality. An inner reality that is a reflection of the soul."

And that was why Clara believed that music would bring colour, a painter's palette of colour, into her soul. If only she could use her music the way an artist does his paints, then that colour would reflect in a prism of light out of her.

"On yer knees the both of youse! God listens even to the ugly ones, so long as youse are pure of heart!"

The albinos' mother, Faye, stared out at the waves. The girls would be coming later and this time she felt confident that she could handle their visit. Nurse Elaine had prepared her, reminding her daily for almost a week of their upcoming visit. When Faye looked at her without any sense of understanding, she reinforced a memory of them by showing Faye their pictures. Two pale white girls with unblinking pinkish-blue eyes with dark red pupils stared out happily. Of course. Her girls. Yes, she was prepared for it. She could do this.

There were memories that were lost to her forever. Moments that would never be retrieved. There was a calmness in that. Like the days when the water was still and the waves were almost non-existent. It was peaceful. No churning water. No grey waves. No undertow. Just a gentle rock without a ripple to be seen. That was how it felt to her once the resting time was done and she could return to the little yellow cottage. She rarely remembered the treatments, only the fatigue that came afterward. And the confusion that settled in for a time. Then glimmers of the past would re-emerge, without sense, like fragments of dreams lost when the awake time would take over. Flashes of the past that seemed more surreal than concrete.

She did not, at any time, agree to any of this. She never agreed to come here to convalesce. But she doesn't remember the discussions. Doesn't remember what brought her to the yellow cottages in the first place. Cannot really remember a time before the cottages. At times she could remember something like the taste of ice cream, or a mother holding her and telling her stories about fairy godmothers and magical spells. A finger pricked. An awakening kiss. Dwarves and witches. Were they memories or stories? And who was the Big Bad Wolf?

No. No. There was no Big Bad Wolf on the shores of Lake Ontario. Just acres of farmland sloping to the lake. Fresh air, birdsong, and rest every day. Rest until it was time for a treatment in the bigger building. She could remember being taken there, she always remembered that part, but then nothing, again, until she'd wake up, wondering where she might be, and feeling the tired ache in her thigh muscles and back.

She understood that her girls were coming. Two of them. They looked the same, though. Exactly. It could be the same girl posing in two different pictures. How was she to be sure that there were really two? They looked like the same child. Same white hair, same white, chalky skin, same pink eyes. Same sweet and shy smile. Surely there couldn't be two children who looked so very strange?

Flash. Yes, she remembered. She had twins. Two snowflakes, so wee and tiny that they looked more like porcelain baby dolls than babies. They couldn't hold their little heads up and so they looked like a pair of bobbleheads, with tufts of white hair growing straight up and out of their pink scalps. Right, there were two of them. And when she first held them she worried she would get them mixed up. Confuse one for the other after she named them. So she just called them her wee ones. She put one then the other to her breast, but they were too weak to give suck because they came too soon. Almost six weeks early. Always early, those girls. And now they were going to come to visit today. And she wasn't really ready, after all. It was too soon.

Mustn't tell them the truth, she thought. If what she could remember was actually the truth. Her father said it wasn't the truth, though, just crazy talk. But still. Still, there must have been some reason as to why she didn't want them. Why she feared them when they were growing inside of her and how she had wanted to tear them out of her body. But there they remained, pushing up against her heart, pressing down onto her pelvic bone, kicking at random whenever they liked without a thought of the host who carried them. How exactly did they get inside of her? Two of them. If her memory was wrong, then how did it happen?

"I was asleep with my mouth open and I accidentally swallowed a star and that is how you were planted in my belly. The star broke into two and each of you is part of that star and when you are together, that star is whole again." That was what she whispered to them as she held them, swaddled tightly, to her chest when they were little. And now the star was coming. The fragmented two pieces of one star would be there. A white star it was. It must have been, to produce such white babies.

Her girls. Now she could remember the pieces of the puzzle. The babies were hers alone. Clara and Blanca. She had named them herself. They belonged only to her. One day, she would leave the yellow cottages and reclaim them. They could live happily ever after. And the ogre and the henchman could just stay away.

But to do that she would have to leave her lake.

Clara wanted to sing to their mother. Wanted to make her happy with the joy of their sound, but Blanca was worried that their mother might be hurt and jealous that another woman was teaching them manners and how to sing. Blanca was also worried that their mother would somehow read her thoughts and know that she wished that Esther was her mother instead of her. How she secretly longed for stability. One room that was theirs, and not a single bed in their grandfather's stinky living room. Food that wasn't fried and fatty, or reheated. Food that didn't come from a box or a can. Just last week Esther had made them a huge salad with apples and walnuts. In a salad! Who puts fruit and nuts in salads? Salads had always been that anemic thing you pushed out of the way so that you could smear ketchup closer to the fish and chips. Salads had never looked so colourful, so pretty, in all her life as they did at Esther's. She could get used to food that had colour, and flavour. And music, and art, and nice smells. Blanca knew that if they brought the music they learned from Esther to their mother, it might open the door to their secret life and it wouldn't be so secret anymore. It would be shared and, like everything else, slowly taken away from them.

"But you could bring her joy. Maybe even make her better," Clara pleaded with her sister on the ride there as they watched the world slip away because they still rode in the backward-facing seats of the station wagon.

Blanca knew how selfish she was being but she just wanted something that was theirs alone. Something uncontaminated by worry.

Something so pure and beautiful that it would transport them from the endless teasing at school. Still, she couldn't help but feel shame and, because she didn't want her sister to know how she could so easily betray their mother, she agreed to sing a duet with her. She even offered to sing the part of the slave girl instead of the part of the love interest from *Lakmé*. The perfect song for two sopranos, equal in size and harmony, one offsetting the other as the two girls, one a servant and the other royalty, gather flowers. The perfect song for a summer's day when there is water nearby, and a fallow field full of wildflowers.

"You mean weeds?" their uncle asked them as they zoomed closer. It was his turn to drive them and, even though they could have sat in the front, all important-like, they still sat rear-facing.

"Ah, c'mon, girls," he had said to them when they took their usual places, "I don't bite!"

And they had all laughed. Uncle Bob made biting gestures and they had laughed all the harder. How wonderful it had been staying the night at his place, eating all together as a family at the dinner table with their cousins. And then, all of them, watching their favourite TV show, *Bonanza*. They never watched *Bonanza* with their grandfather! And then the two boys wanting to play cowboys and Indians, but, of course, they both had wanted to be the cowboys and so Clara and Blanca offered to be the Indians because of their long braids.

"Are you gonna visit her, too?" Blanca asked him as the car passed through the impressive iron gates.

"Naw, your uncle Bob is in need of a pep-me-up. Gonna go inside where there is a café and put back some joe."

"Joe?"

"Another word for coffee."

"Oh," they both said fake-knowingly, leaving him at the big building as they rambled toward the lake.

They ran to their mother at the water's edge but slowed as they neared her, not knowing if they might startle her. How pretty she looked with her long, long hair. So many mothers had sensible hair-cuts, with a wave falling by their chins or shoulders and the top feathered or teased just a bit for height. But their mother had hair that fell past her waist, in ripples as gentle as the calmest waves before them. How brilliant it was in the summer light. Burnished and bright and glorious. It reflected the light in a way theirs never would. The white was just too opaque, too uniform. But, as the wind moved their mother's hair, they saw myriad colours, from gold to red to light brown. Like a painting the woman downstairs, Esther, might collect.

"Mama!" they cried out in unison as they neared her.

Faye saw them. Dropped to her knees and opened her arms wide. Yes, she was ready for them. *Oh, just look at them*, she thought to herself, *like white angels or fairies*. Yes, that is how they got there. Changelings from the fairy world! One day she would have to hide them so the fairies couldn't steal them back.

"Come to me, my beamish girls!" She laughed, opening her arms wider so that she could catch them both in her embrace.

To them, her hair smelled like sunshine. As they flung themselves into her grasp, her hair fell around them like woven umbilical cords. This is how it always was. This is how it should be.

"Why can't we stay with you in the yellow cottages and look at the water all day like you?" Blanca asked.

"Because there is no school here. You have to learn things and get smart."

"I hate school. They are all mean," said Clara.

"Yeah," Blanca concurred. "Last Hallowe'en two boys dressed up as us. They painted their faces white and put mops on top on their heads!"

"Well, you have to learn things," Faye insisted. "How are you going to grow up to be smart if you don't go to school?"

"We are learning things, but not at school!" Clara blurted out, and Blanca started to shake with anticipation. *Please, please don't tell her!*

"Are you better yet, Mama?"

"Almost. I will be home soon. Now, are you going to sing for me?"

The girls began the familiar "Flower Song" with the purity only young voices have. Voices without bravado. No scoops, no dips. Just pure sound. And all the time Faye just stared at the water.

"It sounds like water," she told them when they finished. "Like mermaids singing, or sirens inviting you into the water. You have to be careful of the sirens. They are very tricky."

"It takes place at the water's edge, but not a lake, a river. And the two go off to get flowers."

Faye grabbed up their hands and began running with them to the fields where snapdragons, Queen Anne's lace, and goldenrod grew in abundance. The three picked and picked till their arms were heavy with the wildflowers. Then Faye began to braid them into crowns for the girls.

It was so much fun that they didn't realize how long they had been outside, in the sun. The sun, an enemy to the fair-skinned. An enemy to the girls. Sun was their greatest threat; it could kill them. But it had all felt so very good until their white, white skin was pink and starting to blister. When Faye hugged them they cried out in pain. How, oh how, could she have been so irresponsible? How would she ever be able to care for them?

When they returned, Bob was standing there, waiting, hands on his hips.

"What the hell, Faye? They're all burned up. What in God's name were you thinking? Oh right, you weren't thinking! You never do." He pulled the girls away. "Get into the car, I got a little something I want to discuss privately with your mama."

"No, I don't want to talk to you." Faye crossed her arms.

"Oh, you're going to talk to me all right. A little chat for old times' sake."

It seemed slow motion, but too quick to do anything to stop her. Faye bent over, scooped up a rock, and threw it at her brother's head. It hit right above his eye, splitting the skin. And in no time at all, a goose egg rose up from his forehead.

"What the fuck, Faye!"

On the way home the girls sat facing backward. They sadly watched as their mother receded into the distance. And with her diminishing form, all hope of ever being reunited with her receded, as well.

Gareth could hear his parents talking in the next room. Sometimes their words would blend together like the hum of an engine. A sweet engine. An engine that never had to be gunned or revved. Gareth knew that his parents loved each other, and their murmured talk at night reinforced that. Their words a blanket that wrapped around him.

"You should have seen them, Mark, little things. Twin albinos. And they were so happy to see their mother. It was all looking so positive till she snapped and threw that rock."

"I wish you didn't have to work there, Elaine. So many sad stories."

"Well, we need the money. At least till the factory is up and running again," Elaine reminded.

"Yeah, stupid me, going into management. At least when you are on strike you can picket and get paid."

"Why don't you stop fretting and just go back to school? You're smarter than what you are doing. Go into mediation or labour law. Remember all the dreams we had when we first met in college?"

"I just want to take care of you."

"Oh, please, it's a modern age. Women are burning their bras now!"

Gareth could hear laughter and what sounded a bit like wrestling.

His father laughed. "Well, don't you get any crazy ideas!"

"Too late for that, darling! I married you!"

Gareth was straining to make out all the words this time, only because he had heard the words *albinos* and *twins*. Could it be that his mom was the nurse to the mother of those fairy girls he met at the eye doctor's almost eight years ago? He wondered how they looked now. If they were as magical and as beautiful or if they had become as awkward as the twelve- and thirteen-year-old girls in his school. How many times had he tried to conjure up their faces as he drifted to sleep. And sometimes it made him feel all funny … down there.

"I just don't think that she will get out as early now. I think that the doctors will order up another round of the treatments."

"Love the way you just say treatments instead of electroshock therapy," Mark quipped.

"Oh, it's come a long way. Anaesthetic now, muscle relaxants. They don't even feel it."

"Could we, just for once, leave your work at work? It always presents itself no matter what we're doing."

Gareth could hear kissing sounds, so he put his pillow over his head and tried to conjure the image of the albino twins.

They float above the ground. Because the earth cannot contain them. They hover, tiny wings aflutter. They approach him. Beckoning. Then one, the one who had given him the colouring book, holds her hand out to him.

"Away with us he's going," says the first one.
"Away with us he's going," echoes the other one.
For he comes, the human child,
To the waters and the wild
With a faery, hand in hand,
For the world's more full of weeping than he can understand.

* * *

At the time the walnut cake had tasted sweet. With hints of orange and vanilla and a generous, aromatic cinnamon rising from the top. Inside there were tart apples and, of course, walnuts. It was Esther's favourite cake.

"Tastes just like my *bubbie's*. And when I smell it cooking, I can remember being a child again. Being so loved and embraced by my family. But they are all gone now."

"Where did they go?" asked Blanca.

"Well, they were taken away to a concentration camp."

For the girls, a camp was a place where more fortunate children got to spend their summers. Girl Guide camps. Sports camps. Swimming, arts and crafts, and explorer camps. The camps were endless and they were always excluded from them. Even if it were subsidized, the twins could never go to a camp. It was too risky. Too much sunshine.

"They took them to a camp?" Clara asked.

"And they never came back?" Blanca chimed in.

"Very few ever came back from the concentration camps," Esther replied sadly.

"Doesn't sound like a very good camp."

"Why did they go, couldn't they concentrate?"

Esther marvelled at what sheltered lives the girls had led. How could they not know such recent history? They really were little savages, these girls. Wild and untamed. They smacked their lips when they chewed. They had to constantly be reminded of their manners, their pleases and thank yous. They laughed at the nude paintings and made, what seemed to her, crude remarks. They ran about like hoodlums. And yet …

And yet there was something extraordinary about them. They had curious minds. They had the voices of angels. And they loved each other.

When they took her family, Esther was hiding behind the piano. She could see them, pushed and shoved as they were taken out. She wanted to run out, to yell at them, "Don't you treat my parents like that," but she had promised that, no matter what happened, she would stay quiet; she would stay hidden. Her older sisters, both married and living in their own apartments, may or may not have been taken, as well. She was told not to go to them. Not to check. Oh, how she had loved her sisters. Envied them with their thick dark lashes and long, wavy dark hair. Esther didn't have their sultry colouring. She was fair like her mother. A dirty blond, really. Her hair was lank, straight, and unruly. A cowlick at her crown that made her hair grow out in different directions. And so, like the twins, she mostly kept her hair neat in two braids while her sisters' hair flowed and cascaded in thick veiled curtains to their waists. But it was her hair, her lank and second-rate hair, that had saved her. Her hair allowed her to blend so that she was not given away. She did everything she was told to do. She took the papers from inside the piano and she began to walk. To walk and walk and walk, until she made it to a border crossing. She handed over the papers, spoke perfect German and waited, fingers crossed inside her coat pocket. With a stamp on the second page, she turned away from all she had ever known. But what she had known didn't exist anymore, anyhow. She left her home, her country, her family, and her piano behind. Not knowing where she would go and how she would survive.

"I like the cake. May I have a little more? Please."

Yes, they were learning, after all. Esther cut another slice. Topped up their teacups and offered them milk and sugar.

"Not too much, though, you'll want to taste the tea."

"You always say that!" The girls laughed together.

Esther didn't make it to Canada until long after the war. There had been a quota and Jews were being turned back by the boatload so, during the war, she waited out her days by caring for Swiss children, teaching them piano and vocals. They were always very polite, those Swiss children. They bowed, took your hand, curtsied. You never had to tell them, any of them, to remember their *p*'s and *q*'s. But none of them, not one of them, could sing like these strangely white and unruly twins.

"Did you sing for your mother?" she asked them.

"Yes, she loved it!" said Clara.

"We sang *Lakmé*!" Blanca added.

"And which part did each of you sing?"

"Oh, we switched it up to make it fair. Why did they always make the songs in different languages in the olden days?"

"Well, it is just the language it was written in."

"But it's never in English," complained Blanca.

"We should sing in our language!" enthused Clara.

"We could find something nice for you in English. Some Purcell, perhaps?"

The girls looked slyly at each other. They were reading each other's minds. Could she be trusted? Should they let her know, let her in on it?

"We have our own language," Clara confided.

"What do you mean?" asked Esther.

"May we please be excused?" they asked together.

The girls had come to emphasize the polite words. To reinforce that they were trying, that they were good. Worthy of Esther's efforts.

"Yes ..."

They stood together and Clara snapped her fingers one, two, three times. When they started it was a chorus of familiar but unknown sounds. Vaguely English but not. Like nonsensical poetry. There was something rhythmic about it, and yet their voices carried the notes as though on the wind. Esther could hear how the hours of making them listen to opera had inspired them. But what language was it?

The girls stopped as abruptly as they started.

"Something like that; we are still working on it," Clara announced.

"And that nonsense language, what is that?"

"It isn't nonsense! It's what we speak to each other when we don't want other people to know what we're saying." Blanca was defensive.

"Yeah, it's our safe language," Clara added.

"Are you saying you just made it up?" Esther asked.

The girls didn't know if they had, perhaps, done something wrong. Esther was so full of questions and, really, adults only asked questions when they were trying to trick you into admitting something. First it was the questions, then it was the strap on the bum.

"We didn't do anything wrong!" Clara yelled at her.

"We thought we could trust you, but you are just like all the other grown-ups!" Blanca added.

"We thought you would like it, we made up the song for you!"

Esther was stunned. She had no idea that her questions would upset her little guests. She looked at them, intently, making sure that her expression was as benign as possible.

"You know, you two ask me a lot of questions, too. I don't think I have done anything wrong when you do."

"Yeah, but you are a grown-up."

"Not really. I just look like one! It is a disguise!"

The twins relaxed. Even smiled.

"When someone asks you a question, sometimes it isn't to get you into trouble, sometimes it is because you are interesting. I think that your song is the most interesting thing I have ever heard. Like an ancient language. Now tell me how you made it up."

"It just grew out of us," admitted Clara.

"Well, it is something you should share with the world. You must continue to sing in your language. People sometimes lose their language and, when they do, they lose a little of themselves."

Esther remembered how she drove the Yiddish out of her, preferring only Haute Deutsch, until she could blend like everyone else. But these girls could never blend. They would always stand out, be different. *Hopefully these will be kinder and gentler times*, she thought.

"If it is okay, could we have just a bit more cake? Grandpa isn't home so I don't think there'll be supper tonight."

"Did you forget something?"

"*Please*," they both said in unison.

She put two big slices on the plates. She could always make another cake for David. She watched with contentment as the girls ate happily, and greedily, not knowing that her walnut cake would later leave a bitter taste in their mouths. It would, later, trigger the memory of the saddest day in their little lives.

Come away, oh human child,
To the waters and the wild
With a faery, hand in hand,
For the world's more full of weeping
Than you can understand.

*   *   *

Faye had once known love. Young love. Pure and uncontaminated by expectation and responsibility. It was carefree, like a gentle breeze through her troubled life.

Timothy had been in her grade all the way through the primary-school years, but, in high school, their friendship changed. They stopped seeing each other as someone to tease and torment and began to see each other with new eyes. Faye was no longer the girl with the know-it-all personality who, every time she put up her hand and answered a teacher's question, ended her responses with the words *of course*. And Timothy ceased to be that nuisance, that class clown, who obviously couldn't concentrate enough to actually pass any of his subjects. Instead, he became the one who could make her smile, even laugh at times. He became the one to pull her from her darkness, to see the world as a place full of promise. She, in turn, was his thoughtful muse. A girl so deep in her emotional being that she was a constant inspiration for him. He wrote poetry about her. He picked up the guitar and started to write songs about her. She imagined that they would marry one day, travel far away from Cobourg, and see the world together.

Little had transpired between them physically. A few fumbled gropes, a bit of exploring with the hands, and lots and lots of kisses, stolen in safe places, in the shadows, away from disapproving eyes.

Yes, Faye did know love once upon a time and, as she stared out over the lake, she could taste it on the moist air coming off the lake water.

"Step back a bit, Faye! You are not allowed in the water," Nurse Elaine warned.

They were always close but, because Faye had been there so long, she had grown used to the constant presence of guards and nurses. There was a constant feeling of eyes watching from a discreet distance, analyzing every move, disapproving of anything out of the ordinary. But how different was that from her childhood? There were always eyes on her. Making her feel ashamed.

Why had she been ashamed? She was sixteen then. She had a boyfriend. She loved him, yes, and she felt that he loved her back to an equal level.

"Faye, I won't tell you again! You don't want to have to go into the big building, now do you?"

She did not. After she threw the stone at her brother she had been taken there for a few days, for observation. Those days seemed long and claustrophobic without the lake to keep her company. The walls seemed to close in around her, the air felt stuffy and suffocating, the other patients seemed too far gone. All she wanted, while she was resting there, was to be out of there. There were no dreams of future days in the big building. There were no dreams of happiness in the big building. Only a yearning to go outside and lose herself by staring out at the water. There's an infinity to water. A large body of water can carry your soul to impervious shores, serene, untroubled, and vast. Looking out over the water, Faye could feel herself lift away from her own body in order to hover across that body of water, reaching shores where there were no judgments, no consequences, and no reminders of all that had been lost.

She was still young. Barely seventeen when she had the twins, that would make her what now? Clara and Blanca had to be about twelve. So still under thirty. Still in her youth, really. There was time. Time enough to live again. Time to make things right.

Except that she threw a stone at her brother's head. She hit him. She drew blood.

Faye remembered the rage that had suddenly consumed her. She was upset, yes, that the girls had suffered such a bad sunburning but that was tempered by the joy they had shared. One emotion was overlapping the other, like the coming and passing of waves. But then she saw him there, hands on his hips, and her heart started to pound in her chest. It echoed in her ears and she could feel the lava of resentment rise in her to a crescendo where she had no control over it. It was heating and rising and rising and heating and filling her, consuming her until it had to burst through in a violent eruption.

She had felt that panic and rage before. It was no stranger to her. One moment she would be fine, coping, even happy and, the next, she'd react without thought or censure. Her emotions could always take hold and spiral her away, whether that hold was one of happiness or despair. But the power her emotions had over her was fed and given supreme power the day of the big incident.

She was just sixteen. She was juggling two emotions, desire and trepidation, and desire was winning. Timothy was lying across her, mouth on hers. Her breasts were bare and his hands were all over them, cupping them, stroking them, pinching their pale, small nipples. She could feel herself giving way, lost in the moment of experience, losing her sense of what if? Then a shadow fell across her. It snapped her back, and there he was with his hands on his hips, judging her. She grabbed at Timothy's back, as if by pulling him closer to her she could hide from the imposing shadow. But a larger hand was there, as well, on Timothy's back.

There are parts of the story she has blanked on. Parts that have been erased with treatment and time. She has a flash of Timothy being lifted away. Timothy being thrown down the stairs and his leg twisting at an extreme angle, making it impossible for him to run from the blows, but she didn't see that. Only heard the stories, the rumours afterward. She never witnessed Bob raining down on his head, pummelling him till blood spilled from his nose and his lip split. That's a part of the puzzle that is missing for her now. And so is the moment that her brother, Bob, returned from beating Timothy.

Faye was lying on her stomach, her head in her pillows, crying. She felt a tender stroke on her head. She felt his hand rub her cheek.

"There, there now. Don't cry. He's gone. It's all okay now. You're safe."

But cry she had. Her whimpers had grown louder and louder as she gulped for air.

"Shh. Quiet now. No more crying. Hush."

He hadn't bothered to turn her over. Just pressed her flat with his wide palm on her slender back. He'd kept the other hand on the nape of her neck as his knees pushed her thighs apart. He unzipped himself but didn't pull down his pants. He just took his penis out and began pressing it into her.

"It's not right. Not right," he had told her. "First time's gotta be with someone who loves you."

She'd struggled but his weight was upon her and he was so much bigger, so much stronger than her. And the more she struggled the harder his grip, the more he pulled her hair and pushed her face into the pillows so she could hardly breathe.

"Gonna hurt if you struggle. I want it to be nice for ya. So just relax and enjoy it. It only hurts a bit at first. Then it'll feel nice. Real nice."

And once she'd stopped struggling, once she was exhausted with all her fighting, only then did he take his hands, lift her hips upward, and start to fuck her from behind. At first, he was almost gentle but after a few thrusts, he intensified his efforts, ramming her as hard and as deeply as he could, all the while breathing in her ear, "You're my sister. Mine, not his! Mine! Who loves you, Faye?"

Faye had said nothing. It was as though her spirit had left her body and was watching from above.

"I said, who loves you?" And he thrust hard into her. When she didn't respond he asked again and again, each time ramming into her all the harder.

"I said, who loves you?" he had yelled at her as he slapped her backside with an open hand.

"You do. You love me," she finally had whimpered.

Faye never did return to school. She did not say anything about her brother. She remained inside and in shock. And then she missed her period. And then another. And as her belly began to swell she tried to cover it by wearing long, flowing dresses. She tried drinking peppermint tea to get rid of the baby. Tried punching herself in the stomach. Over and over again as hard as she could. She tried everything. She stopped eating and drinking. She closed off, shut down. Became catatonic. She lost weight, began fainting almost every morning. And so she was brought to the *doctors*. That was when her pregnancy was divulged to her father. He told her he would like to beat her senseless if only she weren't pregnant. He made her pray, many times a day, on the hard floor. She said she was going to kill herself. She had a plan. And that was when she was first brought to the cottages. That was when she had her first treatment, assured that the electroshock would not affect the pregnancy.

Although she can't really remember her more recent treatments, that first one she would always remember. Pads on either side of her head. Something to brace her neck. Gauze in her mouth. And then her body in an epileptic convulsion that went on and on and on until every muscle in her body ached. No anaesthetic then. No muscle relaxants. Those luxuries would come a few years later.

When she returned home from that first treatment, she had told her father the truth, wanting him to protect her and accept her. But he could not, would not, believe her. It had to have been those treatments muddling up her mind. He always knew it was that good-for-nothin' Timothy who had knocked up his darling girl. Either she was protecting her lover or she was mad. Madness was the easiest option. There was no way that his son was such a depraved monster. Not his first-born. Not possible. He was married to a nice girl and she had a child on the way, as well! He was sure that, although the treatments helped her emotional being, it did rattle her brain quite a bit.

"Faye," Nurse Elaine called out to her, snapping her back to the present. "Last time. Get away from the water. You're up to your thighs!"

Faye backed away. Knew there would be a time. A time when there would be a disturbance elsewhere and the focus would shift and she could be one with the lake. She retreated and sat on the shore, feeling the solidity of the earth under her. She felt around her. She was centred. She was sure in her memory.

She picked up a rock, not unlike the one she threw at her brother. She put it into her pocket. Every day, she vowed, she would take another rock and sneak it to her room until she could fill those pockets with dull, smooth grey rocks. Then, she would wait till the gaze turned from her. And then, all she would take with her would be the memory of the sound of her girls singing.

FOUR

"THERE IS A WILLOW GROWS ASKANT A BROOK,
That shows his hoar leaves in the glassy stream.
There with fantastic garlands did she make,
Of crow-flowers, nettles, daisies, and long purples,
That liberal shepherds give a grosser name,
But our cold maids do dead men's fingers call them.
There on the pendant boughs her cornet weeds
Clamb'ring to hang, an envious sliver broke,
When down her weedy trophies and herself
Fell in the weeping brook. Her clothes spread wide,
And mermaid-like awhile they bore her up,
Which time she chanted snatches of old lauds
As one incapable of her own distress,
Or like a creature native and indued
Unto that element. But long it could not be
Till that her garments, heavy with their drink,
Pulled the poor wretch from her melodious lay
To muddy death."

Mr. Birch closed the book, peered at his class, and waited for a response. Gareth shifted uncomfortably in his seat. He had heard of such a thing. A deliberate drowning. Heard his mother telling his father about it in hushed tones a couple of years ago. Gareth couldn't quite comprehend it, being so young, but it stayed with him like a haunting. His mother's sobs sounded in his head because he had never heard her cry like that before. Crying, Gareth had assumed, because she had walked away from the lake in order to tend to another patient who was making a fuss, crying and screaming. Then the woman with the long red hair was gone, nowhere to be seen. There was nothing but the sound of the hungry waves.

"What do we know from this speech?" Mr. Birch asked the class.

Johnny put up his hand. He seemed more confident now with his glass eye. No longer did he look away when his name was called. No longer did he slide along his chair to hide behind his desk when a question was asked. He was far more present. And this eye didn't weep or crust over. It sat confidently alongside the other. Not matching it exactly, but as a complement.

"John?"

"Well, first of all, it is interesting that it is Gertrude who is telling Hamlet about the suicide because Hamlet was once close to his mother, but now he feels betrayed by her because she married so quickly after Hamlet's father died. Every son hates the idea of his mother being with someone other than his own father ..."

Johnny was old enough to know that there had been little passion between his parents for some time. He felt much closer to his mother than his father but still, still, he could sense that when they were in Germany she was different in the presence of the ocularist. He liked Siegfried, really liked him, but he wasn't his father. That is what made it all the worse. He liked Siegfried a lot. The first year he was unaware of the flirtation between his mother and Siegfried, but, during the subsequent trips to Germany, Johnny became aware that there was, perhaps, something between them.

Maybe it was because he was starting to become aware of girls himself. And so his glances, his appreciative looks, were more apparent when echoed in the ocularist. Those weeks they spent in Germany his mother seemed more awake and alive. When she was home, in Canada, she was merely counting the minutes, the hours, the days until she could return to the home of her youth.

The truth was that since Johnny had returned from his first trip his father had been kinder and more attentive to him. He had started to include him in his activities, even let him join the bowling team. And Miss Argyle was there, looking as fetching as she had when he was in first grade. No wonder all the boys loved her. Now he was her peer, bowling alongside her. Almost an equal. Johnny did wonder why she was there and not his mother, but he excused it as a cultural difference. His mother just could not understand the value of bowling. Besides, his father was probably protecting her from ridicule. All those years in Canada and she still had that heavy accent. Changing her *y*'s for *j*'s and her *w*'s for *v*'s. How hard could it be to make some simple adjustments? The fact was that his mother just wasn't trying hard enough. Yes, Johnny could understand how Hamlet would turn against the mother who had given him life. The mother whom he'd adored. Hamlet's mother had betrayed him when she betrayed his father.

"John, I think you are missing the point. We have already discussed Hamlet's relationship with his mother, but what do we know of Gertrude's relationship to other women?" Mr. Birch wanted to keep Johnny on track. Johnny was a deep-thinking student, more so than any of his classmates. One insight always led to another for him. Was that because of his accident as a child? Did those feelings of seclusion and otherness make for a more thoughtful student? If so, was it worth it?

"Oh, she doesn't care about other women. Ophelia is insignificant to her, even if she might have made her son happy. She doesn't care about her son's happiness; only her own needs. The thing is that Gertrude's passions are not pure of heart. Gertrude is warning Hamlet that there is no place in her world for the pure of heart. Ophelia is a delicate flower. Her mind may have been polluted but her soul remains pure. Even in death."

"That's a very romantic notion, but, at the time, suicide was considered a crime. It was a sin against God."

"Only if it was done in sound mind. But if someone is mad they cannot be responsible, and so Shakespeare has once again proven that her soul is pure and without sin."

Was there any woman, or girl, in Johnny's life who was as pure as Ophelia? Surely not Miss Argyle, as much as he might wish it. She was such a flirt with everyone, especially his father. His sisters were not pure. Too self-serving and hurtful. One of them, Margaret, actually said to him, "You think that Dad missed you and that's why you get to go bowling with him? No, it's just because your new eye isn't as embarrassing now. You almost look normal." And there it was, a truth he did not wish to admit. His father could only love him because of the acceptable glass eye that the man his mother desired had created for him. Without Siegfried, his father could not accept him and yet with Siegfried, his mother's affections were elsewhere.

"An interesting take, Mr. Wagner. Anyone else?" Mr. Birch looked at Gareth, daring an answer.

Gareth thought about the woman who walked into the lake with rocks filling her pockets. Did she float at all or did the rocks make her sink under the water right away? Was there a moment when she thought, *No, I have changed my mind. I cannot do this.*

"Gareth, do you have anything to add?"

"Yeah, I think suicide is dumb. How did drowning help anything? Didn't help her. Didn't help Hamlet. It crushed Laertes, and, well, Polonius, but he was a fool, anyhow."

"Polonius was already dead at that point."

"Oh. Yeah, right. Well, probably a good thing because hearing that his daughter offed herself would've killed him, anyhow.

Imagine having to tell a father that his daughter drowned herself on purpose."

Gareth thought about how cold the lake had been that October two years ago. There was a constant chilly wind and the water was already colder than usual. There were waves crashing up and an undertow. No, she did not choose a calm exit. It had to be deliberate. A slow walk, step by step, and then she was taken as she threw herself at the water, rocks pulling her down, her lungs filling with water, wanting to cough but unable. Her ears must have filled with the cold, cold water so that the world she was leaving was finally quiet. Her eyes were surely closed, he imagined.

Gareth never mentioned to his mother what he had overheard that night. His mother felt enough sorrow and guilt as it was. It would be so much easier if he told her how he could hear their conversations, how he pressed his ear to the wall, struggling to make out their secret words. But he would have to keep that to himself. His mom would feel betrayed if she knew. And betrayal was the last thing he wanted to bring into their home. Besides, her talk about work had been his only link to those two girls. His white angels. The twins.

Johnny had his hand up again. Gareth knew that somehow he would contradict what he just said. He didn't care about Hamlet and his self-centred whining. Selfish prick with all his introspection and holier-than-thou pronouncements. Blaming everyone else and taking no responsibility himself. It was his fault Ophelia drowned. No one else's. But no, poor Hamlet! Hamlet was a selfish asshole, plain and simple.

Gareth thought that perhaps a woman's demise was always a man's fault. He knew it wasn't his mother's fault that the red-haired woman drowned. It was a man's fault. It had to be. A monster who was as selfish and as evil as Hamlet. There were whispers. There were things he'd overheard.

Gareth kicked at the legs of his desk.

"The tragedy of *Hamlet* is that we have to spend so much time studying it. Everyone dies, nobody learns a thing. All this self-reflection is worthless. It only brings sadness. Why can't we study *A Midsummer Night's Dream* instead? You know, a comedy with warring fairies. Drinking. Revelry. Fun. The difference between comedy and tragedy is that in tragedy everyone dies, and in comedy they all get married."

"Assuming you don't think that marriage is a tragedy, Gareth," Johnny trumped him again.

Gareth still liked his friend but all this overanalyzing, all this self-reflection and talk of purpose, had become so very boring. Everything had to do with fate and destiny. It was as if Johnny saw himself as some kind of philosopher-king. Some all-knowing pompous guru or something. All Gareth could think was how much more likable his friend was when he'd had his ill-fitting, ugly old crusty acrylic eye instead. Ever since he was outfitted for a glass eye in Germany his friend seemed to have changed.

Johnny knew he was outgrowing his friend. Their interests were changing and they were growing apart. And when he looked inward, honestly, he knew he was just a little sad about it. But there was nothing Johnny could do. You cannot fight against destiny.

It was an epiphany. A woman with bleach-blond hair, a raspy voice, and the charisma of the world's best evangelical preachers was tearing up the charts. She was being featured everywhere from billboards to magazine covers. Bleach Blond. Thus the name of the band: Blondie.

When the albino twins first saw Deborah Harry on Video Concert Hall, it was as though their own personal goddess had descended with a message for them. There she was, a created version of what they were and could be authentically. They were bleached without the bleach. Blonder than Blondie. And they could sing. They had been developing their own sound. But the rest had to be acquired.

There had been a history of the bleach-blond goddess: Marilyn Monroe, Jean Harlow, Lana Turner, Kim Novak, Sandra Dee, then later the rock stars and musicians of which Deborah Harry was just one. But she was the one who used her bleach-blond persona as the name of her band. She made her look and her style a part of her sound and it resonated around the world. No longer the pouting, strutting male front and centre, here was a woman baring herself in an utterly raw display of unapologetic verve. If nothing else, that is what Clara and Blanca wanted. To exist without apology. To make no excuses for who and what they were. They had spent too long out of the sun — it was time for them to step into the light. They couldn't blend, so why try? They would never be accepted. Why remain an apology for a grandfather who was ashamed of them, a project for teachers who pitied them, and a joke to the boys who ignored them? They could be goddesses. Adored. Everyone knew that adoration trumped love every time.

The girls needed a look. They needed to lose the pastels of childhood and focus on something a bit edgier. Dark red, midnight blues, and mostly black came to mind. Something that would contrast their white, white hair, their pale skin, their translucent thick eyelashes, and invisible eyebrows.

"We should start wearing eyeliner and darkening our lashes," Blanca said. "We can copy Deborah Harry's look. Eyeshadow, dark liner, and red lips. Everything else pale."

Makeup was strewn across the counters: rouge, lipsticks, eyeshadows, and pencils. Clara took a cobalt blue, pulled down her lower lid and inked a line over the inner pink of her lid. It felt waxy and irritating, but the effect was perfect. A dark inner line sat in contrast to all that was pale. Blanca reached for the pencil, copied her sister. And then they stood, looking in the mirror at their handiwork. A contour below the cheekbones, but every contour was too dark for their white skin, so eventually they just opted for the lightest ivory, and that was dark enough to hollow out their little cheeks.

"Oh my God! It's amazing! We look completely different!" Clara exclaimed to her sister.

"We need to outline our lips. But on the outside to give us a big, full, pouty look."

By now they had loosened their hair so that it fell in braid-waves down their backs. Lips were blood-red, eyes were cobalt blue with a blue-black mascara on the lashes, cheeks were contoured and the whole picture was somewhere between goth and Tammy Faye.

They donned ripped black jeans they snuck from their aunt's closet and tight-fitting T-shirts they found in their younger cousins' drawers. Then practised strutting in front of the long mirror. If nothing else, it was fun. Fun to experiment with their aunt's makeup behind her back. Fun to see themselves in a different way. Fun to dream of a life as rock stars.

"What in God's name! You look like a pair of cheap tarts!"

It was their uncle Bob, home a bit earlier than expected. He looked horrified, as much by the mess in the bathroom as by their painted faces and tight, tight clothes.

"Your mother would roll over in her grave if she saw you like that!"

It had been the familiar threat for a couple of years, ever since their mother had died mysteriously at the yellow cottages. Clara and Blanca hated it when their uncle mentioned their mother. It made them feel guilty for any pleasure they might have. Made them think that they should have been nicer, better, more attentive as daughters. Worse, they felt that if they hadn't been born, then their mother would not have suffered because they knew, they knew, that they were the cause of her endless grief.

Bob grabbed a face cloth and threw it at them.

"Wash that shit off your faces. You think you look good like that? You look like a couple of sorry clowns. Sorry slut clowns. You don't look good, you look pathetic. Wash it off!"

"Sliffy midwists umper stash," Clara whispered to Blanca.

"Yep. Sliffy umpteen thrice upper den."

"And stop with that gibberish. You know it's just made up and nonsensical. You just do it to piss me off!"

"Dinger immer and jammer, stingerly," Clara said, in defiance, and Blanca understood every word.

"Keep it up and I'll wash your mouths out with soap! Jee-zus!"

He hated that they were wearing makeup, growing up. The world wasn't a safe place, he knew that only too well. No matter how many times he smacked his boys, he could see them leering at the girls. Probably because they were walking around like a pair of sluts, showing off their suddenly evident, perky buds. Yes, they would have to stay full-time at their grandfather's apartment now. There'd be no one to blame but themselves if something happened to them there.

"Now get that shit off your faces and put on something decent."

As they rubbed, the colours smeared and bled across their faces. Black mascara streaked into the blue and the red and the pink, making them look as though they had been beaten. The more they rubbed, the worse it got, until their little faces looked bruised and raw.

But they knew it was all wrong, anyhow. They knew that their look depended on their differences, not their ability to mimic someone else. And so there would be no mascara; the lashes would remain, full and white, in a dense fringe around their pale, lightly rimmed eyes. Eyes that had steadied considerably over the years and had come to look more violet than pink. Eyes so intense that they needed no adornment. Gone were the thick glasses. Contacts would keep them seeing at their 40 percent vision and that would be just fine. Good enough to get by.

They removed the tight black jeans and the T-shirts. Blanca pulled white sheets from the bed and draped them, tightly, around their thin bodies. Yes, that was right. They would make tight white dresses that would fall from their bare shoulders to the ground. Or perhaps something gauzier. It didn't matter as long as it was white.

"White. Everyone is wearing black and tight. We will wear all white from top to bottom. And our only makeup will be lipstick."

And so the look was created. Two white goddesses with blood-stained lips. White brows, white lashes, white hair.... Everything white except the backup band. Yes, they would find the best musicians to back them up, one day.

"Add a little funk to the opera and the punk!" Blanca declared.

"Punk and funk opera!" Clara agreed, a conspiratorial smile across her face.

They began to try out their look on an everyday basis. They wore white to school. White T-shirts and jeans and white sneakers on their feet. Never again did they braid their hair; they wore it loose, sometimes as straight as a pin and sometimes in waves. They brought a tube of lipstick with them at all times and often dashed off to the washroom to touch up those lips so that they could be seen coming from a mile away. At first, there were whispers and pointed fingers but, in time, it was accepted. Accepted to the point that no one even remembered the awkward two with the thick glasses and tight braids. They were just a vision in white, striding in tandem down the halls, hanging out in the drama and the music rooms. And strangely, for the first time in their lives, they began to make friends. Kids wanted to hear them sing or they invited them to hang out. Somehow, the more they tried to differentiate and not to blend, the more accepted they were.

"What will you call your band?" a cool boy two grades older asked them.

"Bleach," Clara replied. It was supposed to be a joke, but the moment it left her lips, her red-stained lips, she knew that indeed, they would be Bleach. And they would turn heads.

* * *

The art teacher sat with her hands placed in front of her, one over the other, in a nonthreatening but not entirely open manner. She waited for Gareth to explain himself, to shed light on why the student who had won the art award the previous year was now failing her class.

"It isn't that your work isn't good. Quite the contrary. You get As on everything you hand in. The work you hand in is excellent. But you hand in so little."

"Why don't you just mark me on what I hand in?"

"Because you are not doing the work. If Susan, for instance, who doesn't have your degree of talent, is working really hard to get better and she not only hands in what is required but goes beyond the call of duty, why should she get less of a mark because the few pieces you hand in are better?"

Gareth knew she was right. He handed in one out of every five assignments. It just seemed to take him longer. If they had an exercise in class where they had to sketch ten quick still lifes in thirty minutes, Gareth would complete two. But what he handed in were not simple sketches. They were never quick. Gareth was incapable of showing anyone anything that wasn't a study in detail.

"Let me ask you something, Mrs. Beacon. If you had to have an operation, say, on your heart, and you had two doctors, one who did three operations a day but lost one or two of his patients and you had another doctor who only did one every two days but never lost a patient, which doctor would you choose?"

"Clever question, Gareth, but it is hardly the same thing. Saving lives is not the same as making art."

"Maybe that's why you're a teacher and not an artist."

"I am an artist, as well!"

Gareth shrugged. "If you say so, but you don't take art seriously." And then he imitated her, "Saving lives is not the same as art, after all."

Mrs. Beacon wanted to slap his impertinent face, just to wipe the smile off of it. But no, there was something she could do that was far, far worse. She could fail him. She could decide to not recommend him for art college and say that he was too lazy to be a true artist. That he lacked discipline.

She pressed. "How can you improve if you do not do the work?"

Gareth opened his binder, which was filled with handouts and assigned work from other classes. There, where the science notes should have been, were drawings of faces and eyes and body parts. She could see her fellow teachers' expressions in the doodling. In the math Duo-Tang, it was the same. In physics, where equations should be, there were more sketches. History class had illustrations in every margin. Again and again, in every other class notebook, there were pages and pages of faces and details of eyes everywhere.

"If you just put these into your sketchbook for a mark you wouldn't be failing."

"And what kind of a mark would I get on these sketches?"

"I don't know. At least a seventy-five or an eighty percent and that would bring your whole mark up to the high eighties."

"That's exactly why I can't hand them in. I can't have you judge something that isn't perfect. Why would I? I'm just doodling to relieve boredom. It isn't worthy to be considered my work. I would rather get a zero for work not handed in than to get anything less than ninety percent on something I did feel worthy of being judged."

"But you are failing and that could ruin your entire future."

Gareth knew that she could never understand him. She couldn't see that there was work you played with, knowing it would be discarded and never seen, then there was the work you put out into the world.

"You could give Susan a better mark even though you know she's average. And you could fail me, if you want. But does your mark make me less of an artist?"

Why were her best students always the most difficult? That young confidence was something she couldn't fathom. She was, even at this late stage in her life, always seeking approval. Always trying to imitate greatness. And so her work was competent, in the style of this artist or that, but she knew that what she lacked was the very thing this boy had. That was the thing about genius. Genius never made a good student. They were the ones who came in, knew what they needed to learn before they learned it, took what they wanted and discarded whatever didn't apply to their vision. How are such creatures made in this world? And why didn't she have that quality? She should have admired him for his youthful confidence, his talent, and even his impertinence, but she couldn't. He was a walking, breathing slap in the face.

"Then you will fail. Perhaps when you go home, you should take a long hard look in the mirror and practise saying, 'Would you like fries with that?' Good luck, Gareth."

"You're gonna retire in a few years, right? And you'll have lots of retirement money. Now if you pass me, you'll retire the same way as if you fail me. You have in your hands the power to affect someone's destiny and either way it'll make no difference to you."

"No, your destiny is in your own hands. It is up to you. There is nothing predetermined. There's only hard work and rejection and disappointment. You, Gareth, are an arrogant little prick. Now get out of my class. You've ruined my weekend."

Gareth looked at his adversary. Maybe she was young once. Maybe she had dreams once. But there in her face, all he could see were pools of regret weighing down the corners of her downturned lips. This is what it meant to defer. This is what it meant to compromise. This is what it meant to rush and ignore detail. It meant a life of comfort and content, but the price was regret. And an ugly mouth.

Gareth sat at the kitchen table, an open quart-bottle of milk in front of him and, as there was nobody home, he could see no reason why he should reach for a glass when the milk was in glass, anyhow. Besides, he knew he would finish it off, which was fine as he had just carried in the fresh bottles that had been delivered and left on the doorstep.

He wondered if that bitch teacher would actually fail him, just to teach him a life lesson about effort. But what kind of a lesson was that? To rush and to accept less than your very best? That quantity was more important than quality? That was the type of lesson that produced the workers of the world. The factory workers, the clerics, the teachers.

Gareth felt a bit guilty for his thoughts. Hadn't his father worked in a factory to support him and his brother? He never shied away from shelling out for whatever interest took their fancies. Cameras for Tristan and paints and canvases for him. And didn't his mother work long hours as a nurse to provide for them all? It was her extra shifts that allowed his dad to return to university to follow his dreams. His mom did all that, caring for others and caring for them and doing whatever she could so that everyone else could reach their full potential. His father would be a labour lawyer in another year, all because his mom worked the extra shifts. His brother would be going to school in Toronto to get a degree in film studies, all because his mom worked extra shifts. And so how could he possibly tell her that he may fail art because he didn't put in the extra time, when all she did was put in extra time?

He took a long pull on the milk, swallowed with a gulp, and wiped the white creamy moustache from his upper lip with his sleeve. "Wear a crazy T-shirt, wear a cutaway skirt, but wear a moustache." He hummed the milk ad song as he opened the top cupboard. There, on a plate, were freshly made oatmeal raisin cookies. His mom had even baked before going to work, where she would be changing patients, holding straws for them, and giving them medicine, saying, "There, there, it will all be okay."

Gareth grabbed four cookies, picked up the milk bottle, and went to his room. In the corner stood an easel, in his closet there was a 3x4 canvas, and in his toolbox there were oils and brushes. He thought of Ophelia and the flowers. He thought of the lake and the wind. He thought of the albino twins. But no matter what he thought, there was one image that he could never shake from his mind: the image of his best friend's body, twisting as though in some *danse macabre*, falling from the branches of a tree.

He mixed blues first, adding a little black and a dash of Carmen red. Next to that, he placed the greens and greys. From a tube, he squeezed a long line of white. *This*, he thought, *this will be my answer for my failing mark. This will be my reasoning, my excuse. And anyone who can see will understand its meaning.*

A woman stands with hair blowing in the wind, her dress billows around her as the grey-toned waters lick at her ankles. Behind her is another woman, in white, a nurse running, but she is so far in the distance that it is hard to tell if she is indeed a woman or a wisp of a cloud. Before her is the expanse of water, in greys and blues and greens, but from the water, there is a rock and on the rock are two girls — or are they mermaids? It is hard to tell, as only their torsos are above the water. Their mouths are open as though singing a siren's song. One combs her hair and the other reaches out toward the woman, and, in her hand, she holds something, an offering of sorts. Here Gareth puts the most attention. Here are the details and the point of the whole painting. Here she holds out an eye to the woman. And in the eye is the reflection of the entire world.

Gareth worked furiously, with intent. The paint hitting the canvas in globs, colours rising from the white background, almost three-dimensionally. The water's waves seemed to curl to the end of the canvas so that the viewer could almost walk in, along with the woman who was being seduced to her death.

If a picture is worth a thousand words then this would be what Gareth would hand in to Mr. Birch as his essay on the demise of Ophelia. This is what he would give Mrs. Beacon as his reason for all those assignments not done. And who cares, who really cares what mark he would get, anyhow? There it was, everything he felt responsible for, but could never really comprehend.

"You have been working for hours. Didn't you hear me come in?" his mother asked. "I brought you up some dinner."

Gareth stepped back. Away from the canvas. He was tired and covered with paint. His mom, Elaine, looked at her youngest son. How tall he had grown this past year. He was on the precipice between boyhood and manhood and sometimes it was hard for Elaine to know if he needed the hug or cuddle of youth or if he wanted to work things out for himself. Gareth had always been the one who kept things inside and only broached topics when he was ready. When he was tiny he seemed to stare off into space if he didn't want to discuss something. He looked far, far into the distance, as though he could place all his sorrows on the horizon, only to revisit them when he was good and ready. So many times Elaine had wanted to check in, make sure things were fine with him, but a quick hug and off he would go, as though replenished and ready to embrace a new day. Still, there were things that were buried in her son. She worked in a psych ward; she knew the signs of suppressed memory and emotion, but as long as he carried on as though he was fine, Elaine chose not to push him too far emotionally.

"I'm failing art, Mom."

Elaine looked at the painting for a very long time.

"No, you are not failing art at all."

* * *

"Strrrr-rike!"

Johnny's ball roared down the lane, took out the lot! He had another two goes and he knew he would do it again, and again.

"How does he do it?" Miss Argyle squealed. Although she had ceased to be Miss Argyle some time ago and had become Jean. Teammates now, and so first names were fine, just fine!

"Can't touch us!" Johnny replied, doing a premature victory dance. "This year the cup is ours!"

"All because of you, John Jr."

John Jr. He had outgrown Johnny, even though his mother still called him that, and yet John Jr. didn't quite work for him, either. He may have started to spend more time with his dad but, although he liked the newly found closeness, he hardly felt like his younger clone.

"I was thinking …" he tried it out for them, "I was thinking I would like to be called Jack. You know, it's another way of saying John, and Johnny is just, well, you know, just too kiddy."

"Tell you what," his dad said, smirking, "you get another two strikes and we will call you anything!"

"Anything but late for dinner!" Jean joked and the other fellers laughed, too. How they all loved her!

Johnny, or rather Jack, knew he would make the next two strikes. Monocular vision was an asset for anything requiring aim. Shooting darts, pool, and archery were all easy for him. And now bowling. Maybe Siegfried was right all those years ago. One eye looks ahead and the other, the blind eye, looks within. The blind eye knows. It is the one that places the ball while the other sees where it should Strrrr-rike!

"One more and your name is Jack! Forever Jack from the moment they hand over the cup!"

"Doesn't matter, we've already won the championship. There's no catching us now! Better get used to calling me Jack from this moment on!" Jack laughed, happy to be free of his old name. Yes, he was a Jack, through and through. Happy to be rid of Johnny.

"Yeah, but sometimes it's not enough to just win. Sometimes you have to destroy the competition."

"Oh, John, you should have been in something more competitive than the school system. You've got the killer instinct!" Miss Argyle exclaimed.

Jack picked up the ball. Slipped his fingers into the holes, readied himself. He took two steps back, lifted the ball in front of his face and focused on where the ball should be placed, down the long lane. He could see it. He brought his right leg behind himself, looking almost graceful in this pose, as he held it for one, two, three seconds. But then he thought he saw something. Something on the glass eye side. He had an inner vision. There his dad and Miss Argyle, Jean, sat safely on his blind side, but he knew, he knew that there was something else going on. Something other than mere team spirit. He moved his back leg farther behind and then swooped it over so that he pirouetted and stood there, ball before his face, in front of his father and his former grade one teacher. What was it? Not an embrace. Nothing so obvious. No, it was far more dangerous because it was so casual, so accepted by all. It was clear an arrangement had been going on for some time. There was Jean, taking a sip of his father's drink, and his father, sitting, one lanky leg crossed over the other, but in such a way that their knees touched. And then there was his arm draped loosely on the back of her chair as though that is where his arm has always belonged, had always been.

Silence. The team waited.

"Go on, lad, take your last turn," his father's pal said, his stomach rolling over the top of his belt, his shirt only half tucked in.

Jack laughed. He kissed the ball. But just when they thought he was going to finish up with his final strike, he walked over to the team. He stood as tall as he could and looked down on the sitting pair. Jean shifted a bit. Moved her knee away.

"I already won your cup for you. You're the team captain, Dad. If you want to destroy, I think you might be the better man for it. So why don't you just take the last turn?"

He dropped the ball. Hard. Into his father's lap. John Sr. couldn't help but wince as it hit his jewels.

The only place Jack wanted to be was at his friend's house. Gareth's home. Sure, they hadn't been as close since they started high school, but still, there were all those years. The shared comic books, the giggles, the make-believe. Would it be strange to just show up at this late hour? To suggest they have a Coke together and just hang out. He didn't want to go home. Didn't want to show up there without his father and raise suspicions.

But perhaps his mother already knew. Didn't she get all quiet on bowling nights? Practically throwing dinner on the table and eating without the pleasure of small talk and niceties. Every Thursday it was the same: a quick casserole, either tuna or chicken, with an iceberg lettuce side salad, and then a bowl of ice cream scooped from the carton. On Thursdays there were no butter tarts or deep-dish pies, no *Kuchen* or meringues like the other nights of the week. All the other nights his mother delighted in putting her latest creations on the table. Two veggies, potatoes done in a variety of ways, steak, meat pies, knackwurst.... But on Thursdays, the food was very, very North American, prepared and slopped onto plates. Yes, of course she knew.

Which came first? His father's distraction or his mother's detachment? Did she already suspect something the first time they had gone to Germany? Or did his father suspect that his wife's heart had always been elsewhere and so he had to try to find some attraction away from her just to heal his bruised ego? Perhaps he needed to feel that middle age hadn't taken ahold of him and so he looked for attention, some harmless flirtation, from the opposite sex. The prettier, the better. And who was prettier than Miss Argyle?

Of course, Jack couldn't go home. Home wasn't even home anymore. The Christmas dinners, the oversized tree, the holidays, the evening dinners, it all seemed no more than a charade to keep the lie alive and to keep the children happy.

But he wasn't happy. If both of his parents found love elsewhere, he should be happy for them, but he couldn't be because every hope and dream of eternal love, every possibility of it, had been shattered by their selfishness.

Of course, he couldn't go home. But Gareth's house was perhaps not the best place to be, either. His parents always seemed more like a pair, better suited than his parents had ever been. Didn't they go on weekly dates? Together! Yeah, Gareth had it made compared to him. A happy home, a mother who worked and baked cookies, a father who loved his mother, an older brother who worked at the cinema and got him in for free, and no mean older sisters ... so if he had so much more, then why did fate have Jack fall from the tree and not Gareth?

It was all a lie. True love, fate, destiny. Fairy tales for adults so that they could get through the day. Because the truth was, the truth was that it was all pointless. As pointless as a bowling tournament.

"What do you mean you don't know where he is? How could you just lose our son?" Hilda yelled at him.

"Well, he's hardly a little boy now. He'll be fine. He'll find his way home. We just had a little disagreement."

"A disagreement? At bowling?"

John sighed and collapsed onto the couch. He could stay up reading, waiting for John Jr. — no, Jack — to return and, providing Hilda went to bed, he could have a word with him man to man and convince him that he had mistaken friendly team spirit for something else. But whom was he protecting in doing that? His guile was a shield to protect whom, exactly? Him and his structured world, with a family, a wife, and a girlfriend on the side? Miss Argyle and her reputation in the community and with the school board? Or his wife, Hilda, who had been a stranger to him in bed for so long that it was hard to think of her as anything but a mother and a roommate. Or was he protecting his son from the muckiness of the adult world? He could easily tell a lie and leave him the security of family. After all, hadn't he been the last man out for so long? A misfit with a misfitting eye. Even in the discomfort of the situation, John had to chuckle at that one.

"What did you argue about?" Hilda persisted.

Her accent irritated him. How was it possible that at one time it was so charming? Her funny emphasis. Her direct speech, her back-of-the-throat sounds that were almost a purr. Once those things trapped him and now he could not abide the sound of her voice. Of course, everything about her irritated him because she just wasn't Jean.

John didn't even know how the affair started. It was all so innocent at first. Harmless fun, really. In fact, he still felt love for Hilda when it started. Jean was there one night, bowling with some girlfriends, and none of them were any good at all. She was part of a clutch of young women laughing. But the joy was intoxicating. Laughter was something he hadn't heard since his son had lost his eye. And there it was, like bells ringing in the air and circling all around him. He found himself smiling. Smiling! For a moment all that existed was their laughter, their silliness, their attention. He rolled his ball down and it hit all but two pins, one on either side. One of the other girls, not Jean, had called over, "Good luck getting those two."

"You don't think I can?" he'd challenged back.

"No, they are so widely spread apart!"

And there it was, the first innuendo. Except it wasn't Jean. But Jean had looked at him when her friend said that and she smiled, shyly. They knew each other, outside the bowling alley. He was a school inspector and she was a teacher. Apart from the year his son was in her class when they would meet during the scheduled parent-teacher interviews, he also saw her in a work setting where he had the upper hand as her performance inspector. On those visits, she would be sitting primly behind her desk at the front of the class while he sat in, usually at the back, for the lesson. Then he would walk up and down the aisles, asking the children to put their hands on their desks so he could make sure they were clean, sometimes pausing to quiz a child on something he or she should know. And always he had a ruler in his hand, as though he could, at any moment, give someone a stinging thwack. If only he had his handy ruler now!

"I'm very good at dealing with spread … pins," he said, picking up the ball, and, as he looked at the younger women, he slowly and deliberately eased his fingers into the holes of the hard, reddish ball. He moved them slowly in and out a couple of times.

"Tight fit." He had smiled at them, in a boyish way, without a care in the world.

Two steps back and then a little twinkle-toed run up and he released the ball. It sailed down the lane, looking like it would roll right down the centre, clean between the two pins. But at the last moment, it curved and took out the pin on the right. The pin closer to the girls' lane.

"Aw, too bad!" That time it had been Jean teasing.

"I still have one ball left."

And the three had giggled. "Let's hope you have two, sugar!"

The women had then joined him and his mates for french fries and drinks. Jean Argyle had taken off her bowling shoes to rub her instep.

"I have such high arches. I have this problem with lots of shoes. It's my insteps, see? They are like ballerina feet, really."

And it had been then, when he looked at those high arches, at the perfect instep of her narrow foot, that he felt the first stirrings in a very long time. When was the last time he had looked at Hilda and felt a tingle in his groin or had an unexpected, spontaneous swelling? Hard to do that when she was always running around to ophthalmologist appointments, cleaning fake eyes, and putting eyedrops into their boy's eye, always then describing it to him in the greatest detail. Why, when she could just do it and keep quiet about it, did she have to describe it all to him? Then there was her secret crying. He tried to ignore it, hoping it would go away. Hoping that his indifference wasn't the cause. He wasn't indifferent, though — he was overwhelmed. It seemed that if they had any joy at all, it was a betrayal to the suffering and teasing their son endured. And so all emotional intimacy had been lost, all closeness denied, and any attraction erased, until it was only grief that bound them.

By the time Jack had a proper eye, a glass eye, things had just gone too far. He had rubbed those perfect arches too many times and his massaging fingers had made their way up the tight calves to her knees. When his teammates were up, his hand would venture farther, under the hem of her skirt, to the rim of her stockings. She said nothing, stared straight ahead at the bowling action, but she never took his hand away. And so, he pretended to look at his teammates while secretly he walked his fingers to the start of her panties. She sat a bit more forward, opened her thighs a bit, encouraging. He pulled away the material and felt the outline of her cunt.

It had become a weekly game for them. Her keeping the score and him sitting beside her, telling his mates that she still didn't understand the scorecard and he was helping her get it just right. Then, when they were up, her knee would move to touch his and he knew that she was ready to play. She wanted his hand to explore more and more. She wanted it to climb higher up her skirt. She yearned for danger. She wanted his fingers inside her. And every time she seemed wetter and wetter to him. Until finally, finally, one evening, she said that her car was in the shop and it was late and she was afraid to walk home at night in case someone accosted her or took advantage. So he acted chivalrously and offered her a drive home.

It was just supposed to be a bit of fun. A distraction, that's all it was! It wasn't that he didn't love Hilda, it's just that the Hilda he loved seemed so very far away from him. Duty had taken his lover and had given him a partner instead. How could he ever possibly say to her that he no longer wanted to be her husband, but he would love to run away from the worries that were drowning them, he would love to have a little room somewhere where he could rediscover her as a lover, where he would love to fuck her as he had in the early days. But, as that would not and could not be, he had found a replacement. A keener. A woman who wore cashmere and pearls and straight skirts to her knee and, under all that, there was a wet, wet cunt encouraging him with anticipation and secret desire. A woman who wasn't afraid to push his hand higher and higher and higher still, all the while writing down scores, smiling at his mates and telling stories of the goings on in primary school.

If only Hilda could be so naughty.

It should be easy to have both. To not give anything away and to have it all! But as time went on, and the affair escalated, he couldn't help but resent that Hilda just wasn't Jean. She wasn't rushing into their bedroom for anything other than sleep. She wasn't hanging on his every word, telling him how clever he was. Yes, he resented Hilda because she no longer looked at him with wonder. No longer trembled with want. No longer shut out all other concerns when he was with her. When he got promoted to school superintendent she didn't say, "That's amazing," as Jean had. No, all she asked was how much more money they would be making because replacing glass eyes could be expensive.

"What did you argue about?" she asked for the third time.

"The bowling balls. He had one that was too small. I wanted him to use mine."

Hilda stared at him.

"Really?"

"Yes, really! You know I am a bit of a perfectionist when it comes to choosing the perfect bowling ball!" He was shouting. It took them both by surprise.

"Well, if you love your bowling ball so much, why don't you just fuck it? It has holes that are big enough for your little pee-pee, I'm sure."

Thank you! Oh, God, thank you! That was all he could think. *Thank you for finally being so vile that I can leave you with a clear conscience.*

He was now Jack. It was decided. He would never go back to being Johnny or John. He was now independent, separate from his parents and his bitchy sisters. He was free. Free and terribly sad.

Jack sat on Tristan's bed, surrounded by movie posters, actors' pictures, and autographs that were tacked up, neatly, on his walls. He had arrived an hour before, found out that Gareth had gone out with other friends and, when he turned to leave, Tristan asked if, perhaps, he wanted to hang out.

"God, you must really love films."

"What do you think that each of these filmmakers has in common?"

"They all made a shit-ton of money in Hollywood?" Jack suggested.

Tristan laughed, leaned back into his pillows, and crossed his arms.

"You and I have more in common than you and Gareth. We're both blind in one eye."

"I am not blind in one eye; I have one eye missing. You still have yours. There's a difference."

Tristan shrugged. *Semantics*, he thought to himself. What was the difference if an unmoving glass stand-in was in Jack's head and a symbolistic but useless real eye was in his? Neither of them would ever understand the magic of 3D.

"Has having only one affected … you know?" Jack asked.

"What? No, I don't know."

"Getting a girlfriend?"

"I've never had a problem getting interest, but then, I can get anyone into the cinema for free so I guess I have a leg up on you!"

How was it that Tristan was so easy about it all? So nonchalant about his monocular vision when it was a constant source of despair for Jack? He wanted to see things, everything, in a balanced, even, and symmetrical way.

"Which do you think is a better name for me? John or Jack?"

Tristan narrowed his gaze and thought for what seemed an eternity.

"Jack," he finally said. "Definitely Jack. No doubt at all!"

"Cool," Jack agreed as he relaxed back into the pillows. "I think my parents might divorce."

"Aw, that sucks. Your poor dad, your mom is so hot."

Jack looked at Tristan with shock and disdain. Was he being antagonistic or was he just crazy? How was his mother hot?

"I mean, come on! She has a voice like Marlene Dietrich. Who wouldn't find that hot? When I was twelve or so and your mother would say, 'Come here, little Tristan,' I was like jelly. I didn't know if she was a spy or something! For real. God, she's like a cross between Marlene Dietrich and Hildegard Knef!"

"I don't even know who those people are."

"Then your education starts here!"

Tristan pulled out all his books about films. He showed Jack his cameras, a collection that included a 1955 Hasselblad from Germany, a Minolta Hi-Matic 7s, and a Yashica Electro 35.

"I bought this one myself from the money I made at the cinema. See how big and old-fashioned it is? But it takes great photographs."

Jack looked through the eyepiece. Turned the camera as he tried to find a good shot.

"And you know, the benefit for guys like us is that we never have to close one eye."

Jack took the camera from his face. He turned it around to look at the front of it.

"The camera is a bit like us, isn't it?"

"How so?" asked Tristan.

"Well, the camera is also a Cyclops. It has only one eye and with it, it tries to hold an image forever."

Tristan thought about the idea of the Cyclops. Of course, the Cyclops had always seemed to be something to be feared. A monster with one eye, something that could be disarmed with one well-placed poke of a stick or a flaming torch as Odysseus had done. But maybe, just maybe, that was a myth written by the two-eyed folk who thought a little less of monocular beings. Maybe it was the Cyclopses of the world who would capture the most memorable images.

"You want to start a photography club? We could make a dark-room in the basement. Or at your house. Then I could spend some time trying to cheer up your distressed mother," he joked. "Older women are so hot."

"Thought you were interested in movies?"

"I am, but you cannot frame a movie if you cannot frame a still. Every other Tuesday? Deal?"

"Deal!"

FIVE

DECREE NISI. Hilda wasn't even sure what that meant but, because it said something about a decree absolute following in three months' time, she could only assume that it was an unnecessary step between being married and divorced. A three-month purgatory where one is neither free nor in partnership. How ironic that their engagement had also been three months long all those years ago.

Why now? Why, after all the years of knowing someone. Why change at this time of life? But there were signs that John was discontent before; Hilda just didn't want to admit it. She thought they could weather the storm, that things would be better as the kids became more independent.

"I don't want to drag this out and make it any messier than it needs to be. We can mediate this. You stay in the house, keep everything," he had told her, his voice filled with a concerned tone.

Of course, John let on that he was being generous, but all Hilda could think was that he wanted out so badly that he was willing to leave with next to nothing. Wanted out so badly that he could not run from her fast enough. If there were any ties, any lingering affections, why wasn't there a fight? Deep down, she wanted the court case, the messiness and the chance to stand up and say that he had betrayed her. To have an ear for her hurt. An outside ear. Someone who was supposed to be neutral but couldn't help but side with her. But, instead, she agreed to the mediation and the quick process because she knew that messiness would only hurt the kids and divide their loyalty. And so the brave front. The businesslike efficiency of just getting on with it. The stiff upper lip.

"But then I would have to agree on the grounds of incompatibility, when we both know it is because of adultery, John."

"Yes, but then you would have had to have filed and not me. If you want it on grounds of adultery, are you willing to do the paperwork?"

"No."

"Then incompatibility it is. You just need to sign that it's uncontested."

"But we are not incompatible."

"We are incompatible." He smiled tightly.

"I don't agree," she argued. But then she couldn't help herself. "You are just trying to make yourself look less dishonourable than you are. Fucking *arschloch!*"

That had been six months ago. Then the process. A few meetings with a mediator. And then the many signatures. And now here it was. An opened official envelope, with a seal and everything, declaring that she was divorced, in principle. Three months' wiggle room.

Hilda wanted to cry but didn't have it in her. Every step had seemed a drama that would end at any moment. The greasepaint could come off, the costumes could be put away, and everything would be normal again. In three months, though, the drama would be complete. The curtains closed, the players offstage, and the audience all back at home.

Hilda put the envelope in her bureau drawer. She decided that it would stay there, alone, until the decree *absolute* joined it in three months.

Three months. Didn't Jack need a new eye fitting in three months' time? Wasn't he due for that? Why wait around for something that was going to be final, no *absolute*, anyhow?

The ocularist prepared, as he did every day. The face-washing, the brushing of the teeth. The shave, the aftershave, and then the daily contemplation of the hair remaining on his head. It wasn't so much balding as it was a revealing of the forehead. Wasn't a high forehead a sign of intelligence? And his was getting higher every year! The widow's peak was becoming more pronounced, with a deepened *V*, the upward spikes reaching almost to the top of his head now. If the point wasn't there, the entire top would be thin, almost bald, and he would have that around-the-back-of-the-head scruff that so many men walk around with, sans apology. *Why*, he wondered, *is God always portrayed as a man?* Surely one male would not be so cruel to one of his own sex! Unless, of course, he had mounds of long, flowing hair and an ample beard, all in curls. Yes, that is what made them all cruel gods, whether they were the one and only God or one of the many patriarchs on Mount Olympus. They all had the locks, the curls, the ample hair, everywhere but on their bodies. *How contrasting that is to the middle-aged German man*, he thought. Siegfried had developed a few tufts of hair growing out of his ears, something he quickly remedied the very moment they sprouted. His chest hair was certainly present with a few new grey individual ones emerging amongst the darker ones. Then the hair became more sparse as it travelled over his belly and downward.

Did women prefer the smooth skin of the gods, those maniacal beings with their damned perfect hair? Did any woman want a man with less body hair than her? A man with smoother, silkier legs? With better, fuller hair on his head? No, of course not! The woman was the creature to be admired and adored, not the man. But if that was truly the case, then why did he feel so insecure, so undesirable?

Today Hilda would return, with her teenaged boy who now wanted to be called Jack. Well, why not? Jack was a perfect name for him. After all, didn't Jack climb the beanstalk just as Johnny had the apple tree? Didn't Jack face down the giant, as Johnny would one day? Didn't Jack have a mother who loved him? A mother who raised him on her own? Just as Hilda had with her Jack.

Hilda. He had only seen her a few more times since that first eye fitting. He had told her to come back every year to two years because of the changes in the growing eye. But that wasn't necessary, really. The human eye grows very little over time, the greatest growth happening by three years of age. The eyeball grows rapidly, increasing from about sixteen to seventeen millimetres at birth to between twenty-two and a half and twenty-three millimetres by three years of age. By age thirteen, the eye attains its full size. Siegfried knew this. He knew that replacing Jack's eye on a regular basis was no longer needed. His eye could take him through many years and into adulthood. Oh, the sclera would need to be darkened perhaps because a child's whites were whiter than an adult's. And perhaps a few lines of subtle veining could be added through the years. But the fit would not change much. And Hilda's visits would be fewer and fewer. Well, they would be, anyhow, as the boy eased into manhood.

Why was she always so present in his mind? What had transpired between them, really? Some talks about the past. An arm around her waist as they walked along. A bit of flirtation. Four visits was all there had been. And always with the boy present. No, there was no intimacy of the physical kind. But there were letters and, over time, they had become more and more frequent. Some were no more than a few lines. Others were pages, written on flimsy blue airmail paper, talking about a walk along the lake, or a sunset that was particularly beautiful or a detailed description of a cake she had made. Those were the letters he held dearest. Not the newsy ones, but the ones that described her every day. A meal made, a walk, a laugh with a neighbour. These were insights into how she travelled through her life. These were a taste of her day-to-day.

Siegfried had tried to respond in kind, but his days were so similar that he found he was repeating himself. The same breakfast, the same walk to his studio, the same ritual of blowing glass and creating eyes. Of course, it was fascinating to him. Of course, he was obsessed with each and every eye, but how could he write that to her? How could he say that Mr. Weiss had developed a yellowing in his sclera so he needed an eye that reflected the change? Remember, he was the one whose eye was somewhere between grey and green, but had a ring of brown around the outside of the iris and was shot through with gold specks? Why would she care, this woman who walked barefoot in the cool May sand while icy waters chased her feet, this woman who decided to add a little coffee to her chocolate icing and it was marvellous, this woman who told off a teacher for being mean to her son, this woman who could dispatch and dress and cook a rabbit all in one day! This was a marvellous woman! And it was only through her letters that he learned who she grew to become because when he did see her those few times she came to Germany, he always just remembered who she once was, as a girl.

Siegfried took off his shirt, looked at his torso, and assessed it. The chest was broad enough. The shoulders were square. There was perhaps a bit of flab over what was once a tight, lean body, but it wasn't bad, you could see the muscles there still. Underneath. A little bit of a paunch. Damn that evening beer, he should have given that up as soon as he knew she was coming. But if he stood taller, breathed in, then it wasn't so bad.

Who was he fooling? His shirt wasn't going to come off. There had never been anything more than a kiss and that was lovely while it lasted, but then it quickly broke off when Johnny, no, Jack, was heard returning from the wash-closet. And then there was nothing but awkwardness between them. And nowhere in any letter was there ever a mention of it. Nor had there been a mention of that first flower he had included. Was he just a foolish romantic, projecting an imagined intimacy simply because he had failed so badly at romance in his actual life? Then again, her letters always ended with "Be Heartily Embraced. As ever, Hilda." Was there greater meaning in those words?

No, they inhabited different worlds and the infatuation had been silliness on his part. Something they both enjoyed to break the monotony of their lives. But he needed more, much more, and he knew it. He has known this for some time and that is why he joined a dance club and went every Friday night. There he met newly divorced women, all eager to dance. And always there were three women to every man and so he was always danced off his feet. Never had a moment to sit down. He took an array of women into his arms, women of all sizes, women who all smelled of different perfumes, women who dressed for the night wearing everything from evening gowns to simple little slips of a dress. Strappy shoes and high heels. Scarves and dangling earrings and necklaces. And on all of them, a bare fourth finger, some with a lighter circle where the ring was recently removed. There were a few he preferred. A few he met outside of the dance club for a coffee or a drink. A few he even bedded, making the dance club a hornet's nest of gossip and jealousy. And those women seemed to like him, too, although he never showed them his drawers of glass eyes. That could have been a deal breaker for romance. No, he just pretended that he was an optometrist and that was good enough for them. They had no complaints; he was a professional, after all. A good catch! But they weren't Hilda. None knew him in his youth. No one else could look into his eyes and see him now, where he stood, but also as he once was. Hilda was the only one left who knew the boy he had been. And, because of that, there was a shorthand, an understanding and a shared loss that no one else could ever understand. But why should that be important? Why shouldn't a look to the future be the only thing that really mattered? How you choose and what you choose on this day and how you write your ending was the key to all happiness, right? That was what all the books said about relationships and soulmates. A look to the future should be the only direction, not the grasp the past has on your present. And on your heart.

Yes, it was now time to move on, he understood that in his mind. He looked at his image, the image of a middle-aged man and not a youth. He was no longer what Hilda remembered; time had passed. He decided that he would see her this one last time. He would tell her how he had always loved her. And then, he would tell her goodbye. No more letters. No more visits. He just couldn't do it anymore.

Once she returned back to the life she'd created in her new world, then he would go, sheepishly, back to the dance club. He would look for Gisela with her dark brown eyes, her short but shapely strong legs, her hearty laugh, and her earthy sexuality. And if she had moved on then there was always Antje with her blond hair, her light-blue eyes, and her small breasts. He could ask either of those women out again, maybe buy a nice meal and drink some wine! Why not? Yes, it was time to put the past behind him in order to lose himself in the possibility of a future.

But only after Hilda leaves, he thought. *Only after this visit is done.*

"The greatest gift is not vision, did you know that, Jack?"

"What do you think it is?" Jack asked the ocularist as he polished the iris of a newly finished eye.

"I think it is sight. You can have vision but not really see anything at all. You have no vision in one eye but you have better sight than most with two eyes."

"I thought vision and sight were the same thing."

"Entirely different."

Jack wandered over to the cabinet with the drawers filled with eyes.

"Why do you make so many extras?"

"Ah, good question. There was a time when Germany supplied all the glass eyes of the world, but, of course, people could not come all the way here all the time to be fitted. Now the best are custom-made eyes. They are always preferable. But we also exported eyes of many shapes, sizes, and colours so that in America and England, even in Canada, eye doctors could simply look for a close match and fit. Not optimal, perhaps, but I think it is still better than the acrylic eyes because so many people have allergic reactions to the plastic. You did. That was your problem."

"But if they don't do that anymore why do you still make the extra eyes? I mean, if all eyes are custom-fitted now, why do you have so many extra eyes?"

Siegfried knew Hilda was listening in. She always did and then pretended to be surprised if he repeated himself, acting as though she had heard it for the first time.

"Why do I still make the extras? I guess it is because I have a hard time letting go of the past."

Siegfried reached over and pulled a chocolate out of thin air, from behind Jack's ear. Jack was wise enough, old enough, to know that it wasn't magic, after all. That it was sleight of hand, and yet it brought back the memory of that first visit, of how he had once been delighted, and in the memory, there was still magic. He laughed and grabbed at the chocolate but the ocularist threw it into the air and it disappeared.

"Open your hand, Jack!"

And there it was, in the palm of his hand. Maybe it was magic, after all.

"You know you always act like you are so wise and all-seeing, but you really are short-sighted when it comes to what is right in front of your face."

Siegfried stared at the boy. He could see the cleverness of early manhood creeping into the way he held his mouth when he spoke. But there was also the impishness of boyhood in his eyes. There was some peach fuzz signalling a proper beard yet to come. But between the struggle of boyhood into adulthood, there was a look that said, *I know something you don't know.*

"You know my mom is listening in at the door."

"Yes, I know. She always does that."

"And so I can't tell you."

"You shouldn't tell secrets, anyhow, my friend, or how will you be trusted?"

"Oh, but you must trust me. I have an honest eye!"

Jack leaned in, motioned for Siegfried to lean in closer, and then he whispered in his ear so that Hilda could not hear the information being conveyed. It didn't matter, though, because Hilda knew what secret her son would delight in telling him. The very thing she had told him not to say. But Jack was at an age when he could no longer be told what, and what not, to do or say. Hilda was losing the last bit of control she had over her youngest child. He was at the age of rebellion. The age of knowing his own mind and rejecting the input, and, sometimes, the feelings, of others. That was how it always was and would always be. The breaking away, the tearing apart, the differentiating. A painful process. A process that would only allow for healing once the separation was complete.

"I see," Siegfried said. "But that is not why you are here. You are here to be fitted for your grown-up eye. I understand you are now Jack, no longer little Johnny, so now you must have an eye that reflects this."

Siegfried set to measuring his pupil, writing down the smallest fractions of measurement. An occasional clearing of the throat, as though he had found an interesting change, something of note.

"Your eye has not really changed so much and it probably reached its full size two years ago. But when I look into your eye there seems to be something different."

"I think my old eye is still good. I like it. If I could, I would like to have an eye that looks completely different than the real eye. You know, like David Bowie?"

"David Bowie does not have a prosthetic eye, though."

Jack didn't care. He wanted eyes that were two different colours, like a husky dog, or a lone wolf. David Bowie had that and he was ultracool. He could spike his hair, wear long duster coats, and walk along, without apology, with two mismatched eyes. The difference would appear to be a choice instead of a random accident. His glass eye could be a trademark instead of an apology.

"People will look at me and think that I chose the different eye on purpose. Don't you get it?"

"But that would be a lie."

"So is the glass eye a lie! A bigger lie, in fact, because you try so hard to make it look like a real eye. But it doesn't function, does it? It isn't like a fake leg you can walk on, or a fake arm that has a claw on the end for grasping things. It isn't even like a pacemaker. It sits in the eye socket just for show. It's for the benefit of other people, the ones looking at me. It makes them feel comfortable. But it isn't what I want! If it's about honesty, then you should just stitch up the socket and wear a patch. That would be way more honest."

The ocularist stepped back. He had never thought of his profession as dishonest. As trickery. Perhaps the boy was right. It took his breath away. The better made the eye, the more likely it was to deceive the viewer into believing that it functioned. Trick those who gazed into the subject's eyes into believing that the glass eye was organically set into the eye socket as honestly as the seeing eye was.

"Then why don't you do that? Just get an eye patch? Why bother coming all the way here?" Siegfried tried to sound nonchalant, but both Jack and Hilda could hear the hurt in his voice.

"My mother insists on the trip. Says you are the best and that we need to come for upkeep."

"So you do not want to be here?"

"I didn't say that. I said that since what you do is just for the sake of appearances, then why not make me an eye that I want? I'm the one wearing it!"

Siegfried removed the glass eye from Jack's socket, leaving a fleshy whitish interior, a placeholder over which the glass prosthesis usually sat. The muscles of Jack's eye socket had moved about it over the years, accepting it as though it were part of his body and, because of that, Jack was experiencing some movement now in his enucleated eye. The fake eye was beginning to follow his real eye. Siegfried examined the socket closely. It was clean, no signs of inflammation or infection. Hilda must have been heeding his instructions well. A cleaning once a week, but if there were any signs of eye gunk, then a morning rinse until the condition passed. Colds, flu, and fevers meant more frequent cleanings, but because the glass had good wetting, the tear fluid could build a regular film onto the glass surface and the glass eye would practically self-clean. Siegfried wondered how often the North American acrylic eyes had to be cleaned. How strange to wear an eye that could not be wetted because fluid could not flow evenly and naturally on a synthetic surface. So unhygienic. So unnatural. And then the scratches on the surface of the plastic eyes. Now that had to be irritating! Those eyes had to be sanded and polished yearly, just to make them look acceptable. Siegfried was sure that those plastic-eye makers (he refused to call them ocularists) would be only too happy to make fake eyes as fashion accessories. Cat's eyes. Snake's eyes. Eyes that look like a deck of cards!

"When you came to me, you wanted an eye that would be a companion to the eye you had. You wanted more comfort. You wanted to not be teased. And you wanted an eye that reflected your soul."

"No, I didn't. I wanted an eye that could see! But that's never going to happen, is it? So now I want something cool."

Jack reached into the drawer and pulled out a handful of stock eyes. Eyes that would never go anywhere. Wasted eyes sitting, unseeing, in a drawer, for what?

"You don't even have to make a new one. Why don't I just sort through some of these and see if I find one I like?"

"*Prêt a porter* eyes, you mean?"

"Sure, I guess."

"I will make you a deal. You can see if you like any of these eyes, but I will also make you a new one to match what your seeing eye has become. I need to make an eye that is harder, less innocent and slightly disrespectful. How do you say it? An impertinent eye, yes? But keep your old eye, as well. It still fits you, and perhaps in time, you will return to your true essence. Go ahead, look through the eyes. But not the ones in the middle drawer, okay? Now I will go and have a coffee with your mother."

"You think I lost some of my innocence? Well, it's called growing up," Jack responded.

"Then I hope I never do that."

Jack laughed. How he had liked all the talk about destiny and purpose when he was younger, but now everything was different. He still wanted to believe that there was a divine reason for his fall. He still wanted to believe that there was a reason for everything and that, by some magical hand, a greater purpose would reveal itself to him. But now he also understood that everyone was just stumbling through life. A father, whom he was just starting to know, had moved out after being with his mother for over twenty years. His sisters were both away at college and there he was, stuck in a country house in the middle of nowhere. Still, there were a few good things. Friends a bike ride away. More freedom. And, of course, Cyclops, his camera. His real other eye. An eye that allowed him to see things in a slightly different way than how he saw things with only his seeing eye. His mom had bought him that camera. Saved up and bought it for his birthday. Made the extra money selling eggs and rabbits.

Jack sifted through a handful of eyes. His eye was a hazel grey, so an eye with a bit more green would be nice. His father and his sisters had green eyes and so he would have one eye that matched his mother and one that matched the rest of his family. How ironic that his seeing eye was more like his mother's eye. How ironic and how perfect at the same time.

Jack regretted how he had spoken to Siegfried. He imagined that he and his mother were now in a small café with the smell of fresh coffee rising from fine German porcelain mugs, with just a splash of thick cream stirred in, until the dark liquid was lightened to a mocha colour. And then there would be a slice of cake — *Kuchen* — with berries or apples or poppy seeds. And fresh whipped cream to top it all off. But now he had to just sit and wait for them to return with filled bellies and knowing smiles while he sorted through drawers of eyes, looking for a few possibilities. How much more fun it would have been if Siegfried had agreed with him and the three of them could have shopped for the fun eye together!

When Jack opened the middle drawer he saw organized trays of eyes, labelled by the year. Eye after eye the same colour, the same shape. Even the flecks and details seemed to be echoed, eye after eye. There was something familiar about these eyes. He knew them, knew the glint, the darkness of the pupil, the other thing that one could not put into words. Yes. It was a drawer of glass eyes made to look just like the ocularist's eyes. Jack looked through them, one after the next, seeing them in chronological order, seeing how each year had engraved its experience on Siegfried's psyche. One eye had an extra vein of tension or regret, etching ever so lightly over the sclera. Another saw his aging as the white was shot through with a tinge, ever so imperceptible, of yellow. Every eye was a history, a story, of what had happened to the man. And yet there was no language or meaning to it. It spoke to Jack the same way that listening to his mother's opera did. Of course, his mother understood every lyric of every opera she listened to, but when she would go to explain the context and the story to Jack, he would always protest because he didn't want to know the literal meaning. He just wanted to feel whatever it was the music was alluding to. Context meant nothing to him. He wanted to understand the world in snapshot emotions. And here they were in every eye the ocularist had created for himself. Like photographs left lying around, waiting for interpretation. But why? Why had he left a record of his life, and in a drawer of glass eyes?

Jack started to close the drawer but then, after looking over his shoulder to the closed door, he reached in and stole one of the eyes. An eye that was, perhaps, six or seven years old. An eye that looked to have new hope in it. An eye that he must have made shortly after the first time they had visited. Yes, he would rob Siegfried of the memory of their first meeting. He would take it away.

It was understandable. Yesterday when Jack mentioned that he might want to be an ocularist, Siegfried had told him that he couldn't. That it was necessary for an ocularist to have very good eyesight, that it was impossible for someone monocular to do such detailed and exact work because of the depth perception.

"But it is an asset when I take photos!" Jack had protested.

"When you use a camera you are using two eyes, your lens and the camera lens. When you shoot a gun, you look through a sight. With all of these things, you have an advantage. You do so because the apparatus provides the second eye. Oculary requires two functioning eyes. That is the sad irony of it. But I hear that your photos are very good."

Jack put the hopeful eye of the ocularist into his pocket, then looked for a perfect green-gold eye to contrast his hazel-grey one.

*   *   *

Hilda and Siegfried sat at a small round table. The place was crowded and the heat of all the bodies caused the windows to steam up. Hilda felt claustrophobic in the tight space, aware of how close she had to sit beside Siegfried just to hear his words above the general din.

"He is in a rebellious stage. I think, perhaps, we let them be children too long and then it is harder to break apart and so they have to be rebels." Siegfried sounded unaffected by the exchange with Jack, but his decision to not eat cake spoke differently.

Hilda crossed, then uncrossed, her legs. They were long, shapely, with full calves, and so when she crossed one over the other, the curve from the knee to the ankle was most becoming. A leg man would say that she had gams like Betty Grable.

"What do you want? Another war so that they grow up as quickly as we had to?"

Hilda pretended to concentrate on the dessert menu. Cakes of all sorts, mostly tortes. This cake-eating every afternoon would surely show on her body. A moment on the lips, a lifetime on the hips. Still, it was worth it. Those cake bottoms, nowhere near as sweet as North American cakes with their heaps and heaps of white sugar and baking powder, were divine! This was a taste of her youth. The cakes, themselves, were somewhere between a crust of bread and a traditional cake. Then the fruit! Everything from plums to berries. Real cream, not from a can. Hilda thought of how Siegfried would panic if he ever saw, or ever had to use, a spray can of whipping cream. She imagined him struggling with the nozzle, trying to spray the cream out without it going all over the place, as it had with her the first time she tried canned whipping cream. How she had shrieked and her husband, John, had laughed at her and then, taking the can from her, he had sprayed her until it was an out-and-out whipped-cream fight, which led to raucous, crazy sex. How long ago was that? A lifetime.

Siegfried noted her change of expression, saw her eyes focus away from him, on some distant thought or memory. He had to do it now. Find the strength to bring up the subject of the whispered secret.

"What do you think your son whispered in my ear? I know you were listening at the door, so do not pretend you were not," he teased.

"He probably told you that my marriage is *kaput*. That I am getting a divorce."

Siegfried was taken aback by her blunt admission. There was no coy asking him for a hint, no skirting around the issue. There it was, on the table in front of them, sitting uncomfortably beside the freshly served torte.

"And are you all right with that?"

"Of course not. I have put almost twenty years into it. But it is what it is. I can be upset or I can just accept things and move on. I am too old to waste my time obsessing over it."

This was her brave front. Her way of saying, *Do not worry about me. I am capable.* Still, it ate at her that she had stood by him, even as things got complicated. And what was it all for? Twenty years, her best years, gone and never to be returned. She felt robbed by it all.

"The girls are gone to college and have their own lives. Jack seems to hate me half of the time. I thought that, at least, I had my marriage, but he threw it all away for a poke at a cheap tart in a bowling alley. Bowling, really? Couldn't he do better than that?"

"Do you want him back?"

"No, I could never trust him again. Even if he professed his love to me, even if he were to become passionate again, I would never feel that I was enough for him. You know, it isn't about the sex. I mean, fine, get it out of your system, have an affair and be done with it. But when you delay that satisfaction it becomes much more. It is all about how someone can possess your mind even if you are with someone else. He ceased to be present long before he actually left."

Siegfried sat quietly. How many times had he reread her letters, smelled the envelope, hoping to breathe her in? How many times had he waltzed or foxtrotted with another woman in his arms and his mind had drifted to her? He would imagine her standing across the room, watching him and perhaps feeling jealous. How many times had he hoped and wished that all was not as promised as it seemed in her promised land?

"Why did you not tell me in your letters?"

"Oh, because I wanted to bring you joy in the letters. To tell you about the nice little things. Why would I want to write upsetting things? Why give it that much power?"

"Because we are friends, old friends. And friends share with each other."

"When your father's a war criminal and executed, you learn not to share so much." Hilda could feel the familiar gripping in her chest.

"But I am the one who knows all of that. I know your darkest secrets and love you just the same."

Silence. The word *love* had escaped his lips and it hung over them, in the overly busy and cramped café, like a zeppelin. No matter where Siegfried looked the zeppelin loomed over their heads. He had said the word before, but that was different somehow. She was a married woman then.

The coffees came and he reached for the sugar, his hand brushing past hers. He awkwardly scooped two teaspoonfuls and watched the granules fall from his spoon into the hot liquid where they would melt, each granule no longer being an individual but a part of the whole thing. He stirred and watched his coffee with such intent that Hilda thought that there may be something wrong with it.

"Everything okay?" she asked him.

"It is. It is okay."

Hilda cut through her torte with her fork, careful that an equal amount of pastry, fruit, custard, and whipped cream balanced on the tines. Every mouthful could be perfect. Why was she concentrating on something so arbitrary as a mouthful of cake? It was easier, perhaps, facing a cake than facing her tenuous future. There was something to committing to the present and living in the moment, as those irritating, meditating Buddhists would say.

"You see, I have to come to terms that I am just a woman. I am average. Not a modern woman. Not a sexpot and not a career woman. He has left me for a more modern woman. A woman with a career. Unlike me, she has dreams and ambitions, apparently."

"Oh? What does she do?"

"She's a teacher."

"Well, you know what they say: those who cannot do, teach."

Hilda laughed and covered her mouth with her hand as she had just taken a bite and did not want to spray him with crumbs and cream. Siegfried reached across with his white linen napkin and wiped a bit of cream from the corner of her mouth.

"There, now you are perfect again."

"The *Kuchen* is very good. Want to try it?"

Hilda set out to get the right combination of fruit, cream, and cake once again. She lifted it in an offering, gesturing that Siegfried have the bite. He opened his mouth and she slid her fork between his lips.

"I think my friend likes you," Hannah spoke above the sound of the music and general noise of the bar.

Jack looked across the room to where Sabine, a tall girl three years older than Jack, swayed to the music playing — blasting — from an overhead speaker. Her chestnut hair was parted in the middle and fell, like a curtain, straight to her shoulders, and every once in a while she threw her tresses back so her hair fanned out straight from her head.

"She's okay, I guess."

Hannah leaned in, pretending to not quite hear him. Jack breathed in lavender along with the pub's smell of beer and knackwurst.

"You smell nice."

"Lavender. Very relaxing. It gets rid of stress."

"You have a lot of stress?"

Hannah shook her head. "No, not really. I know lots of ways to relieve stress."

Jack shot a glance over at Sabine. A new song, the same moves. The sway, the hair being thrown, a little wiggle of the hips. Jack could see that he wasn't the only one watching her, but he was the only one she looked at when she opened her eyes from her reverie of the music, singing along to the familiar lyrics of "You Sexy Thing."

She was a sexy thing. And very intimidating. She knew every nuance, every move, that could seduce an entire room. She seemed to be a regular; everyone knew her name and kissed her cheeks in greeting. And she kissed everyone back in return. She owned the place, owned the room, owned herself in a way Jack had never seen in young women back home. How comfortable she was with her sexuality. How obvious she was. There was no labelling of "slut" or "flirt" or "bait." Just a young woman enjoying the movement of her body, without apology or shame.

"Why did you ask Siegfried if I wanted to come out with you?"

"I didn't. He asked us to take you out and show you around. Said that it must be boring for you being around old people like him and your mom."

Ah. So Siegfried had planned it all, wanted him out of the way. Wanted an evening alone with his mother. Jack took a big gulp of his beer. And then another. He wouldn't be allowed to drink for another year yet in Canada, but here it seemed to be no problem. Everyone drank beer like it was water, yet they all seemed to function perfectly fine. Unlike Jack, who was starting to feel the floor move with every beat of the music.

"I'm not feeling great, I think I need some air."

"I will go with you," Hannah offered, slipping her soft hand into his.

"Your English is so good."

"It should be, I've been studying it since I was eight. Then when I was eleven I had the choice between French and Latin."

"Which did you choose?"

"French, of course. Latin is a dead language."

Jack imagined how Latin might have died. Daggers in the back like Caesar. A slow, painful death of some degenerative disease. A jealous rival lover, Italian perhaps, shot Latin in its vernacular! Of course, it would have to be the last option. Italian, that usurping language! Once all Romans spoke Latin, and now in Rome, they all speak Italian. God, he hated usurpers. Siegfried was probably kissing his mother right now!

Jack opened the door for Hannah. Her blond curls caught the night air and rustled just a bit. She passed by him, so closely that her body brushed him.

"Feeling better?"

"Yes. I'm not used to drinking so much beer. I don't know how you do it," Jack admitted.

"Well, our mothers drink beer when we breastfeed as babies, so we are all weaned on it!"

Jack would have laughed if he could. But her mouth was suddenly on his. Not gently, but with purpose. She had pulled him closer by the arm so that his body fell toward hers. Then, there it was — lips, mouth, tongue pressing, exploring, demanding. He felt her hand move up his trouser leg to find his crotch, where his hard-on affirmed his attraction.

"You want to go back to our apartment?"

"You have your own apartment?"

"Of course. Sabine and I are here studying, so we got·a flat together." Hannah started laughing as she wrapped her arms around him in an embrace, pushing her body into his. My God, she was like a cat in heat.

"But, I am only here for another day. This is so fast."

"If you are only here one more day then it has to be fast."

"What about Sabine?"

"She's a big girl, she knows how to get home. Either she will bring someone home or she may join us."

Jack was as panicked as he was aroused. What could be the worst-case scenario? He makes a fool of himself, he doesn't know what to do, he cums too quickly. But if any of those things happened, he was leaving in a day, anyhow, and would never have to see them again. What happens in Hamburg, stays in Hamburg.

"I love your eyes," she said. "Like David Bowie."

"Yes," he replied, wondering if she was aware that the left eye was a fake.

Hilda understood why he had arranged a night out for Jack. She knew Siegfried wanted their last night there to be spent together, talking about old times and remembering a time before Jack. A time when she existed as an individual, unhampered by progeny. Did painters or writers feel like that sometimes? That as much as they loved their finished work, whatever they produced defined who they were while the limitations of expectation closed in all around them.

Hilda didn't know why she thought about writers and painters so often. She never aspired to be either, although she did take first place in a national poetry competition once. So, then, what did define her? She had no vaulting ambitions, no great feats she wanted to accomplish before she died. There was no bucket list that she referred to, striking off experiences as they happened. Very North American, that. Her husband had a bucket list. She wondered if sleeping with Miss Argyle had been on it.

Miss Argyle. Her second. No, her replacement.

It wasn't the affair that bothered her. It was to be expected. Twenty years, a man has to get a little bored and want another flavour. Hadn't she been bored herself? Hadn't she imagined other lovers and had her own fantasies when she was left alone to pleasure herself? No, it was something else that ate at her. The times they could have gone out, and didn't. The times they could have had a laugh, and didn't. The times they could have sought out joy in each other, and didn't. It had nothing to do with him fucking Miss Argyle. It had to do with the fact that the things he had been denying her, bit by bit over the years, those inconsequential little things, were the things he so easily gave to another woman. She had no problem sharing some intimacy, but that it was withheld from her and generously shared with Jean Argyle was the thing that ate away at her ego.

Ego. She knew it was all about ego. It had to be because she asked all those questions: Was she prettier? Was she funnier? Was she sexier? Did she do things that Hilda would not do? Hilda had to laugh because with that always came the memory of her grandmother, her *omi*, on her mother's side. She had adored her when she was a child, not realizing how very embarrassing she was until her teens.

"See that ugly *Mädchen* there?"

"*Ja, Omi?*"

"Do you know why that handsome man is with her?"

"*Nein, Omi.*"

And then her *omi* would get all conspiratorial, motioning for Hilda to come closer so she could whisper, but never quietly enough, "Because she takes it up the *arschloch.*"

It was many years before Hilda even knew what that meant, but, one thing she did know, because her *omi* had told her, was that it wasn't something to be done. It was not clean. And besides, only ugly girls had to do that. Hilda knew that her reputation as a beauty depended upon never doing something as unclean as taking it up the *arschloch*.

John only attempted it once. His pecker exploring and poking around, missing the usual spot and pressing gently there. Hilda wondered if it was a mistake because he'd had too much to drink. She reached behind to redirect him, but he moved back, pressing a bit more. It was only when she verbally said no that he ceased to try and they never spoke of it again.

Miss Argyle was pretty. She was lovely and perky and full of life. Surely she didn't have to do that sort of thing. Or did she? Imagine that! A sex-crazed seductress at night in the bowling alley and then Miss Prim-first-grade-teacher by daylight!

Hilda went downstairs to the hotel bar to wait for Siegfried. A change of scenery might clear her head from her relentless thoughts. John was gone, no longer a part of her life. It was time to move on. And it made no difference now whether or not Jean pleased him with unclean sex when she would not. Too late to start that kind of thing now.

Perhaps all men liked nasty sex. Dirty talk, fantasies, and the pushing of boundaries. Perhaps the first blush of love, where each partner wants to consume the other, became boring the moment sex became a marital activity, or worse, a marital obligation. Not that she bored of the same old, same old. She liked the intimacy of having her husband inside her, moving in her and her enveloping him. She didn't really need the conversations he seemed to like about sharing her with other men or having a woman join them from time to time, just for a bit of fun. She saw sex as an enjoyable bodily function. No mysteries. No imagination needed. Simply a joining of bodies in a physical act. Two individuals coming together and then letting the winds of heaven dance between them once again. It was no different from enjoying a meal with someone. It was as natural as anything else the body needed and required. So what was she to do now without an outlet for what her body needed and required?

She knew that Siegfried was a fantasy, a projection of everything she missed without the reality of everything she had purposely left. German men were blunt, telling the truth when a little white lie, as they say in America, would be just as good. For instance, when a German man loves you and you ask him, "Do I look fat in this new dress?" a German would easily say, "Well, you have put on a few pounds over winter," while a North American would say, "You look beautiful in whatever you wear." God, could she possibly endure that level of honesty again?

But look at what guile had brought her! Her eyes were so shielded that she never saw the betrayal coming. Confident in the protection of tactfulness, how was she to see the bulldozer that would flatten her existence, levelling twenty years of what she had built until, like an old building replaced, one could only wonder what really was there before the destruction.

Oh yes, Miss Argyle was a goer, all right. Weren't all schoolteachers, with their "You'll do it again and again till you get it right" motto?

Hilda ordered a drink: Pernod and water. She carefully combined the two, watching the pastis effect, enjoying how the two seemingly clear liquids created a white, milky cloud when combined. *Yes, that is how it is. Two things seem to be one way, but then together, blended, they become something else, for better or worse, except that for better or for worse does not mean forever.*

"I rarely drink Pernod, that milky thing it does really creeps me out!"

Siegfried had slid in beside her on the next seat without her noticing, so preoccupied she was in distracting herself from her thoughts.

"Why?"

"Because, well, it is silly ..."

"No, tell me," Hilda insisted.

"Because it reminds me of the milkiness that comes with age or with blindness in the eye. It often means the eye must be removed. Now I know that is good for my business, but I do find it very sad."

Hilda pushed the glass away. A moment before it had been so enticing. Something that she would never have at home. The country demanded more substantial, more honest drinks like beer and cider and wine. Not something that filled the glass and changed its properties, creating a white, floating, creamy ... *Oh*, mein Gott, she thought, *how the drink looks like floating semen!*

"I think we should go. Maybe walk somewhere and have something to eat."

"Yes," he agreed.

It was a temperate night with a definite breezy warm breath of air all around them. How carefree this weather was. How undemanding! No coats. No scarves. No gloves. Perfect. Siegfried took her by the elbow and steered her in the right direction.

"Why do you like me? I am not special. I have no great accomplishments, no big dreams. I am not a carefree modern woman."

"Don't be silly," he responded.

"No, I am serious."

"Because you always have hope and you never give up. Because you embrace the big challenges and the little wonders. And because you make me laugh."

"How do you know I don't give up? I am giving up on my marriage."

"His choice, not yours."

"Yes, but I am not fighting for it."

"For that I am glad. I will tell you something. When you were a girl, I used to try to teach you to stand on your head. You could not do it. But you practised and practised and on my side of the wall I could hear your feet hitting the wall before you fell over, again and again. And that is when I knew you were special."

They stopped walking. People passed by them. Siegfried pulled her closer by the elbow until they were touching and he looked at her face for what seemed a very long time, as though he were etching every feature into his memory. And then he lifted her chin with one finger, moved his face nearer to hers, and kissed her mouth. It was simple, sweet, and predictable. Exactly what she needed.

"If you didn't try so hard, if you could just do that headstand, I would not have loved you all those years ago."

Hilda stepped away from him. Stepped off the sidewalk and onto a sliver of grass in front of an old walk-up five-storey apartment building. It seemed to her that every window was watching as she tucked in her knee-length skirt and squatted. First a tripod position, hands shoulder-width apart on the ground, between her squatting knees. Then she put her head between the hands, making sure her elbows were bent like a ledge. One knee on each elbow, and, there, she balanced a moment before contracting her stomach and squeezing her thighs and her buttocks while she straightened first her back, then took one then the other knee off the elbows. Straightening, straightening, balancing, concentrating, until she was, surrounded by people, standing on her head in the middle of Hamburg. Legs in the air, skirt blowing away. And there was clapping and whistling. Even Siegfried must have been clapping. But then she wavered a bit and knew it was time to come back down. She tried to catch her balance at the last moment, but she fell just the same. And Siegfried was there to catch her.

"Superb," he said, his arms around her in the grass. "How could anyone not love you?"

Jack awoke with a start, his surroundings completely unfamiliar. There were nice sheets over him, and a fluffy duvet with flowers on its cover. Pillows all around him, as though he were a baby and he needed to be barricaded in so he wouldn't fall off the bed. He shut his eyes and the room moved and swayed. His head could not keep pace with the imagined movement, so he stretched his leg out and put his foot on the floor to steady himself. Better. Slightly better.

Where were his pants? He threw off the duvet. Indeed, he was completely naked, except for his underwear. He looked around the room. No sign of his shirt. No jeans. But his shoes were neatly lined up at the edge of the bed.

He could hear a voice reinterpreting the actual words to Tony Orlando and Dawn's "Knock Three Times." There was a confidence in the voice, even when the word *feeling* was substituted by *ceiling*. But who was singing? Surely not Hannah, so it had to be Sabine. Had he spent the night with her and didn't remember any of it? He reached down and felt his crotch. A morning erection defied his hangover. *I'm alert, I'm perky, I'm rarin' to go!*

"I vant you, I vant you," another voice joined in. Surely that wasn't the backup lyrics. This was all wrong. The song, the two girls, the lack of clothes, and his early-morning erection. Damn. How embarrassing!

"Hello!" he called out.

Wafts of fresh coffee were teasing him awake. Ah, that would be so nice. Hot coffee, a little cream and sugar.

"Ah, the prince awakes!"

The two girls came into the room. Bright and beautiful, with freshly cleaned faces and daytime clothes on. No sign of the party girls from the night before. These were now transformed young women, committed students, with appropriate buttoned shirts, jeans, and softly draped sweaters, the arms tied at their necks.

"Umm … where are my pants?"

"No worries, we are washing them. And your shirt." Hannah smiled.

"Why?"

The girls started to laugh and Jack felt awkward, vulnerable in his white Stanfield underwear. How boring was that, white Y-fronts? Boring and oh-so Canadian. Why couldn't he have that carefree attitude he saw amongst these European students? Drink and party, maybe even fuck all night, then just carry on the next day without worry or commitment. Sit in corners, arguing politics or literature. Well, he would have to learn something about those subjects, wouldn't he? And everyone spoke English. Why didn't he speak another language? Well, French. He had some French, coming from Canada. But it wasn't real French. Not conversational. How many times did he have to repeat "*Henri est un enfant terrible*"? He spent year after year, looking at the Leduc family poster, with the children and the house and the little dog, Pitou, repeating the familiar phrases about the Leduc family as the French teacher pointed at the cartoon family and all he could think was, *What was the thing that Henri did that labelled him* un enfant terrible? Had Henri gone home with two horny German girls only to wake up unaware of the night's activities? Perhaps it was his older brother, Jacques, who was the real *enfant terrible*. Jack is a horrible child.

"Don't worry, nothing happened, you weren't up to it!"

"No, not up at all. Not like now!" Sabine looked down, toward his underwear.

"Oh, leave the poor boy alone! He is probably hungover," Hannah chided, handing Jack a much-needed coffee. Perfect. Just the ticket, as they say.

"You Canadians don't know how to drink beer?" teased Sabine.

"We do ..." Jack stammered, more a weak protest than a statement.

He had to believe them, that nothing had happened the night before and for that, he was relieved, not because he wouldn't have liked a story of his first conquest to take home with him, but because he would like to remember the details of his first time. No story. No memory. A promise of magic and then all vanished.

Poof! Too much to drink and what came of it? Not confidence, not jacked-up courage. Just disgrace. Two beautiful girls, stripping him, leading him to the bed and then what? Tucking him in? Or worse. God, they were washing his clothes. A flash of kneeling before the toilet, their strange toilets with the presentation ledges instead of the simple bowls like at home, and retching, over and over again, until the contents of his stomach were emptied. A pull of an overhead chain and *swoosh*, the presentation platter was efficiently cleared.

"We cannot stay and play with you — we have a lecture to attend."

"That's okay. Have to get along … my mom is probably worried."

Oh, God, did he actually say that? His mom? Really? Jack was feeling more embarrassed by the minute.

"Perhaps you should call her. Let her know you are okay. Sabine, go get his clothes, they should be dry by now."

What a debacle! He could never imagine having an opportunity like that again. If there was fate at work, or divine intervention, then he could only hope that at least the gods were entertained. Not the Greek gods of thought, myth, and philosophy but the dark gods of this place. Norse gods. Loki, Tiwaz, Frigg. Yeah, Frigg, because his luck was a friggin' joke. Always had been. Gareth would never have gotten so drunk. Gareth was well-balanced, after all.

"You can let yourself out when you go. The door will lock itself!" Hannah's voice was cheery, with no judgmental tones whatsoever.

Jack took his clothes from Sabine, still warm from the dryer. He slid his legs into the pants, pulled his shirt over his head.

"Thanks so much for this, and I am so sorry about last night."

But they were both gone, and Jack was leaving later that day.

SIX

GARETH HAD HIS EAR to the wall. His mother was talking, as usual, recounting her day as they waited for the heaviness of sleep to overtake them. This time was theirs, the stolen moments at the end of the day belonged to just them. No responsibilities, no burdens, no clients or patients or even kids. Well, at least that is what they thought, but Gareth was present, though unseen, on the other side of the wall.

"Oh, Mark, no one told those girls the truth. They showed up wanting answers about their mother. I mean, it had been a few years. What was I to say?"

"What did you say?"

"Well, I took them aside and told them that it was very sad, but that their mother committed suicide. I mean, they are almost eighteen now, almost adults. I don't know why they were lied to. All those years!"

"You did the right thing."

"Oh, I don't know, Mark. It could cost me my job."

"Fine. You work too hard, anyhow. Besides, I am working now. Maybe it's time that someone supported you."

Gareth curled down into his blankets. Let the feathers of his pillow rise up to encase his head. He stared at the painting he had done. There she was, the woman who walked into the lake and never walked out again. And her daughters, beckoning to her. Had his mother not understood what he had painted? Had she not seen herself there as a wisp of wind, unable to help, unable to change the woman's fate? Why had they never discussed his painting?

But, more importantly, she had seen them, spoken to them, the albino twins. Gareth wondered what they looked like now. If their pink eyes still darted back and forth and if they still wore those heavy glasses. And how were they wearing their thick, white hair? Surely not in those tight braids they once sported.

Gareth had a girlfriend. She was good at science and French and swore that one day she would study medicine and then work in some third-world country, maybe for UNICEF, saving children. Hopefully in a French-speaking country in Africa somewhere. Sometimes Gareth thought that his girlfriend was just too good. It seemed to him that she talked about her lofty goals whenever he was going in for a kiss or angling to cop a feel. Her goodness was a turnoff. Why did he have to choose so well? She was the marrying kind, not the type for a first girlfriend. He should have chosen someone failing school, wanting no more than a clerical job at a bank or in an office. Now that kind of girl might be more game and just a little less intimidating.

When Gareth thought sexy thoughts before bed, he never imagined his girlfriend. He always imagined the albinos. Both of them. He willed them to him, imagining that they would both love him equally. That one day he would have a house and they would both live with him. A huge king-sized bed for all three, but also separate rooms for when they wanted privacy. But how could that ever be when it was his mother who saw theirs walk into the lake that day?

"What did they say, when you told them?"

"Well, Mark, that is the saddest thing, really. They talked about a kitten their grandfather had drowned. The one girl said that they had taken in a cat and it turned out to be pregnant and gave birth to three kittens. Their grandfather told them to pick a kitten each. The one girl picked an all-white kitten because it was like her, but the other girl, the one who seemed a bit more sensitive, chose the ugly kitten because she felt sorry for it. She said she thought it was the sort of kitten that nobody would want. And indeed she had wanted the other kitten, but knew it was cute enough that someone would want it. So she took pity on the homely one. Then the grandfather said, 'Are you sure?' 'Yes,' she said. And so he picked up the other kitten, the one she had really wanted, and he drowned it in the bathtub. Held it down until it was dead. Then the other girl said that they never wanted to take a bath again and the first one said, 'I guess we can never swim in the lake again.'"

Gareth could hear his mother sobbing now, really crying, and his father was soothing her, telling her it was her time to do something for herself, telling her to take some time, to stay home and just relax.

Gareth had to see the girls. He had to find them so he could paint them. Not the young girls of his memory, but the young women that they had become. He no longer felt desire for them, but something else. He felt that they were bound somehow and that only by finding them could any of them be truly free. He didn't know why, but somehow he knew that they held the key that would free him from the guilt of telling his friend to climb higher all those years ago.

The twins took the bus from downtown Oshawa to the Pickering station, where they boarded the GO train to Toronto Union Station. From there they'd take the subway north to Dundas station and then try to find Massey Hall. They had it all written down in large, clear letters.

They had made it through the first round. They had sent in a cassette tape, Esther having played the piano behind them as they sang their strange and haunting music. Part operatic, part punk. Nothing raw, though. Music that showed their vocal range, music that showed their ability to harmonize. But beyond that their music was a poetry of loss that sprang in half-spoken and half-sung lyrics, but then, just as you thought it would be predictable and go into a familiar chorus, the language would change to their secret language, a nonsensical "Jabberwocky"-style language filled with words that seemed familiar but were not. Here is where they sang with their greatest emotion, as if they were saying that their experience of life was too full, too rich, and far too painful to put into words.

They had gone through the first round and were now in the finals. They had their white dresses. They wore their hair loose, in waves like white rapids down their backs. They knew that they just had to keep it together, that they were unlike anything anyone had ever seen.

Clara rubbed her eyes when they entered the hall. She had never seen a real theatre. A proper theatre. Only the Little Theatre in Oshawa and the school auditorium. The heavy wood, the red velvet seats on the chairs, the steep incline of the seats … it was all too much, not to mention the lights of the dressing rooms where round bulbs shone all the way around each mirror. Imagine that!

They had no idea what a sound check was. No idea what a technical rehearsal would be like. All they knew was that it seemed that there were a thousand butterflies in their stomachs, swarming around, looking for a place to rest, finding none.

"Tonight," Clara said, "tonight we sing for our mother. Tonight we will sing so beautifully that she will hear us deep beneath the waves."

The girls had never discussed what could have driven their mother to the water's edge. They never questioned why she started a walk that she would not, could not, stop. It was just a fact for them. Somehow they knew that she was not long for this world and, at best, they hoped that somehow the lake she had stared at for so many hours every day had somehow embraced her in the end. Did they miss her? No, what they missed was the dream that one day they would have a mother. But they did not, could not, miss a mother they never really had.

Esther would be there, though. She was taking a later train with her husband. Said she wouldn't miss it for all the world. (As if anyone was offering her all the world!) And that was enough for Clara and Blanca. They knew they would be singing for a mother they never really had and for a woman they had wished had been their mother.

"Hey. I'm Ernie, the stage manager. Now, I will give you a heads-up before it is your turn. You need anything?"

"Some water would be nice," Clara requested.

"There's water for all the talent in the green room."

All Clara heard was the word *talent*. Wow, they were being called talent, how amazing was that? "The talent," the man said. But Blanca was confused, because as hard as she looked, none of the rooms was painted green and she wasn't quite sure where she should go.

"Excuse me, Ernie, where is the room that is green?"

Ernie laughed. Of course, the room wasn't green. It was actually a dove-grey room with big sofas, coffee tables, and snacks everywhere.

"Why did you say it was green?"

"It's what it's called. The room where the talent hangs out is called a green room, even though it's rarely painted green."

Blanca nodded knowingly, which really pissed Clara off. How dare she pretend to know such things when she was as just as naive!

But really Blanca was nodding because she was so damned pleased that he used the word *talent* again.

"Anyhow, I have your placement. You're the third act up. So don't get too comfortable."

People were doing vocal warm-ups in the corner. "Paul has a head like a ping-pong ball, Paul has a head like a ping-pong ball, just like a ping-pong ball … Many men, many men, many men-men-men." Then there was the blowing through loose lips so that they looked like aggravated horses. Head rolls, body shakes, rolling up and down through the spine, and breathing exercises including soft-palate plosives, in through the nose and out through the mouth, and panting. How very intimidating, all those warm-ups. The girls felt so very unprepared.

The speaker in the green room was turned up just loud enough that they could hear what was going on in the auditorium, but not so loud that it interfered with whatever preparation the acts needed. Band members and soloists lounged about, some with carefree confidence and others with nail-biting anxiety. There were makeup artists waiting to do touch-ups or to completely cover the artists with a fresh coat.

"Would you like a bit of mascara, perhaps, some eyeliner?"

"No. Thank you." Blanca was adamant.

The makeup artist moved off, shrugging. "Suit yourself, your eyes will be lost under the bright lights."

The host could be heard, announcing the lineup, introducing the judges, and revving up the audience, demanding applause from them.

"There will be solo acts and singing groups. Bands will not have the chance to set up their own equipment and will have to use our amplifiers, drums, and equipment. This not only makes the competition more fair, it also saves time between acts!"

Light laughter.

"Let's get started with our first competitors. They call themselves RPM!"

Clara and Blanca listened to their competition. A group of four, two men and two women. They sounded like an ABBA rip-off. ABBA had just hit the charts and had taken the world by storm with its inane rhymes and sentimental music. Very poppy, and so were these four. Hummable music, something everyone likes, but where was the edge? Where were the boundaries being pushed? Where was the innovation? Clara figured it was a love song of sorts. A why-can't-you-love-me-as-I-love-you type of song. She looked at the other acts in the dove-grey green room. Nonplussed. No, these were no competition.

There were obvious punks in the room. Indie sorts who had been garage-band hopefuls. Then there were the rockers, the Bowie types and the Fleetwood Mac–influenced bands, the hard rock types who were obviously influenced by YES and Genesis, and even Black Sabbath wannabes. There were the folk singers filled with earthy sincerity, and a couple of boy bands, relying on cuteness and bubble-gum charm. The room was a representation of every sound that was on the late-1970s airwaves. Clara wondered why they were even there. What niche could they possibly fill?

A soloist took the stage. A young man with spiked hair, piercings, and leather pants. The girls couldn't see him strutting across the stage like Mick Jagger. They only heard the sour notes from time to time and wondered why it was that the crowd seemed to love him so much? But as his song progressed all they could hear was the beating of their hearts in their ears, knowing that they would be next.

"Clara and Blanca, you are next up so come wait in the wings. What are you called again?"

"Bleach. We are Bleach."

"Bleach? Okay, if you say so."

The lights blinded their pale eyes. Blanca squinted and tried to focus as Clara blinked repeatedly. They stood for what seemed a long time until someone yelled out from the audience, "Come on, already!"

Blanca held her tambour and, with a flat hand, hit the skin three times, very, very hard. Clara stepped toward the microphone and keened a note that was so high and so pure that the audience stilled and anyone could hear a pin drop as it sailed up over the seats to the rafters. Three more hits on the drum and Clara's fingers found the keys on the keyboard and played the chords, slowly, as they began to harmonize in sound alone, trilling scales and haunting everyone who sat on those red velvet seats.

Here is the sound of a kitten drowned. Here is the sound of a mother away, beneath the cold waves. The sound of fear and teasing and the sound of love withheld. Here is what it means to transcend the ordinary and to embrace difference. And now we speak, in what seems like tongues, but has no God within it. This is the anarchy of our song, this is the discord of life. And then again, a harmony and a bit of *Lakmé* thrown in. This is the sound of peace after a storm. The sound of life renewed after despair.

As much as their song was a reflection of life, it was also a giant fuck-you. Fuck you for laughing at us. Fuck you for leaving us out. Fuck you for knowing what is cool. Fuck you for our loneliness. Fuck all of you. We are the White Queens. We are Bleach.

Sweat dripped off Clara's nose as she played the last notes, her fingers spreading as far as she could stretch them. And while she did, Blanca stared out at the audience. There was no sweet smile on her face. No look of a desire for their approval. Here was the look of defiance. A dare to all. *Here I am*, it said. *I am an albino with pinkish eyes. I am whiter than snow, more fragile than crystal. My lifespan is shorter than any of yours, but I will burn brighter, as bright as a star, and then one day I will suddenly expire and go out. I know it and you know it ... so just use me up now.*

At first, there was nothing. No clapping. No sound at all. As if the audience had no idea they were finished. They sat in their seats, anticipating more. Not knowing what to think or feel. They had never heard anything like it. The opera, the virtuosity, the anarchy of outrage! This was what the punk movement aspired to, but rarely had the chops to achieve. It was the sound of a generation that was tired of war. The sound of sexual freedom. It was the sound of the young who were tired of expectation, labels, and gender definitions. It wasn't just music; it was a movement. These young women were to be feared and admired. They were as fierce as Vikings, as awe-inspiring as goddesses, and as beautiful as a blanket of fresh snow. But how would anyone ever market them?

Esther wasn't quite sure who clapped first. She stood, hands poised and ready to go, but, as no one joined her, she paused, hands ready, eight inches apart. She waited for someone else to show the respect the two deserved. Could they not hear the virtuosity? The vocal range? Did they not realize that something wholly original had emerged right before their eyes? This was the first act that wasn't derivative and yet, and yet, it borrowed on aspects of what was already established. These were trained voices. Esther knew it, because she had trained them.

Esther's world closed in all around her. The relatives gone, her sisters dead, but there was more to it than lost family. There was the guilt that she had lived all those extra years when her family hadn't survived the horror. Not even a generation later and it was all gone. Unbelievable. Her sisters with their lovely dark hair and lashes and their perfect singing voices, gone. While she still lived. Her own sweet father who could play the piano with such skill and confidence and a mother who often sang after dinner while guests sipped on sherry, both gone. While she still lived. An entire life now forgotten, except by her. What was it all for, the lessons, the love, the work, the practice, the rituals, if they were so easily lost?

Now there seemed to be an iota of sense to her unlikely survival. Now she saw that she had some purpose. In these girls was raw talent trapped in feral little bodies. They knew nothing beyond their rough surroundings and the discrimination they endured because of their lack of pigmentation. They only had each other and so how could they learn or become cultured? What chance did they have to rise up from the shit of their circumstance? Except for her. She knew that it was because she was barren, because she was in a land that wasn't her home, because no one cared about what was near to her heart that she had taken in these ruffians, these rude little heathen girls, and moulded them into what their essence dictated. In doing so she gave them their true worth. But she also gave them a piece of her life. A life that was filled with as much guilt as it was with art, culture, and meaning,

She stood with her hands eight inches apart until the thunder roared all around her. Stamping feet and bravos and applause. And then the word she had always longed to hear for herself, a word she had never experienced in her life of loss. A word she had only ever dreamed of. The word *encore*.

Esther didn't know that the first clap came from a young man, a boy in his late teens, who had taken his camera from his face, let it hang from a strap around his neck so that his hands would be free to applaud heartily. It was only when his camera was away from his eyes that one could see that they were two different colours. One a hazel colour with a grey outline and the other quite green with a few brownish-gold specks in it. He clapped hard, not caring if anyone else clapped or not. His heart was beating and his hands were keeping the tempo of the rhythm within him. Until the rhythm caught and spread like wildfire.

Jack was there, in front of the first seats, because he had been invited to go along with Tristan, who was filming the event for a university assignment. Unlike Jack, Tristan hadn't stopped his recording in order to clap. No, he turned his camera on the audience, caught its reaction, then he grabbed a quick shot of Jack, his glass eye outshining his natural one, caught in the reflection of the footlights.

Jack stopped clapping and took a quick series of shots. Clara and Blanca standing side by side, a study in white, almost overexposed by the harsh stage lights. There they stood like queens staring down at their subjects. And then the word *encore*, and there it was, the first hint of a smile. One that started with the slightly taller one and then transferred to the smaller twin. When the audience didn't sit down the smiles spread wider across what had been focused and stern faces until it was all laughter and the white queens were holding their stomachs as they convulsed in glee, as if to say, "We did it!" Flash. And they are smiling. Flash. And they are laughing. Flash. There is a high-five. And finally, flash, and the taller one holds up her hand to hush the crowd, to settle them again. What power. What grace. What sovereignty!

"We would love to do an encore, but we were only allowed four minutes and so we cannot."

"Right. We are good girls, we follow the rules." The smaller one, the piano player, smirked. Clara.

Then the biggest laugh of all and the audience was on its feet again, giving these beautiful creatures love. What was it? Magic? A spell cast over everyone like an encompassing fog of devotion? All Jack knew was that they pulled him to them with their siren song, until he was trapped by the illusion they had created.

There may be one, there may be more, but they are called the Lorelei and they can trap a mortal man with the sound of their song.

Jack didn't care. He wanted to be trapped. He wanted to believe in magic once again. He scribbled down a note, with his name and address, telling them to be in touch. He would use his talent behind the lens to bring them to him.

"The twenty-third pair of chromosomes are two special chromosomes, X and Y, that determine our sex. Females have a pair of X chromosomes, whereas males have one X and one Y chromosome. Chromosomes are made of DNA, and genes are special units of chromosomal DNA." The teacher, Miss Reynolds, held her chalk in her hand, pausing for emphasis, as though she had just relayed a great secret to the class, enlightening them. She was the antithesis of what Gareth thought of when he considered a science teacher. Yes, she was keen on a lot of boring stuff, but, if he were to ever take another science class in his life, he would want her to teach it. Not because she explained things better than Mr. Swatasky, whose heavy Polish accent made science seem grave indeed, but because she had an enthusiasm that spilled into how she spoke, her childish joy as she would toss the chalk in the air when she felt she said something clever, and, mostly, because she never wore a bra. Now, with the weather warming, she often showed up in an Indian cotton printed shirt, loose-fitting but falling in drapes over her curves, and a peasant skirt that fell almost to the floor. In every way, Miss Reynolds looked more like a peace-and-love hippie, passing joints around a campfire, than the keeper of the secrets of DNA.

"How does that affect recessive genes?" It was Jack who asked. *Of course*, thought Gareth, *Jack can feign interest in almost anything if it serves him somehow. The teacher's pet!*

"Good question!" And up the chalk went, landing flatly into the palm of her hand. "Never gets old!" she said. "Okay, so … a recessive gene is a gene that can be masked by a dominant gene. In order to have a trait that is expressed by a recessive gene, such as blue eyes, or better still, red hair, you must get the gene for blue eyes or red hair from both of your parents."

Jack raised his hand.

"Yes, Jack?"

"How is it that two blue-eyed parents can have a brown-eyed child, then?"

"Well, because the two must carry a brown-eyed gene as well as the hidden blue-eyed gene. It is more complicated with eyes. So let's, for argument's sake, look at red hair as our example. With red hair, both parents must carry the red gene, whereas with other hair colours only one parent needs the gene. So there are two available hair genes in each parent. The child has to grab the red gene from both parents, even if the parents are brunette or blond. So in a family of, say, three children, one might suddenly pop out with red hair even though there hasn't been a redhead for generations, because the parents each have a recessive red gene hiding in them. With eyes, there can be many differentials and there are some scientists who believe that blue eyes are not recessive. They think that it is all about the amount of melanin, or pigment, in the eye."

Gareth was listening, although it did seem as though he was not paying attention. It was a problem he'd had from the earliest grades. Teachers assumed that he wasn't listening because he always doodled in his books and rarely looked up at the teacher. When he did look at them, he was distracted by their gestures, their choice of clothes that day, their quirks, their looks. With Miss Reynolds, it was her looks. How could he hear what she was saying when her nipples could be seen through her cotton shirt? Better to just doodle in his notebook. Had they mentioned eyes and eye colour? In the margins he'd drawn eye upon eye of every sort. Fringed in thick lashes, crying, old and wrinkled. But those were just the exterior trappings. Gareth liked to draw the eyeball with expression and accuracy.

"Are you listening, Gareth?"

"Yes, to every word." He looked up and there she was, in front of him. She leaned over and looked at his notebook filled with drawings. The loose peasant neckline of her shirt fell forward and Gareth had an optic nerve–full of neckline and cleavage. He looked down at his book.

"Seems to me that you are doodling instead. Perhaps you would like to tell us where we left off."

"Miss, I concentrate better when I doodle. Anyhow, we were talking about genes and what it means to have two recessive genes in creating red hair or blue eyes. But I do have a question."

"Yes?"

"What about pink eyes?"

"You mean like pink eye, the condition?"

"No."

"You mean like what rabbits have?"

She actually liked Gareth. He did well on tests even though he never paid attention. It had occurred to her that he might be cheating, but she had watched him closely and could never figure out quite how. And even though her great passion was talking about genetics and biology, when she wasn't meditating or smoking pot with her friends, she had to admit that the boy seemed to have a great talent for drawing. Those eyes stared right off the page.

"I want you to leave your notebook with me over the weekend, Gareth, to see if you are doing the required work."

"Yes, ma'am."

"Don't call me ma'am. I am only twenty-seven. Not a ma'am yet."

"Are you going to tell me about pink eyes?"

"No such thing."

Gareth sat quietly. How could she say that? Of course, there are pink eyes. He had seen them. They had stayed with him throughout his life. Little pink eyes, darting back and forth as if vibrating within the heads of those girls.

Jack raised his hand, but their teacher ignored him and so, when she turned her back, he spoke up anyhow.

"I know quite a bit about eyes and eye colour and you are both right and wrong, Miss."

Miss Reynolds turned slowly. The cloth of her shirt moved over her slim waist and it seemed to Gareth that Jack's impertinence must have excited her because her nipples hardened and poked through the cotton.

"And you are an expert, how exactly?"

"I'm pretty tight with an ocularist, actually. In Germany," Jack informed, with a slight cockiness in his voice. "Anyhow, most pink eyes are very, very pale blue, but with so little pigmentation that what you are actually seeing are the blood vessels behind the eye.

In the retina. But if someone loses an eye and a replacement has to be made, like mine, then the ocularist has to take into account the pink shades that are very obvious in certain lights."

"And who are these people with pink eyes?" she asked.

"I'll show you."

Jack went into his backpack and pulled out a manila envelope. He carefully removed a stack of 8x10 photos. Photos taken at the competition. Photos of Bleach.

"See, in this light their eyes look very, very blue. Pale and piercing like a wolf's. But in this one, with a slight change in direct light, the one here looks to have pink eyes. And it isn't because of the camera, picking up red tones. Cyclops doesn't do the red-eye thing."

"Cyclops?" Miss Reynolds asked, fully aware that she had lost control of her lesson some time ago.

"My nickname for my camera because it only has one eye, like me."

Miss Reynolds had not noticed that Jack only had one eye as Jack always wore the matching eye to school. The David Bowie look he saved for special occasions. Miss Reynolds looked directly at Jack. She wasn't old enough or experienced enough to know that looking at someone with curiosity wasn't always the most subtle and acceptable reaction for an educator.

"Which one? No, don't tell me, let me guess. It's that one. Of course, that makes sense. I see now that it doesn't move as much. Quite extraordinary, though."

Gareth had stopped sketching. He stopped listening to the banter. All he cared about was the fact that his best friend had pictures of the albino twins. It had to be them. All these years later and there they were, in a series of photos, in the possession of his friend. What a betrayal that Jack hadn't told him!

Miss Reynolds looked at the photos. Jack was right, the eyes went from a blue to a violet to a pink depending on how much light was being let into their eyes.

"Well," she said, "they are albino. Everything about them is recessive. Both parents would have had to have carried the albino gene. But that doesn't mean that they would be sure of having an albino child, because they would also be carrying a non-albino gene, assuming that the parents were not albino themselves."

Now she was excited, drawing charts on the blackboard and explaining probabilities.

"So if both parents carried the gene it would seem the probability would be, assuming they had, say, four children, that one would be albino, two would be carriers, and one would not be affected at all. However, it is estimated that one in three hundred carry the gene and so if you do the math, the probability is one in twelve thousand children. And most often both parents look unaffected."

Gareth thought of the red-haired woman in his painting. Pale, yes, but unaffected. And so her daughters, the twins, must have a father, somewhere, who carried the albino gene, as well. How likely was that in a small town? Gareth thought of the whispers he had heard on the other side of his bedroom wall.

Jack placed the photos back into the envelope and carefully put it back into his backpack but, because Gareth was sitting on the side of his artificial eye, he did not notice the jealousy in his friend's eyes.

Clara stretched out on their grandfather's sofa. He was off on his tricycle, peddling his wares up and down the streets. Up to no good, the girls now understood. All those years of believing it was special vitamins he was selling. But no! Supply and demand had nothing to do with vitamins. Something to get you up wasn't vitamin B12. Something to put you down wasn't melatonin, after all. Dear old grandad was the town's geriatric drug dealer. Nothing could have made them cleaner, more straitlaced teenagers. Drug use would be very uncool if it was something their grandfather approved of ... and traded in.

"You know, we never really talk about Mom," Clara said, seemingly out of nowhere.

Blanca looked up from her homework. They were coming to the very last of the exams they would ever have to write in their entire lives. All those years of study and confinement almost over. So very close now they could almost taste the freedom.

"I mean, I felt bad. I felt it was unfair, but then, I guess, I felt like life wouldn't be that different without her. She wasn't really in our lives."

"That is so cold," Clara said. Sometimes she wondered why people thought of them as the same. Why people got them so mixed up because it was clear to her, and clearer every day, that they were very, very different. Oh, perhaps not to look at them, as they really were carbon copies. Blanca being that bit taller, but still, the faces, the body shape, the hair, the eyes — all identical. But it was inside that was different. Blanca was much more practical than Clara. She could move on and get over things. She could forget the past and plan ahead, getting her ducks in a row. She didn't question everything the way Clara did. Things were what they were, best to accept them and use them if possible. Blanca could even see their albinism as an asset. Something to be exploited for fame and profit.

"I just wonder how different we would be if we had known her better. If things weren't the way they were."

"Well, you cannot change the past. You just have to accept it. Hey, what doesn't kill us becomes art, right?"

Clara shrugged. Moving forward wasn't her most present thought. She wondered when her sister changed her focus. Didn't they always ride backward in the station wagon, seeing what had been instead of what was ahead of them?

"Ever wonder who our dad was?"

"I have my theories, but I am not going to tell you. You would just freak out and I have to study."

"You think you are so much smarter than me. Why don't you just tell me?" Clara pestered.

"Maybe it is someone who prays so much for forgiveness. Then again, maybe not."

"Oh, God. That's disgusting! Makes me feel unsafe around him."

"Naw. Our white skin is repulsive to him. He thinks that God punished him by giving us white skin and pink eyes. Our albinism is a blessing. It's a shield of protection."

Clara couldn't believe how Blanca was talking. It was all too much for her. She started to cry softly but, because Blanca wanted to finish the year with the same high marks she had achieved throughout, she chose to pretend that she did not notice.

He waited. The door had been unlocked and a few overhead neon lights were turned on just so that he would not be in complete darkness. They would come in and find him once his mother let them inside. That was his plan. Let the twins see him in his domain, where he ruled, not as a teenaged boy living with his mother on the outskirts of town. Here he could be king, in a room he designed and created himself, for the purpose of making magic.

He started out by developing his photographs at night until he quickly learned that developing photos could be time-consuming and, on many nights, he found himself still fiddling with the images until the morning sun started to stretch its long-reaching fingers across the lightening sky. Daybreak could be beautiful, but to Jack it was no more than an intruder, ruining a night of work and concentration. At least in the countryside he didn't have the inconvenience of streetlights to ruin his work, but still, that eager, unwelcome sun!

He needed a darkroom where he could work any time of day or night, without having to wait till natural darkness occurred. A place where there was no sense of time, like a Vegas casino where there were no clocks, no windows, and oxygen pumped inside to keep the gamblers gambling. Not that he had ever been to a Vegas casino. But his father had. He'd taken one of those all-inclusive trips with Jean and, upon his return, made a date with Jack so that he could make a huge announcement. But Jack ignored the announcement, choosing, instead, to ask questions about the desert, the climate, the quality of the light in the Southwest. Even the gambling rooms, the cheesy shows with the high-kicking gals, the buffet, and the over-the-top descriptions of the neon lights were of more interest than the news the couple had for him. News that they were busting at the seams to deliver. They had done that other thing folks so often do in Vegas. And they had done it at the Elvis Chapel, no less! Married by an Elvis impersonator. Wham, bam, thank you, ma'am.

It wasn't that Jack would have attended a ceremony if they had actually had one in Canada. It wasn't that he wasn't a part of the ceremony, being told after the fact. Well, hey, they both claimed that it was a very spontaneous moment, another way to have the full Vegas experience, top to bottom! *Sure, it was top to bottom*, Jack thought to himself. *Top to bottom, then you rolled her over, you old, disgusting dog.* It was that Jack felt a betrayal that his mother was replaced by someone fun but insubstantial. Something shiny and new. It was like trading in a perfectly cared for, humming Mercedes for a shiny new Ford. And it would be just a matter of time before he, too, was replaced by a brand-new boy with two working eyes and a goo-goo-ga-ga non-judgmental love.

It was right after the announcement that Jack mentioned how he needed his own darkroom. His father offered to create one in their second bathroom in their newly built, cookie-cutter condo, but Jack impressed upon him that he needed access to it at any hour of the day and that his comings and goings would be disruptive for them, newlyweds and all. He also said that he would have to trouble him or his mom for a ride every time he needed to work and that photography was his only hope for his future, and building a great portfolio was the key. John pretended to be disappointed but Jack read the relief on both their faces. Perfect. He knew that guilt was the key to getting the needed funds from his father. He could get the required drywall and labour out of his dad. If he put the room in his mother's mudroom off the kitchen he would be able to access water and put in deep, heavy sinks. He would just have to section off where the washer and dryer were. Washers and dryers have a way of removing all magic from darkrooms as equally as marriages.

He would need to make the room light-tight, using blackout curtains or blackout blinds for the small window to keep that bit of light out. Blinds were probably better, but to be safe he told his father that he would need both. Even the slightest leaks could cause problems with light-sensitive photo paper. And so his father provided those first things, but there was so much more to building a functioning darkroom. A darkroom that would be his place, his sovereignty, his church.

Now, in his true domain, Jack sat on a chair with wheels and no back. A homemade moveable stool that he often used to move from one side of the darkroom to the other. One side was his dry side, with the electrical outlets, where he kept equipment, paper, and his enlarger, a second-hand Meopta Opemus 6 enlarger, a gift sent in a package from Germany. Jack was fully aware that his parents' divorce actually helped him achieve this darkroom. Both parents wanted to assure him of his worth, while their own worlds were changing and crumbling.

Jack pushed back, his foot pressing on a cabinet drawer until he zoomed over to the wet side of his darkroom. No equipment here, just the two large sinks and the chemicals. And these things were kept quite, quite separate from the dry things, as though a line were drawn down the centre of the room like the line that had been drawn between his parents. Things on one side could never, ever, cross the line to the other side. Never.

Jack heard voices outside his darkroom. His mother's deep, accented voice welcoming the girls and then their softer, gentler voices making niceties. How he wanted to run out straight away but he had already waited weeks, what was another five or ten minutes? *Oh, do be quiet, Mom, with your offerings of coffee and sweets. Just show them to the mudroom!*

He placed a sheet of photographic paper beside a tray filled with his magical chemical solution. All photographic processing uses a series of chemical baths. Processing, especially the development stages, requires very close control of temperature, agitation, and time. Jack was ready. He made sure that when they arrived, it would be little time before the image first emerged from nothingness to the first faint ghostly outline.

"Your guests are here!" his mother called out.

"Just show them in. I'm just mixing chemicals and I cannot leave it right now!"

He wasn't mixing chemicals, all the prep work was done. He was simply waiting, on his wheelie stool, holding a piece of photographic paper in a pair of tongs.

There are few times in a teenaged boy's life when things go as planned. Few times when a rehearsed event actually works out. But this wasn't just performance, it was science, and he had been meticulous. The right image waited to be transferred onto the paper. A picture of the two of them, just as they had started to laugh, that very second before the release of their mirth. A picture of contained joy, held in the heart for a few seconds before it was released into the world, and then diffused into the ephemeral. The moment, as with all performances, was gone and even forgotten by many. It had been offered as a gift, accepted and held for a moment, and then evaporated and lost. Only through his magic could the moment be reclaimed, made permanent and held beyond its short lifespan. This was his gift to them. This was his power.

"Hi," said the taller one as they stepped through the doorway. Clara or Blanca? He really would have to get them straight.

"Hello, hello, come on in. I was just about to make a copy of a picture of you!"

The girls smiled awkwardly and entered. Jack reached up and turned off the lights and suddenly the room was darker than either of them had ever imagined. Clara assumed that they must be glowing in the dark but, as she looked at her sister, she could barely make out where she stood.

"I am transferring the image to this paper now," Jack told them, "this is the most crucial part of all. If any light penetrates the film then all is lost."

"Why?" asked Blanca.

"Photo films and papers are made from salts of silver that darken when exposed to most light."

Clara closed her eyes. No darker than when they were open. She knew that he had invited them to his darkroom, but she had no idea just how dark it would be. It was a darkness she had never known. More than dark. It was an absence of sight. She reached out her hands till she felt the cool, metallic edge of a sink or something. How sensitive her fingers suddenly felt now that she could not see at all. And the sounds! There was a fan on, she could tell by the constant, even whir of the rotating blades. And there was a drip in one of the sinks. She hadn't noticed that before the lights went out. A sharp smell of chemicals. Not nice. And the sound of breath. Her sister's. His. Hers. Each slightly different. Hers was steady, once she touched the sink. His was uneven but that came with the sounds of his body movement, as he went about his photography stuff. But her sister's was jagged, uneven, and abrupt, as though she held her breath and then remembered that she had to breathe. Was she frightened in the dark? Claustrophobic? Excited? It was hard to tell without sight or light. It was the look of flushed cheeks or dilated pupils that could give such feelings away. Not breath alone.

Suddenly the room was alive in a red glow. And Jack was smiling.

"Perfect. Next step."

Clara noticed that Blanca seemed all rosy. Her face, her hair, everything was bathed in a pinkish glow. How beautiful she looked! Clara assumed, and hoped, that she looked as lovely as her artificially blushing sister. But then she also noticed that her sister was standing much closer to Jack than she was. So close that they almost touched. Did she know that she was so close or was the proximity just something that happened naturally when the room was darker than Hades?

"I thought you couldn't have light, so why did you turn on these red lights?" asked Clara.

"Photo papers are sensitive to blue and green light, mostly, not red. You can't see infrared or ultraviolet light even though some other animals can, like snakes and fish. It's the same idea with photographic materials: they vary in their sensitivity to different colours. Mine can be used with a red light."

"Okay, enough about snakes and fish, what's the next step?" Blanca asked, her voice a whisper like she was in church or at the library. Blanca had never been thrown out of the library. Not even once! *She is always in better control*, thought Clara. She could tell a joke and not even crack a smile. But Giggle-Guts Clara would always laugh out loud before she even reached the punchline. So it was only inevitable that she was always in trouble for her laughing and fooling around. *Why can't you be good like your sister?*

"Well, the exposure of the image onto the sensitized paper is first. We use the enlarger for that. Then comes the processing of the latent image using a chemical process. Then, at just the right moment, we stop the development by neutralizing or removing the developing chemicals. Then we fix the image by dissolving some undeveloped silver halide and finally we wash the paper to remove the processing chemicals, which protects the finished print from fading."

"Wouldn't it just be easier to send the film in to be developed?" asked Clara. "Seems like a lot of bother for the same results."

"Where's the magic in that?" asked Jack.

"Yeah, Clara, where's the magic in that? So, Jack, you said you did the transfer, but I don't see anything on the paper." Blanca seemed far more interested in the process.

"Oh, just you wait! The image is there, in the paper, but now comes the magic!"

He held the paper with tongs over the tray and then, slowly, let it drop into the liquid. Clara and Blanca came closer and watched as he made sure every inch was completely submersed.

A ghostly image, an outline, was seen first. Two bodies, perhaps, seemingly above where the camera was placed. The girls watched as more and more was filled in. Features going from vacant, to visible, to lively. Bodies, first almost transparent and ghostly, changing until they were full of life and presence. Even the background, the performance curtains, took their time, making an entrance fit for stars. Unfocused and unseemly at first, but slowly the details, the patterns, emerged before their wondrous eyes.

"It really is magic!"

"It's science, Blanca. It's a process," reminded Clara.

"It is a bit of both," Jack added, allowing both girls to be right, although he preferred to be thought of as an alchemist more than as a scientist. As an artist more than a technician. And so he couldn't help but like Blanca just a little more than Clara. And Clara knew it.

"I'm feeling a little crowded in here. When it's safe maybe I'll just step out, get some fresh air and help your mom with tea. Blanca can witness the rest of the magic."

"Oh, don't be like that!"

"Like what? I'm not being like anything. Just trying to be polite, Blanca."

"Okay, you can go out in a few minutes, but the paper is still sensitive."

"Yeah," said Blanca, "not only the paper!"

Was it no more than a joke? Hard to know because Blanca never cracked a smile when she was joking.

Gareth was covered in paint and dry chips of colour. It was everywhere. His clothes, his hair, and even his face bore the residual shades of his efforts. He had been aggressive with his work, throwing great gobs of paint onto the canvas, and then sanding the colours down to create a patina, a backdrop to the smoother figures he would place in the foreground. It was a huge piece, the largest he had ever done. A fuck-you to his teacher before he graduated. Who cared what the gatekeepers really thought? He would ruin her day, ruin the last days of her pathetic little life, by painting something that would haunt her into her retirement because it would remind her of her mediocrity. It would tell her, *You could never do this, you silly little woman, and that hurts you, doesn't it? Why? Because those who can't do, teach. That's why. Those who cannot do, teach, bitch!*

Gareth was afraid that he wouldn't get into OCA, the Ontario College of Art. He had his acceptance but it was contingent on his final mark. He'd had his interview, submitted his portfolio, and all of that went well. But when they looked at his third-term marks, there was concern. How could someone with his portfolio be getting an average mark? The school prided itself on accepting only the best, only the most promising up-and-coming artists. If Gareth wasn't at the top of his class, his acceptance was in jeopardy. Suddenly his art was about future opportunities, not about expression, opinion, or escape.

Gareth knew that art had been, amongst other things, an escape for him. He could draw other worlds, create beauty where there was none, justice where there was none, and understanding in the face of confusion. He had painted with love in his heart as a child. Had picked up his pencil, his brushes, his tools, with an expected ease and joy. But this painting was not something that sprang from joy or love. He was painting from a new place. He had a new muse. A muse who was demanding, prolific, and present. A muse named Hate.

Mrs. Beacon, that small-minded imbecile, had invited in his new muse. She was the source of his latest inspiration. How did she unmask this darkness hidden within him? This unknown hatred? By diminishing his miniatures.

Gareth had become obsessed with painting miniatures.

Such tiny precise work, every bit as detailed as a full-sized painting, but so difficult to do it without it becoming as dismissible as it was small. But that is exactly what Mrs. Beacon did when she saw them. Dismissed them. Each student had a wall for the culminating exhibition. White and bare. Some makeshift walls were added to the room, on wheels, so that everyone had their own space. Students hauled in their many canvases, 11 x 17 inches, 20 x 28 inches, 24 x 32 inches, 27 x 40 inches. All the usual sizes and dimensions. Nothing too big to transport. And certainly nothing too small to smuggle in.

"Where's your work?" Mrs. Beacon had asked Gareth.

He patted his knapsack confidently, knowing that the small pieces were, each and every one, a treasure. He had even made tiny frames to go around them, covering them carefully in gold leaf so that, when viewed, every painting seemed like the inside of a jewellery box. Each miniature was an eye. Some fringed in lashes. Some so close up that it became almost an abstract. They begged the viewer to come close, and then, unexpectedly, they peered right back at the viewer. It was a commentary on whether art sees the viewer or the viewer sees the art.

"That's it? These little things? Hardly proper canvases, now, are they?" Mrs. Beacon had scoffed.

Gareth put up his show. He watched as people stepped closer, curious about the miniature paintings. Parents and students, and even other teachers, approached him and talked about his installation but it didn't matter; his mark was barely above passing. Well, if those miniatures weren't to her taste because they were small, then she would have to deal with this work, almost the size of a movie screen with the same strange ratio of width to height. It would take a truck to get it there. A truck, and at least two people to carry it in.

Gareth didn't hear the knocking. The sander was going and he had earphones on.

"Gareth!"

Gareth continued to sand. So all Jack could do was to walk around him and stand in front of him until he looked up and jumped with a start.

"Oh my God, you scared me!" Gareth held his heart before removing his protective glasses.

"Aren't they for your stereo?" Jack gestured at the earphones cupping his friend's ears.

"Yup, but they are as good at keeping noise out as letting noise in."

"You mean music, don't you? They let music in."

"Yeah, I guess."

"Well, come out of the garage, I have someone for you to meet."

Gareth unplugged the sander, shook the paint dust from his clothes, and walked into the early June sunlight, blinding him after hours in the garage. So blinding that, at first, he didn't understand what he was looking at. Two figures. Unworldly, but that could be just the adjustment to the change in light.

Slowly he understood that there were two fairy images, large as life and twice as beautiful. Had he done it? Actually painted another world and, by some trick of light, walked into his own imagination? And Jack, who was he in this dream? A guide, perhaps? His own personal Virgil?

"This is Clara and this is Blanca. I got it right, didn't I?"

The girls laughed and nodded. A stereo gesture of harmonized sameness. God, it was them! The imagined muses, the image from his childhood. The elusive twins who skirted all around him, but never made themselves known to him since that first sighting in the eye doctor's office. They were exactly the same, but older, taller, without the thick glasses and braids. Their eyes no longer darted about like crazy marbles, separate from their thinking brains, independent. They were almost settled, with the slightest vibration, which only seemed to give them hyperreal life. As though their eyes, their violet eyes, had breath.

Clara raised her hand and waved in that awkward back-and-forth way of a child. A wave that is hesitant and says, *Do not make a fool of me by not waving back.* And Gareth mimicked the gesture, knowing full well that she, too, remembered that first meeting.

Elaine was happy to have both boys home. A few short months and the house would be quiet and lonely; Tristan back at York University studying film and Gareth at the Ontario College of Art, hopefully. Surely he would pull off a respectable enough mark in his art class. After all, Mrs. Beacon did say to her at the last parent-teacher meeting that Gareth was one of the most gifted artists she had ever taught. Those earlier marks were no more than a threat! Surely his final mark would reflect his talent. His acceptance depended on it.

She shone the cutlery on her shirt, removing any spots left over from the dishwasher. What a thrill that was when they bought it! Just fill it, turn it on, and *voilà!* No more fights about whose turn it was to wash or dry. Of course, there wouldn't be any fights at all soon. Just peace and quiet. Serenity. Silence. God, she would go out of her mind.

Timing. What a silly notion that was. If there really was such a thing as good timing then Mark would have gone straight to school before the boys were born, and not spent his time labouring in a factory. He would have been a professional early enough that, perhaps, she could have been the one who was home more, watching them grow in infinitesimal increments. She could have been the one going over the homework and greeting them at the door after their day was done. Something that she did do, once every three weeks, as her rotating schedule allowed. Only then, there was normalcy. Every day.

She was home, full-time now, straightening pictures, dusting the furniture, and rearranging things. A macramé wall hanging came down and was replaced by one of Gareth's larger paintings, one he had done of the woman and the lake. The throw cushions on the sofa were all re-covered in a muted flowered chintz, petals in a blush pink on a dusty-grey background. All the chipped mugs had been tossed, replaced by some English bone china mugs. She even had the broadloom cleaned in the family room, but some stains remained, though faded. Memories of a twelve-year-old's missed birthday party here and an unattended young artist's spilled paints there ... Elaine rearranged the furniture to cover them. To ease her conscience.

The boys were growing up and away, and now, finally, she had agreed to be a stay-at-home mom. Where was the sense in that? The years when she should have been home have passed her by. Those were the years she was too busy bringing home the bacon. She had overcompensated with gifts and homemade goodies. Everyone thought she was a marvellous mom. It was easy; it was part-time. She knew that the only reason that she could create the illusion of being a perfect mother was that she had an escape. Work allowed her to be more present when she was present. Work allowed her to be more interested, more doting, more understanding. She wondered how Jack's mother, that German woman down the street, managed to do it, day in and day out, without pulling out her hair. What stamina she must have. What tenacity! Well, she was German.

"Mom?" Gareth poked his head in, through the tear in the screen door. (Something else she could fix!) He was covered in dried paint, but, as that was now the norm, there was no point in mentioning a shower to him.

"Hey, it smells great in here! Is there lots? Because I invited some friends for dinner. Well, Jack, but he's here half the time, anyhow. And a couple of girls."

"Girls? You mean your girlfriend and a friend of hers?"

"Ah, no. Some other girls. You'll see."

"There's always lots. You know that. I'll just set a few more places."

She was creating a perfect Sunday meal. Potatoes, roasted in the oven, alongside a roast, peas on the stove, and an iceberg salad on the side. But the treat, her favourite thing, would be the Yorkshire puddings. Something that would surely smoke up the house with the melted hot fat in the oven, but oh-so worth it! She would open the windows and doors before she put in the cupcake pans, each round cup with a tablespoon of lard in it, under the grill. And then, if that wasn't enough, she had defrosted a Sara Lee cheesecake for dessert. One of the new ones with cherries and sauce on top!

But it wasn't enough for her. Mark had gone back to school; she had nurtured and facilitated that years ago. So now, what about her? At forty-five years old, what was she to do? There were only so many cherry-topped cheesecakes she could defrost.

If only I could have made more of my patients trust me. If only they could have opened up to me. The ones whose words failed them.

Elaine knew that Mark was looking forward to quieter days where it would just be the two of them again. Him coming home to her and there never being an empty house or lonely bed ever again. But surely he would tire of that. Surely they managed to keep their love and passion alive because she wasn't always readily accessible. Yes, she would have to tell him that she might have other plans. But not tonight. Tonight would be a perfect family dinner.

Elaine stood, back to the door, pouring flour into a bowl, followed by the other dry ingredients, a pinch of salt and a tablespoon of baking powder. Yorkshire pudding was a very easy recipe and the results always brought smiles, as if it were more of a task than it actually was. She could make them more often, but then they wouldn't be special, and the family would catch on that, perhaps, it wasn't a magical recipe, after all.

"Yorkshire pudding! My favourite! Is Tristan home?"

Elaine turned, milk bottle in hand, and saw Jack with two girls. Two white, pale, thin, almost ethereal girls. She felt she was looking at a spectre, or rather two identical spectres. Here they were, the girls whose mother had sacrificed herself to the waves. Was it a test, a message, or a sign, perhaps? Elaine believed in signs, even though she prided herself as a woman of science. She would, for instance, never admit to anyone that she always stepped over every crack in the pavement. Don't step on a crack or you'll break your mother's back.

"This is Clara and Blanca, friends of mine. I met them at the concert with Tristan a few months ago. They came in second."

"Nice to meet you." The taller one extended her hand.

They do not recognize me. Or are they pretending? Should I say something or just hope for the best? I was the messenger, the one who told them the truth and broke their little hearts.

Elaine glanced at the painting in the living room. There they were, sirens in the water, as younger girls. And their mother, walking into the waves. She would have to devise a way to remove it before they noticed it. But how?

"Jack, why don't you go upstairs and see Tristan. I know he is dying to see you. Bring the girls, too."

"Okay, if you say so. Should I tell him dinner is almost ready?"

"Sure."

They passed by her, went to the stairs, and seemed not to notice the painting over the fireplace. Before Elaine could get to it, Gareth was there, lifting it down and stashing it behind the sofa. He frantically looked for something to hang in its place, but his mother waved him off.

"Go on upstairs, I'll find something."

"Thanks, Mom. You know I didn't paint it to upset them."

"No, of course not."

"But I did have to paint it. And I can't hide it forever."

"Give me five minutes, then it's dinner. I'll go find the macramé. That couldn't offend anyone."

"Well, really, Mom, it does offend anyone with good taste."

Elaine shooshed him out of the way with her tea towel. She opened the smoking oven with its fat-melted cupcake trays, plopped in her doughy mixture, then looked for the macramé wall hanging.

And all that time she thought about the woman with the red hair who walked into the lake and never returned. How she had planned it secretly and all they thought was that she collected rocks. How naive! How trusting! Elaine wished that there were such a thing as a time machine. If she could go back, she could change things. She would listen harder. She'd pay heed to every word said after each and every treatment, knowing that there were always clues. But she was only a nurse. A caregiver and not someone with power.

As she lifted the ugly macramé, she knew that one day the girls would have to see her son's painting. *But not today*, she thought, *not today*. Today there would be a perfect Sunday meal.

Tristan was lying on his boyhood bed, surrounded by his old movie posters. He opened his drawer in the bedside table next to him.

There it was, the patch he had tried so many times, covering his good eye, willing the lazy, substandard eye to perform better. Had he not tried hard enough? Not wanted it badly enough to suffer through the exercise? He was just too vain to cover the good eye. Or maybe he just gave up too easily?

School was getting tough. All the deconstruction of old films and the overcomplication of examining why the director chose a particular shot or lens was a constant frustration for him. *Because it looks cool.* But that didn't cut it with his professors, they wanted essays and a thesis on the effect German expressionist films had on modern-day American cinema. Well, of course, he knew that they affected film. Hadn't he seen every Fritz Lang film available to him? Even the early ones like *Die Spinnen,* and *Der Müde Tod,* films he had made before he met Thea von Harbou, his collaborative partner, his love, and his writer till she died. And what a looker she was, with wide-set intelligent eyes, a full mouth, and that perfectly coifed hair coming off her face, away from her high forehead! Wasn't that a sign of intelligence, a high forehead? Everything about her said, *Here is a woman who is as smart as she is beautiful.* Surely she had been his great muse. And why not, a woman like that!

Tristan tried to conjure the perfect muse. A woman like Thea von Harbou, smart and insightful. But even she did not inspire the feelings he desired. He popped his top button on his jeans, keeping his seeing eye focused on the door and his blind eye focused on his fantasy. He reached inside, beyond the soft denim, and imagined the perfect V-line, like an arrow pointing southward. Then he thought of jeans falling away to reveal a young man's hips. A trail of downy hair from the belly button downward like a sacred path. He yearned to follow that pathway with his mouth, while his hands traced the V-line of his imagination. And then jeans would fall away from his body, revealing an equal excitement. Yes, this is his muse. Someone who could meet him in every way as an equal.

Someone to mirror him. His hand was now his muse's hand, stroking, touching, and stroking again …

"Trist? Hey, it's Jack!"

Tristan leapt from his bed.

"Just a minute," he called out.

"I have some friends here."

"Okay, give me a sec!"

Tristan took a few deep breaths to calm himself. He sat on the edge of his bed and did the only thing he could to quiet his excitement. He shut his seeing eye and, as the world ceased to exist around him, his erection ceased, as well.

He opened the door, happy to greet his brother's best friend.

"Ta-da! Remember the twins?" Jack asked, presenting the girls with a flourish.

Clara and Blanca entered Tristan's bedroom. The space seemed tight and cramped with the four of them, but perhaps that was because of the many movie posters pressing down upon them. Clara approached one, *The Quiet Man*, because she thought Maureen O'Hara looked like her mother. Or at least the way she would like to remember her mother.

"What's this one about?"

"About a boxer who kills someone then runs away to Ireland, but falls in love with a crazy redhead."

"Did he kill him on purpose?" Clara asked.

"No."

"Why Ireland?" she persisted.

"His family was from there originally. And then there was some argument about land and this other guy hates him, but then he falls for the guy's sister."

"Sounds like every star-crossed romance. Misunderstandings and then it all works out," said Blanca. Clara knew that Blanca was just showing off again. How many movies had they actually seen?

"I guess it does," laughed Tristan. "But this is the one that really made John Wayne a star."

Blanca shrugged. No big deal. She'd never seen a John Wayne film.

"By the way, I thought you should have won. You know, that night at Massey Hall? You two were the best. But second prize is pretty good, right?"

When they came in second that night, when the emcee called their names and said "Bleach," the crowd cheered for them. They had been the favourite. They had stepped forward, leaving whomever would be the winner standing alongside the unnamed losers. They were set apart, no longer in that nerve-wracking position. They were told to stand beside the third-place Bowie lookalike, on stage right. There were some "bravos" shouted out. But all that Clara could think was, *We've lost, we didn't come in first*. There is first place and then there is everyone else. As they stood there, Blanca took Clara's hand and squeezed it hard. So hard that Clara could only think of her fingers and not about coming in second.

"It was a great night. We got lots of exposure and I am sure something will come of it," Blanca replied politely, but deep down she was just as disappointed as her sister.

"Dinner's ready, we're just waiting for my dad!" Gareth shouted up the stairs.

"Better wash my hands," Tristan said. "Don't be touching my stuff while I'm gone."

"Oh, Trist, you know I'll have my hands all over your stuff." Jack smirked.

The boys started laughing and, for the first time in their lives, the twins understood what it was like for other people to be on the outside when they were together and in sync.

"Did this movie win any awards?" Clara asked, indicating *The Quiet Man* poster.

"Yes, it won the Academy Award for best direction," Tristan replied.

"Oh." Clara smiled. "And who came in second that year?"

They came in second in a music contest. So what? The judges probably felt sorry for them. Pathetic little things! Couldn't have won first prize because that would be too encouraging, but a second place was just right. It was just a bit of kindness toward those ugly little ducklings. Yep, that's what they were, all right. Noisy little ducklings with white, uneven feathers, struggling and fighting to get their share of the stale bread.

Still, those big notions should never have been put into their heads by that woman downstairs in the first place. Singing and playing the piano and all that talk about how to behave if the Queen invited them to tea. It was fine when they were nine and ten, but it should have stopped ages ago. The best they could hope for would be to get jobs as checkout girls at the grocery store. This was all just tomfoolery! Musical tours and audiences and all that crap!

The old man sat on the edge of his twin-sized bed. He really should slide the rest of the way down to the floor, to kneel and pray before God, but everything ached. Pancreatic cancer was a bitch. He was half his usual size, shaky and disoriented much of the time. Of course, his self-medicating cure, half a bottle of cheap cooking sherry every morning to chase down the two heaping tablespoons of curry powder, did leave him just a bit off-kilter for the whole day. *Note to self,* he thinks, *no tricycle-riding today and maybe three tablespoonfuls of the curry powder.*

He knew it was working. He could feel the cancer being beaten down by the curry and sherry. Like they were attacking where the doctors with their medications and cures could not. He might beat this bugger yet. Sherry, curry, and faith in the Lord. There would be no chemo for him.

"Oh Lord, forgive me for not getting onto my knees. I fear I would never get up again," he spoke out loud, but then regretted it. Surely the Lord would give him the strength to rise up after his little talk.

"I got a few things on my mind. Ya see, my awkward little granddaughters … well, ugly, really … but I shouldn't say that since ya made 'em. But hey, ya can't hit it out of the ballpark every time, can ya? I mean, look at all those sunsets ya do, night after night! Ya can't be on all the time. Now, look, they are sweet, even though they are hard on the eyes, God. But that's the thing, right? If ya let me die, who will they have, eh? Who else could bear lookin' at 'em? Even my son, Bob, is starting to find them … well, you know, creepy. He thinks it's a sad thing the freak show don't exist no more. Heh! Said we could'a sold 'em to them. Now, you know he was jokin', right? So, anyhow, ya gotta let me live, because someone's gotta take care of your failures and I am that man. Your humble servant. Amen."

That should do it. Give the big guy in the sky an unselfish reason and surely he would let him live a while longer. Although there was a bit of truth in his prayer. He was worried about the twins being at their uncle Bob's if something happened to him. Not that he believed the stories (no, lies, all lies!) from the devil-tongued daughter of his. She weren't evil, though, he knew that much. But evil had penetrated her and she'd suffered for it. God rest her troubled soul.

Besides, if there was something to it, she silenced herself, didn't she? And wasn't that a sin? But who was to know what really happened? All in the past now. Now his concern was to keep gossip away and make sure the girls were safe. They needed him, after all. Just to watch out and keep an eye on them. Keep rumours and threats away from them.

But these crazy ideas that they could be famous singers! Sure, there were some freaky-looking singers these days, but they wouldn't last. Didn't they know what real singers looked like? They looked like Tammy Wynette, Patsy Cline, Loretta Lynn, and Emmylou Harris. Women with big hair, fresh faces, and healthy bodies. Women without pink rabbit eyes.

"Lord have pity on my granddaughters" he added to his prayer. "Let them down easy. And stop that Jew-woman downstairs from filling their heads with nonsense. Singing contests. I'd be damned! Amen."

The old man reached for some painkillers and washed them down with the last few ounces of the leftover sherry from the morning's bottle.

Esther was cleaning up the evening meal plates, stacking the white dishes one on top of the other, largest to smallest. It had been a simple meal, the heat stopping her from cooking and heating up the apartment. Even with a cross-draft, it could get hot in there. So it was cold plates with a beet salad, greens, and some smoked fish from the delicatessen. Weird food, the twins had proclaimed the time she tried to introduce them to smoked fish with sour cream and dill on the side. Well, you cannot change Rome in a day, as they say. And they had learned some manners; they'd learned to fold their napkins and which fork to use at the right time. They had come a long way. They had come so far that they would soon be far away from her, as well.

Esther had seen how the old man was suffering upstairs. Cancer eating away at his body, leaving him weak and dizzy. Twice last week she had helped him upstairs to his third-floor apartment, the air growing hotter and more stale with every step. It was the first time she had peered into his flat with its low ceilings, stained carpets, and general debris. There were dirty clothes and linens in a pile on the floor, dishes with half-eaten grilled cheese sandwiches and ketchup beside the TV, which was on and blasting. The bed was unmade with stained and faded sheets. What could have been a sweet apartment, a quirky place like so many she had lived in during her youth, was a mistreated home, smelling of smoke, grease, and dirty feet.

"Where do the girls sleep when they are here?" she had asked.

"On the bed. I sleep on the sofa when they're here. It's a big sofa so I'm okay with it."

"Both of them? In a single bed?"

"Well, they are skinny little things and they're used to it. Been their bed since they were toddlers. When they weren't at their uncle's. We used to share them. Now they're here mostly."

"I see."

Used to it doesn't make it right, she thought to herself, but her demeanour did not betray her. She simply supported him with her arm and helped him to his disgusting little bed with its one lumpy foam pillow.

No wonder the girls were her constant visitors throughout the years. She had always thought the visits were solely because of their love of music and their desire to learn about the world, but no, it was as much about escaping as it was about glimpsing what was possible. Escape could be as good a muse as love or misery or heartbreak and, if anyone knew about escape, it was Esther. Annihilation can come in many forms. A holocaust. A smothering of identity. The killing of dreams. The erasing of the soul.

Self-preservation is strong in the young. It has to be. When others have perished around you, there is the thought you carry all your days, that any life thrown away is a mockery to those lives that have been lost. If you survive then you have to live life harder, with more love and forgiveness in your heart. You cannot waste a day on hate or revenge because, if you do, then evil wins and your survival means nothing. She had an obligation to survive for everyone who didn't and so she ran faster than reason, faster than duty, and faster than the love that bound her. Only when she caught her breath could she take into account what had been lost.

If her hair had been dark like her sisters', if the guard hadn't turned a blind eye because she was good-looking, if a letter hadn't arrived from a long-lost uncle and found her in Switzerland … all of these ifs brought her into the life of these two girls. Their birth into abuse was as arbitrary as her survival had been.

Esther looked for her stationery, a cream-buff paper with a gold edge. A request always demanded style and reverence. She fetched her address book. A proper apprenticeship was what they needed. She still had some contacts in Europe, after all.

When Jack came home from dinner at his friends' house he was careful not to be noisy, tiptoeing in, quietly removing his shoes, slipping past his mother's bedroom so as not to wake her. But there was no reason for it; he could hear the soft, stifled crying on the other side of the door. Surely it wasn't about his father, that had been ages ago now and she was better off without him.

"Mom?" He knocked on her door. No answer, but the sniffling stopped abruptly. "Mom?" he called out again. "I know you're awake."

"You were out late. You had a good time, yes?" She did pretty well, but there was still a small crack in her voice, giving away the night of tears.

"Can I come in?"

He didn't wait for an answer, he walked in and sat at the edge of the bed. There was a heap of tissues piled on the bedside table, evidence that it had been a long night of tears.

"What happened, Mom?"

"Nothing. Nothing at all. That is the point."

"I don't understand."

"Sometimes it is better not to have a taste of something new because then you want a whole meal of it, and perhaps deep down you know that it isn't good for you. You know you will never be satisfied with the food you normally eat. The food you need for survival."

"Mom?"

"Yes?"

"Do you think that for once you could just tell me what's going on instead of always speaking in food metaphors?"

"It's okay, I am just being silly. Go to bed."

"Okay."

Jack kissed his mother's forehead and then left, shutting the door behind him. He wondered if it was just moody woman-stuff or regrets. What could possibly make her, the woman who had always seemed so strong to him, cry herself to sleep? Was it that he was off to college the next September and suddenly she felt unneeded?

Jack opened the fridge, got himself a glass of juice, then sat at the kitchen table. There, stacked in front of him, were letters to be mailed. A few bills being sent off to be paid. And then the familiar pale blue of an airmail envelope. To Siegfried, no doubt. Jack pulled the envelope away from the others and held it up to the light, trying to see what was inside but having no luck. Then, somehow, he just knew. He looked inside with his unseeing glass eye and felt that, inside the envelope, there was sadness. The letter was the cause of sadness and the bringer of sadness. His mother was crying because she was ending her love affair with the ocularist.

Jack didn't know why he acted the way he did. Why he made such a rash decision. All he knew was that his mother had cried too many tears. Here she had a chance at happiness and she was giving it up. He filled the kettle and waited for it to boil. He held the letter over the steam and loosened the grip the glue had on the seam where the body and the flap met and joined. He carefully pulled it away until it was open and took his mother's letter from it. Hilda was from that generation who had, all over the world, been forced to spend hours practising the curls and dips of cursive. Without a line to guide her, each sentence was perfectly straight, every letter even, slanting slightly to the left. Every stem from a *p* or a *q* or a *g* hit the same spot. But the *w*'s looked like *m*'s and where there was a double *s* it looked like a capital *B*. Whatever missive was in the letter was as hard to crack as the Enigma code. He should have taken German in high school, but Jack was feeling too rebellious then. What he did know was that there were some ink smears, places where tears must have hit the thin, flimsy airmail paper, and the words became weakened by the water, one blurring slightly into the next. He saw the word *genug*, then *untröstlich* and knew that those words meant "enough" and "heartbroken." Finally, there was a big smear of ink from what must have been a huge tear, beside her ending salutation, *Meine Liebe, auf Wiedersehen*, Hilda.

Jack put the letter into his pocket. He opened the mudroom door and unlocked his darkroom. His hand reached overhead and pulled the chain that illuminated the room in red light. He was on a mission and had to work quickly.

He opened his files of pictures, early photos of carefully placed things and found objects. Stolen objects. There, almost at the bottom of the drawer, it was. A small jewellery box and, inside, the glass eye he had stolen from Siegfried. Underneath the box was an envelope with a photo of the eye.

He put the photo into the airmail envelope, and added a little note:

"If you ever want to see your eye again, you'll have to come here to get it."

He resealed the envelope. It looked a little tampered with, but who would possibly be looking for that? No one would suspect a thing. Then he slipped it back between the phone bill and the electricity bill.

It had been good to see Jack, to catch up over dinner. He looked more and more like his mother who, God knows, looked like a

German movie star with those cheekbones, full lips, and intelligent hazel-grey eyes. Why were Tristan's imaginary muses all German? Marlene Dietrich, Romy Schneider, Hildegard Knef. But the one Hilda was most like, he decided, was Hanna Schygulla. Yes, same oval face, same unpredictable look, and that same voice. Jack's mother could have been a movie star in another time, another place.

Tristan imagined a relationship like Hanna Schygulla and Rainer Werner Fassbinder. The goddess and the most important filmmaker in Germany. What magic they made together. He remembered the night he lined up at the Carlton cinema to see *The Marriage of Maria Braun*. Two-dollar Tuesdays, it was. Every Tuesday he would take advantage, watching, making notes, studying. But on this Tuesday it was Hanna Schygulla who caught his imagination. She was his discovery that night, more than the director or the movie itself. He remembered squirming as the husband of Maria Braun entered the room where his wife, played by Schygulla, was undressing her African American lover. How tense, how sexy and suspenseful. And then when the fight broke out between the two men, and Maria was sure that her husband, her true love, would die, she smashed a bottle over her lover's head, accidentally killing him.

Yes, Hilda could be capable of doing that. He had seen her dispatch a rabbit as easily as opening a can. She could easily smash a bottle over someone's head, and still look sexy when she did it.

Tristan loved screen sirens, far more than their male costars. He loved their strength. He loved their glamour. They were all so much larger than life. Deities of the celluloid. So why didn't they excite him?

SEVEN

HE HAD NOT HEARD from her for weeks. Three weeks and three days to be precise. Usually her letters came at a rate of two a week. Glimpses into her day, her thoughts, and her heart. Some were pages of descriptions, others no more than a few words. Words that encouraged him to believe that she might return soon, even though she no longer had the excuse of having to go to refit her son's artificial eye.

Siegfried poured himself a beer, tilting the glass at the perfect angle so that there was no head at all, till the last second, when he uprighted the glass, allowing for a two-millimetre layer of foam. He sipped and a bit of the foam tickled his upper lip before the amber liquid slid past his mouth and down his throat. Why hadn't she written?

He went to the fridge, found some leftover potato salad and some cold cuts, and he set out to make a simple meal. Shaved ham on rye, mustard, and the leftover salad. He placed it neatly on a plate, with nothing touching. Why hadn't she written?

He bit into the sandwich and thought the bread was a bit on the stale side. Should have toasted it. A bit of extra butter, though, would make it edible. Or more mustard, perhaps. But after his attempt to fix it, he gave up and threw the sandwich away. He wasn't hungry, anyhow. Why hadn't she written?

It kept coming back to the same question no matter how many times he busied himself with normal activities. No matter how many times he got on with things, it all came back to the question of her, Hilda. He didn't even realize how much he had depended on the letters, how much he looked forward to them, how they had, over the years, become the thing he most looked forward to. And now she was withholding his greatest joy with the same ease in which she had once given it.

He hated the question that kept coming back into his mind because it made him consider all the reasons. She may have had a *rapprochement* with her ex-husband. And why not? He could easily have seen the great mistake he had made. She may have met someone else. Someone younger, perhaps, with more hair and a little taller. She may have decided it was foolish, there were too many miles and too many differences. She may have had a change of heart and simply stopped wanting him. That was the hardest possibility for him to accept, and yet it was also the one he thought most plausible.

If he could only reach her by thinking of her. If every time he imagined her, she would also think of him, wherever she was, and remember their times together, then, maybe then, he might stand a chance.

He did write to her. Two letters, in fact, after she had stopped writing. One was quite romantic, recounting their intimacy and telling her how he missed kissing her mouth and that his arms ached for her. When he got no response he wrote a second, asking if everything was all right. Nothing. Silence.

Could she possibly be dead? Surely Jack would think of letting him know. Surely Jack would get a message to him if she were ill or in the hospital.

Siegfried changed his shirt, buttoning it to the neck and then undoing the top button. A periwinkle blue to enhance his eyes. He found his favourite sports jacket, tan suede, butter-soft and loose-fitting. He decided he would go and dance her out of his thoughts. His life couldn't stop simply because she blinked or looked away. Just because he wasn't in her sight, didn't mean that he didn't exist. He thought of Gisela and Antje and wondered if they might still be going to the dances, eager and willing to dive into the possibilities of romance or a relationship. Why should he wait for something so fragile as a long-distance affair? It was crazy. Wonderful when they were together, but the months and months apart were difficult and lonely. It wasn't real. It was a fantasy. And fantasies were easy to walk away from. Easy to abandon when the substantial, the real, presented itself.

He smoothed the strands of his unruly, thinning hair, having sprayed a bit of hairspray into the palms of his hands first. He reached for some aftershave. *Something earthy but spicy*, he thought. Then he stepped back to evaluate the full effect.

"Who are you kidding?" he said to his reflection.

He took off his shirt, folded it, and put it onto his chair. Stepped out of his trousers and put himself to bed, snuggling down into his pillows, imagining that Hilda's face was there, on the pillow next to his, looking at him. Smiling.

Hilda couldn't remember where she had put the letters. Surely, she had left them on the kitchen table, but they weren't there. On the desk perhaps? No. The letter was gone and, she feared, posted.

"Yeah, I mailed them on my way over to Gareth's," Jack told her.

Hilda sat down hard on her chair. Well, it was meant to be. This back and forth was just amusement, a fantasy, because neither of them would budge and make a move. They were both too rooted in their lives. Her with her family. Him with his business.

It would be too much to ask after all the years they had both dedicated to carving out their separate lives.

But wasn't sacrifice the currency of love? She had sacrificed for John, but that wasn't enough. Eventually every sacrifice she made for love was spurned, mocked, rejected. It was as though everything she did to prove her love became the future instruments of resentment. Finally, there was no way to win. If she didn't do things for the family, didn't put them all first, they wondered what was wrong with her and resented her for letting them down, but when she did put them first, they resented her for not having her own dreams and desires. She would not allow herself to fall back into that rut. She would rather have a tearful but romantic ending than the slow death that came with familiarity. The old saying was right, familiarity did breed contempt. Hilda knew that contempt was a far worse fate than heartbreak.

She decided she would push it all from her mind. If the letter was sent, so be it. He would find someone else and when he became bored with her, his new woman, then he would think of Hilda with nostalgia and longing. How much better was that than him rolling over for a comfortable, easy fuck? The only problem was that she would never know if he longed for her. She would never have the satisfaction of knowing that she was still wanted. Desired.

Why was desire more important now than simple physical satisfaction? It had never been that way for her before. She loved sex, loved the smells and the touching. Loved the tired and spent sensation that came afterward. And the calm. Sex was like a vacation from real life. For those moments of sensation, the troubles of her world didn't exist. So why would his longing for her mean more to her than any other man's touch?

Because she longed for him. And she didn't like it. Didn't like how, on a perfectly fine day, as she walked the dog along the beach, he would penetrate her mind and suddenly the walk wasn't as perfect as it had been. She didn't like that when she made a cake she wondered if he would like it if he were to eat some. Or a joke she might hear, would he find it funny, too? She hated that her life was now measured by what he might think or how he might experience something she was doing if he were there. She hated that she no longer felt complete without him.

I must get on with my day. Accomplish those tasks that define me, she thought. And so, she decided on making Jack's favourite dessert, *Pflaumenkuchen,* a plum cake with, perhaps, a runny custard to pour over it. Her daughters were coming for the weekend, too, so why not make it a celebration? Hilda counted the eggs and realized she needed a few more, so she went outside to see if there were any in the little coop at the back. How sweet the air felt this morning, with the aroma of lilacs wafting in the breeze. An early-morning rain had only encouraged the scent, made everything fresher. The grass was damp underfoot, so she slipped off her shoes and pressed her foot into the coolness. She could never have done that in Germany. Barefoot in the grass? Her mother would roll over in her grave! How could Hilda ever give up the feeling of cool grass on a hot summer's day? There were freedoms here that were beyond her imagination. And so much open space. Elbow room, as she liked to say. Did Siegfried ever consider just how huge this land was? Here you didn't have to drive to the Black Forest to experience nature, you just had to open your back door!

Hilda remembered one of the worst nights of her life since coming to Canada. The night John left her, declaring that he wanted a divorce. Once he had taken his suitcases, thrown them into the back of his pickup truck, and sped down the street, kicking up clouds of gravel dust, Hilda went onto her back deck, alone. She sat until late into the night, the chilled air wrapping around her. She didn't care. She had a hot cocoa to warm her and steady her nerves. She sipped, so lost in her thoughts that, at first, she hadn't realized that she had company. Slightly up the hill, but downwind, was a young coyote. No longer a pup, but not yet fully grown. He had the kind of curiosity only the young possess, where the desire to know is greater than one's safety.

"Hello, little coyote," she had said.

He cocked his head, as if listening closely. But made no move to run off.

"I am so very sad," she had told him. "I feel like I haven't a friend in the world."

The coyote sat on his haunches and continued to watch the silly lady talking to him.

"They say you are magical. That you are a trickster like Loki or Mercury. Is that true?"

The coyote flicked his tail.

"I think it is true. I think that you have been sent here and that now you know what's in my heart."

The coyote walked toward her. So very close. Slowly, hesitantly. With curiosity. Then, when he was in touching distance, he ran past her, his fur brushing her bare leg.

Yes, she thought, *this has become my home with all its clumsy beauty. I would take the wide skies over the cobblestone streets, the lake the size of a freshwater sea, over all the little lakes with sailboats, the unbelievable autumn leaves in their crimson, gold, and orange over the dull browning of a German fall.* Even the extreme seasons had become a part of her psyche. How could she give all that up for better coffee and superior cake? How could she give that up for opera and architecture? How could she give that up for love?

There were three fresh eggs. Hilda put two in her pocket and the third she placed at the edge of the fence for her coyote friend.

It would be a great cake, because that was something she could do. She could keep the taste of her past and the beauty of the world she had run to. All she had to do was make a perfect batter, cut the plums evenly, and her world would be in order.

She went back into her kitchen, turned on the oven to preheat it, and decided to throw in a load of laundry while it warmed. She grabbed everything in the washroom hamper, then went into the bedrooms to gather the rest. Jack had left his shirt on the floor. She picked it up and sniffed the armpits to see if it needed a wash. It did. She emptied the chest pocket. The few dollars she placed onto his dresser. And then, two sheets of flimsy blue airmail paper. She unfolded them. Her goodbye letter to Siegfried.

Not in his plans! Yes, he had agreed to the marriage, it was the least he could do once it had become apparent to everyone that he and Jean were involved. How else could she keep her job? And what a great job it was for a free-and-easy modern couple. Good benefits and lots of time off. Entire summers just for them. Long Christmas vacations and a spring break. There could be travel and road trips. Afternoon sex. It was so much to hold on to.

John had to create an image of decency even if that wasn't the thing that had attracted him to her in the first place. It was the dichotomy of it all. The double life. The appearance of one thing to the world and another reality for just them. That was the excitement of it. And so, the marriage was the get-out-of-jail-free card. He could pass Go and still collect his money. Keep his job, be the poor divorced man who had to put a life back together again while proving to be the more generous one for giving the house to his ex-wife. Nobody had to know that Hilda's inheritance from her mother had paid off the large mortgage. By the time he married Jean, he was the man back on top with a new start and a new wife. A wife who shared his interests. A wife who understood him, not some foreign woman with an odd dress sense and rabbit hutches behind the house. No, now he could be a man about town, with a fresh, pretty wife whom everyone adored. Except that this go-around would be so different. This wife wouldn't become too preoccupied with what was expected in the home to forget about what really mattered. Connection. Adventure. And fun in the bedroom!

Except now she was starting to change her tune. She was moving the goalposts and already John could feel the suffocating constriction of marital expectation.

"We agreed, Jean. I have already had my kids. Three of them. And they are pretty much grown up. It's my time now. I don't want all that mess and concern again."

"Can't we even discuss this, John?"

"It's just not going to happen. You are surrounded by little kids all day, for fuck's sake! You would think that that would be enough for you!"

"I just don't think my life would be complete without the experience of motherhood."

"Trust me, you have no idea. Of course, you love them more than anything or anyone you've ever known. I would kill for my kids. But they are dream-killers. Your life will never be the same."

"Maybe I don't want my life to be the same. Maybe I'm bored."

Bored? How could she say that? They had one adventure after the next! Flew off on last-minute flights on a whim. They had a new circle of friends and lots of laughs. How could she possibly be bored? Did she actually know what was boring? Being kept awake all night because the baby had colic was boring. Driving to piano lessons and sitting outside the room, where the next arriving parents would strike up conversations about how well their kids were doing with the lessons, was boring. Cheering them on at sports events. Boring. Birthday parties where inevitably one kid threw up or another started crying. Boring, boring, boring. My God, she didn't know boring! How about playing Barbies with a daughter and after she calls you boring, you add a little conflict between the dolls and she ends up crying and telling her mom on you. Now that is boring. Boring is not afternoon sex.

Boring is not going to the movies whenever you like. Boring is not being spontaneous.

"I know, let's go to the Caribbean this spring break and try scuba diving."

"John ..."

And there it was. That sentence left dangling. The name said in that teacher's way, implying that he should know better. And he did know better. He had made a mistake. She was so yummy, so fit and sexy, and so very forbidden. Twelve years younger and full of life. But a younger woman just meant that she would eventually want those things other women had. The problem was that he didn't really want another wife — he wanted a lover. A lover who could be legitimized in the community but still his private little tiger in bed. In the home she could be his alone. Now she was angling to destroy that. She wanted to introduce someone else into the mix. Someone she would be able to love more than anyone else in the world. A little dream-killer.

If he had only held on another year with Hilda. The kids would all be gone, Jack being the last off to college. In just two short months she would have that beautiful old house all to herself. There, she could start to become the woman she was before the kids. She would be free, unencumbered. But no, he went for young and, in doing so, he had to take on her ticking biological clock. Damn, damn, damn.

Perhaps he could go back. Say it was all a midlife crisis and that he had just made a terrible mistake. Tell Jean that she needed a younger man and that he shouldn't be the one to rob her of her maternal dreams. Then he and Hilda could have the life they deserved. The kids, home at Christmas in the big house, with a feast that only Hilda could cook. And then they could be a united pair when the girls got married or when Jack graduated university. But when they weren't there they could talk to each other, rediscover what they once had. If it was a new start he so badly wanted, why didn't he just wait for a little bit and have a new start with her? Because having a family with Jean wasn't a new start, it was a rerun. A rerun of a hackneyed sitcom.

Of course, Hilda would have to forgive him first. But that could be fun. They could have months of angry sex in the process. Her fucking him with a rage that could only come from a female betrayed. But what about Jean? She would hate him, of course, but she would move on in time, find someone else. Would that bother him? Would he be jealous thinking about her with another man? Probably, but he would keep that a secret, that jealousy, and bring it home with him. Use it to fire his passions with Hilda.

Hilda. He missed her. Even her blunt, almost crude remarks, he missed. Go fuck a bowling ball! Ha! It was funny now! After all the earnestness and all the words of enthusiastic encouragement, after all the kind reinforcement he had to endure with Jean, he really missed Hilda's tactless honesty. There was nothing coy about her. Jean was a study in coy and, because of that, she was a master of flirtation. Not Hilda, though! Hilda was more likely to say, "We should have sex now, yes?" than to mince about suggestively, talking sweetly, or — God forbid — pouting. Suddenly, all this talk of having another baby and all he could think of was a straightforward fuck with his ex-wife!

Jack! Yes, Jack would know his mother's emotional state. He could tell him if he had a chance with her. A spontaneous lunch with Jack was just the thing. Perhaps at the golf club? Yes, golf! Jack should learn that sport next. That required aim, a steady hand, and a strong follow-through. Jack would be good at golf. He could make something out of his one-eyed son yet!

Jack held the loupe in front of his good eye as he skimmed through the contact sheet. Here, this one. And this one, maybe. He circled his favourites with a waxy red pencil and then, after re-examining his initial picks, he put a dot on the corners of the favourites from those. He eliminated, chose, and discarded with great care until he was down to the final dozen. Half in black and white and half in colour. Two headshots each and the rest with both girls together, in a variety of looks and poses, from quiet and reserved to fresh and saucy. But in every picture, they looked as though they held some ancient secret.

He was on a mission. He would create the most extraordinary portfolio for both of them and then one for himself. His plan was to approach the modelling agencies, as a rookie photographer, offering free sessions for their best models. He would show them samples of his work, mostly pictures of Clara and Blanca. Anyone with an eye for the beautiful but different would snap them up in a nanosecond. But he would always be the one who discovered them. He would be their maker. Yes, he knew that they wanted a music career, but surely some high-end modelling couldn't help but raise their profile and put them smack dab in the middle of the public eye.

His father wanted him to concentrate a little less on photography and a bit more on his future career options. He wanted him to get his B.A. and from there go on to teachers' college. He encouraged him to play it safe with a career that had a strong union to protect him, the benefit of a good medical plan, and a future retirement package that was solid. But Jack felt that he had played it safe for too long already. *Careful, Jack, you'll put your eye out!* was all he ever heard. *Careful, careful, careful, Jack. Be safe.* Well, he was sick of it. He wanted to take chances now. To jump like a dreamer believing he could fly. He liked that image and repeated it to both Tristan and Gareth. Gareth said nothing but Tristan replied, "I think we have already ascertained that you cannot fly, and you have the glass eye to prove it!"

"It's a metaphor, asshole."

Jack had no intention of attending teachers' college. He would, instead, as a compromise, attend university, study the arts with a focus on photography, and, while he was doing that, try to get a foot in the door of fashion photography.

Jack looked over the contacts again. They were the perfect models. Slightly bored and unaware of the camera due, in part, to their extreme nearsightedness. They only really read things in extreme close-up, in their faces, and so when Jack used a long lens it was as if he wasn't there at all and the pictures seemed to tell an intimate story.

He loved them. Both of them. But Blanca just a bit more. He had touched her bare arm, to guide her two steps over, before he took a shot. His skin was already taking on a sun-kissed look, so easily and quickly he tanned. But his flesh touching hers was extraordinary. A golden olive, rich and dark, in contrast to the pure white of her skin. He imagined a summer of swimming or lying on the beach so that his tan was deep all over his body and then, just lying naked with her, their contrasting skin intertwined. But even as he thought it, even as he imagined their bodies wrapped together, he could not help but think what a wonderful picture that would be.

"Jack!"

It was his mother's voice, calling from outside the darkroom.

"Yeah, Mom?"

"Come out now, I need to talk to you."

Jack put the contact sheet and the loupe safely onto the work table. They could wait a few more minutes.

"What, Mom?"

Hilda stood before him, holding the pages of her letter in her hand.

"Sorry, Mom. I know it was wrong, I just thought ..."

But before he could finish, Hilda threw her arms around her son and hugged him tightly.

"It's all about the fall. Don't you get it?"

Tristan was looking at his brother's epic painting, not quite understanding it. Why the fire and wings and torment?

"It's Icarus with melting wings, falling because he's a bit too confident," Gareth continued to explain.

"Or, it could be Lucifer with scorched wings. Hard to tell, really. Is it, perhaps, a bit too pretentious?"

"By whose standards? My teacher's?"

"I'm not saying it isn't good, but who really cares about Greek mythology?"

"But it's not just Greek mythology. It's Jack, falling from the tree. Don't you get it?"

Tristan took a step back, away from the painting, and tried to see its value outside of his brother's narrative, but all he could see was Gareth's guilt, painted, once again, onto canvas.

"Jack doesn't have wings, you know. He isn't an angel and he sure isn't a god. At some point you have to let it go. I think he has."

"Well, it's easier for him, isn't it? It wasn't his fault." Gareth crossed his arms.

"Really, Gareth? Really? Easier for him? You are such an asshole sometimes."

Tristan walked away, leaving Gareth in front of the giant painting. Was it really Jack's face he had painted? It wasn't the face of a child, that was for sure. It was a man's face. But the expression was that of surprise. As if falling had been the last thing on his mind. It was all wrong. Gareth took out his toolbox filled with oil paints. He grabbed a rag, dampened it with a mixture of linseed oil and admiral spirits, and then he rubbed out all of the features of the face. He placed a mirror beside the canvas. Peered at his reflection and then, stroke by stroke, he repeated his image, from his face to the mirror to the canvas. He was Icarus, not Jack. He was the one who dared to fly too close to the sun. The one who made every mistake with two eyes open.

* * *

It seemed that the sherry and curry powder were no longer work-ing. Their grandfather lay on the single bed, barely moving. Blanca took one of the cigarettes she had rolled that morning, put it in her mouth, then lit the end. After a long inhalation and a slow exhala-tion, she sat on the edge of the crusty bed and put the cigarette into her grandfather's mouth.

"What are you doing, Blanca? He's got cancer, are you crazy?"

"He's not going to make it, Clara. And smoking's one of his few joys."

Clara couldn't believe her ears! How many times did it look like Death was knocking and then, somehow, the old man tricked him. Told Death he wasn't home, to call back later. Then it would be all the sherry in the house and three tablespoons of the curry powder for a week and, sure enough, he would be up and at 'em again. Wheeling through town on his man-sized trike, offering things to get you up or take you down.

"Go down to Esther's. There's no rush, take your time. Tell her that I said it might be close. She will know what to do."

When Clara left, Blanca took her grandfather's hand, gave it a squeeze, then put the cigarette to his mouth again. He opened his eyes and smiled at her.

"You're such a good girl. Always a better-behaved girl than your sister. Your uncle always said that. Always preferred you. Said you were the smarter one."

"Yeah. Look, Grandpa, you have things you haven't told us. You know who our father is and you need to tell me before you die."

"It was that boy …"

He shook his head. Mum's the word. Let her think what he chose to think all those years before the doubts started to creep in. The twins didn't need to know what he had begun to suspect. The whispered secrets would have to go to the grave with him.

"Because if you don't tell me now, Clara and I will get onto our knees, every day, without the comfort of a cushion under them, and we will pray that your soul spends an eternity in Hell. Understand?"

The old man chuckled one of those weak, silent, raspy laughs. The air caught in his lungs so that the exhale came out with a high keening sound. For a moment his face turned quite red and Blanca jumped up away from him, thinking he might die right then and there. It was a good thing that she had told Clara to go downstairs. They all thought Clara was the naughty one, but she was just the one who was too often caught. She was the sensitive one who felt bad when they misbehaved. She made mistakes. Didn't lie very well. And all the time they thought Blanca was the better-behaved, but she knew that she was always the one with more power. The stronger twin.

"Not all angels are beautiful, Grandpa. Did you know that? Not all angels are sweet. You are going to die, and I bet you're afraid. Afraid to meet your maker. Guess what? I'm the angel who stands between you and your maker. I'm the last face you'll see before you see God. So, you had better tell me the truth, you nasty old man."

He was no longer laughing. This was a side of Blanca he hadn't seen. So in control. She lifted the cigarette and he thought she would give him a drag on it, but, instead, she took a puff herself and blew rings into the attic room.

Perhaps they were not human, after all. Perhaps they were angels from God. Fierce, unforgiving angels. Angels of retribution, and he had mistreated them. How could he denigrate an angel of God by telling them those terrible rumors? By repeating all the crazy talk of his devil-tongued daughter?

Blanca viewed her grandpa with little empathy and a lot of impatience. It seemed unreal to her, like a movie, where she was on the outside of the drama and yet still witness to it. Yes, he was a man suffering, struggling to breathe, holding on to life by those last, dubious, dangling threads, but it was hard for her to see him beyond his condition. She brought the cigarette to his mouth and told him to go ahead, have a nice long drag on it. Then she picked up the lumpy pillow from under his head. There was little point in fluffing it for him, the foam wouldn't allow it.

"The secret cannot go to the grave with you. You have an obligation to tell us. Everyone deserves to know their past."

Her grandpa shook his head again, refusing. Blanca brought the pillow toward his face.

"It would be an act of kindness. Put you out of your misery. No more struggling to get up and down the stairs. No more struggling to breathe. It could be so simple. Now, tell me, who is our father?"

There was something that always creeped him out when he looked into their eyes. He understood, from the appointments with eye doctors, that the darker pupils were quite normal in albinos, but still, up close, they seemed to be preternatural. Like the eyes of a demon or a succubus. Yes, that is what they were and they were sucking the life out of him. Her and her sister.

"If you do not tell me I will assume, all the rest of my life, that it was you. It has to be someone carrying the recessive albino gene. I am guessing it was family because albinism is quite rare in North America."

He couldn't believe that she suspected him! Okay, yes, he did live somewhat outside the law. He sold acid and pot, he cheated on his income tax, he even stole extra cream from the diner, but that was so far removed from anything she might be thinking! How could she believe for a minute that he would hurt his daughter that way? That would make him a monster, an absolute monster, and he wasn't that. Didn't he care for the two of them, love them to bits even though they were ugly little things? Didn't he protect them from harm and teasing and the sun's harmful rays?

"You are dying. The cancer is growing, Grandpa. It will swallow you up soon. Only the truth will set you free."

She gently put the lumpy foam pillow back under his head. She knew she was making some progress and so she began to quote from the Gospel of John.

"You are from below; I am from above. You are of this world; I am not of this world. You will die in your sins; you will indeed die in your sins."

She took his hand one more time.

"It could be so easy. I could make the pain go away," she reassured him.

He tried to sit up higher but didn't have the strength, so Blanca leaned in close, so close she was breathing in his fetid breath, smelling of curry, cigarettes, and death.

"I cannot be sure, but there was some talk. And your mother made some horrible accusations."

"Yes," she encouraged, bringing the cigarette close enough that he could smell it.

"There was talk. But that's all it was. Gossip and talk. All lies!"

"Fine. Burn in Hell. You were never a good father and an even worse grandfather. I will pray and curse you to an eternity in Hell. And one day you will be thirsty and I, and Clara and my mom, will walk by you and give you not so much as a drop of water!"

He felt the world closing in on him. His breathing became almost impossible, every inhale was a stab in his chest. He reached for his chest, gasping. This was it. Hers really would be the last face he would see before meeting his maker. He tried for air, popping his mouth open and closed like a freshly caught perch. Suddenly he remembered the first time he brought the girls fishing. Bob and his boys were there, too, all with lines in the water, but there wasn't much in the way of nibbles. Two sunfish and a nice chubby perch. He cast out again, telling the girls to keep an eye on their catch. They'd have a great fry-up that night if they could just catch one or two more! Clara sat silently by the bucket, water barely covering the day's catch. She was staring at them, their mouths opening and closing over and over again. Blanca put her little line back into the water. Suddenly the bucket was empty and there was little Clara, crying, with the empty bucket

in her hands. Then it happened. Bob yelled at her, full of unbridled rage. Right there, at the side of the road, he pulled down
her pants and started to spank her, her white bare bottom changing to a crimson red while his boys covered their laughing faces.
Clara was screaming, kicking and struggling, but he went on,
thrashing her bum, over and over and over again until her body
went limp and he dropped her in the gravel.

"Bob. It was your uncle Bob."

It was all too much for him. He lay back down and closed his
eyes, believing that death would now take him. Hoping to escape
the room, the pain, and the spoken truth. But it didn't. The air
rushed into his lungs and he could feel his life force returning.
Suddenly he was as relieved as those fish must have been, at the
hands of his granddaughter Clara.

All Blanca could think was that Clara must never find out. It
was too terrible. They really were freaks, after all. All those years
of cruel teasing and name-calling and, now, it turned out the slurs
were all true. They were cursed, marked, inbred. If only she could
take Clara away, far away from it all. Somewhere they could start
again, where they could create a new history. A history uncontaminated by the truth. That is what she would have to do. Run away
and protect the weaker twin.

"I have come for the eye."

Siegfried stood at her kitchen doorway, three large suitcases on
the ground beside his feet. He looked a bit tired from the journey,
but there he was, as big as life and smiling like an idiot.

"What do you mean, you've come for the eye?" Hilda asked
him. "What eye?"

"The eye that was stolen from me. The one you are holding
hostage."

"And you need three suitcases to retrieve one small eye?"

"No, I need three suitcases because it is going to take a very long time to get my eye back. Now are you just going to stand there blocking the doorway or are you going to invite me in?"

"Very presumptuous of you."

"Yes, I know. But you did send a ransom letter."

Hilda knew that Jack had tampered with the envelope, but had no idea what Siegfried was talking about. Eyes and ransom letters? Madness.

"I know nothing of a ransom letter or a stolen eye, I promise you."

Hilda was suddenly self-conscious. No warning! The house could be cleaner. There could have been a cake ready for coffee time. She would have bathed, put on a nice summer dress, one that showed off her lovely legs, and maybe even a bit of lipstick. But here he was, unannounced, and she was unprepared in a white T-shirt and pair of loose-fitting jeans. A pair of flat summer slip-ons made out of canvas. She was everything she wasn't in Germany, where she dressed properly, every day, and presented her best self to the world. His surprise arrival left her bare and vulnerable.

She carried one of his suitcases and told him to follow. Up the old farmhouse stairs, each step creaking underfoot. Past the smaller bedrooms and the washroom, with its old claw-foot soaker tub, to her room. At least the bed was made.

"Put your suitcases there, on the chair, I will clear out the drawers for you." But they were already cleared out. They had been cleared out a year and a half ago when John left.

"You are putting me in this room?" the ocularist asked her.

"Yes."

"But it is your room, yes?"

"Yes."

"I thought you would put me in the guest room at first."

"Did you come here so you could sleep in the guest room?"

"No … I came to retrieve my eye."

Hilda wrapped her arms around him. Fate had a strange way of unfolding and sometimes it needed a little bit of help. Jack's interception, his foresight, and his disregard for privacy had brought her a second chance at love. Of course, he would know better than she when it came to her heart. She had carried him high in her pregnancy, and he rested near her heart for those long nine months and somehow rested there still. But there was room for more than one person in the human heart and Hilda knew that the time had come to loosen the grip on motherhood and embrace this new gift.

"Liar! You didn't come here to retrieve your eye. You came here to retrieve your heart."

"Perhaps. Yes."

He popped the top button of her jeans, ran his hand down the rounded curve of her stomach.

"I will have to get used to this North American dressing," he said, slipping the denim over her hips and down off thighs and calves, till, with a gentle step, she was out of them and yanking her T-shirt over her head.

"Mom!" Jack's voice came right after the sound of a closing door. "Dad's here. He wants to talk to you!"

EIGHT

THE NEWS CAME QUICKLY. Gareth sat for a long time with
the envelope in front of him. It was thin, a single sheet inside. He
knew that the first few words would be one of either two things:
"We are pleased to inform you," or, "We regret to inform you."
What power there was inside that regular 4 1/8 x 9 1/2 white
envelope. Gareth knew that the right response was to rip it open,
see what fate had in store for him, but he didn't. Not out of fear.
Not out of worry. Not even because he wanted to expand the
moment. What was it then? Why did he simply turn it over and
over again in his hands?

"I hold my fate in my hands," he said out loud, knowing full
well that he didn't. His fate had been decided by committee, and
not by him. And the truth was that he wasn't so sure, anymore,
that he even cared. He had been through the wringer trying to
prove himself. He had been accepted conditionally and then it
all came down to one person. A person whose opinion did not
matter to him. Why should she have been the one to determine
his fate, and not him?

What did he want? Was his lack of excitement due to the time he had to wait? He remembered once ordering some comic books. For one reason or another they never arrived and so his mother contacted the distribution company and had them send another package, but once it arrived, everyone else had moved on to the next series of Spider-Man comics. He was a month behind. Now it was already July. Everyone else had announced where they would be heading to school in September. They all made plans and, during that time, he waited. Now that it was his turn to see if he would be going to his chosen school, it was past the time of announcement and excitement. Everyone had moved on. They were enjoying summer. They were deciding about housing on campus or sharing an apartment with a friend. No matter how he looked at it, the train had come and gone and he was left waiting for the next one on the schedule.

It could have been a joyful time, seeing his acceptance, because already he was feeling confident that it would be an acceptance. His huge painting of himself falling because of his pride had won him top marks and he sat at the head of the art class for achievement. But it should never have come to that. His miniatures should have given him the mark he needed the term before. His acceptance should never have been a question.

"I hold my fate in my hands."

Gareth had no idea what the future would bring. He had no idea what he wanted to do next. He just knew that he didn't want to be a last-minute addition. Not in an art school and not in life.

He lit the corner on the gas stove. He held the envelope away from his face, over the sink. He stood there, holding his fate in his hands until it was nothing but ashes.

The eye was a symbol of life in the ancient world. In Egypt, bronze eyes were placed on the closed eyes of the deceased. The Romans and Greeks decorated statues with artificial eyes made of silver. The idea of a figure without eyes, without the eyes of beauty, was something abhorrent, even if the eyes were unseeing and artificial.

Siegfried often thought of Jack's accusation, that his glass eye creations were deceitful. It pained him. He was an ocularist and the accusation seemed an assault on his very identity. He had been raised in Lauscha, a mountain village five hours from Hamburg, known for its excellence in the art of glass-blowing. *Glashütten* were established all over the town, producing drinking glasses, vases, and glass beads. The unusually fine sand was harvested from the nearby Steinheid quarry. It was a magical sand. Sand that took on the colour of the human eye's sclera when heated. In 1835, a glass-blower named Ludwig Müller-Uri invented the first artificial human eye from glass made of that magical sand and it changed the destiny of the whole village. Lauscha soon had a worldwide monopoly on glass eyes.

Siegfried could never go home to Lauscha. At the end of the war, Lauscha became part of East Germany, but the skills he had learned in Lauscha were something he kept with him in the West. He pushed himself beyond what he had learned, adding more pieces of glass to each eye, in order to better capture the complexity each individual carried. He wanted to create each eye to fool the person who gazed at its host; he wanted a truth within his work so that a part of the person was reflected in the glass he created. Mostly, he wanted his work to mask the injury because, he felt, it lessened the trauma of losing an eye. Now he wondered if the ancients were more honest with their gaudy colours and shiny stones. They never pretended; it was all ornamentation. But for an ocularist, any ocularist worth his grain of salt, the greatest compliment was when an onlooker assumed that the person could see from one of the prosthetic, glass eyes. Mein Gott, he thought, *maybe I am no more than a trickster, after all.*

Jack now had three eyes he could use. One was his daytime eye, with a slightly smaller pupil than his nighttime eye. And then there was the David Bowie eye. This was his special eye for meeting dates, going to concerts, and showing off. Siegfried noticed that he was wearing it more and more and it saddened him that Jack saw his life's work in the same way that one might view a jeweller's craft.

Siegfried missed his workroom with its drawers and Bunsen burners and heavy oak doors. He missed the careful work and the chance to bring relief or confidence to his clients. How he had to comfort and ease them as they sat through the process of creating an imprint with the soft, warm material. He never showed anything but calm, even as he stared at their fleshy, rounded orbs, created from a ball that was covered and wrapped in the muscles and tissues left around their eyes. The best of these connected to the muscles so well that the prosthetic eye could move with the seeing eye, making the deception all the more real. Jack, being so young at the time, and having such an extensive wound, had limited movement, but enough to fool many, provided they did not stare for too long. Yes, he had given him confidence, even though all he really wanted was sight. It was, the ocularist thought, as though the eye, in all its perfection and beauty, was no more than the consolation prize for Jack. The Miss Congeniality award, when indeed, it was the crown that was desired.

He knew that he couldn't just stay in the country house with Hilda, that at some point he had to resume his work, as flawed as Jack may think it. But how to find that balance? And certainly, leaving now would be a big mistake because her ex-husband was having second thoughts and Jack was about to leave for university. Besides, it would certainly be nice to have some time alone with her, without Jack bursting in or her daughters coming by for weekends. Oh, they all seemed to like him well enough, but there was an underlying resentment because, as long as he existed in Hilda's life, any notions they had of putting the family back together again were over.

He had listened in that first day, Hilda's ex-husband having no idea of his arrival. He had heard his words: *mistake, return,* and *sorry*. He had not heard a response from Hilda, though. Only a silence. All those miles he had just travelled, the grand romantic gesture of just showing up, the risk he took for love! Within an hour of his arrival it could all be taken away with one word only. *Family*.

When John had said, "Think about the family," Siegfried heard the harsh sound of a cup hitting the table, hard. And then more silence, until the sound of the door opening and then the slam that followed. Only then had he heard Hilda's voice. "Think about the family? You *arschloch*! I have done nothing but think about the family, while you were chasing skirts! You are the one who threw the family away. For what? For what? For your ego!"

What a woman, Siegfried had thought then. *What a temper!* He quietly vowed to himself that he would never give her the opportunity to be that angry with him. But there was so much mistrust in her, so much disappointment. He knew that he would still have to win her over.

"I told him it was a bad idea."

Jack had seated himself down on the top step beside Siegfried, an amused look on his face. His daytime eye was catching a bit of light coming in through the hallway window.

"Hello, Jack. It is so good to see you."

"I was wondering when you would get here," Jack had replied confidently.

"I think you are the one who sent the ransom note for my eye. Isn't that so?" Siegfried had asked him, already knowing the answer. The fine handwriting on the envelope didn't match the chicken-scratching in the inside.

"I'm not the only one who listens in on private conversations!"

"Well, we both learned from your mother. Do you think there will be a *rapprochement* now?"

"No, she loves you, you knucklehead."

"How did you learn so much about love, Jack?"

Jack had then pointed to his glass eye and winked. "Oh, I have an eye for it!"

Perhaps Jack had always been on his side. Or perhaps he had always been on the side of his mother's happiness. It was the daughters he would have to win over if he were to have a life with Hilda. And he would have to put his old life, with all his familiar comforts, smells, and memories, behind him.

Now, almost two months of staying in the old farmhouse near the Great Lake and Siegfried still could not feel a connection to the vast, strange land. He could see its beauty, its untamed power, but it never felt like home. It was too open for him. The landscape did not wrap around him with soft hills, the buildings and streets did not hold him safely. He felt like a man out of sorts, until nightfall, when the clothes were stripped away, and he climbed into bed beside Hilda. Only then did he no longer feel lost in a vast and unfamiliar land.

The alien watches as John Wayne kisses Maureen O'Hara in *The Quiet Man* on a television screen before him. The alien gets excited by what he sees, his little hairless body shaking at the sight. Then the boy, Elliott, who isn't even there, kisses a pretty girl in his class. He likes the girl but the only reason he kisses her is that he and the alien are somehow emotionally and psychically connected. Whatever the alien experiences, he experiences. They are one, in spirit and experience.

Clara sat beside Gareth, aware of his every movement. He was holding the popcorn, but she was too shy to reach over to grab a handful. It was on his lap, after all. What if her poor vision affected her aim? Best not to eat any popcorn than to make a mistake. Also, popcorn could be a noisy thing to eat. She glanced at Blanca, sitting on her other side. Jack's arm was over the back of her sister's chair. Not touching her, though, just poised and ready. All that had to happen would be one really scary or sad thing and that arm would slip around her sister's shoulders and she would allow it, welcome it. She knew her sister's thoughts. She was like the boy in the movie.

It bothered Clara that the alien had to be hidden in a closet, that he wasn't easily accepted just because he was different. And people were laughing at the little guy, like it was a joke or something. Like the movie was a comedy, which was strange to Clara because everything from E.T. being displaced, to the dangerous curiosity of others about him, only proved that the film was actually a tragedy. Clara only saw the injustice of being set apart. She hated that E.T. was kept hidden in order to be kept safe. She wanted to get out of her seat and gather up the little alien and tell him that it would all be fine. That he was lovable, even though he was different.

But the alien did have friends and the kids did love and accept him, without really understanding him. That part was unbelievable to Clara. How often had she and her sister been ignored, treated like pariahs when they were small, as small as E.T.? Yes, she identified with the film's extraterrestrial. How often had she and Blanca been called aliens, ghosts, or freaks?

By the time the alien was taken for scientific studying, Blanca was quietly weeping and Jack had made his move. A reassuring arm to cradle her. That arm said that he understood her, that he felt her tears. That arm saw an opportunity to get closer to her sister.

Why hadn't Gareth done the same for Clara? She hadn't even looked at him during the film. She just sat there, hoping that he, too, would have a reassuring arm for her. But no such luck. Perhaps he didn't like her. It was a double date and she was just a convenient fourth. If he didn't like her that way, then why be afraid to look at him? She turned to him, her face coming close to his. Just to see if he thought her as ugly, and as repulsive, as the alien had been on screen.

He was weeping. Quiet tears fell down his cheeks and he quickly wiped them away. Why should the film upset him so much?

"I'm sorry. It's silly. Just so unfair," he said to Clara.

Gareth seemed like the kindest person Clara had ever met. She wanted to tell him secrets, just so he would know that it would be safe for him to tell her things, too.

"You don't like popcorn?" he asked her, changing the topic to cover his sensitivity.

"I do like popcorn."

"Why didn't you have any?"

"I was too shy," she answered honestly.

"Me, too. I'm shy, too."

In that moment both of them knew that the night would end in a kiss. An awkward kiss where Gareth would first ask permission and Clara would nod with a blush, averting her eyes. Of course, they would have to step away from Blanca and Jack, who both seemed so much more at ease with the game of flirtation.

In the foyer, people moved about, some exiting, some waiting for their friends making a last-minute visit to the washroom, some tossing unfinished drinks and candy wrappers. Clara and Blanca excused themselves.

"Just going up to say hi to Tristan in the projection booth." Jack said. Gareth thought he should probably also go but then who would wait for the girls?

It was then that he saw her. His ex-girlfriend, out on a date with someone new. She was laughing, a little too loudly, obviously for Gareth's benefit. She wanted him to know that she was happy, had moved on. Living well is the best revenge and all that.

When the twins came out her laughter stopped abruptly. She stood, staring openly.

"Take a picture, why don't you?" Blanca shouted over to her.

"She wasn't staring," the new boyfriend shouted back.

"It's okay," said Gareth. "Let's just go."

"It is not okay," informed Blanca. "We are not freaks!"

"I thought you two were in costume for the film," the ex-girlfriend replied.

Gareth went to grab Clara's hand, to move her away, but she was wringing her hands and biting her lip.

"Fuck off, you PIGmented waste of skin!" she yelled with such a sudden rage that Gareth was taken aback. Where did that come from? One moment, shy and sweet, the next it was as though her one-hundred-and-ten-pound frame could rip the head off a giant. Her whole body was tense. In a situation of fight or flight, it was clear which choice Clara would make.

"Yeah, you better look scared, because I'll put a hex on you, bitch." Clara made a *V* with her fingers, first pointing at her eyes and then to the ex-girlfriend's.

"It's okay, Clara. Against stupidity even the gods fight in vain," Blanca announced. Wasn't she the one who started all this?

Gareth's fantasy of the shy and awkward kiss evaporated. And yet, he found her, in her rage, all the more beautiful.

He took the hands of both the twins and led them to the projection booth, away from the stares of the lingering audience.

Gareth hung the painting back up on the wall. Art has a way of speaking, of revealing truths and of changing the course of history, often personal history.

"We should talk about that sometime soon," his mother said.

"What is there to say about it? I knew that the woman killed herself by drowning and I knew she was Clara and Blanca's mom. The rest is imagination." Gareth knew whatever dark secret his mother held on to could change his relationship to Clara and Blanca. He had ceased calling them the twins weeks ago.

"But why the eye?"

"Because they are the mirrors to the soul. Right? Or you could say, because they have a way of showing up in all my work. Gee, I wonder why?"

Elaine wondered how much her son might know. Certainly, the painting didn't give anything away, but it did speak of an uneasiness in a questioning soul. She had bits of the story, the bits that were missing in the painting and perhaps those bits, like missing puzzle pieces, could fill in the parts left out. She had heard things, fragments from Faye, as she awoke from her treatments. Usually the patient was quiet, worn out afterward, their body feeling like they had undergone a strenuous workout, every muscle tensed and released, worked over until only exhausted rest could remain. But the brain doesn't let go as easily as the large muscles of the thighs and arms. The brain releases in its own individual way. And Faye had spoken her release, her words painting a picture of her memories. An Impressionist painting, made up of seemingly different strokes so that the story only made sense when one stepped back far enough to see the whole picture. Elaine had done that. She stepped as far back as she dared until it became clear to her that Faye should never have been there at all. She had been put there to be kept quiet, out of the way, proclaimed as crazy so that her indicting words could not hold power.

"I think you like those girls and so you need to know this. Under that sweetness and that vulnerability there has to be some bottled-up rage. They are the product of rape."

Clara still could not understand why they were suddenly going off to Europe, running away, right when everything seemed to be happening for them here, at home. Their portfolios would surely get them an agent. They had booked a few gigs as Bleach, and even an A&R guy had tracked them down to talk about recording a demo tape. Why leave now? Why run away from opportunity?

Why run away from the sweetest love?

Clara had written those words in a new song she'd been working on, chording with her left hand on the piano, harmonizing with the right hand, and working out the song vocally. She knew it was silly. A first love. A young love. Perhaps nothing at all had happened, and surely, she would be over it quickly, but still it was an experience that was being whisked away from her before she had a chance to experience it. It was as though Clara had been invited to a feast and then told she couldn't eat.

Esther was impressing upon her, once again, that it was an opportunity like no other, that Bleach was a nascent start to other things. Better things. Never mind the career opportunities, it was a chance to see the world.

"Yeah right, see the world. You know we only have forty percent vision."

"All the more reason," Esther replied. "And with that forty percent you'll have a chance to see more of the world than anyone else in this town. What you lack in vision, you make up for in talent. Do not hide that in the dark. Go into the world. See the world. My time for adventure is over. It is your time now."

Blanca was nodding. It seemed that the plan had been devised behind Clara's back and she resented the fact that she never seemed to have a say when it came to their musical decisions. It was always Blanca and Esther. Wasn't she the one who wrote the majority of the music? Wasn't she the one who played the piano? Oh, it was easy for Blanca to agree to apprentice with an opera company in Berlin because she wasn't the composer, she wasn't the musician. For her it was all about vocals.

"Besides, you should spend some time in a proper city," Esther continued.

"Toronto is a proper city."

"No, only cities that have rivers running through them are proper cities. Paris, Budapest, Vienna, Berlin ..."

"What about the Don River?"

"Hardly a river! There are no cafés alongside it. No artists painting on its banks. No museums. There is a whole world beyond what you know and now you have a great chance to experience life, while you are young."

It was something Esther had hoped for them, even before Blanca had sat down with her and explained how they needed to go away, and soon. Blanca thought that Esther would be sad to think of them going, but she wanted it for them, had secretly been reaching out to her European friends, hoping that the twins would leave their home in order to grow and become what they were destined to be.

Clara could cry. She didn't want to leave but she knew that she couldn't stay behind, alone.

John saw the wrapped gift and wondered if he had forgotten something. It wasn't his birthday. Not an anniversary, was it? Jean had dates for everything.

"Don't you remember that was our first kiss?"

"That was the first time you stayed over."

"That was the first time we met at school."

"That was the first time you slid your hand under my skirt," which was, of course, weeks before that first kiss. Wow, it almost made him horny for her all over again, thinking of how he had explored and learned all about those other lips before he had kissed, or even touched, the usual lips.

He picked up the small, narrow gift. There were no hints what it was for. What was he forgetting?

He could hear her in the kitchen. It wasn't usual for her to cook, she was too career-minded, hoping to be a school principal within a couple of years! Yes, she was a woman with ambition, which was why they had become so used to TV dinners with their little compartments. Here is the meat and, over here, a serving of fake potatoes.

And here is the mystery vegetable in the smallest compartment.
What is it? Anemic peas with cubed, mushy carrots? She usually
gave him the Salisbury steak. How misleading was that? You'd expect
it to be steak, of sorts, and it turned out to be just a fancy way to say
hamburger! She almost always opted for a chicken pot pie. And then
jelly or pudding for dessert. It wasn't like the meals Hilda would
plan and make. Hearty, substantial, and everything from scratch.
But then, Hilda didn't have a job, so it was to be expected.

"Smells good in there. Are you cooking?"

Jean emerged with a big, shit-eating grin on her face. A
cat-who-ate-the-canary look of smug satisfaction.

"I am making you something special to celebrate! Homemade
spaghetti and meatballs. And I have chocolate cake for dessert."

"You made a chocolate cake?" John was incredulous.

"Don't be daft, John! I picked it up at the IGA. But freshly
baked, you know?"

"What's the occasion?"

Jean had wanted him to wait. To be sitting with her perfect
homemade dinner and a glass of wine and then, only then, the
opening of the gift, but she couldn't contain herself any longer.

"Oh, just open it!" she enthused. "You'll see."

He shook it, looked curious, and then slowly, gently removed
the tape from the bottom. He slipped it out of the wrapping paper.
It was a stick of sorts. Plastic. Blue on the bottom and white on the
top. And there was a little oval window. Inside the window there
were two lines. One quite purple. But the other line, the second,
more telling line, was a pale lavender.

Jean threw her arms around his neck. Kissed him with more
passion than she had shown him for a few months.

"Isn't it wonderful? We're going to be parents!"

* * *

From the deck one could see the horizon on three sides. When Siegfried squinted he could see where the land and sky met in a hazy line. Purple rock to the north and water to the south. On some days the blue of the sky and the water blended so that he could not tell where one started and the other ended. If he had been a boy growing up in such an open land, would he have wanted to bike or run to where the two met, land and sky? Or would the openness and vastness be as intimidating as it was to him now? Siegfried wondered how much the landscape moulded one's character. He looked at the infinite space before him, the flat fields, then the gentle roll of the hills, then horizon so far away and unattainable because, once you travelled toward it, it became farther and farther from your grasp.

When he didn't fixate on the distance, on the horizon, when he looked closer to where he stood, he saw Hilda's cherry trees and apple trees a little farther off. When he first arrived, it was cherry season. Sour, semi-sour, and a few sweet. The sweet ones never made it as far as the kitchen door — Jack and his friends would grab them as soon as they'd ripen and fill their mouths. What they didn't eat was consumed by birds. Starlings, finches, and fat, oversized robins that looked nothing at all like their smaller, more delicate European cousins. Just one more thing he would have to adjust to. The birds also ate the semi-sour ones, but the sour ones were, for the most part, spared. Hilda would pick first thing in the morning and breakfast would be hot coffee and cherry soup. Yes, she had found a balance of sorts, bringing her German recipes with her and adjusting them to the raw materials at hand. She was like the coyote she fed, adaptable. But when she arrived, she was so much younger than he. She came at an age when one is just starting to create and define life, while he was set in so many of his ways. He would have to balance his life, not so much by bringing the old world with him but by keeping one foot in each world. It was a conversation they would have to have.

He had one more thing to make his time with her possible. He would have to make her agree to an important promise. He would first tell her how much he loved her, ask if she felt the same and then, with that established, explain to her that she would have to make a difficult promise that she couldn't break. A promise she would remember, always. A promise that meant more to him than almost anything else. One that would give his life meaning. Meaning beyond the infinite and unattainable. A gesture filled with significance.

He sat on the top stair of the deck, the lawn spreading before him. The late-August sun had warmed the wood so that he could feel the heat through his light summer trousers. The sun was still to the east, but already powerful in the morning. How easy it would be for him to suggest that they sell this place, get a home together without the past of her first marriage colouring their surroundings. But as he sat breathing in the morning air, he started to see the land, the orchard, the lake, through her eyes, not his, and he knew that this land had indeed shaped her, moulded her into something that held both the mythology of Bad Oldesloe and the possibilities of the southern Ontario countryside.

Yes, he would go back and forth. He would find his home in her while in Canada and be home when he was in Germany. Perhaps, in time, she, too, would split her time between her past and her future and, in doing so, find balance and contentment in the present.

"Did you hear? I'm going to have a new brother or sister." Jack announced, plonking himself down beside Siegfried.

"No, I hadn't heard that. Your dad and the schoolteacher?" Siegfried carefully kept any joy or relief from entering his expression.

"Jean. Yes. Three months now."

"And how do you feel about this?"

"Okay. I mean, I'm off to university in a few weeks, so I'm pretty much out of the drama here," he laughed. "Hey, take a look at these and tell me what you think. They are for my friend Gareth. I'm going to get a coffee. Need a refill?"

Siegfried nodded and took the stack of pictures. He flipped through the first few — large but impressive paintings, especially for one so young. Then he saw that Jack had done a series of details, extreme close-ups of sections of his friend's paintings. This Siegfried found more interesting. The zooming in of every brush stroke, every thought expressed with a bit of paint. But it was the next few pictures that really caught his attention. Close-ups of miniature paintings. Eyes painted with such precision, such expression, such feeling. Who was this boy?

"You want cream in it, Siegfried?" Jack was yelling from the kitchen.

"*Ja, danke.* And bring a coffee up to your mother. She is sleeping in for a change!"

Jack would be a few more minutes now. Siegfried laid all the photos of miniatures along the deck so that he could look from one eye painting to the next. There it was, right in front of him.

What a morning! Jack's father was having another child. No chance of him coming back into Hilda's life now. And Jack's best friend was brilliant at painting eyes.

Siegfried looked out to the horizon. It no longer seemed quite as far away.

"I am here to see the eyes."

Elaine took in the ocularist for the first time. Not as tall as she had envisioned. Handsome, yes, but not in that healthy, boyish way that had become popular in North America. There was an all-American look that said, I am the same man as I was in high school; I am a boy-man. Like Robert Redford, who was so different from those earlier male stars, with his naughty smile, tousled blond hair, youthful, wiry body. There no longer seemed to be a large differential between the young and the mature, neither in Hollywood nor in real life. Life had become more relaxed. Clothing was casual wear. Khakis or jeans instead of proper trousers. Lacoste shirts with their little alligators and turned-over collars, which were no more than a dressed-up and expensive T-shirt, acceptable because, instead of slogans or pictures of rock bands, they were pastel colours, subdued and calm. And the alligator was discreet, although oh-so present. Even her husband had taken to wearing the alligator casual wear. Fridays, at work, were casual days for him now and he always went in soft denim jeans and his light pink or turquoise-blue Lacoste T-shirt. Happy to be out of his monkey suit, and well worth the two-dollar donation for some charity, tossed into an office money jar! But what kind of a lawyer dresses himself like a kid? If she had dressed like that at the psych ward when she was a nurse, what confusion there would have been! No, there were uniforms and accepted dress for a reason.

Here, before her, was a throwback to an earlier decade. A man in summer linen trousers, slightly wrinkled from his drive over in the heat, an open neck, proper button-down shirt, and a light cotton jacket thrown over the top. A bit warm for the jacket, but, perhaps, he was wearing it because he was visiting someone new. He was, likely, a man aware of first impressions.

"Ah, you must be Siegfried. I was wondering when I would meet you. Hilda has been hiding you away, keeping you to herself."

"No, not really," he answered, not understanding the New World familiarities.

"So, you want to look at eyes? Did Jack mention something to you about Tristan's blindness?"

Siegfried once again had no idea what this pleasant but strangely confusing woman was on about.

"The paintings," he stammered then gestured with his hands that they were small. Tiny, in fact.

"Oh! You mean Gareth's work? My mistake. I knew you were an optometrist or something so I assumed when Gareth said you were coming over that you wanted to look at Tristan's eyes!"

"No, I am an ocularist, not an optometrist. There is a huge difference. I wanted to see Gareth's paintings. He invited me."

"Yes, he is upstairs listening to music. He's a bit lost. It's almost September and we haven't heard from the college. So that is a stress."

Again, Siegfried was confused. Had Jack's friend not been over just a few days ago, railing on about his acceptance, talking about how he had burned the letter without so much as opening it? Something about gatekeepers and mediocrity. Something about selling out and being lost in a world of mass-produced objects. How cynical for someone so young! And yet, the more Gareth had spoken, the more convinced Siegfried had been that he had found a kindred spirit in the boy.

"Why?" Gareth had asked. "Why settle for passable? Why say something is nice or pretty, without seeing a deeper meaning in it? Yes, technique is important, and sure I could learn better technique at the college, but what about the other thing? That intangible thing? What about that?"

"Do you mean, the soul inside the work?" the ocularist had asked the boy.

"If that is what you want to call it. I prefer the word *essence*."

Siegfried had then glanced over at Jack, who was sitting uncomfortably with it all. Left out. He was staring at his plate, moving his last two potatoes lazily from one side to the other, one chasing the other, in a pointless cycle. Siegfried doubled his efforts to bring Jack back into the conversation.

"It is hard to know if that essence was something I saw because of your paintings or because of Jack's great ability as a photographer."

"Only one way to know. Come by my house and see my paintings! I think you might like my miniatures," Gareth had enthused, a charming smile spreading across his face.

Hilda smoothed any ruffled feathers of jealousy in her usual way, knowing that sometimes speaking to the stomach can distract one from the sensitivities of the ego.

"I would guess it is a bit of both. I am destined to be surrounded by talented men! Now who wants a big slice of raspberry torte? I have whipped some fresh cream for the top!"

The following day Siegfried was at Gareth's door, explaining to Elaine why he was there, uncomfortable that Gareth hadn't explained it to her better.

"I will be honest with you, madame. I believe that your son has what it takes to be an ocularist, and I am here to see his work and, if he wants, to mentor him."

"Mentor him?" Elaine was taken aback.

"Yes, it is a skill that is still passed down from one generation to the next …"

"You mean it's a trade? No, no, no. He is going to college or university. We saved since he was a baby for this … for him. He is going to get his degree."

"Is this your choice for him or his?"

Siegfried walked over to the painting above the fireplace. He had seen it in Jack's photos. How much more alive it was in person! The photos had flattened the surface of the painting and only now did Siegfried see how the waves almost rolled out of the canvas toward him, beckoning him to enter the image, maybe even to also walk into the water with the doomed woman. He went in closer, studied the work, the brush strokes, the colours, the subject matter.

"And what do you think of this painting?"

"I think it is beautiful," Elaine replied, "which is why I was hoping he would go on to study art at university."

"Yes, but how would you make it a better painting?"

Elaine wondered how Hilda could have possibly let go of her ex-husband, John, to go for such an abrupt and impolite man. Sure, he had a beautiful voice and he was almost handsome, definitely stylish, but what unusual manners! So straightforward. Did he not know how things were done here?

"It is perfect. Why would you want to change it?" Elaine crossed her arms, covering that part of her stomach that always twisted whenever it seemed to her that conflict was on its way.

"I wouldn't. It is you who thinks he needs to learn how to paint. Not I. I just think he just needs to paint more. Make mistakes, take risks, and do it again. Be critical enough to throw away what he doesn't like, and then try again. He is an artist. Now tell me, how is his glass-blowing?"

"He has never blown glass." Elaine was confused.

"Ah. So." Siegfried shrugged.

"What?"

"Well, that is something he could learn, then. Okay. I see."

"What do you see?"

"Perhaps a degree means much to you and you would like him to have that success. But, perhaps, something else in life means more to him. Perhaps a degree is not his ultimate calling? One cannot escape one's destiny. And his destiny was set the day he told his best friend that he should climb higher. He chose a path away from one you could possibly imagine for him that day."

Elaine had no idea why she was crying. In fact, she had no idea that she was crying until the ocularist handed her his handkerchief, with S.V.P. embroidered on its edges.

"*S'il vous plait?*" she asked.

"Siegfried von Pichler. Apparently Pichler is derived from the word *hills*. So, I guess I am Siegfried of the Hills. Although not so much here." He smiled.

She began blowing her nose into his perfect hankie, gobs of snot filling the pressed linen. But he didn't say anything. He just waited.

"He can never give his friend the sight he lost that day. But they were just boys. And boys climb trees ..." Elaine stammered.

"Yes. All over the world, boys climb trees."

"And Jack fell," she continued.

"Yes, Jack fell. He climbed too high. He was not meant to climb so high. But Gareth climbed that high and he did not fall. Now Jack is going to university and Gareth is floundering. Such is the irony of life," the ocularist said with a shrug.

"Yes," Elaine sobbed, "but what if I had been watching them? What if I had paid better attention? So that is twice in my life that I wasn't watching closely enough. The day Jack lost his eye and the day that woman," she pointed to the painting, "the day she walked into the lake."

"And can you save her now?"

"No!" Elaine stared at him, tears still rolling down her cheeks, cutting a path through the rouge blush until white rivers ran in lines through the light pink.

"And can Gareth make eyes for all the children who might lose one, from doing what boys do? Climb too high, play too hard or, worse, have an eye removed because of cancer."

Elaine collapsed in floods of tears and the ocularist opened his arms so that she could cry into the light cotton of his summer jacket. How awkward, a woman he had just met, clinging to him as a stream of salty tears poured from her. He patted the back of her head with an anemic there, there gesture. Was he too harsh in his approach because he saw in her boy an answer to his greatest desire and selfishly set out to acquire it so that he could pass his knowledge to the next generation? To have someone, even though he was not his own son, take up the history of his family and hold it safe? Foolishness, it was. A crazy notion that was already wreaking havoc in another person's home. Why could it not have been Jack who had the promise of the continuation? But Jack was the capturer of moments, caught in a second of stillness. He was compensating for an eye lost, using the camera's lens as an extension of himself. Besides, he was not enough of a perfectionist. Not exact enough. Not seeing in two eyes. But Elaine's youngest son was a boy who had an eye for detail, and could work in the smallest, most delicate strokes. How he wanted to settle this woman, so that he could see the miniatures Gareth had done, and then, only then, he would know for sure if what he sensed in his soul was real.

Elaine pulled away self-consciously with stammering apologies. She handed him back his wet, used hankie, which Siegfried reluctantly put back into his pocket. How embarrassing! But the tears had been a long time coming and once the dam was cracked there was no end to it. She knew that the dreams she had nursed for her son, as early as she had nursed him, were not the dreams that would be his reality. And yet, yet, in the arms of this stranger she felt comfort.

"You looked away. That is not a sin. It was an accident. Not a mistake," he consoled her.

"It was my fault."

"You know, it was not Gareth's fault that Jack climbed too high. It was Jack's choice, even if Gareth told him to climb higher. And it was that woman's choice to walk into the lake that day, even if you looked away. When we take the credit or the blame for another's actions, we diminish their choices."

Elaine turned away from the stranger. What if it hadn't been her fault, after all? What if she had no control over those events that day? What if she had no control over anything at all? She went to the foot of the stairs and called up to Gareth.

Siegfried looked through Gareth's work, studying each and every painting for what seemed an eternity. When he was quite satisfied, he closed Gareth's portfolio and sat back. His fingers pressed against one another as though in their own contemplation. Gareth waited, silently, unsure of what the ocularist was thinking. His heart fluttered and he knew that this could be his answer. To see the world, to live abroad. To be unlike anyone else and to be far,

far away from his childhood. How could he not accept the opportunity if it was offered to him?

"Couldn't he just learn to blow glass here to see if he even likes it? It seems a big step for someone who has never even worked with glass," Mark interrupted, entering the conversation, late to the party.

"Well, yes, but it would not help him to become an ocularist. We do not work in front of large furnaces. We do not design the glass in the same way. Besides, there is the making of the object, but then he will also have to learn how to measure and fit an eye. There is much more to it than blowing glass. It is as much a science as an art."

"Yes, which is why I don't understand why it isn't a university course. You would think that he would at least get a Bachelor of Science for studying this. I mean, you are working with people's eyes, so why isn't it a medical course at a university?" asked Mark, not wanting his son to live so far away.

Siegfried was not one to brag. He rarely spoke of his work, unless it was during a consultation, or if that rare person showed an interest and brought it up in conversation. But now he felt the need because somehow Gareth's parents had to know the value of his work and the importance of the offer.

"I am considered one of the very best ocularists in the world. I have devoted my life to it, as did my father, my grandfather, and his grandfather. It is more than a respectable choice for someone who is a talented artist. It is a chance to help people, on a deeply emotional and psychological level. You understand that, for most people, the loss of sight is one of the greatest of fears. But there is more to it when it is not just sight but also the whole eye is lost."

Siegfried remembered Jack when he was still young Johnny. How hopeful and frightened he was then. His weeping eye, his curiosity, his shy demeanour. How changed he was once he had an eye that fit him properly. An eye that suited him.

"I had to be very sensitive with Jack. When I gave him back an eye, I gave him another opportunity at life. Isn't that what you do, Mark, when you defend someone in court? And you, Elaine, don't you help those who are troubled? I think that Gareth, here, has both the temperament and the talent to do this. I think that, one day, he could be a great ocularist."

Elaine shifted her weight uncomfortably. She knew Siegfried was right.

"What do you think, Mom?" Gareth asked. "I think I would like to give it a shot. I think it's what I am supposed to do."

"Then do it." Elaine took her son's hand; it was no longer the little palm that fit inside of hers. Now her hand seemed lost in his.

Clara didn't know why Gareth wouldn't return her calls. The summer had passed. It was late August and all the time that they could have shared had passed them by. And now she was leaving.

She knew that Blanca and Jack had been having kissing sessions all summer. Clara didn't understand how Blanca could move on at this time. How could she walk away from Jack? How could she abandon Bleach? Or the big house? And Esther, what about her? How could she leave the lake where their mother slept for all eternity?

Of course, Clara never told Blanca how often she would go and speak with her mother. Sometimes the words were silent but spoken so loudly in her head that surely her mother could hear her. Other times they were simply whispered on the wind. It was her private secret. And it was the secret she wanted, for no logical reason, to share with Gareth. She wanted to tell him how she had a life apart from her twin. That it was okay for him to like just her because, even though they looked the same, they were so very different. She wanted him to see those differences but he had closed her off. Didn't return her calls.

"Hey, Clara!" It was Jack, calling down from the cliff above. The two must have climbed up, leaving her below on the boardwalk, the lake at her feet. She squinted up at them. They were waving, arms above their heads, as if they were stranded on an island and she was the rescue boat.

"We're going to drive you to the airport! Tristan and me. I asked him yesterday."

"Not Gareth?"

"No, haven't you heard? Gareth's going to Germany with Siegfried. So he's too busy getting ready to go!"

Clara turned her back on them. So she would not see him before she went. The door to first love was opened a crack and then nothing happened until the wind blew it shut again. Yet she knew it wasn't quite over. She, herself, was on her way to Germany. They would be in the same country! If it was meant to be, it would surely happen!

"Mama," she whispered, "let me be lucky in love and let me know the happiness that was denied to you."

"Clara!" Blanca called to her. "We gotta pack!"

"Coming!"

She looked out over the water one more time, then she pointed to her heart and said, "You'll be right here." She picked up a smooth stone and held it to her chest.

He wasn't sure if it was the sherry or the admission, but ever since he told Blanca the secret he began to get his strength back. It was as though God was draining him of life and now, because he had faced his great fear and given power to the words of it, the life was coming back into him. It was clear that he had a purpose. A calling. He had a second chance and reason to be alive. Perhaps he would retire from peddling his wares from his tricycle. Why give happy pills and mood-altering drugs to teens when he could give them a greater high? And what could be a greater high than Jesus? He would go every day to Victoria Park and he would stand on a wooden box, ready to talk to anyone about the mysterious power of God.

"Look, here I am, a dead man walking just weeks ago, and now as alive as live can be! I am the physical proof of a miracle!"

It wasn't too much to ask, to be given his life back. And a place at the table of the Father. After all, he had been forgiven, reborn. All his sins had been cleared, the slate was clean. It was a brand-new day! There was no point in even seeing his doctor now. He knew those tumours were shrinking away. He could feel it!

But why, when he had changed his ways, were his precious flowers leaving him? Going to Europe (Germany, of all places!), to sing that crazy music no one could understand? What was the purpose of that? Yes, they were his precious flowers and they belonged with him. They were no longer the manifestation of shame, but the blossoms of truth. The blessings he needed. They were his road to Damascus.

Suffer the little children so that they may come to me. That was why God created them so freaky-looking. They had the power of forgiveness. The awful acts of his son could only be forgiven by the two white angels his seed had produced. There was only one thing to do: bring his son to his knees and have him ask them for forgiveness.

Blanca refused to go upstairs. She had been very clear with her grandpa that if their uncle showed up it would be the last time he would ever see them. And now here he was, at the big house, expecting to say their goodbyes. Clara saw no problem with it, thought it would be the right thing to do, to say goodbye to someone who had cared for them and loved them. Weren't some of their best times at his house, watching TV and playing with their cousins?

"No. Clara. They were not good times."

"Yes, they were. What is wrong with you?"

Esther said it was fine for them to wait downstairs. She could go up and gather their things for them, but Blanca said they could wait. The boys could do it. Esther had already done more than enough. She had taken them for their passport photos, had done all the paperwork, applied for their work visas, and then paid for their fares. The whole process had taken time, but Esther went step by step, taking care of every detail.

"It is the start of your new lives. The lives you were meant to have. Who knows, maybe one day you will get to Buckingham Palace!"

"Well, at least we will know our manners because of you," Clara said, throwing her arms around the older woman.

"Hey, get yer little white heinies up here now and say yer goodbyes!"

It was Uncle Bob's voice. Clara started for the door, but when she saw Blanca shaking she stopped herself. What was going on? Her sister wasn't shaking from fear, she could see that. It was rage that made her body quake. Esther put her hand on Blanca's shoulder to steady her.

"You know something," Clara said.

"No. But you can't go up there. He's drunk and angry."

"But we should say goodbye."

"We already said goodbye to Grandpa," Blanca said.

"It is better if you just go. Goodbyes can be too hard. Let the boys get the last of the bags," Esther advised.

"Well, there's someone else I have to say goodbye to and you're not stopping me!"

Clara ran past her sister, past Esther, and out the apartment door. She didn't go upstairs — she ran straight to the lake. She took off her shoes so the cold of the water could kiss her feet. She let the wind from the lake blow through her hair, the white strands lifting away from her face. Then she reached out her arms as far as she could, so that her fingers were just over the shoreline. She stood like that for a very, very long time. But her mother did not rise up from the waters. She did not awaken from a dream. She did not come to her even when she sang out. And Clara finally knew that her mother had left her a long time ago.

Jack and Tristan had gathered up the last of the suitcases and were heading down the steep stairs from the attic apartment. The twins' grandfather had been helpful, but Uncle Bob was uncooperative and insulting. Even as they descended the stairs they could hear him, complaining and speaking in tones only possessed by the righteously drunk.

"I don't fucking get it! You make me come all the way out here to see them off and then they don't even come up and say goodbye. Been down there at the Jewess's place all this time. You know, I coulda drove them."

"Maybe you should go down and say goodbye to them, then."

"They can bloody well come upstairs. Lazy little bitches. Everything I've done for those ingrates!"

Bob helped himself to the sherry. Not very good, but that was all that there was. He wished the old man had gotten it into his head that vodka or tequila would be the magic cure instead of bloody cooking sherry. Fuck, the place stank! He hated going to his father's apartment. Hated the drive. Hated the nosy woman downstairs, always interfering, but, mostly, he hated seeing his father's emaciated body. It wasn't pity or empathy he felt. It was rage. Why did he have to drive over there to see his revolting, dying body?

"You got any percs or 'ludes?"

"No, I told ya. Not doing that now."

Outside the apartment, on the landing, Tristan paused. He couldn't help but listen in. This was real life, not dialogue, but still he thought that he might be able to use it in a script one day. He put his finger to his lips and crept back up the stairs to hear a little more.

"Little bitches. You know it's that woman downstairs with all her lies she's put in their heads. Like the Holocaust. Like that really happened. Oh, maybe a few hundred, a thousand even, but come on! Six million? That's bullshit. Just a way for them to whine to get more stuff. The whole fucking world bends over backward for that lot and they still control the banks. Now my daughters won't even say goodbye! Fuck her."

And there it was. Holy shit. Tristan turned to Jack who stood stock still in fear and stunned amazement. The next thing the boys heard was the horrific sound of a dying man crying. The wheezing sound of an old engine, fighting to turn over, losing its power. Then there was the sound of things breaking. Bob must have been in a rage, knocking things over, or throwing things. And yelling. More yelling.

"You have to make amends. You have to say something. Make this right," the old man pleaded.

"Fuck off! I didn't do anything. You know that. Your daughter was a whore. Mark my words, those girls will end up like her. Slutty and crazy like their mother!"

"You called them your daughters! You admitted it. You did it to Faye. You ruined her! You're a monster! I never wanted to believe it. Now she's dead and it's your fault. Monster!"

"Stop it, Dad. I'm warning you …"

"MONSTER!"

When Tristan heard the sharp sound of a slap, he could no longer stay listening on the other side of the door. He burst in to find the old man, crumpled in the corner, grabbing at his chest.

Bob turned quickly and told Tristan to get the hell out. But Tristan held his ground. Went over to the old man to help him up.

"We all need to just calm down," he said.

Bob turned around in anger. The past was the past and he'd more than made up for it! Wasn't he good to those ugly white things? He took them to see their crazy mother. Made the drive every other week! He had done his share of atonement, goddamn it! Every time he looked at them it was an act of atonement. Their pink rabbit eyes with the zombie-red centres. Their colourless flesh. Like they were something from *Night of the Living Dead*.

"Just go downstairs and take those ugly zombie girls away. Never want to see their freak faces again! Fuckin' freaks."

"They aren't ugly. Don't ever speak of them that way!" Tristan objected.

"Or what?" Bob challenged.

Bob grabbed Tristan, one hand at his throat and, with the other, he grabbed a dirty, discarded fork and held it at Tristan's eye.

"You didn't hear shit up here. Understand? The old man's a fucking liar. If anyone fucked Faye, it was him. He was always a perv. Selling drugs to kids so he could have his way with them."

Tristan would have closed his eye, but he didn't actually register the fork because he didn't see it. Didn't really understand the threat till much later. What he did see was Jack. Beautiful Jack, who moved with ease and grace as he burst into the room, reached over for the empty sherry bottle, lifted it high in the air and then brought it down, full force, on Bob's head. Bob was down. A pool of blood streaming from his nose and mouth.

Jack stood, in shock, not believing what he had done, his heart pounding in his chest. He stared at Tristan, at the dropped fork, at the unconscious man. He didn't see the old man rise. Didn't feel him take the bottle from his hand. Didn't know that he wiped it on his dirty sheets, then held it in his own hands, wrapping his fingers around the neck.

"Tell Esther there's been an accident and to call an ambulance. Then take the girls straight to the airport. Don't look back, ya hear me? Don't look back."

Tristan took Jack by the arm, led him past the suitcases and down the stairs.

"Do you think I've killed him?" he mumbled.

"I don't know. I don't think so. I think you just knocked him out. But what I do know is that you saved me. Oh my God, you were just like Hanna Schygulla in *The Marriage of Maria Braun!*"

And Tristan also knew that just like in the case of Maria Braun, it would be someone other than Jack who would be taking the blame. He never would tell Jack that the monster had held the fork to his bad eye and that it hadn't really been a threat to his sight. That would remain a secret that would stay a secret and, in time, as the story would be told one day, it would become his good eye that was threatened by a madman holding a fork. But the story would not, could not, be told for a very long time and then, when it was, it would have to be disguised as fiction.

The twins sat in the car. Clara in front with Tristan driving, and Blanca in the back seat beside Jack.

"What happened up there?" asked Clara.

"Your uncle was drunk. Got into an argument with your grandpa. He said just to take you to the airport," Tristan answered, his concentration on the road before him.

"But we should have said goodbye. We may not be back for months, maybe even longer!"

"Yeah, I thought so, too, but they really didn't want to see you. Said to just get you freaks out of there so that they'd never have to see your ugly faces again. I'm sorry. It's so cruel."

Blanca knew there was more. She reached across and held Jack's hand. It was shaking. She looked at him, caught his eye. They both knew that this would have to be their goodbye. Possibly forever.

As they drove, Clara realized that they were all looking ahead, eyes on the highway before them. There was no receding landscape. No view of what they were leaving. She knew they would never sit facing backward again.

*   *   *

Siegfried was packing his clothes, arranging his passport, money, and paperwork in his billfold. Everything was in order. He hated leaving Hilda, but there were so many things he had left unattended, so many clients to check up on. Besides, he knew he had to get Gareth to Hamburg before his parents changed their minds and convinced him to go to a community college for a year.

Everything was good, except that Hilda had refused to go with them. She said that she wanted to stay close to home in case Jack didn't adjust well to university. She said, in time, she would come and share their life between two countries. But not just yet. And so Siegfried got down on one knee and asked her to marry him and she promised that she would think about it.

Siegfried had reached into his small bag of toiletries, and drawn out a small green velvet pouch and handed it to her. Hilda carefully loosened the strings and reached in to find a jewellery box. She pushed open the top, and found, not a ring as she had expected, but the match to the eye that Jack had stolen.

"This is the other one. I made eyes every year, you know, just in case," he said, laughing, "but I stopped the year I met you because, if I ever went blind, I would want the eyes I had the day you walked back into my life. That was the greatest thing that ever happened to me. If ever I were to lose my eyes, I wouldn't want to lose the sight of you. So I hope I caught that when I made these. Ask Jack for the other one. He has it in his dark-room. Put them under your pillow every night so that you dream of me when I am away. That way, you will not forget me."

Hilda took the eye in its box and placed it beneath her pillow. What a strange man she had fallen in love with. And yet, nothing could have seemed more romantic to her.

"I will get the other one from Jack. But, you know, I still

expect a ring. Not expensive, but it has to be gold. Cheap metals turn my fingers green."

"Of course. And I will not expect an answer until I return with a ring. A gold one."

When Jack returned from the airport he was in no mood to discuss eyes and their whereabouts but promised his mother that he would retrieve the match. He wanted only to speak with Siegfried, alone, before he flew off the following day.

Siegfried noticed that he was wearing a younger eye. An eye that still fit comfortably, but was not as hard as the last one he'd made him. It was the eye of the open-hearted Jack he was wearing. Not the show-off Bowie eye. Not the confident in-control eye, but the eye of the more sensitive young man.

"You told me to destroy the Jabberwock."

"Oh yes. But that is a metaphor. The Jabberwock represents our greatest fear. The monster we must all face. Sometimes it is the monster within and sometimes it is an external obstacle."

"But I did face the monster. A real monster. And I destroyed him. And the girls still left and I will probably never see them again. I thought that if I killed the Jabberwock, they would love me."

"You thought it was about love?"

"Yes," replied a very sad Jack.

"And you have killed the Jabberwock?" Siegfried had no idea what Jack was on about. He knew nothing of evil uncles and ogre grandfathers. All he knew was that Jack had changed enough that he had the courage to wear his most vulnerable eye.

"*Und schlugst Du ja den Jammerwoch? Umarme mich, mien Böhm'sches Kind!*"

"You know I don't speak German," Jack replied.

Siegfried opened his arms and embraced Jack.

"I said come to my arm, my beamish boy!" Siegfried laughed.

"I don't know what happened or what you did. I may never know. But I do know that you have changed somehow today. I also know that for you, it was never about love. I never promised you love when I gave you that first eye. I promised you courage."

"But I wanted love."

"No, you wanted courage. And that is what you got. Now go and find that other eye for your mother. It is very important that she has both eyes before I leave."

The house was strangely quiet for the first time in Hilda's experience. No sounds and, more poignantly, no anticipated sounds. Only her own footsteps, her own breathing, her own rustling of the newspaper as she gazed from the kitchen window past the deck. The leaves were just starting to turn, their outer ruffles picking up the slightest tinge of orange and red. This was her favourite time, when the sun still beat hard upon the earth, the air held the slightest chill, the leaves were still on the trees but turning a range of fire colours, and her garden was in its highest bloom. Indeed, her garden always was at its height just as others were harvesting their last shares. There were still tomatoes and basil. The root vegetables were still in abundance and the wildflowers she had planted, poppies and daisies mostly, were blooming abundantly between the veggies. And all around it was a border of marigolds. Not that they did much good because the aphids still made their way in and gobbled here and there. Then, of course, there were also the rabbits, both the wild and the escaped ones, nibbling at anything green. Some deer from time to time with their spotted fawn visited and feasted. Squirrels, too, helped themselves. Yes, she was feeding them all! Hilda never minded. She was good about sharing.

She knew that the monarchs were staging and readying themselves for the long migration to Mexico. That the geese would be flying endlessly in their *V*-formation. And that very soon the mornings would bring a layer of magical frost, a glimmering coating on the green, that would melt away by the warmth of the sun touching the earth with a mere stroke.

It was a difficult choice. To be alone in the big old house or to be with Siegfried in Hamburg for the autumn.

"Why can you not train him here?" she had asked him.

Siegfried just shook his head. They both knew better. He had all his materials and equipment there. Everything needed to train the young man was in his workroom. Besides, he had clients waiting for him. There was unfinished business. He had jumped a plane quickly for the sake of love at the start of summer, but he had left so much unfinished there in Germany. A large old apartment in Hamburg, the oculary, his workroom and all his equipment. They were all waiting for him as she had once waited for him.

It was only in the quiet of the house and in the view to the garden that she realized how great was her preference for the autumn season and how her late-blossoming garden was a reflection of her life. Only now did she feel full, confident, and strong. Strong enough to live alone. Strong enough to not fear the next day. Strong enough to know that being away from her love did not mean that love didn't exist.

On their last night together, Siegfried held her close as they slept. She could still feel the imprint of his body upon hers, even while he was away. Perhaps this was why her alone time was equally enjoyable. Missing him was as sweet as having him.

Next week would be Thanksgiving and she would cook a feast. Jack would be home, and Margaret and Elizabeth with their significant others. Margaret seemed quite serious about this one and so he would be shown off, first at her dinner on the Sunday and then, doing it all over again, turkey, potatoes, and all, at their father's the next day. If Jean could cook, that is. So full and uncomfortable carrying those twins in her belly. Hilda wished that they could move beyond the acrimony. Eventually share grandchildren as friends and not have to subject the kids to two sets of holiday meals. But the last time she tried to speak in a civil manner to John, he complained about his small house and suggested that they come to an arrangement so that he could have the old farmhouse back again.

"And who would feed the coyotes?" she had asked him. "You know, they come quite close now. They are fearless. You wouldn't want your new little babies to be carried away as a snack!"

She hadn't seen him since but there was an uneasy feeling that he might come after the house, demanding half of it now that he had twins on the way and their children were now grown. How unfair when her inheritance had paid for most of it.

Hilda wondered what Siegfried was doing right that moment. It would be six hours later there, pretty much time for coffee and cakes. She wondered if he was introducing Gareth to the things he had shown Jack once. Opening his eyes to an older world with its tastes, cultures, and slightly different customs.

There was nobody there to see her and so, instead of a healthy breakfast, she helped herself to the last thin slice of pound cake. Threw a few raspberries on top, just to make it healthy, and then doused it all in cream. She grabbed her coffee and sat in the cool air of the morning. It was fine. After all, it was coffee and cake time in Germany and her heart was there!

Beyond the garden she heard a rustle. The long grass moved and there he was, her coyote friend. With a fat brown bunny in his jaws.

Gareth strangely felt as though he had found his home. Sure, the language was a challenge and he often looked out of place but, still, as he walked around the city, he somehow felt that he belonged. He loved the trains through the town, the business on the streets, the food, the clubs, the shops! He liked going from store to store to buy what he needed, instead of just going into one big superstore.

And, of course, there was the freedom. Eighteen years old, away from home, in another country, and making a little money, too! How much better was that than being in a dorm somewhere, attending classes, competing with other students.

His day was set up in a very organized way. After a breakfast, usually consisting of coffee, fresh bread or rolls with unsalted butter, cheese, a boiled egg or a few slices of meat, and a small, three-ounce glass of juice, he was to go into the oculary to watch and learn.

"You must train your breath. You have the ability with your eyes to capture the likeness of another's eye, but it's no good unless you work on your breath control. You blow too fast and hard."

"Well, maybe I can make the eyes faster, then. Up our productivity to two or three a day."

"Fast is not the desired outcome. Perfect is. You cannot do the part you like, fixing the colours and detailing the eye, if you cannot blow an orb worth painting."

As long as Gareth put in a satisfactory morning he had his afternoon off to paint and explore. Afternoons usually started at two o'clock, after the main meal of the day. That was one of the biggest changes for Gareth, eating so much at the start of the day and then having not much more than a snack in the evening. Siegfried kept telling him how much healthier it was for him, but Gareth just felt like he spent the first three-quarters of the day stretching out his belly, only to leave it empty at bedtime.

In the evenings Siegfried would write letters or read a book. He'd constantly encourage Gareth to go out, suggesting that he befriend Sabine next door. Gareth usually refused to go out, preferring to spend his time, late into the night, painting. He worked on smaller canvases as he didn't have a garage or a big workspace. But the room he was given for painting was beautiful, with large windows looking onto *Glockenblumenstraße*. It had white walls, hardwood floors, and high ceilings. Off his studio was his bedroom.

It was small, with a three-quarter-sized bed, something between a single and a double. But it was fine. The mattress was firm and the duvet was overstuffed with feathers. Gareth was happy.

"Why do the Germans just string words together? I mean, why not have an adjective separate to the word? Like the street your apartment is on. It's like three words strung together as one word. You could have the word *street* by itself, but no, you have to just keep adding words onto words till they are too big to pronounce. What does it mean, anyhow?"

"Bellflower Street. It isn't so hard. I think you will take a German class every day, as well, now. Just so that you get used to stringing words together. If you want to take over this business one day you will have to learn German."

There it was. An opportunity to move from an apprenticeship to a business, without having to build it up from scratch. Gareth often wondered why the ocularist was helping him. Why he had chosen him. He had not been in the world of oculary long enough to understand the custom of passing on the art of the glass eye from one generation to the next.

"What about my painting, though?"

"You will do both. And you will do both well. Tomorrow I have a friend coming from Berlin. A very nice woman who likes to wear leather from head to toe, but do not let that influence your judgment of her. She has a gallery in Berlin, so she will look at your work, yes? I made an eye for her mother years ago. A very nice brown eye with light green flecks and a darker, almost black, rim around the iris. That does not matter. What matters is that you concentrate on your morning work. Today you will learn how to breathe properly. Come, lie down on the floor and we will do some breathing exercises until you have better control. Think of yourself as a flute player. A flutist doesn't blow. The passage of air is controlled. It is all about control."

"Anyone ever call you a control freak, Siegfried?"

"Yes, all the time. Thank you!" He laughed.

Yes, he would have been happy to have had a son like Gareth. But Gareth had a father already. It was Jack who needed the love. He would have to continue to make Jack a priority even as his affection for Gareth grew.

Gareth was eager to have a perfect orb in his hand, hot glass he could turn over and over, shaping it, manipulating it, and then that part that seemed like magic to him. The colouring of the iris and pupil with so many colours of hot, temperamental glass. He lay down on the floor, pressed the small of his back into the hardwood beneath him, and began to inhale on Siegfried's slow count to ten, feeling the movement of his diaphragm as the air filled him to capacity. He then held the breath for another count of ten and exhaled as slowly as he could, through his mouth, with his lips open and his teeth closed, making a hissing sound for a count of thirty more seconds.

"Good. We will do that three more times. Oh, and I think we should go home for Thanksgiving. I have so much to be thankful for."

"Really? Home already?"

"Yes. Don't you miss it?"

"Are you kidding? I'll be on wurst withdrawal if I go back. I mean, it's sausage everywhere here. I think I am addicted to currywurst."

"Yes, well, it is the thing I miss most when I am in Canada. And also the pretzels. When you finish breathing I think we should go and get some."

"You know, sometimes I think you just brought me here to eat with you because you're lonely and hungry all the time."

"Maybe it is you who are lonely here, homesick, yes? If you do not take over the business I will sell it and you can start your own in Canada, but you will have to go toe to toe with the people who think that plastic is better. One day, we will go to East Germany, maybe, and you will see Lauscha, the town I came from, where everyone makes things from glass. It is where the Christmas-tree decoration originated. It is the most beautiful village in the world. Filled with sparkling, coloured glass. Like magic. Now let's breathe some more. On a count of ten …"

But all Gareth could think about was going to Berlin. Having an art show in a gallery. And maybe, just maybe, finding the twins, Clara and Blanca. He finally felt ready to see them again.

"Siegfried, when you think you love someone, do you think you have to be honest with them all the time?"

"Well, I think you cannot lie. But I also think it is fine to have your own secrets. Love requires a little mystery."

Gareth started his slow inhale. This time his exhale would be perfect, slow and steady, like a whistling kettle, or the slow telling of a deeply rooted secret.

Jack threw his knapsack onto the kitchen table and plonked himself on the futon. It was their sofa by day and his bed at night while Tristan had the small room, with a double bed, off the kitchen. It was a bit cramped but they had everything they needed: two closets, a desk, a galley kitchen. It was fine. Most of the time they were out, anyhow. The apartment was just a place to sleep. They didn't live just there, they lived in all of Toronto.

Their apartment was over an Italian coffee shop on St. Clair Avenue, near Dufferin Street. There was a deck off the back bedroom and, as long as the weather was decent, Tristan and Jack could sit outside to drink their morning coffee. There were some wooden stairs off the deck that took them to the back, where Tristan had his rusty Ford Pinto parked. It was needed for getting up to York University. Jack had suggested a closer apartment, but Tristan waved him off, saying that they needed the experience of living in the city. And so, St. Clair West, in Corso Italia, it was, and Jack soon became a regular in the downstairs coffee shop, spending hours nursing one cup as he wrote and studied. It was someplace where he could be surrounded by people and be completely alone at the same time. He never imagined that he would feel more solitary in a busy city than he ever did in the country.

It was the noise he liked. The constant hum. When he slept he could hear the streetcars throughout most of the night and, although it was very different from sleeping in his bed in the country, he was soothed by the sound of the metal on the tracks. It was a comfort; it drowned out his thoughts.

He had killed a man. In a split-second decision he had robbed a woman of her husband and teen boys of their father. He had changed their fate when he'd taken a life. He tried and tried to drown out the voice in his head that reminded him of this act, but the more he did, the louder the voice became.

"Do you think I should go to the police and confess?" he asked Tristan.

"Why? He was a horrible man."

"Yes, but that still doesn't give me the right. For fuck's sake, Trist, I killed a man."

"No, you saved a man. What would you prefer? That he killed me and you let him live? Would that have been better?"

"No. But still, it's wrong."

"What else could you have done? He was strangling me, I couldn't breathe. And he had a fork at my eye! Besides, you didn't kill him, he died later. Who knows what happened when we left. The old man said he did it. Went temporarily crazy and beat on him. Did you not see that in the paper?"

Jack had wanted to believe Tristan, but what if that wasn't quite the truth? How would he ever make amends?

"Trist? I don't think that fashion photography is for me. It seems so superficial."

"Well, yeah, of course, it is. It's fashion, not brain surgery."

"I think I have to do something else with my life. Make a difference."

At night, when he couldn't sleep, Jack would see Bob's face looking down at him. He would smile and a trickle of blood would fall from his mouth, drop by drop, onto Jack's head, like water torture, until he would awaken to find comfort in the streetlights shining through his window and the sound of the streetcars rolling along.

It was only at those times that he could reassure himself that he was not an evil young man, that he had acted on impulse to save his friend from a man capable of anything. A man who had raped his own sister, a man who caused his sister to kill herself, a man who was beating up his own father and who was about to kill his best friend.

It was at those times that he would imagine what would have happened if he had not acted. How life would be if Tristan was strangled instead. Or if the twins' uncle had stabbed Tristan's eye, blinding him. It was only late at night that he knew how much Tristan meant to him. Could he imagine a world without him? It was only the thought of Tristan that gave him peace.

Hilda had invited Elaine, Mark, and Tristan even before she knew that Gareth and Siegfried were returning for Thanksgiving. Elaine was delighted by the invitation. She was so busy studying her courses to become a therapist that she hadn't even thought about a Thanksgiving dinner.

Jack would be home, and the girls, so the house would be full, with people everywhere. How strange, after the quiet, to have a full and rowdy household. Strange and welcome. She treasured both the quiet time and the social gatherings. *Balance*, she thought. It was all about balance. Something Jack still had to learn. Last week he had called in despair, but the week before he had been excited and happy. The peaks were high with him, and the valleys were low.

"I think I need more from life. Fashion photography is fun, but who cares? Maybe I should add some journalism or writing courses the next semester. I was always good in English class," he had told her.

"You just need a focus," Hilda had responded, not sure what to say.

"I need more than focus, Mom. I need a challenge!"

"And how is rooming with Tristan?" Hilda had asked, thinking how odd it was that they were now the best of friends while Gareth was away with her lover in Hamburg.

"It's great, Mom. I love living with him. Tristan's the best."

"He is respectful? Lets you study?"

"He's the best, Mom. He's coming for Thanksgiving, right?"

"Yes, the whole family. And Gareth is coming home, too. And Siegfried, as well, so it will be a full house!"

She was pulling out all the stops. Three different tortes for dessert. After all the years she had spent in Canada, she still didn't understand the allure of pumpkin pie. Why turn a vegetable into a treat? Pumpkins, she found, were best when pickled, not served sugary-sweet with whipped cream. She loved Thanksgiving and its customs, but she hated pumpkin pie with every fibre of her soul. Every year she overcompensated with wonderful desserts and yet, still, they all asked for pumpkin pie. Well, this year her kids could enjoy pumpkin pie the next day at their father's house. Surely Jean could make a pie out of that canned pumpkin goop and an empty frozen pie shell. No, she would probably buy a premade one at the grocery store. *Die Slacklinerin!*

Hilda knew that she should cut Jean some slack. Jean was close to her forty weeks of gestation and as big as a barn. Those twins must be huge in her belly. Hilda had seen her shopping a few days earlier. Jean was in full waddle, holding on to the cart for support, but still wearing that perky, optimistic expression. Damn her! Hilda could easily wish her well now, offer her an outstretched hand of goodwill, if it weren't for that perky, happy face of hers. If only her face could wear that usual haggard look of pregnancy, then Hilda could make the effort. But that pretty, perky, pasty, pesky face just wouldn't allow her to do it. So Hilda slipped out of view and headed down the fresh fruit and vegetable aisle. No chance of Jean finding her there!

At the checkout, though, there was no escape. Jean saw her and politely waved. Hilda nodded back and smiled tersely. That was what it all came down to in the end. This woman, two check-out lanes over, was carrying half-siblings to her own children. The two women had shared the intimacies of the same man, both making a domestic life with him, and all they could pretend to share in public was a polite wave and a nod. Hilda smiled to herself, thinking of how they knew the same smell of the same man's sweat, the same noise he made when he orgasmed, the same feel of the same cock and yet they behaved as though they barely knew each other at all. They probably knew more about each other's intimacies than anyone else on earth! They could have a coffee and laugh about the face he made while he pumped away. Or amuse each other imitating that growly sound that rattled in his throat when he came. They could joke about how his socks never matched his clothes or how he might wear a brown belt with black shoes. But, no. They had both carried his children in their bellies and yet something dictated that they be cool to each other. *Why?* Hilda thought. *I have a man I love and I no longer want John. So why should I have any resentment at all? Because she won and I lost. It is only my pride.*

Hilda had hurried to the door before her and kept it open so that she didn't have to struggle too much. Jean walked past barely saying a thank-you.

"Jean!" Hilda had called out after her. "How much longer?"

"Any time now," she'd replied. "Looks like boys, from the ultrasound."

"Twins! Congratulations."

"Thanks. John is happy. Glad to finally have boys he can play catch with!"

What had she meant by that? That Jack was soft somehow? That he was less of a boy because of his eye? Because he'd spent his childhood being careful, protecting his good eye, just in case? And now he wanted to be a photojournalist, putting himself into dangerous situations for his work. He had said that was his intention. To cover stories, worldwide, wherever history was being made. And all Hilda could think was that he was overcompensating. Trying to prove his manliness to his father while shrugging off her overprotectiveness.

Hilda glanced at a local paper, thrown on the top of the grocery bag. How much happier she would be if Jack would choose to stay closer to home to cover the local stories about town. She picked up the flimsy paper and looked at the headline.

MAN ACCUSED OF MURDER DEAD OF PANCREATIC CANCER.

Jack insisted on going to Esther's the day before Thanksgiving and convinced Tristan that it was a good idea, telling him that it would rid him of his nightmares and help him move forward. He knew the reasons he gave were filled with guile, but hadn't Tristan been guileful about the events of that day? Hadn't he made the threat that day seem greater, the actions more justified than they really were? The only way for him to understand the craziness of that day was to go back.

His heart pounded as they pulled into the drive and stopped the car. The place seemed strangely quiet, deserted. It seemed that all the tenants had vacated and the big house was like an empty film set. The scenes were shot, the crew had moved on, and nothing of the performance was left except what was to be edited together at the hands of someone who wasn't even there. Jack was desperate for some clarity. He needed to know that Bob was still alive when he was taken from the house in the ambulance, but there was nobody there to ask.

"It's for sale," Tristan announced. "Look, there's a FOR SALE sign."

"Write down the number."

Jack walked the edge of the property. He could smell the familiar freshwater and seaweed scent wafting from the nearby lake. The air was chilled, the sun was hot; it seemed like a perfectly normal, beautiful autumn day. Except that the house itself knew things. It held secrets.

Later, at Tristan's house, they called the real estate broker. A chirpy voice answered with that happy, eager tone of someone hoping to make a commission.

"Yes, a beautiful house! Yes, lots of character. Original details and wood. The downstairs apartment is gorgeous. Upstairs needs some work. But you could make it a single dwelling again and it would be quite the estate!"

"Yes," Tristan replied, putting on his most mature voice, "and, of course, I am not superstitious at all, so I'm not worried about the rumours. I mean, if it means I can get a better price, then bring them on!" He laughed with the most rich-real-estate-tycoon laugh he could fabricate, something between a chuckle and a clenched, mouthed snort sound. "I mean, I don't care if someone was murdered there if it means a quick and profitable transaction!"

The woman laughed on the other end of the line. Now here was a client she could work with!

"Oh, he wasn't murdered there, he died later in the hospital, so no worries! It was a domestic dispute. Father and son. Both drunk on cooking sherry! Imagine, cooking sherry! Not great tenants, I'll admit. But they are gone now, so if you do want to rent it out, we can help you to get better tenants! So many uses for that building, though. Lots of potential!"

"Tell me something, the other tenants are all completely gone, right? Wouldn't it be better for resale if it were tenanted? You know, cap rates and all."

Jack watched his friend, gobsmacked. Cap rates? Come on! Where did he learn to assume another persona so well? Ah, yes! Thousands of hours of watching films, over and over again, studying them, and putting them to memory. Every great line ever uttered, Tristan knew and could recite at whim. Parties would often end with Tristan in the kitchen, tossing off lines from the movies the guests would shout out.

He winked a cocky response back to Jack. He was enjoying himself, going in for the kill.

"Well, we just thought that it would be better to sell it empty. Not all the tenants were great. A fresh start for a new owner, right?" the agent qualified.

"Right. But I did make the acquaintance of the woman downstairs some years ago. Esther, was it? And she seemed like she would be a good tenant. I would like to invite her back. Well, you know, if I like it enough to buy it."

"Unfortunately she moved away. It was very sudden. Went to Sweden. Or was it Switzerland? One of those countries that start with an *S*. But there are always other good tenants. So, can we book you in this weekend?"

"Ah, no. That won't be necessary," Tristan replied and quickly hung up.

So that was that, then. Esther and her husband moved on and the old man was dead.

"Only you and I know what really happened that day, and it goes to the grave with us, Jack. Nothing was your fault. You acted in self-defence. Now let's never speak of that day again. Promise me."

Jack knew that he had to promise Tristan. He had been the one who'd introduced him to cameras. He was the one who'd talked him through his parents' divorce. He had introduced him to his new life in Toronto. Two years older and so much wiser. But still. Still. He had killed a man.

Jack knew that he, too, would also have to leave. Travel to Europe and beyond to find the places where change was about to happen. Take photos of Serbians after the death of Tito. Photograph the after-effects of Mount St. Helens. Capture moments of history in the making and tell stories through a still image. Use his other eye, his Cyclops eye, as an extension of himself to illuminate the events of the day. He was alive in a time that would one day be history and he knew that his purpose was to make a tangible record for others to see.

"Whatever happened that day dies with us. We don't really know what happened after we left. The old man could very well have beaten him to death after we left, just like the paper said. It was all craziness that day. So now let's just move on and embrace life."

Yes, Jack thought, *let's embrace life. Wherever there is trouble, that is where I will be. I will tell them all at Thanksgiving that Cyclops and I will be leaving. Leaving any shadows lurking in our past so that we can embrace life together.*

"Promise?"

"Yeah, Trist, I promise."

Tristan could never tell him what he felt for him that moment. How he felt so in love with him, his hero, that the death, the old man, and even the albinos faded into the distance of his memory of that moment. The drive to the airport had been a silent one, the twins not really knowing what had happened. Tristan drove, eyes on the road, heart pounding in his chest. Not because of the violence, but because all he could think was that the man he had secretly loved for years had rushed in to save him. That was the real secret that Tristan swore he would take to his grave.

It was a huge table, taken from a church rectory, with heavy, hand-carved legs and a dark walnut finish. And wide across. Wide enough for all the dishes of meat and vegetables and sauces and bread baskets. It filled the whole room. And all around it were chairs. Ten that matched and then two others taken from the kitchen table.

The table was a gift from Siegfried. Not really understanding the meaning of Thanksgiving, he thought it was important to give a gift. He wanted something to do with feasting but also something beautiful. So when he saw the table in a Port Hope antique store he bought it on the spot, providing that they could deliver it before the Thanksgiving meal.

"But that's tomorrow!" the shop owner had replied. He had an English accent, but Siegfried could detect a bit of a cockney tone hidden under the posher accent the man had created for himself.

"Yes, and I did not try to talk you down in price, so if you want to make a sale you must see it is delivered sometime today. Or tomorrow morning. You can buy a big, fat turkey with all the money I just gave you."

"And you can put a huge turkey on that big table," he had countered.

"Well, you know, I am from Germany so I think we will be eating goose, instead. Not that we have Thanksgiving in Germany."

"Nor us in England. But it's a nice custom. Family all together. Fall harvest and all that."

The table was delivered, much to Hilda's delight. Things were moved out of the way and Hilda clapped her hands with joy as it was set up, filling the entire room. Every year, no matter where her children were, no matter if Siegfried was in Hamburg, wherever they were scattered, they would all return here, to this table, at Thanksgiving and Christmas. And she would stay with Siegfried, maybe even marry him, and together they could be an anchor on holidays for the children who roamed the world. There would always be the rectory table to return to. Thank *Gott*, finally she could rid herself of the knotty pine table and the matching bench.

She would give it to John and his schoolteacher as a goodwill gesture. Just to get it out of the house.

They all sat down, the food came out, and they went around the table, each guest saying something of gratitude.

"Your turn, Siegfried," Margaret said. She had just been grateful for her fiancé and their decision to have a child.

"This will sound very strange indeed," Siegfried began, "but what I am grateful for is also something that was lost to someone else, so we must acknowledge both. I am grateful that Jack fell from the apple tree ..."

NINE

GARETH SAT IN THE CLUB, sipping a *bier*, waiting for the opening act. That is what he was there for. He didn't care about *Die Toten Hosen*, it was the first act that interested him. An act that had been getting press across Germany. They had just finished a tour of Europe and were back home, in Berlin.

Und nun freut sich der Underground-Club, eine unserer Lieblings-Acts BLEACH anzukündigen. Man kann sie auch mit Punk Opera spielen sehen, wo sie nächsten Monat eine sehr interessante Interpretation von Carmen machen werden. Lass es uns für Bleach aufgeben.

Gareth had learned enough German over the past six years to be able to read a newspaper and understand most of what was written. He had read somewhere that the twins were singing with an opera company, but had rekindled Bleach and were performing together again onstage. Gareth hadn't seen them in the whole time he had been in Hamburg. He had been working and learning from Siegfried, painting in his spare time, and taking German lessons. He had made only one trip to Berlin in all that time, had gone into the theatre where the avant-garde opera company performed, and left the twins a note. As he heard nothing back from them, he let it drop, assuming that they had all moved on. So, he worked hard. Hard enough to be left for weeks at a time to run the oculary on his own. Siegfried was going to Canada more and more often to be with Hilda, and so the apartment and the business felt more like his than Siegfried's. Even the clients had begun to ask for him and wanted his opinion. Hilda came once a year and stayed only three or four weeks, but Siegfried insisted that the apartment was hers and that it should be kept nice and neat at all times out of respect for her. It was already decided how he would arrange his business. The apartment would stay his and Hilda's, now that they were married, and the business, including all the instruments and equipment as well as the clients, would be passed to Gareth when the time came. Gareth would pay rent on the apartment and the office once the business passed to him. At that time he would have all the profits, but, until then, he would live there for free and be paid a modest salary. Gareth was very happy with the arrangement. Of course, the frequent visits from his neighbour Sabine didn't hurt, either.

Gareth watched as the spotlight came up on the shallow stage. Two women, no longer girls, walked out, dressed head to toe in white. Sheaths around their bodies, wrapping tightly across their chests and falling away from the waist to their ankles. On their feet were white boots, with pointed toes and copper studs running up the legs. Their hair was loose, in white cascading waves, and the only makeup they wore was a stain of matte red on their full lips. The light hit their eyes, turning them from the lightest blue to violet pink. Gareth inhaled slowly, counted to ten, held his breath, and only exhaled as they started to sing.

He assumed that it was Clara playing piano while Blanca stared out, hitting her tambour. The only big difference now was that they finally had their backup band. All male. All black. All excellent musicians.

The talking stopped. The club was quiet. People were listening. And so was Gareth.

"May I sit here?" a strikingly beautiful woman asked him. She seemed about thirty-five, well dressed in that too-hip-it-hurts German way. A small stud in her nose, another piercing through her upper lip. Gareth imagined that there may be a few tattoos on her body and possibly more piercings elsewhere, out of sight. Her dark hair, almost a jet black, was shorn close on one side and then layered so that it fell long, almost to her waist, on the other side, with a thick fringe hitting just above her arched eyebrows, emphasizing her sharp blue eyes. Ice blue, Gareth noted, with a shot of steel grey around the iris. Intense eyes, cool eyes, direct eyes.

"You are alone, yes?"

"Yes, I am alone," Gareth replied. *Alone in a faraway land where nobody really knows me. I have created myself anew and now here I am, in Berlin, alone. Watching two women onstage whom I met when I was six years old.*

There are few parts of us that never leave us. Our red blood cells renew daily. Our liver renews, our skeletal frame is constantly renewing so that it is completely changed every ten years. Skin, hair, nails, they all renew so that there is no constancy with any of them. But the brain and the heart renew very slowly so that they are almost the same, changing very little throughout our lives. But then, there is the lens of the eye, which is with us from start to finish. It is the one part of our body that is never replaced or updated. After all this time, with one look of his unchanging eyes, the girls were back in his heart and would be ever present in his loyal, little-changed mind.

"They are very good," the woman stated. "When did you hear of them?"

"I just came in for a beer. I guess I lucked out," he lied.

"You will have a refill, yes? I will pay. You just say what you are drinking when the waitress comes over. I am Martina, by the way. Also known as the Punk Baroness."

"Okay ... I am Gareth ... Just Gareth. No a.k.a."

The woman waved over to the waitress to bring two more beers. Gareth drained his last one and watched the stage. Clara rarely looked out at the audience, so intent was she on the piano and her harmonies. Even if she did look up she would not see him. The light would be in her eyes and her vision was never very good. So when the song finished he shouted out "bravo" so loudly that the girls had to look in his direction. He knew that he would be no more than a blur, so he raised up his hand and waved in that familiar but awkward back-and-forth motion.

Clara left her place in front of the piano and went over to her sister. She whispered in her ear and Blanca looked out at the audience with a look of bewilderment.

"This is a song Clara wrote years ago," Blanca began. "We weren't going to perform it tonight but my sister suddenly feels moved to sing this one. It's called 'The Sweetest Love.' A ballad, so not quite our usual fare! It is about young love, imagined love. A love that was never to be."

Blanca nodded to the band to let them know they could sit this one out. She struck the drum and Clara keened a high note. A note that could shatter crystal. *Or glass eyes*, Gareth thought. Then Clara began the first verse without harmonies, as a solo. It was her song, after all. As she sang out her feelings, the feelings of the eighteen-year-old girl she once was, Gareth could feel nothing but regret. He had run away because he could not bear to be with her and not tell her everything he knew. He couldn't ruin her life by telling her that her uncle was a monster, but now, as he heard her song, he knew that his leaving was worse than telling her the truth. It was the choice of a boy, not the choice he would make now.

"Why did you wave at her?" the Punk Baroness asked him.

"No reason. I guess I was just swept away by the moment."

Gareth got up, excused himself, and left the club. He walked for blocks until he reached the small gallery where his paintings were hanging. They were almost entirely new works. All done since he had arrived in Germany. Only one painting was shipped from home. And on that painting Gareth put a red dot, placing it carefully between the two young girls who sat on a rock in Lake Ontario, beckoning a mother they didn't know. He would have it delivered to the twins the next day. By that time, he would be back on a train to Hamburg.

The beautiful woman from the club entered the small theatre and turned on the rehearsal lights. The illumination highlighted the dust floating in the air. *Probably not good for the singers*, she thought, *but what else can we afford?* She could be more commercial, perhaps, appeal to a larger audience and cast her net wider, but that would go against everything she believed in. And what she believed in was the power of punk. Her carefully contrived black hair, her piercings in her nose and her upper lip, her tattoo of the tower tarot card on her inner thigh, all spoke to her unshakable belief in the power of punk. It was an uprising for her. A movement. But a movement does not have to throw out all that is good. And so her company, Punkarie, was created, taking what was great about the old world order and turning it inside out. It was perfect, punk and opera together. All the great stories with their over-the-top plots of love and betrayal combined with ideologies concerned with individual freedom and anti-establishment views. She looked for operas with themes of individual liberty and anti-authoritarianism. She, herself, had a DIY ethic, believing in nonconformity, anti-collectivism, and, mostly, not "selling out." For those reasons her company remained small and true to its vision. Operas like *Carmen* and *La Bohème* appealed to her. But performed with electric guitars and aggressive drums instead of the usual orchestra with its organized sections.

When the Punk Baroness had first seen the albino twins, she knew that she had lucked out. They were doing an apprenticeship with the Deutsche Oper Berlin, singing in the background as villagers and maids at night and training their voices during the day. The Punk Baroness saw them in peasant-wear, singing in the chorus of villagers in a production of *Don Giovanni*. She knew the opera by heart, having grown up in a wealthy family who prided the arts above all else. She knew exactly what to expect from the Deutsche Oper Berlin, and yet her love of opera could not stop her from attending. The Punk Baroness secretly had season tickets to the opera, but always went alone. The Deutsche Oper Berlin did surprise her, not because of its directing or staging, but by the casting of two eye-catching albinos. How could anyone look elsewhere? She went to *Tosca* and *The Marriage of Figaro* that season, and there they were, in the background, uncomfortable in the period clothing and yet upstaging everyone else onstage with their presence.

She did not meet them backstage at the opera house, though. She met them, quite by accident, at a dimly lit club, under the arches of the S-Bahn. Bored with singing chorus and small roles, the twins had begun to sing in underground clubs, slowly building a following in Berlin. Martina, the Punk Baroness, was intrigued by them and began to follow them from club to club, finally wooing them away from the Deutsche Oper, with promises of more artistic expression with her grassroots rebel opera company. They were opera-trained women who understood her ideology. Eye-catching, talented, unlike anyone she had seen or heard before. It was fate.

Martina enjoyed the crossover from their following to her audience, but it still wasn't enough to keep the company afloat. The truth was that she had been financing it herself and she was running through her savings quickly, so she agreed to do an extensive tour for which the company would get a considerable government grant. They would have to play in university theatres and music schools across Germany. Was it selling out, or was it simply surviving?

"It's about time you two got here. Just because you did a good show last night doesn't mean you can show up late."

"Sorry," Clara replied.

"*Machts nichts.*" The Punk Baroness shrugged. They were her stars, and she would keep them at almost any cost. How unique the two were. And their voices, together, were unworldly. But they would not be performing together in this next one; they would share the lead, alternating the role of Carmen.

"I would very much like to do an opera of Antigone after this. So on point, politically. No one ever does the one Honegger and Cocteau wrote as an opera."

The twins looked blankly at the Punk Baroness. Antigone, Honegger, Cocteau! What was she on about this time?

"You must have studied the story in school. Even the French saw the play as a stance against tyranny, which is why Jean Anouilh adapted the Greek original. Surely you know it?"

The twins shook their heads.

"Well, there are two sisters, princesses actually, although not your usual princesses. They are the daughters of Oedipus. You have heard of him, yes?"

The twins both nodded, indicating that they had heard of the king who, unknowingly, fell in love with his own mother and took over both her bed and her kingdom.

"You would play the two sisters, Antigone and Ismene, but all the better if they are twins, I think! A young princess who breaks the law because of her ideals and is willing to die for her beliefs and her sister who tries to save her from her fate. Death. It is the perfect punk opera! Anti-establishment Anti-gone! It's feministic."

"How does she break the law?" Clara asked.

"Oh, she buries her brother instead of leaving him outside to rot where everybody can see it."

"Leaving bodies out to rot is a stupid law. Not very sanitary. Who came up with that?" Clara persisted. She had taken to challenging Martina whenever she could. Clara often felt left out of the creative process, that Martina's closeness to Blanca put her outside of the decision-making.

"Their evil uncle Creon," the Punk Baroness replied.

Always an evil uncle, Blanca thought. *An evil uncle who tries to keep control of everything and ultimately causes death and suicide.* Didn't the Punk Baroness understand that she was done with evil uncles? They hadn't run away from Canada to be reminded of evil uncles! Why did she tell Martina anything? Nothing was sacred, everything was potential art with her. She used everything; nothing was sacred.

"Doesn't sound like much of a story," Blanca suggested.

"There is so much more to it. Scapegoating. Making an example in order to manipulate. Read the play, you'll see. I don't care if it's the original Greek or the more modern French version. They are both good. In the meantime, we are doing a quick tour of some universities and schools to keep us going. A performance and workshops."

There was to be no discussion about the tour, no matter how much the twins protested. Clara had her best pout on about it. Why couldn't they just stay in Berlin and make something of Bleach instead? Berlin was becoming such a mecca for music, it seemed crazy to her to be jumping in and out of vans and singing to people whose courses demanded it. Voluntary audiences seemed far more receptive than the compulsory ones.

"Oh, and that came for you." Martina nodded at a large narrow package, wrapped in brown paper, the kind used for shipping packages.

"For me?" Clara asked.

"For both of you. I think it is from the man who was at the club last night. I remember him from a few years ago. I saw him when he left that letter for you, Clara, at the box office. Remember?"

"What letter?" asked Clara.

Blanca looked at the Punk Baroness and tried to signal to her to hush, but it was too late. Clara was piecing it all together, realizing that Gareth had reached out to her years earlier and that she hadn't responded because her sister had kept it a secret. She could feel a tingly heat rising from the lowest parts of her being, through her guts, past her solar plexus, until it gripped her heart and reached for her throat.

"Why, Blanca? Why would you keep that from me?" she accused.

Blanca couldn't answer her sister. Where would she start? All she knew was that Gareth was a link to their past, a past that they had to put to death and bury. She believed that they could create a new reality. Isn't that what Esther had said? That they could be anything they put their imaginations to. And hadn't Esther done just that herself?

"I wanted a new start for us. I was trying to protect you," Blanca stammered.

"Everyone wants me to be safe, but no one wants me to be happy!" she yelled at her sister. "You lied to me and you lied to him! And you lied to yourself, too! Did you really think you could run away from who you are? Doesn't matter where you go, you will always be what you are!"

Clara walked over to the painting, ripped the paper away, and gasped. There they were as children, on a rock in the water, hands reaching out. And there was a woman, from behind, with long red hair, caught in the lake air, walking toward them. And waves that seemed to crash up and out of the canvas.

"Looks like the past found us, anyhow. Now where is the letter?" Clara asked, although it sounded more like a demand.

"I burned it."

Clara started hitting her sister, both hands flying as she slapped and punched.

"Stop it!" the Punk Baroness yelled at them. "Just stop it! We are in rehearsal now; this is not the way we behave in rehearsal!"

"For someone who's so anti-establishment, you sure are good at telling us the rules! You fucking poser!" Clara yelled at her.

"Poser? What is poser?" Martina couldn't help but ask.

Blanca moved away from her twin, wiped her face on her hand. There were tears. Not from the physical assault. Not from the argument. Tears, because Clara was right. Her protection had prevented her sister from knowing any love but hers. It felt like the worst kind of breakup. The top layer of her skin felt raw, down her arms, across her chest and neck, even her cheeks felt like the Velcro of their connection had been ripped apart.

"I'm sorry. I'm so, so sorry. Please forgive me."

Clara lifted the painting and carried it to her dressing room. It would be a difficult rehearsal for her today, if she bothered to do it at all. Martina, their director, would take Blanca's side. She always did. The Bitch Baroness!

"I cannot believe that you kept so much from her," Martina said. "You have to go and speak to her. Make this right. We are going to Hamburg next month. You must get them together somehow."

She looked over to the direction of the dressing rooms. Clara would be a while. The Punk Baroness had tolerated many delayed rehearsals in the past. It was all a part of the more creative temperament. But what could she do? Clara was the more talented of the two. She could compose, and, when she was onstage, there was no doubt that she was totally and wholly the character. The Punk Baroness assumed that it was because she was not as strong a character as Blanca. Blanca was very focused. She put everything in order before she made a move. She was less impulsive than Clara and strangely so much sexier. There was never a question in Martina's mind who was more charismatic. *Less gifted and more charismatic, such is how it goes,* she thought. And there was no question which sister Martina would fall in love with. The taller, the stronger twin was far more appealing to her.

"You know you will have to tell her sooner or later."

"Tell her what?"

"About us. We cannot always sneak around. Besides, I want to love you openly. I only get you in tiny pieces."

The Punk Baroness put her arms around her, pulled her close. She loved the look of her own dark hair flowing onto Blanca's pale skin. Loved the difference in their skin tones. She knew that it had all started as a fetish for her. It was a visual turn-on in the beginning, meant to be nothing more than an affair for her, and probably no more than curiosity for Blanca. Just the thought of her dark, wet, manicured pubic hair rubbing against Blanca's unruly bleach-white plume of hair inspired so many fantasies. Then, one day, after too many schnapps, she had her completely. The swollen purple pink of her vagina was so surprising in that sea of white. And after that, every time she looked at the violet pinkness of her lover's eyes, all she could think of was her other purplish-pink place, hidden away and secret. Yes, she had intended on an affair and had fallen in love, but she knew that it would not be reciprocated to the same degree. It seemed that Blanca easily fell into the arms of anyone who fully adored her.

"Let her have her lover in Hamburg so that I can have you all the time."

Blanca was still crying. Even the comfort of a lover couldn't stop up the flow of her tears. What did Martina not understand? Yes, she might love her, eventually. But her love for another woman could never replace the love between her and her twin. They shared one soul. They were two parts of the same star.

"If I start to tell her the truth, where would I stop? That boy knows. He knows. His mother cared for our mother when she killed herself. If I allow him in, he will tell her things. How does knowing that our uncle raped our mother help her? Tell me that! It didn't help me. It just made me feel like the freak I was always called. How can I possibly tell her that our uncle is our father? It is too awful. I wanted to keep it from her because it has so destroyed me."

"You have to let her decide how it will affect her. Maybe you are wrong about her. Maybe she is stronger than you think. It is not for you to decide. All you can decide is whom you love and how you love them. Do you want to love her in the face of truth or in the face of deception?"

Blanca knew that the day would come when the twins would not be one mind, one soul, one spirit. A day when love and attraction would tear them from each other. But she wasn't ready for that day quite yet.

"If you want a new beginning then you have to separate from your past."

"You don't understand. We are two parts of the same star and when we are together, that star is whole …"

"You know that is a lie. That is a story told to you to bring you comfort as children. But now you are two separate and whole women and you need to let her make her own decisions."

"Where do I start?"

"You start by going into that dressing room and then you begin at the beginning. She will be furious, but I know you both and I can tell you this, in time she will forgive you and you will be bound in honesty instead of lies. You said that everybody lied to you as children. If you want to break from your past, then you need to stop repeating the past. Go, tell her the truth."

The Punk Baroness released her arms, let go of Blanca, and pointed her in the right direction. Why, she wondered, was she so attracted to opera when the life all around her was so much more melodramatic?

* * *

Sabine could stretch exactly like a cat. First unfurling her slender body and then reaching every limb out one by one, finally stretching through her fingertips until everything seemed so much longer across the bed. When she finished her signature stretch, she rolled onto her stomach, her round bottom rising up into the air, above her long, strong legs. Gareth's favourite part of her body, after her astounding bottom, was the muscle that sat like a ball in the middle of her calves. As if she were perpetually standing on her tippy-toes.

"Did you ever see that French movie *Contempt*?" she asked.

"Of course. My brother was a film freak. He made me watch everything."

"I think I would like your brother."

"Trust me, you're not his type."

Sabine looked over at him, turning her head over her shoulder so that her hair flew down her backside as she turned.

"Let's re-enact that first scene," she said. "You kiss my body parts one by one and tell me why you love them. Don't worry, if you get lost along the way I will keep you on track."

"Okay."

"So we will start here." Sabine arched and lifted her bottom upward. "Tell me how you love my ass."

Gareth was game. He kissed her bare bottom and told her that he adored her bum. It was perfect. Like the gods had all designed it together. It was handmade and more delectable than the sweetest treat …

"Like marzipan?" she asked.

"Exactly."

Gareth could feel the excitement returning to his body.

It would be so easy to fall for such a girl who was so comfortable with her body. He tried to turn her over.

"No, you cannot start on my frontside until you are through with my backside. I think you forgot the shoulder blades."

The knock on the door was abrupt. They chose to be quiet, pretending they weren't there. Sabine put a pillow, a square one, into her mouth and bit down hard to stifle the laugher. What fun they had there when Siegfried was in Canada. And those trips were getting longer and longer. Perhaps Gareth would take over soon and she could move in, share the rent. It was a nicer place than the apartment she rented.

"Shhh." He put his finger to his lips and Sabine howled with laughter.

Knock, knock, knock.

"I think I had better get it."

"Why?" Sabine whispered.

"I don't know. What if someone has lost an eye and needs one right away?"

"Right away?" Sabine stuffed the pillow back into her mouth.

Knock, knock, knock.

"*Ja, ja, Ich komme!*"

Gareth did that funny hop-run one only does when trying to hurry to get pants on before opening the door. The last bit, the zipper and the top button, only closing as he reached the door. No shirt, but that was fine, after all it was his home and it was late. He turned the handle and opened the door.

"Hello."

"Hello."

There she was, as real as possible. Dressed from head to toe in white with only a light smear of red across her hesitant lips.

The black walnut rectory table seemed too imposing, too big for a mere four people, but Hilda wanted to sit at the formal family table and not in the kitchen nook. Imposing could be good sometimes.

"The way I see it" — John cleared his throat — "the way I see it, this house belongs to us both. And we both worked hard to have it."

"It was paid for with the inheritance from my mother's house in Germany. She bought this house, really."

"Yes, well, I was working that whole time. Paying the bills. Putting food on the table."

"Yes, that is what you do for your family."

"The thing is, Jean is pregnant again and the boys are almost six now and growing. They need their own rooms. We just don't have the space so …"

"You want to move in here with me?" Hilda asked, shocked. She couldn't imagine a shared space with little ones running around all the time. She enjoyed it when her daughter came with her small daughter, but that was different. That was her granddaughter, after all. And she never stayed for more than two days.

Jean looked at John uncomfortably. She put a hand on his arm, warning him to stop.

"No, Jean," he said, removing her hand. "Fair is fair. We let her have the house when Jack was still here, but now we need it. It is our turn."

Siegfried couldn't believe it. This house was everything to Hilda. From morning to night she either tended the garden, walked the property line, or baked things inside the large country kitchen. John's demands seemed, to him, an act of hostility.

"If you do not agree, I can force the sale of the house. Or I could have an assessment and buy you out."

"Who would like more coffee?" Siegfried asked to break the tension.

"I would, even though I shouldn't," Jean replied. "Let me help you."

Siegfried led her to the kitchen where he ground the beans and frothed the milk.

"Oh, you are so handy. It's so fancy that way."

"You know, it is the details that count. Little things. Ground beans instead of packaged pre-ground coffee. It doesn't seem like much but in the end all those little details add up. Look out at the garden."

"It's beautiful."

"Yes. Hilda thinks it is nothing. That she has no talents. But you know it is always in bloom. She has planted it so that as one flower leaves, another blossoms. It is a knack she has. But I know it has taken her years to get it just right."

Jean started to cry. Said it was the hormones and that she was just a crazy pregnant lady.

"I told him not to come. I feel bad enough that I took her man, I don't want to take her home. I mean, we need the room and all, but still…. How would I feel sleeping in the room where they had sex? No offence — it doesn't seem to bother you."

"No, it does not bother me. But I am not a sensitive woman."

Siegfried spooned extra foam onto the top of her cup, then he went to the cupboard, got some bittersweet chocolate, and grated it onto the top.

"So fancy," Jean repeated.

"Wouldn't it be better if we were all friends? And wouldn't it be better if you were not crying? Let me think of something. You need your own home to make your own traditions. You do not want Hilda's home. And you would feel guilty about the garden because you could not do that, could you?"

Jean shook her head.

"I will buy out his share of the house at a fair price and you can get something new. Something that is all yours, where you can make your own history. There is a big house for sale near Elaine and Mark; you should see that. House hunting can be fun and good for a marriage."

"But John seems so set about it. When he decides something he can be so stubborn."

"I am sure you have gotten your way on a few things! Right now, I bet that John and Hilda are fighting it out. So our cooler heads must prevail."

The thought of selling his last hold in Germany was daunting to him. There would be so many things to set in order. And, of course, it would mean that Gareth would have to strike out on his own. He would give him his equipment, supplies, and business, but still, it was hardly the way he wanted to pass the torch. But what choice did he have? A nasty troll was holding his queen hostage and so he would have to make a sacrifice for her.

When they returned, John and Hilda were no longer arguing. It was far, far worse. John was explaining and explaining, talking and talking, and Hilda had gone completely quiet. His words were falling on deaf ears. Of course, it was a big house. Of course, Jack was never there except for holidays. Of course, the girls had families of their own. It didn't matter to her, though. It was her home and he was trying to tear the foundation down all around her.

"Where is Jack, by the way?"

Hilda refused to answer. Siegfried had witnessed this stubbornness a few times, even when she was a young teenager. There would be no getting through to her. So he answered for her.

"He is in Europe. Documenting what he thinks is the beginning of the end of the Cold War. Last I heard he was in Hungary. That was last week."

John shrugged. Ever since Jack had been going to Germany to get his eye fitted, he had become more and more like his mother and less and less like him. Secretly he blamed Hilda for his son not putting down roots in Canada. At least his daughters had their feet firmly in North America. But Jack had turned his eye away from this home to focus on world politics instead.

"You gotta admit, I do have a point. You have had it all these years ..."

Beyond the dining-room window Hilda could see the fenceline leading to the small orchard where she had planted snap peas and snow peas and the vines were climbing the fence. The small pods were developing tiny white blossoms above the pods. It looked like a good crop was coming.

"However own by tragedy,
Or near the breaking it may be,
My heart can never harden,
As long as I have eyes to see
And windows toward the garden."

"I'm sorry, what's that? You're going to answer me with poetry now?"

"Okay, John. I will tell you what that poem means. It means, would you please get the fuck out of my house?"

Siegfried thought that it was going rather well until that moment. He thought he would be able to strike an arrangement, but John got up in a huff and started for the front door. Surprisingly, Jean just sat there.

"Jean, we are leaving. I can't talk sense into that selfish cow. Come on."

"Just a sec, John. I don't want my piece of cake to go to waste. It's so good." Jean weakly smiled through her crumb-filled mouth.

"Fine, I'll be in the truck."

Jean reached across the table for the bowl of fresh whipped cream and dolloped two tablespoonfuls onto her marble pound cake.

"I must get your recipe."

"Why? Would you ever make it?" Hilda asked.

"Probably not. I am not good at cooking or gardening." She smiled.

"No? What are you good at?"

"Well, I used to be a really good surfer."

Hilda looked at the younger woman, openly scrutinizing her. Was this planned? She would stay behind if things didn't go well with her, just to smooth things over, and then do John's bidding. Hilda picked up the bowl of fresh fruit, raspberries and gooseberries, and dumped them onto Jean's plate.

"It's nicer with the fruit."

"Yes, but what are those green things?"

"Gooseberries. People don't eat them here much, but when I moved here I had some seeds sent from my mother and I planted the bushes and cared for them. Every year they grew bigger till I had so many. When I eat them, I remember her. And, of course, when she died, her house, the house I grew up in, was sold in Germany because John and I had our life here. It was very sad to sell my girlhood house. But we used that money to pay for this house."

"I don't want your house. But John has a bee in his bonnet. And we do need more space."

"It is funny, isn't it, that he will have a child younger than his granddaughter? Your child will be an aunt or uncle the moment it is born."

Jean started laughing, crumbs of marble cake spewing from her lips. Of course, Hilda hadn't meant funny ha-ha. But when the horn started blasting outside all the women could do was start laughing together.

"Another slice of cake, Jean?"

"Don't mind if I do!"

"You know, when Jack was little, when he was still Johnny, and he lost his eye, he only went to school because you were so kind to him. He adored you. And you encouraged him. For that I will always be thankful." Hilda paused, then inhaled. "But you need to know that I will sell this house to a stranger before I give it to you and John. You have to know that."

"I think that is best. Really I do," Jean agreed.

Best? Hilda thought. No, the best would be to let her just keep the house. To let her grow old in it, polishing the large wooden table at Christmas, planting the garden in spring, picking cherries, caring for the bunnies …

"Yes, and I think I will be just the stranger to buy it!" Siegfried piped up, enthusiasm bubbling in his voice. "If you can stand having me around all the time, that is. I will sell my apartment in Hamburg and that will surely pay for his half of the house."

"No, you cannot give up your life there."

"My life is with you. And you love this house."

"I do love this house. And I love you."

Jean polished off her second slice, wiped the cream from her mouth, and got up to go, but before she waddled very far she heard John's engine starting up and the crushing sound of tires on gravel.

"He's gone. He can be such a prissy-pants sometimes."

"He can indeed! And he's your prissy-pants now! I'll drive you," Hilda offered. And she wrapped up the last of the cake for Jean.

Jack found it strange to be sitting with his boyhood friend in the apartment his stepfather owned. His memory of it was that it was so much larger and more exotic, but five years of travelling throughout Europe had made him accustomed to high ceilings, heavy wooden doors, and spiralling staircases. The expansive rooms that had intimidated him in his teens now seemed commonplace. Months in Warsaw, Bucharest, and Budapest had given him a different perspective on architecture. Hamburg was, for him, an odd place. So much had been rebuilt after the war so that modern glass and steel stood in contrast to the old, masculine buildings of stone and brick. Siegfried's building was old, formidable, but no longer as intimidating to him as it was when he was a child.

"I have come for you to check my eye and maybe even make me a new one," he joked, putting on a bad German accent.

Gareth was surprised to see his old friend there. Surprised and uncomfortable. How many times had the thought that they were perhaps living each other's lives crossed his mind? His brother, Tristan, would have loved for Gareth to share an interest in cameras, which Jack did so easily, usurping him as a brother. And Jack, who had once stayed in the apartment as Siegfried's guest and a client.

"So how would you like to buy this apartment?" Jack blurted out immediately.

"Pardon?"

"Siegfried asked me to come and talk to you. He has to sell the apartment because my dad is being priggish to my mom and, as always, Siegfried is trying to make everything right for everyone else. God, it must be hard for him to sell it."

"I'm an apprentice. He doesn't pay me much. And I stay here for free."

"You're hardly an apprentice anymore. Besides, he's giving you the business, so you'll be making decent money. So here is my idea ..."

Jack moved about the space as though he owned it. Knowing where the coffee was, and the schnapps. He hadn't been there in almost eight years, but he held a perfect memory in his mind, as though every room had been fastened to his brain in a photographic image. Gareth could see that the years of monocular vision had made his friend all the better at retaining the memory of how things looked. It was as though the fear of losing his other eye taught him to hold everything he could see in a memory. Just in case.

"Slivovitz or schnapps? Ooh, peach! I could make us Fuzzy Navels!"

"Sure." Gareth shrugged, already imagining how difficult it would be to have to move. He could stay with Sabine, he supposed. They were still friends, although the relationship had become awkward after Clara had shown up unannounced. Sabine, though fully dressed, had emerged from the bedroom that evening with the sleepy-eyed look of someone who had just fucked her brains out. Clara had just stared at her, her pale eyes darting back and forth as they took in Sabine's strong and healthy body, her mane of hair, her confidence, and her overt sexuality.

"Aren't you going to introduce me?" Sabine had asked.

Clara then made awkward apologies for coming unannounced, all the while shifting her weight from one foot to the other. It seemed to Gareth that her eyes had begun to vibrate as intensely as they did in her childhood.

"Don't be shy. Come sit down. I will make some *Kaffe*."

Gareth had wanted to slink away, make himself small, so small that the women could just bat him back and forth the way cats do, playing with half-dead mice. There he was, dying slowly, while Sabine was turning him into a plaything.

"Do you live here?" Clara had found the courage to ask.

"No, no, I am just a neighbour. I was just over, being … neigh-bourly," Sabine had said with a laugh.

And after a coffee and the usual, although not revealing, conversation about how Gareth knew each of them, Clara excused herself, saying that she had an early performance the next morning.

The next morning, Gareth had gone to the university where, Clara said, she was performing. But they had been there two days earlier and Clara had already left town.

Jack listened to Gareth's story, wanting every sordid detail. He couldn't believe that Gareth was sleeping with Sabine!

"Of course, it's been almost ten years since our night," Jack blurted out.

"What? You slept with Sabine?"

"Not exactly. Besides, it was her roommate I liked. What was her name?"

"Hannah?"

"Yes, Hannah! What happened to her?"

"I think she married a psychiatrist or something and moved to Frankfurt."

"Oh, that's a shame."

Jack was looking at all the books Siegfried had collected over the years. Mostly hardcover. And then there were paintings and furniture and dishes. He couldn't imagine having to pack it all up. And do what? Ship it all to Canada? Put it into storage?

"Here is the thing. The future is Europe," Jack proclaimed.

"Says you. I am thinking that I should go home."

"Bullshit. You don't have a gallery willing to show your work in Canada, and even if you did, who's collecting? Besides, they make acrylic eyes there! You would have to train all over again to be an ocularist in North America. But one-eyed people will come from all over the world for your eyes, because Germany is still known for its glass eyes. And you are the ocularist now."

It was true. All of Siegfried's rantings about plastic eyes over the years had made it very clear that to be in the American Association of Ocularists, Gareth would have to make acrylic eyes. He could never do that. It would be a betrayal.

"You know, when I first arrived, Siegfried took me to see the Elba River and said, 'Look here! The Vikings came up this river in 845 and destroyed Hamburg. Charlemagne built that beautiful castle to protect the city against them. But they are very tricky, those Vikings. Very tricky.'"

"Oh, I know, those American Vikings with their plastic eyes!" Jack mimicked Siegfried, "Barbarians, smashing all those beautiful glass eyes! Imagine!"

"But you know, they were stock eyes, though. Not custom."

"Still, pretty brutal. Anyhow, want to hear my plan?"

Jack showed his hand. Explained how he could be a stringer for the *Toronto Star*, but he really needed one foot in Europe and one back home.

"Mark my words, we are on the brink of history in the making. And it is going to happen here. In Europe. And I think it will happen in Germany."

"What's going to happen?"

"I'm not quite sure, but I have a hunch. Look, first there's the EU, then there is Gorbachev, and he wants to bring the Soviet Union into a more modern world. There are protests amongst the young and people want more than what they have. They want more autonomy. They want more freedom. They want more choice. It's happening right across Eastern Europe. So my guess is that East Germany is next. But as I said" — he touched his glass eye — "it's just a hunch."

"How does this hunch affect me? And more important, where am I going to live?"

"Right here. We can buy this place together. Not put it on the market. Siegfried was going to give you the business, anyhow, and he was going to leave me twenty-five percent of this place. We use that money as our down payment."

"I doubt we could get a mortgage."

"Well, I am a citizen. I did that through my mom, but I have no credit to speak of. But you could marry someone German so that you are legit here and together we buy this. It is an amazing apartment. Three bedrooms. A place for you to paint. Your business downstairs."

After a few more Fuzzy Navels it was decided. Gareth would marry Sabine, who always wanted to live in the apartment, anyhow, and Jack would use it as home base, coming and going. Hilda's home would be secured so that they could all go home for Thanksgiving and Christmas. It was the perfect plan.

"Call her."

"Who?"

"Sabine. Call her and propose tonight."

Gareth picked up Siegfried's line and called. Her voice was thick with sleep, gravelly.

"*Allo?*"

"Hey, Sabine?"

"This better be good, it is two in the morning!"

Jack motioned for him to continue.

"Want to come over?"

"Thought we weren't doing late-night, impulsive sex anymore."

Gareth blushed. He looked over at Jack. All was well; after all, he had no idea what she might be saying on the other line.

"Okay, I will be there in fifteen minutes."

"She'll be here in fifteen minutes," he repeated to Jack.

Jack wondered if she would even remember him, the shy but aroused boy whom they had to care for when his youth made a fool of him. Still, they could have a good laugh over it now. Time and distance can turn humiliation into humour.

"I'll get it," Jack announced, rising from the armchair to answer her knock.

To him she looked as exotic and sexy as he remembered. Age had only improved her. The cynical sophistication that she wore like a borrowed dress in her early twenties had become a second skin as she approached thirty. Anything rehearsed and measured had become intrinsically a part of her so that every gesture and move now seemed organic.

"*Guten Abend.* Remember me?"

"*Ja*, of course, I always wondered when you would come back. I heard that Siegfried married your mother so I assumed I would see you again. But it has been — what? Ten years? What happened to your eye?"

"What do you mean?"

"They were two different colours before. Now they are boring."

"Well, hardly boring."

"I mean the same. Like everyone." Sabine shrugged.

Gareth sat, waiting to be included. Were they going catch up the whole ten years, detail by detail?

"You know it's a fake eye, right? That's how I met Siegfried, as a kid. I have three that I change up. Today I was feeling like matching. But I still have my Bowie eye."

"So then you can switch them at whim?"

Gareth was getting impatient. Childhood feelings started to boil up, unexpectedly and inexplicably. It seemed it was always

about Jack's eye. Every shared class ended up with Jack getting
better marks because of the eye. And Tristan, who never openly
used his eye to gain favour, found it easier to bond with Jack
than with him. It was as though Jack had replaced him as a
brother and Tristan had replaced him as Jack's best friend. Now
the woman he'd been sleeping with wasn't even acknowledging
him. Hadn't she gotten out of bed with the aim of having sex
with him? Now it was all about Jack. Jack, Jack, Jack. It had
always been about Jack.

"Well, they aren't wigs, Sabine. They are prosthetics. Some
people lose sight of that," Gareth informed.

"Yeah, some people lose sight, Gareth." Jack smiled pointedly
at his friend.

Sabine thought that it was all hysterically funny.

"Someone get me a drink, and then let's go through that
drawer right there and see how Jack looks in all the different eyes!"

The only eyes in that drawer were the ones that Siegfried had
made year after year for himself. The others were all still at the
oculary. Only Siegfried's had been transported to the apartment.
But that didn't stop them. Jack removed his hazel eye and reached
for the crystal-clear blue eye of Siegfried's youth.

And all around him were dying soldiers. Mud. And flashes of
gunfire. And blood.

Jack took the eye out, placed it back into the drawer.

"No, it's a bad idea. Besides, they don't fit properly."

"Aw, you should have let me see it first!"

"I'm tired," Jack said. "Shall I just sleep in Siegfried's room?"

"Yeah, perfect."

Sabine moved over to where Gareth was sitting on the armchair. She straddled his legs and sat on his lap.

"So, you woke me up from a deep sleep. You better be up for
some sex now."

"Not really. I drank too much."

"I could go sleep with Jack, then?"

Gareth shrugged.

"I know you're jealous."

"A little."

Sabine took his hand and led him to his room. She loosened the tie on her wrap dress and it fell away from her. She really was beautiful. Everything about her pointed upward. Her breasts, full with dark nipples that seemed to flip upward toward the ceiling. Her high and round bum. Even the ski jump of her nose seemed to suggest that there was a heaven and that heaven was up toward the sky. She crawled under the duvet and motioned for him to join her.

"Don't worry. It's just a friend-fuck. It's not like I'm expecting you to marry me," she said.

He joined her and made slow, half-drunk love to her until sleep overtook them both.

And then, he dreams of her. A woman with long red hair, strands of seaweed clinging to her tresses. She is at the water's edge. With wildflowers in her arms. She turns and sees Gareth. She looks so very sad. She turns her back on him, walks into the water.

Gareth got up. He walked about the apartment. It was great there. He loved the apartment, but it wasn't his forever home. It was just a temporary chance to run away from his responsibilities and to shirk off expectation.

"Jack? Jack?" He softly knocked on Jack's bedroom door.

"Yeah," a sleepy voice replied.

"I can't do it. I don't love Sabine. It's your idea, why don't you marry her?"

"I can't. I'm in love with your brother."

Gareth stood quietly, staring at his best friend in wonder.

"Well, aren't you going to say something?"

"No. I'm relieved, actually. All this time I thought you'd replaced me. Guess I got that one wrong," Gareth admitted. He could feel a weight lifting. Jealousy, resentment, even guilt seemed to loosen its grip.

"Yeah. I guess you did."

Tristan stretched across his bed, his hand reaching to the cool, empty spot where Jack had been only a day before. How he came and went and, in those times between, Tristan felt that his existence was just a dream. A period of waiting until Jack, so full of stories and news, would re-emerge, breathing life into their squat of an apartment.

Tristan sat up and looked about the room. It hadn't really changed since they were both students, when Jack slept in the living room on a pullout couch. But then, that one time when Jack had too much to drink and Tristan gave him his bed for the night with a bucket by his head, just in case. After that, Jack pretty much moved in with him, without fuss. No tsunami, no earth-shattering adjustments, just the slow growing together and hesitant exploration of two young men who already knew each other too well. Jack had already killed for him, what other proof of love could Tristan need? The body was given long after the pact was made.

Tristan looked at the room they shared and knew that somehow their surroundings had not changed as they had. So down came the cheesy movie posters of his youth. He was careful as he untaped them and rolled them and put them into his closet. There was, surprisingly, no sadness. He would soon enough have his own posters, with his own name written on the bottom.

The empty rectangles stood out, though, with paint faded around them and cracks on the walls where the posters had been. There would have to be a paint job, some plaster in the cracks, and new decor.

Tristan opened the bottom drawer of Jack's dresser, where favourite photos were kept. He rifled through everything from destruction to nature to fashion shots. He sorted them, looking for three, a triptych, that would work together. Surely Jack wouldn't mind. Here an expanse of water, looking from the cliffs into a moody Lake Ontario, with light bouncing off the water like a mirrored playground. Here the faces of Mexican children in an orphanage outside of Tijuana, looking into the lens of the camera with curiosity and without hope, and here a candid shot of the Live Aid Concert taken in London a few years earlier, crowds of people all together. Photos Jack had taken, in black and white, to be framed and displayed in their shared room.

Before he closed the drawers he took out the file with the word TWINS scribbled across it. He knew what was inside but opened it, anyhow. There they were, over a decade younger, the albino twins. The beginning of Bleach and the start of everything. Tristan stared at them, in their haloed glory. It was the night they had competed at Massey Hall and he and Jack were there to witness them. To capture them. How each of their lives had changed. He closed the file and wondered if they could ever know the truth. Then returned it to the bottom of the drawer.

TEN

SIEGFRIED HAD FULLY PLANNED to sacrifice his past in Germany for his future with Hilda in Canada, but Jack had found a way around it all, suggesting he buy the apartment from him, with his neighbour Sabine. Siegfried's favourite things were sent to him, bit by bit, but he had let the rest go. There was no longer a hold on him. Germany was now far away. He hadn't even been there for two years. Now here he stood, in a land of hot summers and cold winters, with a big sky, and nature creeping up to his doorstep, thankful to be with the woman he loved.

"I will bring in the last Brussels sprouts and make us some coffee and cake. I'll call you when it's ready." Hilda kissed his cheek, gathered up their last harvest, and went inside. How he loved her!

His life as an ocularist also had little hold on him now. This new land had given him his successor, his heir, Gareth, and he couldn't be prouder of him. He had learned everything he could and then, when there was no more for Siegfried to teach him, he went on to experiment more with hot glass, creating more details and nuances than Siegfried could ever imagine. Yes,

Gareth was the ocularist now; he had passed that torch to him. How lucky he was!

And Jack, he was right about him, as well. Hadn't he seen the courage in him, even as a boy? And now he was going to every place where he felt there was change about to happen. A sensitive boy who could see the world through a prism of understanding. Always walking on the precipice of history. How lucky he was!

Everything that had seemed like a misfortune in his life had ended up being a blessing. Oh, to hold on to that with every exhaled breath. It had been almost eighteen years since Hilda returned to his life and ten years since he showed up, unannounced, on her doorstep, only to share a bed and a life with her. And even in the simplest of moments, in the most common tasks of life, he had no desire to be anywhere but where he was, with her. How very lucky he was!

Oh, how beautiful the garden was in the autumn. Hilda's flowers were still blooming. There were some roses and asters and marigolds, of course. The leaves seemed to be on fire, something he could never get used to but had learned to love with all his heart.

All his life he had strived for perfection, to make replacements that were so perfect they would be seen as originals. But now his work was done and the world seemed to wrap its arms around him in an embrace where every loss, every struggle, brought him here. Here to a life with the woman he loved. His heart ached, it was so full, so close to bursting.

How like the glass decorations of his childhood the leaves looked in their rich colours! Perhaps one day there would be a way to go to the East with Hilda, show her his home village, Lauscha. Buy Christmas decorations there, with her. Had he gone back there when the war was over he would have been kept in East Germany, behind a wall built to keep people in. He never did go back to see the Christmas decorations, the vases, and the many, many glass eyes. He had a memory of sunlight reflecting off a blown-glass ball, hanging in someone's window, the light bouncing off, holding the colours of the glass's refection. *As brilliant as Ontario autumn leaves*, he thought. The colours danced all around him. He looked up, through beams of sunlight. Crimson and orange and yellow and green.

His heart kept filling until it could fill no more. It pained him, being so full of love and joy and gratitude. Who knew that at sixty-two years of age he could finally achieve perfection in life itself? But the pain of that perfection, the pain of that joy, was just too much. He put his hand to his chest, tried to slow the pounding, tried to calm the noise, but his heart could not be contained. Siegfried dropped down onto his knees, the colours of the leaves blurred above him, red bleeding into orange and swirling all around him. His breath caught and shallowed and he knew, he knew, he knew he was dying. Dying there, in the garden where he had opened his heart to accept his happiness, held open his arms to love, and then was about to lose it all at the height of his contentment. *No, no, no.* He fought against it. *Just give me one more Christmas with her, one more year, one more night, even.* He felt a surge of incredible pain. A sharp stab into his heart, wrenching it fully open. And then, then there was nothing at all.

Three times she called and he didn't answer, so Hilda went out to find him in the garden, lying still, beside the row of marigolds.

"Siegfried!" she called out. Nothing.

She went over, wondering why on earth he was lying down. Was the gardening too much for him and he was just resting for a moment? Silly old goat! He was having her on. Waiting till she got close then, like so many other times, he was going to jump up and laugh as he startled her.

"Come on now. The coffee will get cold! Stop playing games!"

He stayed still. Not a movement. She knelt beside him, touched his face, held his hand. Then she tried to tickle him. Nothing.

Something was terribly wrong. She felt for a pulse, put her face near his to feel his breath. Nothing. Not the slightest hint of his breath on her cheek.

It was unthinkable. It was a joke. How could he be so unmoving, so unresponsive? Hilda pushed her fear and panic deep inside of herself. It could not be. She would not let it be!

Two quick rescue breaths. Then a two-palmed compression to the chest. Slow and steady, do not panic. Press and press. Press and press. Press. Two more breaths. She continued till sweat poured from her, working as his heart and lungs. Two breaths, press and press and press and press.

"Come on. Goddamn it! You cannot leave me. You cannot!"

She ran into the house and called for an ambulance, then hurried back to the garden, where she continued to be his lungs and heart. Again and again. And with every shared breath, every straight-armed press, she became more and more sure that it was pointless. But she would not give up. She would breathe for him and push down on his heart for as long as it took for a miracle to happen.

Only when the paramedics arrived and told her it was too late did she sit back on her heels, exhausted. Tears streamed down her face. She kept wiping them, but more would appear to take their place. There was an endless supply. There would always be an endless supply.

"Do you have a funeral home arranged where we can take him?"

"Yes, and there is something else that must be done." She remembered. She had made that promise to him. It was important to him. At the time, she had said that she would be too grief-stricken to do what he wanted, but he insisted. Now, it was the time to keep that promise. She ran into the house, then ran up the stairs, two at a time, to retrieve the velvet pouch from her bedroom. She would take it with her to the funeral home.

As soon as the death papers were signed at the funeral home, the harvester arrived and was ready to work. There was a limited time to harvest once the donor had died.

"You may want to go outside for this," he advised.

"No," Hilda said. "They made me wait outside when they removed my son's eye. I can't let that happen again. I will hold his hand while you do this."

"We really don't allow it."

"Do you want the eyes or not?" Hilda insisted.

The harvester had seen it all. People so filled with grief that they changed their minds. Few people saw eyes as functioning organs, as he did. Loved ones always attached some magical thinking to them. Beauty is held in the eye of the beholder. The eyes are windows to the soul. Love is understood in the reflection of the eyes. But the eye was no more than a lens that carried impulses to the brain to register images. And so, to do his job, it was always easier to leave the sentimentality outside the room.

"It is quick. We really only use the cornea, but I will take the whole eye. It does not disfigure the shape of the eye because I will put a placeholder in the socket. He will look like he is resting, with his eyes closed."

Hilda held Siegfried's hand and spoke to him, believing that perhaps his soul was still close to her. She told him how much she loved him, how it wouldn't really hurt. How brave she thought he was. But she had to look away as the optic nerve and the eye muscles were cut. She stared at their entwined hands, hers warm and lively, his cool and still.

"Done," the man said and reached to close Siegfried's eyes.

"No," she said, "not yet."

The man hesitated. He looked kindly at Hilda.

"He has done a great thing today. He has given someone the gift of sight," he told her.

"Oh no, you are wrong. He always gave sight, to everyone. But today, he gave someone the gift of vision."

Hilda took the pouch from her pocket. She opened the box and inside were the two eyes she'd put under her pillow when he was away from her. One eye, the left eye, that Jack had stolen in order to bring Siegfried to her, and the other eye, the right eye, that Siegfried had given her the day he had proposed to her. Both eyes made the year that she had come back into his life.

"My son lost his eye when he was six. Siegfried was an ocularist and he made him the most beautiful eye. It gave him confidence and beauty. It gave him a new lease on life. But it couldn't give him vision. That pained Siegfried. Pained him that he could make such beautiful objects that would never be of use. Eyes that were for looks and not for looking."

The harvester watched as she took out the glass eyes and gently pried Siegfried's lids fully open so that she could lay the glass eyes over each placeholder.

"Here, my love, these are for you. Take them with you to the other side so that you keep an image of me while you wait. I'm just on the other side of the door, like always. But this time you will have to do the listening for me because one day, one day soon, I will come back to you again. As I always have."

She took one last look at his eyes. They truly were his eyes. And for just a moment he seemed alive again. Like a last glance at love. She kissed his mouth and then ran her fingers over his eyelids, closing them to the world.

The harvester put his hand on her shoulder as an act of kindness. "I am so sorry for your loss."

"I was the luckiest woman in the world."

When Hilda went home she was greeted by silence. Silence, the thing she always valued and loved. Silence, which had seemed to be a luxury. But how hollow is the gift of silence without the possibility that it might be interrupted.

She walked into the garden, looked up into the dark, cloudless sky, clear and cold. She stood for a while where Siegfried had fallen. A day can change everything. The garden had lost its aroma, the leaves suddenly seemed to have fallen, and the coyote wasn't there to soothe her. She stepped back, inhaled deeply, but the breath was just a breath and nothing more. Beside her the rabbit hutches contained six or seven bunnies, nibbling or sleeping. Hilda went to them and they reacted, expecting food. She unlocked the cages and opened the hutch doors wide.

"There, have your freedom. Have life," she told them.

At first, they hesitated, not sure if they should hop away or stay in the safety of the cage.

"Go on. Be free!"

One after the next, they crossed the threshold and hopped into the garden. Perhaps they would all be eaten. Perhaps some would survive. It was up to them now. All but one was free and nibbling what was left of her garden. Only a large brown bunny, with a black smudge on its nose, remained in the hutch. A male. A buck.

"Go, go now!" she exclaimed. "Go be free! Go on, you stupid, stupid rabbit!"

He stayed, seemingly content where he was. He had no interest in the garden or the great exodus to freedom. She left him there to choose for himself. She'd just go to bed and check on him in the morning.

Back inside, she stripped down to her undershirt and panties, then wrapped herself in Siegfried's old, worn cashmere sweater. How many times had she suggested he throw it out and she get him a new one? Now it will never be thrown away. It will wrap its arms around her, as he had done, embrace her in familiar warmth, and she will, night after night, press her face into the sweater, breathing in his scent, feeling close to him. Until the day when she's breathed all his scent away and he is exhaled forever.

She slept in his sweater, restless without his head on the pillow next to hers, knowing that it will never be again. She chose the pain of quiet, refusing to call those she loved most ...

She sleeps, dreamless, unaware of the events unfolding in the world.

*   *   *

Humpty Dumpty saß an der Wand,
Humpty Dumpty fiel schwer,
All die Pferde des Königs
und alle Männer der Könige
konnten Humpty nicht wieder zusammensetzen.

It's the biggest party Europe has ever seen. On both sides of the wall, people are gathering. Eager to cross from one side, ready to welcome on the other. There's champagne and dancing. People are singing in celebration. Strangers are hugging. Bare hands, chisels, and pickaxes are assaulting the wall. And cheers in unison of "Let us in. Let us in!" ring out across the West ...

Jack had predicted that something was going to happen, possibly in East Germany. On the seventh of November, just two days earlier, he got up, threw down his newspaper, and suggested a road trip to Berlin.

"The writing's on the wall. Excuse the pun!"

"Why?" Gareth had asked.

"Look, they just announced that there will be a change in travel policy for the GDR. No one knows what that policy will be. It may lead to revolution. It's either going to be bloodshed or celebration. Either way I'm going to be there. I was right about Tiananmen Square and I missed that."

"Thank God you did."

"Sabine, you can drive us. You'll want to be there, just in case, to cover it for the TV station."

"Hardly an entertainment feature, Jack."

All Gareth could think about was a trip to Berlin, three hours of driving with Sabine and Jack, and then maybe, just maybe, Bleach would be playing somewhere and he could see the twins again.

"*Ah, ja*, I saw that girl who came over that night on the music video channel. She has a sister, yes?" Sabine added.

"Yes, twins," Gareth reluctantly informed, but it was unnecessary. Anyone who had ever seen Bleach would realize that the two sisters were twins. There had been so much press about them over the three years. Features on the opera company, pictures of their band, Bleach. They had become ubiquitous.

"They are extraordinary with their white skin and pink eyes. Like sweet little bunnies."

"They are extraordinary because they are wonderful musicians. Trust me, they are anything but bunnies!" This from Jack, who remembered being caught in their song all those years ago. Only Tristan was able to break that spell for him, to untangle him from their enchantment, but Gareth, he knew, was still caught by the sirens' song. He wished it wasn't so. The weight of too many secrets could suffocate his friend.

"We should go to Berlin now and stop by the theatre. Maybe they can put us up for a night or two," Jack suggested, a glint in his seeing eye.

"No, I don't think it's a good idea."

"Why not?"

Gareth looked at Sabine. Sure, she had found someone new to share her bed. That wasn't the issue. But it was just too awkward to imagine confronting Clara again, especially in Sabine's presence.

"Don't worry about me. I knew you still held feelings for her from that time she came over. Besides, I have a new lover on the horizon."

"You always have another lover on the horizon!" Jack joked.

Gareth slumped into a chair and shook his head. How could he possibly go to Berlin and see her again? Twice he had disappointed her and both times because of his own selfishness. What right did he have to be offered another chance?

"Sometimes you just have to accept that some things are not meant to be," he said to Jack.

"Do you think that anything worth having doesn't take courage? How easy do you think it was to admit to myself that I love your brother? How easy do you think it was to kill for him? Now get off your lazy fuckin' ass and let's go on a road trip. If she rejects you again then, only then, can you say it wasn't meant to be!"

Sabine already had her keys in her hand.

"What do you mean you killed for him? That is a metaphor, no?" Sabine whispered to Jack.

"No."

Sabine put her hands to her cheeks. She could feel heat rising from them. Yes, there were many lovers, but would any actually kill for her?

From the moment she met him, the Punk Baroness was completely taken with Jack. His desire to bear witness to history in the making, his belief that a new world, a world of hope and freedom, would emerge soon, was all music to her ears. She secretly hoped for revolution. She was ready to fight, if need be. She was just four years old in 1961 when the wall went up, seemingly overnight. She could remember sidewalks leading nowhere, ending mid-step where she had walked just the day before. And a grandmother she would never see again on the other side.

"But what will these travel laws mean, exactly? We can cross there or they can come here?"

"It means that Germans who have been frozen in time on the other side of the wall might be able to cross into West Germany without going through a third country. Your friends, your relatives. It would mean the end of the Cold War. But, if not, if nothing happens, then we can drink beer, eat pretzels, and nothing is lost."

"Why today and not next week?" asked the Baroness.

"Because there is a televised interview with the committee spokesman tomorrow evening and there will be press from all over the world."

"Then we should be in East Berlin!" chimed Sabine.

"We are right where we need to be," insisted Jack.

The Punk Baroness went into the wardrobe room, started to pull out leather costumes, with bustiers and lace. She found knee-high boots with pointy toes and equally dangerous heels.

"Then we will dress for it! We will go to the wall right after the announcement is made and we will do performance art! If it is good news we will sing in victory, if it is bad news we will sing in rebellion. Either way, we will sing!"

Blanca was keen. She imagined herself at the wall, a sentinel of freedom, an angel presiding over their chosen city. She could be anything she wanted to be, without judgment. She was a new woman in Berlin. A goddess! But Clara sat there, unimpressed, not speaking. She pretended to have no interest whatsoever and refused to so much as acknowledge the guests, let alone contribute to the conversation, until the question of costume came up and the black, signature punk clothes were laid out for them.

"Absolutely not! No! I always wear white in public. I'm not wearing your punk circus clothes!"

"Okay. Fine. I will wear the leather and you two will wear tons of white gossamer and we will either sing for freedom or we will sing against oppression!"

"Or we will just drink beer," Gareth said with a laugh. He glanced at Clara. She met his eyes, held his stare, and crossed her arms.

"Who wants to go dancing? Clubbing?" Sabine lifted her arms above her head in a shoop-shoop dance move. She expected a vigorous response but they all claimed to be too tired; it was late.

"Come on, I didn't drive all the way to Berlin just to talk! Let's go out, have some fun! Dance!"

Jack got up, agreed to go. After all, she had been good enough to do all the driving. He popped his glass eye out and reached into his pocket for his old nightclub standby.

"Oh, *mein Gott!*" exclaimed the Punk Baroness.

"You'll get used to it," reassured Sabine in a stage whisper. "It's just his Bowie eye!"

"You may be due for a new one soon," Gareth advised, not realizing that he was sounding more and more like an ocularist with every passing day.

"How do I look?" Jack asked, primping in front of a full-length mirror. "Do I have your approval, Baroness?"

"Fantastic!" The Punk Baroness was delighted. Jack was lovely and, more importantly, had obviously moved on from Blanca some time ago. *A different church now,* she thought, *and certainly a different pew, as they say.*

Outside the theatre the night progressed and nothing seemed amiss. People went about their business. There was no thought of the wall, the guards watching over it, or the people on the other side. It was life as usual, a city divided as it had been for twenty-eight years.

"Look, it is the same as always. I think you might be wrong, Jack," Sabine told him. "I don't know where you got your crazy idea. Nothing is different at all."

"Yes, I might be wrong. I just felt that something was going to happen. Oh well, let's go to the Underground Metro. I hear the best clubs are there. In the Metro!"

The theatre space seemed much quieter without Jack and Sabine. Clara wondered how Gareth could live with their frenetic energy and secretly hoped that they would be out till very, very late.

"We are doing an original opera of Antigone. Clara wrote most of it. I think it is perfect timing. The dead brothers representing the Cold War conflict, two ideologies, and both having to die. Eteocles is West Berlin and Polyneices is East Berlin. Yes? Do you see?" asked the Punk Baroness.

"Which of us do you think is Antigone and which is Ismene? I bet he gets it wrong!" challenged Blanca.

"That's easy. You're Ismene and Clara is Antigone."

"That is so odd. Everyone sees me as the stronger twin," she laughed, giving Clara a sisterly shove.

The casting was obvious to Gareth, and to the Punk Baroness, as well, he assumed. Of course, Blanca, who always seemed tougher and in control, would play Ismene, the more vivacious, more attractive sister who tries to shield her sister from danger. What a struggle and balance the loving sister has, trying to both support Antigone and protect her at the same time. *It is a great role*, he thinks, *and so often overlooked*. And then, Clara as Antigone, the shy sister, who was so close to having love in her life but then breaks a law that would seal her mortal fate. A rebel princess who chooses truth over happiness.

"It is more interesting with twins because, really, they are two sides of the same woman. We hold two truths at the same time because we are more dialectic than men. Now, of course, I will be the gender-neutral Chorus," announced the Punk Baroness. "The one who sees all, knows all, predicts what will happen, and informs the audience."

"You're a bit like Jack, then!" Gareth noted, smiling at her.

"I guess I have a type," Blanca smiled, knowing that the transition from Jack to Martina had been fluid for her. A mere adjustment. How much more difficult life was for her twin with her rigidity.

Clara cleared her throat, signalling the need for attention. "It is a play about free choice, moral obligations, shame, incest, and truth. The sisters are the product of incest; there is a tyrant uncle, their mother commits suicide. We ran away from the shame of our home, only to put it onstage for everyone to see."

Gareth was stunned by her admission.

"I think it's time for some coffee cake. Yes?" the Punk Baroness suggested. "Come Blanca, we will make something delicious together!"

Gareth didn't know how to get past the years of silence.

"I am so sorry that I hurt you," he said to Clara. "I hope one day you will forgive me."

"I'll give you the odds on that. If the East and West reunite tonight then, maybe, there's a small chance that I'll forgive you."

"Then there is a small glimmer of hope."

"Well, our friend Jack thinks so," Clara said, smiling.

"And so does the Punk Baroness!" Martina announced, returning with a plateful of cakes and sweets. "Now, who is starving?"

The following day, at seven o'clock on November ninth, Jack's hunch becomes a reality because of a mistake in a televised interview, when the central committee spokesman, Guenter Schabowski, unintentionally announces that East German citizens can travel to West Germany immediately. Immediately! On both sides, the news rapidly spreads and everyone rushes outside and heads to the wall. Did he really mean immediately, as in right away? There's both disbelief and a great desire to believe.

Ten people, fifteen, one hundred, a thousand. And more and more coming. Guards try to discourage the Westerners from climbing up onto the wall, spraying water at them to knock them down, but umbrellas come out and the young continue to jump up, dancing, drinking on the wall in a display of the antithesis of the East's ideology.

Gareth decides to go up onto the wall, to see what is on the other side.

"Be careful," Clara calls over to him.

"Why, are you worried I might get hurt?" he tests, jokingly.

"Of course, you idiot! I love you," she blurts out. And why not take the risk? The world's turning upside down and nothing will be the same ever again.

Gareth takes a run at it, springs up, hoisting his body up the wall. From here he can see the chaos, the confusion, the revelry.

Below him are his childhood friends, two white queens and the one-eyed Jack. The twins are clapping their hands, singing, happy to be one with the crowd. To belong, if only in this moment of history.

"You have to see this, Jack, you have to take a picture!" Gareth yells down. "Capture the moment, Jack!"

Jack looks up at his friend. He had scaled the wall so easily. One, two, three, up. And from there, he knew that his friend was witnessing it all without him. His friend, who was always better balanced.

"Come on up, Jack, you can do it!"

Jack steps back, shakes his head. Gareth sees Blanca hug Jack. She whispers into his ear, but Gareth has no idea what her words are, only sees that Jack comes closer to the wall. People bump him, some trying to climb, others just dancing and partying.

Jack attempts, loses his footing. Cyclops hangs, disappointed, around his neck. He tries again, holds on to the wall, halfway up, his legs kicking, scrambling for position.

"Come on, Jack, higher! Higher! You can do it!"

Higher, higher, the words hang in the air between them.

"I've got you this time Jack," Gareth says, reaching a hand down from the edge of the wall. "Take my hand. I won't let you go. I promise."

One, two, three, up!

Jack stands, king of the castle, high up on the wall. It's late in the day and there is no letting up; the party will go on till dawn.

The guards give up. What can they do? There are too many now. They open the gates and hordes of people surge through, met on the other side with cheering and open arms. Jack sees it all. The past begins to slip away with all its dark deeds, and the future presents itself with a breath of optimism. This is the moment. Right here. Right now. It has all led to this moment. Jack lifts Cyclops, frames his shot. He waits. He waits. Steadying his hand and holding his breath. Now. Right now. He holds the image in his one eye and captures the shot, immortalizing the moment forever.

A New Germany

A New Europe

A New World

Hilda wraps Siegfried's old sweater around her shoulders, opens the door, and retrieves the morning paper. It isn't until the coffee is brewing that she glances at the front page. The headline stops her in her tracks.

A New Germany

A New Europe

A New World

And there, below the words, is the image Jack had captured. An image transmitted around the world. Hilda steadies herself, plants both hands on the rectory table for support.

Siegfried is gone. The wall is down. The rabbits are all free.

It is time to go home.

EPILOGUE

Aber zerrissen von der Tragödie,
Oder in der Nähe von rhe, die es brechen kann,
Kann mein Herz niemals verhärten.
Solange ich Augen habe zu sehen,
Und Fenster towrts den Garten.

However torn by tragedy
Or near the breaking it may be
My heart can never harden
As long as I have eyes to see
And windows toward the garden.

— Anonymous

ACKNOWLEDGEMENTS

I APPROACHED THIS BOOK in a very dedicated way, forcing myself to write every single day without fail. I would like to thank those friends and family members I ignored during my writing time.

I gratefully acknowledge my dedicated team at Dundurn Press. Rachel Spence, my acquisitions editor, for championing me and believing in this book from the very start.

Shannon Whibbs, the most thoughtful and precise editor a writer could ever hope for.

Designer Laura Boyle and project editor Jenny McWha for making my book gorgeous inside and out. The publicity department, specifically Elham Ali and Heather Wood. Also Kendra Martin, Lisa-Marie Smith, and Kathryn Lane.

Thank you to my agent, Rob Firing at Transatlantic Agency, for his guidance, advice, and the best coffee meetings.

A big thank you to my cousin in Germany, Frauke Palleske, for reading an early draft, and for verifying and suggesting many of the German references in this book.

To Daniel Matmor for believing in the book and staying out of my way.

And thank you to the muse, who is very demanding and often quite cruel.

I quoted poetry throughout the book, and would like to acknowledge the following poems: "The Stolen Child," by W.B. Yates; "Jabberwocky," by Lewis Caroll; and Gertrude's speech from *Hamlet*, by William Shakespeare.

I gratefully acknowledge the support of the Ontario Arts Council and the Toronto Arts Council.

ABOUT THE AUTHOR

 HEIDI VON PALLESKE was raised on a small farm on the shores of Lake Ontario. At seventeen she moved to Toronto to train as an actor, and is known for her roles in independent Canadian and American films, most recently starring in the feminist western *Bordello*. Heidi has also written poetry, screenplays, and articles for both print and radio, and won the H.R. Percy Novel Prize for *They Don't Run Red Trains Anymore*. She loves swimming in ice-cold water and spends time on both the Atlantic and Pacific Coasts, but calls Toronto home.